The Wave at Hanging Rock

GREGG DUNNETT

This is a work of fiction. Any resemblance it bears to reality is entirely coincidental.

Para Maria,
gracias y siento no haber
hablado de nada mas que
del libro en todo el año.

The Wave at Hanging Rock

one

THE WAY MY dad died was so funny one newspaper gave him a Darwin Award. That's not a real award, it's a joke. They give them to people who die doing something so stupid that it counts as a service to humanity. You know, eliminating their DNA from the gene pool. But the real funny thing was, everyone was so busy laughing none of them realised it was already too late. Because I was already here.

I was twelve years old when he did it. It was a Wednesday afternoon. Normally I liked Wednesdays since we finished school early, and usually Dad would take me to the beach. He'd read the paper for a bit and then fetch up in one of the bars down there drinking beer while I surfed. But things had already gone weird by then. That day we were in the garden, working on his latest project in the shade of the gum trees.

"It'll be good. You and me being together in school," Dad said for what must have been the third time that afternoon. He had his plastic goggles pushed up onto his forehead so his hair stuck up like a porcupine.

"Yeah," I said, meaning no. I didn't like the idea much. I'd been hoping it wouldn't actually happen, but I knew just hoping wasn't going to work for ever.

"Nearly ready for the test eruption." He sounded so pleased with himself.

A couple of weeks before it had been a rocket made of plumbing tubes that was supposed to demonstrate pressure or something. It made an angry whistling noise like a boiling kettle as it sat on the grass launchpad, but when the needle on the compressor's dial trembled into the red section, something sprung a leak and the rocket screamed sideways into the fence. Every one of Dad's experiments seemed to centre on blowing something up. Most of them took out a fence panel or two.

"I bet you've never done something like this in science Jesse?"

"I told you already, we did it in like, grade two or something. In Geography."

A shadow of doubt swam into his eyes but he blinked it away. "Well not like this you didn't. This one is going to blow your mind."

That afternoon we'd stirred chemicals together in one of the big glass bowls Mum used to make cakes on my birthday. We didn't have a bunsen burner but Dad had improvised by using the camping stove. You couldn't see any of this now though since it was hidden inside a giant model mountain made of cardboard and paper soaked in wallpaper paste. Dad had painted it the night before and I had to admit, it looked a bit more realistic now. I mean you could at least tell it was supposed to be a volcano.

"Course I might not get to teach your class, but if I do, that'll be good right?"

Dad had given up his job a few months earlier and was retraining as a teacher. A science teacher, because he knew something about chemicals from the factory where he worked. He said he wanted to do something more worthwhile with his life. I could understand that I suppose. I'd been to work with him sometimes, it was like hanging out in a warehouse with all the stupid kids from school, but older. But even so I didn't like the idea much. I guess I was worried what my mates were going to think of Dad becoming their teacher. Maybe he sensed that. Maybe that explained the experiments.

"Your little pals at school are gonna love this one Jesse," he said. "None of the pussy shit demonstrations that your… what d'ya call him? Mr Carter? Not like the bloody limp-wristed crap he's been showing you. Chemistry is all about drama! Elemental drama! Boom!" He demonstrated this by pouring a quart of something red and oily down through the neck of the volcano and replacing the plug. This was the lava.

"So, if you've been paying attention you'll know what's happening inside our model right now. What reaction is taking place? Jesse?"

I was torn. I didn't want to encourage him. I didn't want to look interested, but if we were done here soon enough there might still be time to get to the beach before tea. And there *was* something cool about your dad coming into your school and blowing away the boring science experiments we had to sit through. Literally blowing them away.

"Messy… Messy zinc?"

"*Mossy* zinc Jesse. Little nodules of zinc cooled in water which have a greater surface area than zinc strips." I nodded. I'd grown up with the garage filled with this sort of shit, ends of runs from whatever it was Dad's work did. "And dropped into Hydrochloric Acid it produces what volatile gas?"

He'd told me so many times. It was just easier to say it back to him.

"Hydrogen."

"Exactly. The agent which will give a little boost to our simulated eruption here." He chuckled and then stopped suddenly.

"Did they use baking powder when you did this at school?" He asked. "When you did this before? They did didn't they? I'll bet they did. Well this ain't baking powder son. We've got a little more power here to play with." He gave the model a friendly pat and I just stared at it without any expression on my face.

It sat there on its plastic sheet, maybe four feet high, a little bigger than the garden table next to it anyway.

"I think we're just about ready. Do you want to light her up Jesse?"

There was only so much enthusiasm I was prepared to demonstrate. I thought about how the waves were good that afternoon and how I was missing them.

"Not really."

He did a good job of keeping it from his voice, but I could see he was hurt. We'd put effort into this. Well, he had anyway.

"OK. Well get the camera. Stand back a little and get filming, and I'll light her up."

I did what he said, backing up till he was happy I'd be able to get the whole eruption in shot with the video camera. If I'd known how famous this video was going to get I'd have tried to hold it steadier.

"Happy?" I could hear my own voice on the recording later. It sounded reedy and thin. Sarcastic.

Through the viewfinder I watched as he gave an awkward smile to the camera and knelt down. We'd left a hole in the side of the model to light the burner. He reached in and grimaced as he struggled to open the valve for the gas. After a while you could see the frustration on his face.

"Fuckin' shit."

"What is it?"

"My hand's too big to turn the gas on. Get over here Jesse and help me."

So I walked back over, gave Dad the camera and stuck my own hand inside the volcano. I felt around for the valve, a little knurled wheel that sat at the back of the stove.

"Got it? Can you feel it? Don't open her right up, just a quarter turn. We only need a small amount of gas or we're going to have a real explosion on our hands." He chuckled again at the thought of this.

I could feel my knuckles sliding against the glass bowl as I turned it. If I'd been paying attention I might have noticed that was wrong, it had slipped out of position, but I didn't notice. I pulled my arm back out.

"All yours," I said, walking backwards to keep the camera pointed on the action.

He picked up the lighter and lit up a long wooden taper. He spent an age trying to get the orange flame to bite into the wood but even though there wasn't much breeze, it kept blowing out. Dad gave a grunt of frustration. Finally he gave up and just stuck his hand back inside with the lighter poised.

"Ready?"

I shrugged. "Let's do it," I said.

You can probably guess it didn't go according to plan. Dad was aiming for what they call a Hawaiian eruption, it's also known as a fire fountain eruption on account of how the red hot lava shoots up in the air like a firework show. They're predictable eruptions. They get the name from the volcanoes in Hawaii where they bus tourists up to watch like it's a show. But what he got was a more explosive eruption, on account of all the gas. Or maybe it was more like a bomb. But then some volcanoes do go up like that. They're unpredictable. I told you, we did it in geography.

Anyway, whatever he wanted to happen, he didn't even have time to pull his arm out before the whole thing just went boom.

If it hadn't been for that glass bowl he might have got away with just losing his arm. But the bowl wasn't even oven-proof, let alone dumb-ass home-made volcano-bomb proof. The bowl blew apart, great big shards of curved splintered glass. One piece flew out and hit the trunk of a gum tree close to where I was standing. They found another piece on the front driveway, it had cleared the whole garage. Most of it hadn't been able to go anywhere though since Dad's chest was in the way. It just lacerated him. His white singlet turned red instantly. Some of the glass pieces stuck in him, some of them went right through, just as easy as they had through the cardboard. I filmed the whole thing, steady as you like. Didn't turn off the camera until I'd got my dad pitching forward, dying hugging his stupid volcano, right in the middle of my frame.

two

IT WAS OUR neighbour who called the ambulance. The one with the broken fence. He must have heard the explosion since he looked through where the panel should have been, a pair of shears in his hands. Then he saw my old man, slumped down, surrounded by more blood than it seemed possible could ever be in one human being. And of course half the blood wasn't blood at all, but fake lava made from red paint and oil. And he dropped the shears so they nearly stabbed his feet and he said "Jesus fucking Christ."

The police said they released my video to the press to warn of the dangers of homemade science experiments, like it was a problem they faced a lot. It was bullshit. They released it because someone decided it was fucking hilarious, or someone got paid, probably both. I saw it on the TV news from the hospital bed they put me in, not because I was injured, just for shock or something. The presenters did their best to look sombre but their best generally wasn't very good. They never played the whole thing, you just got to see Dad's enthusiasm for his shit model and hear my whiny voice whinging about it, and then the tape got blacked out when the thing went up. Because of that it got played everywhere, on all the networks, they printed stills from it in all the papers. Big photos of Dad, somehow they got hold of my school photo too and printed that. For a while the angle they used was about what a terrible tragedy it was, but then this newspaper gave Dad his Darwin Award and it was like that freed everyone up to have a good laugh.

I went to the funeral from the hospital. Photographers followed us to the cemetery and then stood behind some trees taking pictures all the time. It was like some celebrity had died. Like Dad was a legend, not just the stupidest fucking man in the whole of Queensland. Probably the whole of Australia. The priest kept looking over at them and scowling like they shouldn't have been there. But everyone else at the funeral wore this expression that said you might not be laughing right now, but you had to admit it was a proper stupid way to go.

When I got to go home the photographers were outside my house too, camped out like they weren't going anywhere in a hurry. We never really spoke about it, but I always figured that's why Mum made us leave. Not just those photographers, but the whole thing. It was the most exciting thing that ever happened in our street, and she thought she'd always be remembered as the widow of the fucking idiot who blew himself up for a school science project. So what happened next, in a way, was the weirdest thing of all. A week after I came home Mum told me to pack a bag and then we were on a plane heading for London, England. We were going to stay with some family she had there. I'd never met them, I'd always thought of them as the sort of family who sent cards every birthday and Christmas but you never had to meet. Jeez did I get that wrong.

And we never came back to Oz. Mum sold the house and used the money to buy a campsite on the coast in mid Wales. That's Wales, as in the shitty little country stuck on the side of England, not New South Wales. Not somewhere half decent like Sydney. I don't expect you to make any more sense of it now than I did at the time. But when you're twelve you don't exactly get consulted in these things. When you're twelve and your dad's just been blown up you don't argue either. You just go with it.

three

THE DOORBELL RANG making Natalie jump. She looked at her watch, which was unstrapped from her wrist and laid on the arm of the sofa. The unsettled feeling that had been growing all afternoon vanished. Replaced with… She wasn't entirely sure. Relief certainly but perhaps a little trepidation. She'd expected him earlier. She'd certainly hoped he'd be there earlier. She'd begun to imagine car accidents, a motorway pile-up that no one could escape from, no matter how confident or capable, or how quick their reactions were. But at least he was home. She smiled as she pushed aside the essays she'd been marking and she thought of the wine chilling in the fridge, the dinner cooking in the oven, nothing too fancy, but enough to show him she was pleased he was back, despite everything. She doubted the essays would get another look-in tonight. But then the smile left her. If it was Jim at the door, why didn't he just come in? Had he lost his key?

Her visitor was bending in so close to the frosted glass of the front door that Natalie could see who it was before she got there. The smile stayed away, and the anxiety came right back, a new sense of irritation coming with it. For a moment she considered pretending she was out, but it got dark so early this time of year and the lights were on already. Instead she took a deep breath and drew herself up tall, then opened the door. The woman who stood there was holding a tupperware box filled with something green and liquid, a gossip magazine folded in two on top.

"Oh," the expression on the other woman's face fell, she made no attempt to hide it. "I was expecting Jim," Natalie's mother-in-law said.

"Hi Linda. Me too actually," Natalie replied.

"He's not here?" The woman tried to peer past Natalie as if suspecting she might be lying.

"No, he's not back yet," Natalie replied, not adding that he might be any minute. "You knew he was away for a few days?" she added, wondering if she could get away with not inviting her in.

"Yes of course I knew," Linda said. She had a way of addressing Natalie as if she were a rather slow child. "But he said he'd take my washing machine to the tip."

Natalie realised she must have looked blank at this as Linda went on. "The old one. I'm having a new one delivered tomorrow and there'll be nowhere to put it you see."

Natalie thought about this for a moment.

"Well I'm afraid he's not back yet," she repeated in the end.

This generated a sigh from the older woman, and another attempt to peer around Natalie.

Would you like to search the house? Natalie thought, but she didn't say it. Jim talked to his mum like that all the time and made it sound funny. On the few occasions Natalie had tried it she sounded bitter.

"It's not like Jim to be late is it?"

Natalie opened her mouth to speak but closed it again. It was exactly like Jim to be late. Even after the argument they'd had about him going. Even after they'd made up on the telephone. Even after his promise to make it up to her properly when he did get back. "Traffic?" she offered, not wanting to go into any of this with his mum.

"On a *Sunday night*?" Linda was saying, as if nobody ever drove on a Sunday night. "Have you tried calling his what's it called thingy?"

"His mobile? It's out of battery. I spoke to him on Friday from a phone box. He said he couldn't find anywhere to charge it."

For a moment Linda made a face as if this was highly technical information way beyond her grasp, then she gave up.

"Well I can't stop, I'll just pop in for a moment and put these down. I had some left over soup I thought you'd like."

Linda slipped past Natalie with a move she didn't see coming, a kind of feint in one direction then a sliding pass on the other side. Before Natalie knew it the older woman was in the kitchen with the kettle on. Natalie looked up and down the street before she closed the door. It was empty, the neighbours' windows obscured by bright curtains. She was pretty sure her entire evening now depended on whether she could get rid of Linda before Jim came back.

"Charge your bloody phone up next time Jim," she muttered to the empty street.

It was nearly six months since Linda's husband - Jim's father, and her own father-in-law - had died. Linda hadn't taken it well. She went from the sort of mother-in-law who kept her distance to the sort who popped around uninvited several times a week, a bit like elderly relatives did on the TV soap operas she liked to watch so much. Jim had told Natalie to be patient, she'd back off when she got herself back on track, he said. But it was alright for Jim, he was hardly ever there.

"I'll just wait for him a little while. Now that I'm in." Linda said. Natalie never used a teapot but Linda had bought them one and knew they kept it at the back of the cupboard. She'd already washed and dried it and was now re-washing the already clean mugs while the tea brewed. Natalie sat at the table and watched her, glad at least that the kitchen was clean.

"Where's he gone this time anyway? Is it work?"

"No. He's off on one of his surfing expeditions somewhere." Natalie made sure she didn't sound bitter.

"Oh, that's nice."

"Lovely. For him."

If Linda caught the irony here she ignored it.

"And did he tell you when he was coming back? Because the new one is being delivered some time tomorrow you see."

It took Natalie a second to work out she was talking about the washing machine again.

"I don't know. We last spoke on Friday. He said he'd call me on Saturday to let me know for sure. And obviously he didn't. But he's working tomorrow, so he'll be back sometime today."

"Oh dear. And you've made an effort haven't you?"

Natalie glanced at her in surprise.

"I saw the wine in the fridge, and that smell is delicious. Don't worry. I won't stay long when he's back. I'll let you two young lovebirds have your nice evening together." Linda said, sitting down opposite her. "Just as soon as he's moved my machine."

She wasn't sure, but Natalie thought this was a joke. She sipped her tea thoughtfully.

"You know he's a bloody fool if he prefers to go off on silly adventures instead of spending time with you. A bloody fool."

For the first time since Linda's arrival Natalie smiled at her naturally.

"Thanks Linda," she said. Sometimes she glimpsed an alternate universe where she got on well with this woman. She wondered if they'd get there. One day, maybe.

"He's not on his own is he?" Linda was saying now. "I don't like it when he goes off on his own. Is he with Dave?"

"No Dave couldn't..." Natalie stopped herself. "Actually I don't know. I think Dave might have gone after all." Natalie wondered what made her say that. She felt her cheeks flush hot and she blew across her tea so that tiny ripples appeared in the surface of the liquid.

Linda gave her a curious look but then brightened a little. "Oh well, that's good. Jim won't get into too much trouble if Dave's around. He's a sensible one, he'll keep them out of trouble."

Natalie just nodded, but she kept her eyes on the table and away from Jim's mother.

four

"LOOK THEY'VE PROBABLY got into some scrape or another. Or stopped off for a meal on the way back." Linda said a little while later. Her tea cup was empty now. "He gave me plenty of sleepless nights when he was a teenager I can tell you." She gave Natalie a smile that was designed to be reassuring.

To Natalie there was something vaguely insulting in this, though she couldn't say exactly what. Her anxious feeling was back. She tried Jim's mobile yet again but there was still no answer, just the same electronic beep which she thought meant that his phone had a dead battery. She was pleased Linda didn't think to suggest she try Dave's number. When she set the phone down she was surprised to see that Linda was leaving, she was saying something about getting a neighbour to move the washing machine. Natalie had forgotten all about it. For a moment she thought about asking Linda to stay, just until Jim finally got home, but she said nothing. It probably wasn't a good idea anyway. It was getting a bit late for a romantic reunion, and a rerun of the argument was looking more likely now anyway.

Linda bustled herself out of the house. She seemed untroubled by her missing son, reassured perhaps that he was with Dave. But Natalie could take no comfort from this.

With Linda gone the house was too quiet. She could hear a clock ticking and the burbling of the heating pipes. She turned the TV on to drown out the noises and tried to return to her scripts, but she found herself giving them even less attention than before. Instead she thought back to what he'd said on the telephone on Friday night. He was in a phone box outside a pub, the line wasn't great, presumably because he had to keep pushing coins into the slot. They talked about nothing for five minutes, neither of them wanting to re-visit the argument they had when he left. But right at the end he did. He said he was sorry. He said he realised he was being selfish and he said he was missing her. She felt her throat constrict as she tried to reply. Eventually she said the same to him, only to realise he must have run out of money because the line was dead.

"Oh Christ. What have you done?" she said out loud, and threw the scripts down again. How did she end up in this position, with a man who was so damn *difficult*?

"And where the hell are you Jim?"

She sighed. She thought about the last few days. She'd come so close to throwing it all away. But all it had done was make her realise how much she wanted what she had. How much she wanted to make it work. If only life could be a little bit easier she thought, but then she smiled again. How was life ever going to be easy with a man like Jim? Not for the first time she let her mind drift back to the night they met. He'd practically got into a bar fight of all things.

There was an eccentric young man who dressed as if he was an eighteenth century gentleman. She saw him around the town from time to time, where he stood out somewhat in his waistcoats, woollen trousers and monocle. She'd never spoken to him but she'd smiled when he touched his hat on passing in the street. One night, possibly a Wednesday - it was midweek certainly - when Natalie was still relatively new in the city, she and a friend were in a trendy bar where the young man also happened to be drinking. He was alone, as he usually was, and reading quietly from a slim volume of what looked like poetry. They were sitting a little way away, chatting about work. It was a quiet evening, and it would have passed entirely unremarkably had the elegantly dressed young man not somehow managed to offend two drunk young men.

These men had stumbled in a while earlier. They were too drunk already to see how out of place they looked. Too far gone to notice that the sports bar they remembered on this site had been bought out, closed down, refurbished and reopened as a wine and tapas bar. But now inside it was obvious enough from the lack of giant screen TV showing sports and the middle-class huddles of professional people drinking quietly that they'd made a mistake. It was bravado that made them stay. That and one of them remembering drinking San Miguel on holiday in Lanzarote and how it didn't give you a hangover. He persuaded his dubious mate to stay for one pint, only to discover that the bar was too posh to serve pints, and almost too expensive for him to afford two bottles of beer. The two men were now standing rather too close to the table where the young man was still reading, and they were compiling a list of the many faults of the establishment, including the "wankers" who drank there. And it was in this situation that the eccentric dress of the young man really stood out. After a while the two drunk men began to punctuate whatever they said with the expression "fucking freak" shouted every few words in his direction.

Natalie and her friend were sitting far enough away from this scene that it wasn't their problem, and certainly not their responsibility to do anything about it. They could see and hear clearly enough, but it was in the background to their discussion. And if nothing else had happened Natalie might never even have fully registered that anything was wrong. The men were near the end of their drinks. Soon they would grow bored and wander out, presumably to another bar, more their style, and everyone else in the wine bar could relax, and get back to enjoying their quiet midweek drink.

Perhaps Natalie halfheartedly hoped that someone would do something, but it wasn't a conscious thought. Certainly the scene wasn't causing too much concern for Natalie's friend, Alice. She had already persuaded Natalie to stay for another drink, was already at the bar fetching them now. And that's when someone did do something.

It was another man, on his own, who had appeared to be simply walking through the bar, his route taking him close to where the two abusive men were standing. But when he drew level he suddenly changed direction, raised up his hands and shoved one of the yobs as hard as he could, pushing him into a pillar that held up the ceiling. The man crashed into it, and then his feet slipped out from underneath him, and he fell to the floor. He ended up on his backside with his San Miguel spilling onto the bottom of his pastel-pink shirt, and the crotch of his jeans. The man who'd had caused this didn't stop to watch, he just carried on walking past until he reached the bar, and calmly ordered a drink. He was standing, as it happened, right next to Alice.

Natalie saw the whole thing and registered at once the spike in her anxiety levels. What scared her was the retaliation that would surely come. It was obvious how angry the man on the floor was, but also clear how fit and strong he was, she could see it in the way he sprang back to his feet and looked around for someone to retaliate against. But he had a problem, there didn't seem to be anyone there to fight back against. The man who had pushed him was now engaged in conversation with Alice at the bar, as if he were nothing to do with what had happened. And the man who had been pushed looked suddenly uncertain, you could see it on his face. Anger turned to confusion, then to a kind of embarrassment -

at his inability to respond in the way he felt he should when all eyes were now on him, and at the realisation that the large wet patch at the top of his jeans must make him look like he'd pissed himself.

His friend fared no better. He had made the split-second decision to pretend he'd seen nothing, and started laughing instead at his friend sprawled on the floor, as if he thought he had simply fallen over, or slipped. And he too appeared to feel a rush of embarrassment at this. He didn't even glance in the direction of the man at the bar, as if even looking at him might earn himself the same treatment. Instead, when his friend was back on his feet, he began quickly finishing his drink, and muttering something about how it was time to go somewhere decent. It was only when it became clear they were leaving that Natalie realised she had been holding her breath.

As they left some bravado returned to the two young men. The one who had fallen shouted how 'next time' someone was going to get the shit kicked out of them, then he quickly ducked out the door. Natalie watched them through the plate glass window, she flinched when the other man gave it a hard kick. It bowed and for a moment it looked like it might break, but then it seemed to bounce back. And then the men were gone.

The young man reading his poetry, who had barely moved at all during the whole episode now stood up and gave an elaborate bow towards the man who had helped him. In response this man lifted the drink the barman had just put down in front of him. There were a few half-embarrassed whistles and cheers from across the bar, and then everything returned to normal. It was as if nothing at all had happened.

Natalie watched her friend Alice saying something to the barman, then she began talking to the man. They stayed chatting for some time, every now and then looking over to Natalie as she waited at her table. Natalie hoped she wouldn't bring him over. Not because she didn't like the look of him. He was handsome, tanned skin, with very dark hair and sharp features that split every now and then into a warm smile. No, she didn't want Alice to bring him over because if that happened she knew Alice would end up sleeping with him. And he didn't look like the kind of guy Alice needed in her life right now.

Alice brought him over.

"Natalie, meet Jim," she said. "I had to buy him a drink after what he just did."

Jim gave her a smile which confirmed to Natalie that he was as arrogant as he looked, then he and Alice resumed their flirty conversation from the bar. Natalie hardly listened, instead she wondered how long this one would last. Maybe it would just be a one night stand? Maybe she wouldn't have to spend too long supporting her friend when this one split up with her.

And then Alice had stood up saying she had to go to the ladies room, and as she'd passed by where Natalie was sitting she leaned in close to her ear.

"It's not me he's after," And she walked away, trailing one finger along the surface of the table behind her.

five

OUR CAMPSITE WAS just a mile away from the village, right down by the beach. It had three rows of static caravans, a field for tents and another one for travelling caravans. There were two toilet blocks with showers that didn't work very well, and a covered area with a row of sinks where people went to do their washing up. The grass was pockmarked with molehills.

There was a house that came with the site. The main room downstairs was also the shop and reception for the campsite. The rest was just a normal private house, which became home for Mum and me. The windows were tiny and the walls were thick but that hadn't stopped the damp settling into the furniture and carpets over the many years since they'd been laid. From the upstairs windows you could see the ocean, but not the beach, since there was a high bank of shingle that stopped the high tides from flooding the camping fields. Compared to Australia it wasn't much of a beach anyway. The warm blue waters and white sand I was used to were replaced by slate grey sea and patches of dirty-coloured sand scattered among the pebbles.

Mum found out about it from a magazine article that was left on the plane. It was one of those articles that gives suggestions for life-changing adventures that people could do. You know the type, go and count monkeys in the rainforest, or build an eco-house in Mexico. I don't know why she chose the campsite, I was too young to talk about it at the time, and there never seemed much point later on. But it's weird to think I could have turned out a monkey specialist. Or a Mexican drug lord. But instead I was stuck in Wales in the fucking rain.

The campsite was sold as a going concern, which meant there were visitors right from the day we moved in. Mum thought I'd enjoy working in the shop, and driving the tractor around to cut the grass and under different circumstances I might have done, but I was a twelve year old kid, I'd just watched my Dad blow himself up and then I'd lost every friend I had in the weeks afterwards. So I didn't much.

I don't remember much about the first few weeks, and I don't much like trying to remember. I knew the whole thing was insane of course, but I felt it was my fault. I'd fucked up somehow and this was my punishment. I cried all the time, during the day at least, but not for Dad. I cried for me, and where I was. At night it was Mum that cried. She'd bury her face in a pillow so I wouldn't hear, but her sobs were so loud it didn't work.

The day Dad died was the last day I went to school in Australia, and a few weeks later I started a new school in Wales. They were pretty different. There were more kids in my old school than in the whole village we'd moved to. My new school had less than a hundred students. I was probably the first new kid any of them had ever seen, I was definitely the first Australian.

I do remember starting at that school. It felt like arriving on another planet. They spoke English at least, not that guttural gargling Welsh the old folk in the village still coughed up when they queued in the post office, but none of the kids wanted to talk to me, and I pulled a fierce scowl onto my face every morning to warn off anyone who thought of trying. There were twelve kids in my class. Twelve kids was an easy number for the teachers to work with. Six tables of two. "Choose a partner," the teachers would say. Sometimes they'd remember to add: "Jesse, you work alone for now".

Every day it rained. Every day I hated everything and every day it got a little bit worse. But I didn't tell anyone. After school I'd get back to the campsite and I'd tell Mum it was alright, then I'd go to bed early to have a little cry, and I'd try to sleep while all the time hearing her crying in the room next door. The only thing that kept me going in those early days was this idea I got that I just had to sit it out for a while. Eventually Mum would come to her senses and we would go back to our old life in Australia.

But Mum wouldn't take us back. She didn't think we could go back. She didn't think people would ever forget what had happened to Dad, not the way it happened. Plus by then she thought everyone back home would think she was a coward for running away, and then a failure for not making it work. So for Mum the only option left was to make a go of it. And I think she got some relief out of being so busy as well.

There was a steady flow of regulars to the static caravans, a trickle of caravans and tents popping up and down on the grass like mushrooms. There was a regular flow of complaints too, since the site was run down. So Mum jumped in and out of overalls to fix plumbing and electrics and stock the shelves of the shop with brands of food I didn't recognise but had decided I didn't like.

We'd been in Wales maybe six weeks when I finally got that we weren't going back. It was a Saturday. And I turned thirteen years old. Back home on that exact day I was supposed to be having a beach party, only because of the time difference, by the time I woke up it would have already been over. I was so excited I'd already invited a load of my friends, before Dad died I mean. I was allowed as many as I wanted because we were doing it on the beach. Dad was going to do a barbecue and we'd play Aussie footie and I knew for a surprise he'd booked some blow-karts - they're like land yachts that you can race on the beach at low tide. But we'd only do any of that if there was no surf. What me and my mates all hoped was we could spend the whole day surfing and then stuff our faces with sausages and burgers slathered in ketchup, and then watch surf movies all evening. It was going to be the perfect birthday. I wondered if anyone had thought to cancel all those invitations. I wondered if any of my friends had turned up at the beach on the off chance. I wondered whether the surf had been good. I wondered if the blow-kart guy had come with the little yachts loaded in the back of his Ute and scratched his head and then spat on the ground and gone for a beer.

Back in Oz nearly all the boys in my class were surfers, so I was too. The town we lived in was a surfer town. We all had posters of the Aussie surfing legends on our bedroom walls and we hung out by the lifeguard's tower, arguing about whether we'd got tubed or not. We never did of course, we were just groms - that's what the other surfers called us kids. But being a kid you got to pester the pro's every year when the world tour came to town. We'd camp out there all day and beg the guys for autographs when they finished their heats. Sometimes they'd even let you carry their boards.

So anyway, my birthday, my actual thirteenth birthday started badly. The rain had been so heavy overnight the lower toilet block overflowed all over the grass. I actually didn't mind, cleaning up shit with Mum was better than being in school anyway. And when we came in and cleaned ourselves up Mum made me go and look in the little shed at the side of the house. She said there was a surprise there waiting for me. She followed me and watched, and I knew what it was at once. Dad had spent ages talking with the shop guy about this board's volume and rocker flat, he'd worked out that it was perfect for a kid my size, but I'd just fallen for the airbrushed colour scheme, the whole deck was this beautiful morphing from orange in the tail through yellows and reds to deep purple in the nose. I could see it glowing through the bubble wrap now. It was my surfboard. Our old neighbour - the other side from the fence guy - he'd packed it all up for Mum and sent it over. He was a surfer too and he'd packed it real carefully, cutting a polystyrene block to protect the fins.

I cried as I unwrapped it. Mum did too. She thought it was tears of joy, or release, or finally tears of grief over Dad, something like that. But it wasn't. I was crying because I knew I was never going home now.

six

IT FELT LIKE it rained the first six weeks we were in Wales. It wasn't like the rain back home, which came in short bursts but came hard, so the streets would flow with orange-red rivers for a few minutes and then steam as the sun sucked the moisture right back up into the sky. In Wales the rain started when you got up and just hung around all day, right up until you went to bed. Then it did the same the next day. In Wales even the rain was shit.

But then the weather changed. A couple of weeks after my board arrived I came home from school and the sun was shining. You could look up and the sky was blue. I honestly hadn't thought that could happen here. There was something else different too. I heard it first and although I knew that sound it was like I couldn't quite place it. It sounded wrong.

The shingle bank meant you couldn't see the beach from the campsite, but I still ran down to look and my heart was pounding. I held my breath as I climbed the path that led up the bank, I didn't dare to hope too much but it sounded so familiar. And then I looked over the top and there it was. The beach I'd come to regard as permanently flat and choppy and grey was holding a three foot wave. The sun was shining down on the water so it was like a billion diamonds were floating in the bay and playing with that sunlight. But better than that, there was a small pack of surfers out there already, their backs turned to me, bobbing up and down, then turning as the swells reached them and jumping to their feet, riding them back towards the shore. I didn't stop to watch for long. I sprinted back to the house and shouted to Mum as I ripped off my clothes, searched for my board shorts.

"I'm going surfing!" I shouted. I didn't wait for a reply.

It's scary to paddle out in a new place amongst a group of surfers you don't know, even more so when you've just turned thirteen. But I didn't hesitate. This wasn't like the school in the village where weird Welsh country kids eyed me with suspicion every time I came too near. This wasn't the campsite where people on their shit holidays expected me to care if their shower was cold. These were surfers. I *knew* these people. I knew I'd fit in. I paddled right into the middle of them, so excited I spun around instantly and caught the first wave that came through.

Sometimes when you're surfing you can remember the few seconds of riding a single wave for years afterwards as clear as if it was burnt onto videotape. That first wave I caught in Wales was like that. I was lucky, in just the right place at just the right time and I caught the wave easily, and stood up before it even got that steep, then I dropped down the face into a powerful bottom turn, for a kid at least. Certainly I had enough speed to reconnect with the lip with a slashing turn, and then another and another. And then I just pulled into a fast section that nearly tubed on top of me, finally riding out over the dying shoulder of the wave and sinking into the water behind. Even by Aussie standards it was a good ride. Despite, or maybe because of the build-up of emotions inside me, I let out this scream of delight. I sounded like I was an animal or something.

I might have thought I was the same as the other surfers out that day, but in reality they were all staring at me in amazement, this crazy kid in red shorts freezing his butt off while they were all black-clad in wetsuits. I couldn't have been more different. But anyway. That was how it was when I first met John Buckingham.

Actually I didn't notice him at first, right at the beginning I didn't notice anyone. For forty minutes I surfed furiously, taking out all sorts of anger and frustration, and trying to make up for all the sessions I'd missed at home, but then the cold took over, literally grabbing me and forcing my body into a foetal huddle, my arms and chest a mountain of goose bumps. Then he paddled over.

"You're the new kid from the campsite." He was about my own age, but bigger than me. He had a wide smile and blue eyes. Even at that age you could tell he was going to be handsome, I mean he already was. He had muscles like a man, and clear skin, except around his jaw where you could see he was already shaving. He had a face that made you want to watch him. He observed my blue flesh with interest. "You're really good."

I nodded a frozen thanks.

"Are you cold?"

"Yeah a bit."

"You're actually blue." I managed to make my neck work enough to look down. I saw he was right.

"You need a wetsuit. You can have my old one if you like."

I looked at him in confusion, wondering how this could happen. "OK," I said at last. "Thanks."

"No worries," he said in imitation of an Aussie accent. "I'm John by the way."

A wave came along at this point and he turned his board to catch it. He wasn't very good then but he managed to get to his feet and he slid down the wall of the wave until he was too far away to continue the conversation.

The cold had done for me then, I wasn't able to catch any more waves. Eventually I struggled in and I got changed, I ran back indoors and hurried to put on all my warm clothes and then I went back down to watch the other surfers. I'd thought this place had literally *nothing* going for it, but here was something. There was surfing. There was some life.

I hung around when John came in, close enough so he could see me, but not so close that it looked I was waiting for him, on land my confidence had gone again. I watched as he went to where he'd stashed his clothes and bike. I turned away as he changed. He had an attachment for his bike that allowed you to carry a surfboard, lots of guys had them back home, but I hadn't seen any here until then. He strapped the board to it, but instead of peddling away he left his bike propped against the wall then walked over to me.

"Hey, have you got a bike?"

I shook my head.

"That's ok. We can walk. What's your name?"

"Jesse," I said.

"You're from Australia aren't you? I went to Australia two years ago," John said. I learnt later he'd been to most places. "Come on."

"Where are we going?" I said.

"We're going to get your wetsuit."

John lived a ten minute walk away, in the opposite direction from the village, in a house twice the size of anything else around. It was screened by trees and set back from the road so it didn't look too out of proportion. We talked as we walked there. He told me how he'd started surfing. He'd gone on some adventure holiday a few years before and it had just grabbed him and not let go. Surfing does that to some people. Then he told me the waves had been unusually bad that summer, but now it was autumn we would surf two or three days a week at least. He said this matter of factly, taking for granted that I would want to. Then we arrived in his driveway and he stopped.

"Oh Shit." He said. There was a car parked there, a big, new-looking Mercedes.

"What is it?" I asked.

"My dad's home. I thought he was staying in London."

It was all still recent enough that the word 'dad' did strange things to me. It forced images into my mind. My dad's face smiling as he struck the lighter, his body slumped over the sodden cardboard model, blood soaking into the dry earth. I forced myself to keep talking, I didn't know what I might do if I didn't.

"Don't you like him? Your dad?" I asked.

John shrugged. "Not really. We don't get on."

An idea came to me.

"Does he hit you or something?"

John looked at me like I was crazy and I realised I'd said something wrong.

"No. Why d'you think that?"

"I dunno. I just thought…" I stopped.

"Course he doesn't hit me. He doesn't fiddle with me neither."

I didn't say anything to this and John looked at me curiously for a bit but then he shrugged again. "It's alright, he'll probably stay in his study. Come on." He led the way into the kitchen, it was massive and looked brand new, like kitchens are in TV adverts. John went to the fridge and took out a bottle of Coke. "You want some?"

"Alright." I said.

John took down a couple of glasses from a cupboard. He knew just how to pour them so that they filled right up but the yellow foam didn't overflow onto the worktop.

"My dad's in property." He said suddenly. "And restaurants. And hotels. And a few other things too probably."

He said it with this weird mix of distaste and pride. I didn't know how to respond, so I said nothing.

"It pays for lots of stuff, but it means he's a bit of a wanker." He opened another cupboard and began to search inside it. "Or maybe he does all that because he's a bit of a wanker, I've never worked it out."

He flashed me a smile to show he was joking. It put me at ease, it made me feel better. John was a natural at that.

"Do you want some crisps?"

He didn't wait for an answer but spun around and threw a bag at me like he was testing my reflexes.

"I'd live with Mum, she's alright. But she's in London and you can't surf there." He shrugged like I'd understand why this was the deciding factor in where he chose to live. "She caught him banging his secretary a few years back, so they split up. Now she's his secretary and his girlfriend, and we all live out here. She's alright too actually. At least she buys food and stuff."

I nodded.

"What about your dad?" John said with his head cocked onto one side. "Is he over here? Back in Australia..?"

I hesitated at this because Mum had made me promise not to tell people here what happened to Dad. She said she hadn't dragged us half way around the world for his death to follow us. So I could tell people he was dead, but not how it happened. But already I didn't want to lie to John. When you talked to him his eyes would flick over you, like he could see what was true and what wasn't. And most of all I didn't want to give him any excuse to not be my friend. I didn't care that there was something scary about him, his cocky self confidence. I would have done anything to keep him talking to me.

"He died," I said. My voice slewed about an octave higher as I spoke.

John drank his Coke and munched down a few crisps.

"That's a bummer," he said at last. "Was it an accident or what?"

"Accident," I nodded.

"What happened?"

But all the same I was trapped. I couldn't let Mum down just like that, so I looked around the room for inspiration. I could see through to the lounge and there was a painting on the wall, one of the red London buses going over that bridge in front of the Houses of Parliament.

"He got hit by a bus," I said. I should have left it there, but I kept going, I was no good at lying then. "He stepped out without looking. The wing mirror took his head off."

"Shit! For real?"

"Yeah for real."

John stopped eating and watched me for a while.

"D'you see it happen?"

"Uh huh." I nodded.

"Wing mirror took his *head* off." John repeated to himself slowly. "Can that really happen?"

I didn't say anything. I knew I'd gone too far, I felt my cheeks heat up.

"Sometimes I wish my dad was dead." He finished the drink and left it on the side by the sink. "You wanna get that wetsuit? Come on."

I followed him back outside and around to the front of the house. He sat on the shiny nose of the Merc and fished out a key and then opened one of the double doors to the garage. It was dark but he punched a light switch and a fluorescent tube flickered a few times before flooding light into the space. It was filled with bikes and boards and under a tarpaulin there was a classic car, a Jaguar, John told me with a shrug. The suit was on a rail at the back, it looked brand new.

"I've not used it much. But it's too small for me now," John said.

I held it up to me, you could see it was about an inch too long in the legs.

"You'll grow into it," he said, and he gave me another one of his warm golden smiles.

"Thanks... John," I said, wondering as I used his name for the first time if I'd really made a friend like this.

"Is that really true?" John asked suddenly. "Is your dad really dead or did you just say that to shock me?"

I didn't answer for a while. I couldn't meet his eyes either. But then I just started speaking like it wasn't me in control of the words that came out. "He's really dead, but not like how I said."

I looked at John and again I felt how his eyes seemed to be able to bore into me and seek out the truth. I felt that if I lied to him then, I'd be failing some important test. So I told him the truth. I told him everything. As I talked he peeled back the tarp on the Jaguar and we sat in it, cool leather seats and wood panels so smooth you wanted to stroke them. He was the only person I ever told the truth to. When I finished he didn't say anything for a while, then he got out and pulled a bike out from somewhere and wheeled it over to me.

"Here, you can have this as well. The gears don't work but maybe we can fix them."

Then he said. "I won't tell anyone. About your dad I mean. And you shouldn't blame yourself either. Shit happens."

seven

"IT'S NOT ME he's after."

The words jolted Natalie back to the present in the wine bar. She felt a moment of panic as she saw Alice disappear into the ladies, and how Jim was looking at her. She felt her cheeks glow hot. Up close there was something about his looks that brought to mind a fox. Handsome. Sharp featured. Clever too, just not someone you would trust.

He took a sip from his glass and set it down carefully on the centre of a coaster, the bottom of the glass was square and he twisted it so it lined up at right angles to the table edge. His smile revealed very white teeth.

"So Natalie, what do you do?"

This surprised her. Perhaps with an opening line as predictable as that she'd misread him as someone interesting.

"I'm a psychologist," she said. She very nearly was too, at the time she was close to finishing her studies. She braced for the gag. People always had a psychologist joke.

"Why?"

That surprised her too.

"Why?"

"Yes. Why?"

"Why do you ask?"

He shrugged. "I'm interested. I'm interested in people. I'm interested in psychology. Why are you a psychologist?"

"I don't know... That's a difficult question to answer." She stopped.

His eyes were grey but had flecks of blue that caught the light like quartz shot through granite. She felt the heat returning to her cheeks.

"Why are *you* interested in psychology?" She asked.

"I don't know." He said at once. "That's a difficult question to answer."

She smiled. Just a little. Resisted the impulse to bite the inside of her lip.

"Happiness," he said. "It seems like a good idea to dedicate one of the sciences to finding happiness."

"Psychologists aren't only interested in happiness. We study all behaviour. Such as what you did back there. That was very unusual."

His eyebrows arched up towards his hair cut tight against his head, possibly a military haircut? That might explain the over-confidence. She understood his gesture but waited until he spoke.

"Back where exactly?"

"On the way to the bar. You stopped those thugs bullying that poor man."

"I tripped."

"No you didn't."

"Yes I did. There's a loose fold in the carpet, look there." He leaned across so she could sight down his arm as he pointed at the floor. The bar didn't even have carpet. She couldn't stop herself breathing in. She caught the warm smell of soap.

"Have you ever heard of Kitty Genovese?" The thought came into her head and out of her mouth before she knew where she was going with it.

He seemed to search his mind before answering.

"No. Should I?"

"Probably not. She was murdered in New York in the 1960s, I'm sorry this is a bit brutal, I shouldn't have mentioned it."

"It's OK. I'm intrigued. Go on."

Natalie cursed herself silently, but realised she couldn't back down from it now without looking crazy, and something was telling her she didn't want to look crazy in front of this man. She paused.

"It's just her death has become the textbook example of something known as bystander apathy. She was stabbed outside her home in a busy residential street. She screamed and lots of her neighbours heard her, some even saw the attack. But none of them did anything. It took her thirty minutes to die. The man who did it, he even left for a while then came back for a second attack." The redness she'd felt invading her cheeks had receded.

"They caught him a few days later and asked him how he dared to attack a woman with so many witnesses around and he told them this: 'No one would do anything, no one ever does'."

He waited to see if she would continue, and only spoke when he saw she was finished.

"Everyone thought someone else would do something to help?"

"That's right."

He didn't say anything to this, but waited for her to go on.

"And just now in the bar, everyone here was like that. Wishing someone else would do something about those men. But only you did."

Jim sat back in his chair at this, and it was only when he did that Natalie realised how close together they had been.

"It's hardly the same thing though."

"No," she hoped he'd lean forward again and told herself off for thinking it.

"But how did you know they wouldn't retaliate? They could have turned on you. There were two of them, only one of you."

"Ah. Not true. I'm with some friends over there, the rugby players." He pointed at a table where two very slight men were sitting. Boys really. They both wore glasses. Natalie got the joke more quickly this time.

"Does the one on the left actually have a pen tucked into his shirt pocket? Or does he just look like he should?"

"It writes in three colours. They're amazing kick boxers though. Black belts. They do the nerd look to keep the element of surprise."

Natalie couldn't help but smile.

"So you see it was always three against two."

"Are they really your friends?"

"I've never seen them before in my life."

Natalie shook her head, then allowed herself to look into those strange eyes.

"Seriously, how did you know those thugs wouldn't retaliate? I'm interested to know. Maybe you could call it professional interest."

The eyes didn't blink.

"Seriously? I knew they wouldn't. People like that never do."

eight

THE EVENING TURNED into night, and still there was no answer on Jim's mobile phone, just that strange beep that presumably meant a dead battery. She was concerned now. So much that her anger was nearly gone, replaced wholesale by fears for where he might be. Rationally she knew she shouldn't panic. The most likely explanation was that he'd gone for a late surf, then stopped at a pub for a meal and was now driving home. Or perhaps the car had broken down and he was waiting for the AA to pick him up. The most sensible thing to do was go to bed. She'd probably wake up when he came in, if not she'd see him when she woke in the morning.

She dreamt he was there when she woke. It was so real she could still see the image of him lying there, his broad, tanned back curving away from her in their bed. But he wasn't there. She called out, in case he'd already risen and was in the bathroom. But the house was silent, her mobile showed no messages, no missed calls.

Now she was scared. Inconsiderate was one thing. This was something else. Before she was even dressed she phoned Dave to ask if he'd heard from him. The surprise in his voice convinced her she had no choice. She dressed and made herself a coffee, and then she picked up the phone and dialled the number for the local police. She didn't know what else to do.

Right away it felt weird. "I'm phoning because I think my husband is missing," she said. The words sounded like something you'd hear in a film.

The police officer she'd been connected to was a man. He'd told her his name but she forgot it at once.

"OK." He had a grating voice. He sounded young and inexperienced.

"And when did you last see… Mr Harrison?"

"Four, no five days ago. He went away on a surfing trip."

"On a surfing trip?"

"That's right."

There was a pause.

"Was he alone, or was he with anyone?"

Natalie hesitated, thinking of her conversation with Linda the day before.

"He was alone."

"And can you tell me where he went?"

"No. I'm sorry. I just know that he was going surfing. He normally goes to Devon I think. Saunton or Croyde."

"And that's where he went this time?"

She remembered how it had been when they parted.

"I don't know. He might have been going somewhere else. Sometimes he goes down to Cornwall. Or other places," she finished lamely.

The silence the man left went on for a long time and Natalie imagined it filled with accusation, until she suddenly realised it was only so long because he was writing everything down. She could visualise a slow longhand scrawl.

"And how did he travel? Is he in a car?"

"Yes." Natalie gave the details and then had to repeat them several times because the policeman kept getting the registration wrong. The man sounded barely literate but finally they moved on.

"So when were you expecting him to be back?" He asked, seemingly unaware how his slowness was irritating her.

"Yesterday. Sometime yesterday. I don't know exactly when. In the evening at the latest."

There was a longer pause.

"Did he say what time yesterday evening?"

"No, he didn't say yesterday evening, he just said yesterday. I said yesterday evening. That was the latest I thought I'd see him."

This baffled the officer for what felt like minutes.

"So when did he say he'd be back?"

"Yesterday. Evening, afternoon. *I don't know.* He didn't say. But he had to work this morning. He hasn't turned up for work."

"OK." Something had crept into the officer's voice, there was promise in this call after all.

"So your husband works does he?" With the tone of his voice the officer managed to imply he had thought this unlikely.

"Yes, of course he does."

"OK Mrs Harrison, I need you to calm down a little bit now."

"I am calm."

"OK. That's good. Let's try to keep it that way shall we?"

Natalie bit her lip. She realised her breath was coming short and fast.

"So what exactly does your husband do?" The officer asked, as if he still couldn't quite picture a surfer who worked.

"He owns a business operating helicopters out of the airport. He also flies the helicopters. He flew your chief constable to Edinburgh last month," Natalie snapped.

This brought on the longest silence yet on the other end of the line, and when the man spoke again his tone had changed.

"OK... Look normally we wouldn't necessarily list an adult as missing until at least twenty four hours after the person was expected back. But in this case... I think we can put the wheels in motion as it were. I should say now, it's most likely that your husband will come back of his own accord, that's the outcome in the majority of cases like this."

It sounded to Natalie that the man was describing Jim as if he were a lost dog, but she didn't say anything, and she regretted her outburst.

There were more questions before the conversation finished. A description of Jim and his vehicle were circulated around all the police forces in the UK, with particular directions given to those in Cornwall and Devon to look in coastal areas. After she put the phone down she stood at the sink and drank a glass of water, then refilled it but didn't drink any more. She just stood holding the glass. Her face felt flushed and hot. She listened to the silence in the house, the only noise the faint humming from the fridge. She wondered if she had done the right thing. Jim would hate to be the centre of any fuss like this. But then it was his bloody fault.

"Oh Jim, where are you?" she said out loud.

nine

JOHN WAS RIGHT, the surf really did come in two or three times a week, at least for the next few months. We always surfed the same place, the beach right in front of the campsite. Everyone called it 'Town Beach' even though the village was way too small to be called a town. It never exactly got good, at least not by Aussie standards, and even with my new wetsuit I could feel how cold the water was. But it was surfing. And I grabbed it like a rope lowered down to pull me out of my own private hell.

Or maybe I grabbed John. Usually we could only surf weekends, but we'd spend hours in the water, and then we'd come ashore and stuff our faces with cereal and bananas, and then go right back out. It didn't matter if the waves were shit, we'd still want to be out there.

If the waves were really bad we'd be out there alone, but if they were ok there was always a local crew out. I didn't mind, in fact I quite liked it. Back in Oz there were so many surfers that I learnt how to give respect and not drop in or mess up anyone's waves. Back there you saw fights in the line up most days. Normally no one would actually hit a kid even if they did drop in, they'd just swear and shout and generally do their block, but everyone would look at you and know what you'd done. If you were really bad the lifeguards would tell you to fuck off and not come back as you walked back up the beach.

So at first I was respectful, waiting till the other guys had taken a wave before I took one, but most of them weren't that good, so pretty quickly I was taking my fair share too, and then a few more. And it wasn't a problem. I think they thought I was exotic, and it was why we were there, to catch waves, so if I was showing a bit of attitude to the waves, they seemed happy with that. And John seemed to like it. Being associated with me I mean. He seemed to get a kick from hanging out with another kid who could kick up a bit of spray, take on the bigger waves and put down some powerful turns. And if John liked it, I liked it.

Pretty soon I had the other surfers figured out. There was Charlie who was a fisherman who worked off a boat that came into the small harbour in the village. You could tell he was tough, so I kept out of his way. At the other end of scale was Gwynn, an old guy who rode a longboard. He only ever crouched down and trimmed along the waves but he was always talking and shouting encouragement to everyone, like he loved being out there more than anything else. Baz worked in the quarry that was out behind the village. You heard the explosions sometimes when they were cutting new rock and it had made him slightly deaf, so no one bothered talking to him much. Barry and Henry were mates of Gwynn who both also rode longboards and sat out the back. Those were the guys who were always out, and there was another group who made it out sometimes. Usually there were plenty of waves to go around. It was friendly, a pretty cool group.

But sometimes other people turned up too and sometimes that spoiled things a bit. There were often surfers staying at the campsite, or guys who'd turned up from out of town, from the cities down south. If it was just one or two it didn't matter, but when there were too many our pack got a bit more tight knit. We'd kind of unconsciously help each other onto waves, we'd form a little scrum, talking a bit too loudly, making it clear we lived here. Like surfers do. The idea was to keep the visitors off the sandbar in the middle of the bay where the best waves broke. You know, locals only.

There was one other kid who surfed. His name was Darren. I don't remember meeting him, he just seemed to appear from out of the background. Then I realised he was in some of my classes at school, I just hadn't noticed him there either. I don't know why but John had never bothered to talk to him before I came along. Consequently Darren used to sit a little way away from everyone else. He didn't catch too many waves sitting out there, but every so often a good one would come in over where he was and he'd ride it OK.

I don't really know when Darren officially became mates with me and John. He just hung about in the background until we were used to him being there. Eventually it felt weird when he wasn't there. Or maybe just a bit more weird. Darren could be pretty weird when he was there too.

Anyway, soon it seemed that John, Darren and me, the three kids in the water, became our own little group even within the local surfers. At first I was a lot better than either of them but they learnt quick enough. In Australia the lifeguards would coach us all the time and swear at us if we didn't do what they said. We'd had two world champions come from our beach back home, and the lifeguards wanted a third. And I told John and Darren what the lifeguards had told me. How you had to drop faster down the face of the waves before turning back up. How you had to find the steepest parts of the waves to do your moves. How you had to really lean in hard to make the rails bite in the water.

I taught them by showing them, and surfing with them, but most of all I taught them by talking about surfing. John had a massive collection of surfing magazines, and we'd spend hours sitting and reading them and I'd sometimes lean over and point out what the pro's were doing. I think that was one of the reasons John stuck with me at first - he really wanted to learn this stuff, and there was no one else around that could teach him.

That first autumn we hung out a lot in John's place. It was warm and there was always food in the fridge. But then John's dad started coming home unexpectedly. He didn't approve of surfing, he thought John was wasting his time and should be playing rugby or whatever. As a result he didn't approve much of me, and he *hated* Darren, he couldn't even bring himself to look at him. Anyway, John's house was a couple of miles from the beach so we couldn't check the surf from there. Darren's place was no good either. He lived in one of the little terraced houses up in the village. The rooms were tiny and his dad was always there drinking home brew. He'd been laid off from the quarry after he hurt his back. So in the end we often had no choice but to come back to the campsite.

Our house was bigger than Darren's, but because it had the shop and the reception in there it still cramped our style a bit. But John noticed one of the caravans. It was right at the end of the row, and it was waiting for some renovation before it could be rented out. I guess it was obvious it was never going to get it, so John suggested to Mum that maybe we could use it as somewhere to do our homework in. She knew he was taking the piss, but she said yes anyway, and we moved a TV and video player in there, and John brought down his surf movies and some of his surfing magazines. It made a pretty cool base, and Mum never came in, even when she needed to tell me dinner was ready or something, she'd just knock on the door and walk away.

Did I already say John wasn't from the village? Well he wasn't, he wasn't even from Wales. He was born somewhere in London and had been sent to the posh private school that's near here. Then when his parents got divorced his dad decided to move out here rather than upset John's education as well as his home life.

John was the only surfer at his school, he said the rest of them all played rugby or cricket and everyone there looked down on surfing as not something people like them did. Sometimes, when Mum had to go to town to get something from the hardware store I'd come along and I'd see kids from John's school, walking around in their blazers, their black trousers with the crease down the front, with their noses in the air. None of them looked down on John though. He was top of his class in every subject he took, and when he did do their sports he was always the best at them too. Like his dad they were always begging him to join the rugby team but John never would. He didn't want to risk it, he didn't want to have any commitments in case the waves were good and he missed a surf.

I already said Mum liked John too, and she did, she really did. Maybe it was because John was posh, or maybe she was relieved I'd made a friend. Or maybe just because he was *John.* Whatever it was, he could get away with murder. John even called her by her first name.

One time we were in the campsite shop helping ourselves to food - just taking it, we weren't going to pay - when Mum came in unexpectedly. I was allowed to take food from the kitchen, but not the shop since it messed up her stock system. John had his hands full of chocolate bars but instead of looking guilty John just started talking to her like there was nothing wrong in the world.

"Oh hello Judy," he said, not even trying to hide the chocolate. "How are you?"

She gave him a look, like he was busted, but he seemed to smooth right over it.

"You know I was thinking the other day. A lot of people who come camping, they forget how boring it is when they're packing. They forget something to read. What I'm trying to say is you should think about selling magazines in here. It could be a profitable line." Then he put the chocolate down on the counter and started patting his pocket like he was looking for some money.

"Now how much do I owe you?" he asked.

You could see her looking at the chocolate bars, and then at John's face like she couldn't work out whether to be pissed off or to take him seriously.

"Do you really think magazines would sell?"

"Yeah I do." He nodded meaningfully. "You should stock a few surfing magazines too. You get a lot of surfers here. I'm sure many of them would like a magazine to buy. I certainly would. Oh and I'll get Jesse and Darren's. How much does that all come to?" He held up his chocolate.

She smiled at him like she enjoyed the cheek. And this was after she'd given me a right telling off a few days before, about how it ruined her whole stocktake. But she did make him pay.

She tried it though, and he was right. Magazines sold really well. Soon we had a little stand in the corner of the shop, and we got daily papers delivered.

John didn't forget either. Every month he would come in and buy his copy of *Surfer* and take it along to the caravan. Usually he nicked a bar of chocolate too. The thing was John never forgot things like that. Later, when there were things I really wished John would forget, that's how I knew he wouldn't. The bastard wouldn't ever forget.

ten

SHE'D GIVEN JIM her number on the drinks mat from the bar. Classy move. Then she'd cursed herself for being such a cliché as her phone's stubborn silence had taken an ever increasing role in her life. She was working full-time in the hospital at that point, sitting in with qualified psychologists during their sessions with patients. At the end of each session she checked her phone for messages. There were plenty, pictures of the baby from her sister, her mum checking how she was, but not the message she wanted to see. After two weeks she told herself to forget him. It might have happened, but it hadn't. And now it wasn't going to.

It was four o'clock on a Friday when he called. Her session had been cancelled so she was at home, getting in a final couple of hours with the books before calling it a week. She recognised his voice at once.

"I've been doing some reading."

"How mind improving," she replied, telling herself not to sound too keen. "Anything interesting?"

"You wouldn't think so from the names, but bear with me: *Donald Dutton and Arthur Aron.* Come across them?"

"I don't think so."

"That's what I hoped."

'What about them?"

"They were a couple of Americans who wanted to help out ugly guys like me. They did this experiment."

Natalie didn't tell him he wasn't ugly, but the thought screamed out of her mind.

"They found a suspension footbridge that crossed a canyon, wobbly, think Indiana Jones and the temple of whatever. Then they put a female researcher on the bridge, a very attractive female researcher," he paused. "Low cut top, short skirt, nice legs - do you know what I'm saying?"

"I think I understand what attractive means." She'd got up by now and walked to the mirror in the bathroom, she watched her own reflection say this, a flush of colour to her cheeks, she untied her hair with her free hand.

"Good. So this attractive, this *very* attractive researcher has to stop men who were crossing the scary bridge. And she asks them questions. You know, a questionnaire. They have to interpret ambiguous pictures, squiggly lines. They have to tell her what they think they can see in them. And when they finish the woman gives them her name and her phone number, just in case they have any questions about the questionnaire they've just done. I'm sure that's normal for psychologists?"

"Pretty much standard practice."

"Right. Anyway, the same woman then did the exact same experiment again, but this time on a normal bridge, a few feet above a little stream. This time think, I dunno, Pooh sticks. Teletubby land. A bridge you wouldn't feel scared on. And you know what they found?"

"*Misattribution of arousal.*" Natalie said. She remembered the case now.

"So you do know it?" Jim sounded disappointed.

"Yes and no." She said quickly. "I'm not really familiar with it."

"OK," he said slowly. "Well perhaps I should go on. What they found was the men who met the same sexy researcher, same low cut top, on the *scary* bridge were more likely to interpret the images as sexual, and twice as likely to phone the researcher afterwards and ask for a date. What about that? There was a link between fear and attraction."

"Really?"

"Yeah. And you know what the really interesting bit is?"

"No."

"They did the same experiment again, but reversed, so that it wasn't guys being tested but *girls,* and they found exactly the same thing. Put the girls in a heightened state of stimulation - if I can use that word - and they're more likely to link that to thoughts of sex. More likely to find the person they're with attractive."

"That's fascinating," Natalie said. "I must remember that if I ever meet a sexy man with a clipboard on a bridge."

"I think that would be wise."

"Well thank you." It occurred to her for a moment that this was all he'd phoned to tell her, but he didn't keep her wondering for long.

"So anyway, that wasn't why I phoned. Are you busy tonight? I know this great restaurant."

"Tonight?"

"Too short notice?"

She thought of the books. There was a bottle of white wine in the fridge. Half of it had her name on, the other half her flatmate's.

"Not exactly."

"That's a relief as I've already booked it. There's just one problem."

"What's that?"

"The restaurant's in Ireland." He didn't give her time to take that in. "Actually that's not the problem. I didn't tell you but I've just bought my own helicopter. The problem is I got it second hand. It might be a bit shaky, rattly. Some important bits might fall off on the way over. It might be a little *scary* if you know what I mean."

"Slow down. What are you talking about?"

"You've flown in a helicopter before right?"

"What? No."

"Oh. In that case it'll definitely be scary. Flying out over the sea like that. Nothing below you but the churning waves. You'll have to be careful not to let that fear/attraction thing affect you."

She shook her head. She said the only thing she could think of.

"I'll do my best." She wondered if he could hear the smile in her voice.

"Can you meet me at the airport in an hour?"

"One hour?!"

It hadn't been nearly enough time, but she didn't want to be late. She showered with the door open, shouting out to her flatmate questions about what one wore for a first date in a helicopter. They settled on a summery dress with a denim jacket. Matching pants and bra, thank God there was something clean. Then she drove, as he'd told her to, around the side from the airport's main entrance where a smaller road she had never noticed before took her to a little car park. Inside the perimeter fence a number of helicopters were parked up, and further away a collection of light aircraft. He was standing by a gate. He waved her into a space and then punched a code and led them inside.

It was a relief to see she'd called it about right. He was wearing jeans, smart trainers, a shirt with short sleeves, the top button left undone.

"Here she is," he said.

At first Natalie thought he was talking about her, but then she realised he was pointing at one of the helicopters sitting out on the tarmac. He led her out to it, it was bigger than she expected, the rotors were still and drooped so low she could have reached out and touched them. He opened the door for her but let her climb in unaided.

"Like I said she's second hand, but she's had every possible check. Actually she's in great condition," he said as he settled himself into the seat alongside her. He handed her a set of headphones and pulled on a pair for himself. Even on the ground Natalie already felt high up, the windows in the side were much lower than in a car, to give a view down below she supposed. But apart from that the interior of the machine surprised her. It looked like a car, albeit a luxury car with dials and buttons everywhere and leather seats - not like her little Fiat. And the smell was different too. Helicopter fuel she supposed. He spoke to someone through his headphones and pressed some of the buttons. The helicopter began to shudder and Natalie realised the rotors had begun to turn.

"What's it for? I mean, who do you fly in it?" She realised she could hear his voice through the headphones.

"Business people, pleasure flights - people like to fly over their house for some reason. There's a big contract for the wind farm we're hoping to get." He jerked his thumb behind him. "Got six seats in the back, all for hire. We're just glorified taxi drivers really." Then he added like it was an afterthought. "But if that fear/sex thing does kick in, there's a bit more room back there than in a normal taxi."

"I'm managing to keep myself under control at the moment."

He shrugged as if there'd be plenty of time.

"OK, but we haven't taken off yet."

He spoke again into the radio. Natalie didn't understand the terms but got the gist and just nodded when he turned back to her and said: "That's us."

The noise of the engine built from a low grumble to something louder, an incessant thudding behind the cushioning of the headphones. Then they moved sideways. Then the ground began to drop away.

"Jesus!"

She gripped the armrest tightly and watched the airport disappear below them, then give way to a golf course, then fields. The city was already behind them as they headed west. She had an idea of the speed they were travelling from cars not far below, another idea from how quickly the coast came into view.

"We'll head out the Bristol Channel and then out over the Irish Sea," he said. "Flight time should be just under an hour. Are you hungry?"

She had totally forgotten about eating. "I might be when we get there."

"You look nice by the way."

"Thank you."

He lapsed into silence and seemed content to focus on flying the helicopter, occasionally he would exchange words with someone through his radio, and sometimes she glanced across and saw him watching her. When she noticed he would smile then look away.

They left the land behind them and flew out over the water. For some reason she felt less safe with water below them and she thought of what would happen if the helicopter went down, how that cold black water would pour in, how far they were from land even if she did make it out. From the height they were flying, just a few hundred metres up, the ocean seemed endless. She thought of what he'd told her, how people often confused exhilaration and fear for something sexual. She noticed the stick which came up from the floor of the helicopter. Her eyes followed it up until they rested between his legs where his hands gripped it, just a few inches away from the button fly at the front of his jeans. She realised she was staring and she felt more blood flush her cheeks.

The trip seemed to take a long time, the sea seemed vast. Eventually some rocks appeared in front of them, the largest with a slender white lighthouse perched upon it.

"Nearly there," Jim said. "That's Tuskar Rock. A lot of people drowned there before they built the lighthouse."

She watched as it slipped beneath them. From a distance the rocks looked black, but looking straight down she could see they were really dark green from their coating of seaweed. Soon afterwards a lighter green rose onto the horizon in front of them and he told her it was land. Ireland. She felt herself begin to relax, realised how tense she had been while over the water. Jim checked some instruments as they closed the coast until they were finally over the beach and Natalie's breathing flowed more easily. Then they turned right, followed the beach north for a little while until they came to a headland, and, set back from it a large building, its roof a splash of red. They edged out over the water one more time, but here, the sea was shallow and clear and the white sand beneath the water painted it Caribbean blue. The land was lush green.

"Aren't we going to an airport?" Natalie said.

"No need," Jim replied and as if to show what he meant he swung the helicopter around so that Natalie's window was looking almost straight down at the beach below her. Then they levelled off and descended towards the lawn of the building, she went from seeing only its roof to seeing it from ground level, an impressive white-painted building, like a country house. And then with the lightest of bumps the skids of the helicopter found the lawn and then the whole weight of the machine was pushing into the grass. They stopped moving and became a part of the normal world again.

The restaurant was obviously expensive, the tablecloth was thick and heavy, the cutlery shone. The cream walls were minimally decorated with abstract art, perhaps to not distract too much from the view out of the windows, where small waves lapped against the shore. But to Natalie it was the helicopter that stood out most, sat on the middle of the lawn, a constant reminder that this was really happening.

A man in a white dinner jacket showed them to a table. He seemed to know Jim. Despite his dress he wasn't at all formal, they exchanged jokes, him in a lilting accent that sounded fake at first it was so absurdly Irish. He complimented her without embarrassment.

"I've been out here a few times before," Jim explained once the waiter had settled them in and retreated. "Clients. They come out here to impress their girlfriends. They spend all evening telling them how good the breakfasts are. Can you believe anyone would fall for that?"

She hadn't let herself think about getting home until then. But as he spoke she wondered if she was just the latest woman to sit opposite this man, totally at his mercy. She felt a flush of indignation at becoming ensnared in a situation to his advantage.

"Red or white?"

"Sorry?"

"The wine. They say you're supposed to have white with fish, but I say have what you like. It's not like anyone's watching."

"White."

"Good choice."

The waiter came back at the signal from Jim and after a serious discussion, walked smartly away to fetch a bottle.

"So does it always work?"

His frown showed she'd lost him.

"Your *clients*, getting you to fly them out here with their girlfriends. Does it always work for them? Do the women always stay for breakfast?" She smiled at her emphasis on the word, to show him she didn't believe for a moment they were really clients.

He thought for a moment then broke out into a smile. "You don't believe me do you? I really have only ever been here with clients. I usually get to sit in the bar, drinking mineral water, just in case it doesn't go well for them. That's how I know Sean so well. We're the only people here not pissed by midnight." He smiled at her then went on. "Drinking and flying, there's no police up there but it's still not the done thing."

The waiter returned with a silver bucket, the neck of a wine bottle poking out from its bed of crushed ice. He pulled the cork with no fuss and poured a small amount into Natalie's glass for her to try. It was delicious and she said so. The waiter filled her glass then looked to Jim's, but he placed his hand over the glass so that it remained empty. With a nod the waiter settled the bottle back into its bucket and retreated again.

"But to answer your question, I've flown three clients out here. And

I've had three breakfasts. They really are good."

Natalie suddenly didn't care if he was lying. She laughed out loud, then reached over and picked up the bottle. At first she made it look as if she just wanted to read the label, but then she rested its neck against the rim of Jim's glass and watched as the wine flowed out.

"They better be."

eleven

IT WAS LATE summer, nearly two years had gone by since I moved to Wales and we were fishing from the pier. We were going for flat fish - flatties we called them cos that's what they were back home in Oz. We had a couple of crab lines down to get bait. We didn't fish that often, only when there was nothing else to do, but it was that sort of a day - grey, a bit windy, the ground boggy and soaked from rain. Crabs were easy to catch. First you had to climb down the rusty iron ladder on the side of the pier and twist off a few big juicy mussels from the thick wooden legs, then grab a rock and smash them open until the orangey-yellow meat was exposed, bits of iridescent-blue mussel shell tearing into it and releasing the juices. Then tie that to a line and drop it down. The crabs were quick to find it, you only had to wait a minute or so, and they were so stupid they would hold onto the smashed mussel even when you pulled them up out of the water and onto the pier. Even if the wind caught them and knocked them into the pier legs, the crabs would still try their best to hold on. I didn't much like the next bit.

It was ok to smash mussels up, I know they're alive really, but in a way they're not. Killing them was like smashing a nut or something. The crabs were different. They've got little eyes on stalks that watch you, and they'll scuttle away and hide in a corner if you don't hold onto them. But fresh crab meat was the best way to catch flatties, and you had to kill the crabs to get it.

Darren was the best at killing crabs. His brother taught him the technique. He was down in Swansea, training to be a vet, and he was a vegetarian. The technique was to hold the crab by the outside of its shell and quickly stab the knife down between the two eyes then give it a little twist. The legs would kick and clatter on the deck for a bit, but you could tell it was dead right away, and once it wasn't moving it was much easier to cut up, or if it was a little one, to just thread a hook straight through it. Then you could cast it out and although you maybe still felt a little bit guilty, you knew it was out there helping to attract a flattie which you were gonna eat. So that was OK. Even so I was happy enough for Darren to do the killing.

We'd been there maybe half an hour and I'd climbed down to get the mussels and was putting my shoes back on while John and me watched Darren pulling up his crab line. There was one crab on the end, quite a big one, pretty feisty. It was holding on to the bait with one pincer and waving the other in the air like it was warning us to stay back, like it was a dangerous predator or something. With his arms outstretched, Darren swung the line over the side onto the pier decking then gave it a jerk to make the crab fall off. It didn't have far to fall and landed upright, now with both its pincers waving in the air. Darren used the blade on its flat side to hold the crab in place, while he got in a comfortable position to dispatch it.

"Why do you always do it like that?" John asked, from where he was sitting with his back to the wall.

"I told you. Ben told me to do it this way. It hurts them less." For some reason John often got a bit annoyed when Darren mentioned his brother.

"Still hurts though, having that knife stuck in your head."

"Yeah but not for as long. You don't want them to suffer."

"It's only a crab. What does it matter?"

"It's just better this way," said Darren. Ben was nine years older than us and only John ever thought to question the wisdom those extra years brought.

"Maybe it makes them better bait?" I said. I'd learnt by then the warning signs for John's moods, but not how to ward them off. "I mean maybe they release some chemicals or something if they're in pain that puts the flatties off."

"More likely to be the other way round if you ask me," said John, and he scrambled to his feet.

"I mean, think about it. If you're a flattie, you're going to want to eat injured crabs in the sea, cos you're less likely to get pinched on the fin or something, so you're going to want to sniff out those injured chemicals."

Darren looked troubled by this. He was still holding the crab down with the knife, the blade bending under the pressure he needed to use, the crab slowly flexing the legs it could still move.

"I think it's more to do with just not being unfair to the crabs," he said. "Ben says you should try and make them not suffer." He made no move to kill the crab. It was like he knew what was coming and was powerless to stop it.

John said nothing but he crouched down low right in front of the crab and stared at it for a long time. Despite its situation it was still trying to eat a morsel of mussel flesh that it had ripped off from the line.

"Doesn't look too worried to me. Look, it's still trying to eat."

We only had two fishing rods, John's was the best one with a good casting reel. Darren's was a bit old and knackered. I think it used to be his brothers. Mum didn't have enough money to buy me a rod.

"I know," said John, still crouched down in front of the crab. "Let's test Jesse's idea. Pull up the other crab line Jesse, get another crab. We'll put Darren's injured crab here on one rod and a dead one on the other, and we can see which is better at catching fish."

"It wasn't my idea," I protested.

"Yeah it was." The way John said it was all magnanimous, as if he was too generous to take the credit himself. I wanted to argue but I didn't. Instead I moved over to the second crab line and tugged it gently. It felt heavier than just the mussel so I knew there was another crab on it. For a moment I considered pretending I hadn't caught anything, but I felt John watching me.

"That's it, pull it up," he said.

I did so and when the bait broke free of the water there was another crab attached, clinging on with its back legs while its pincers delicately fed it morsels of mussel meat.

"That'll do, bring it up here and kill it Jesse. Darren can injure his one a bit."

You might wonder - with me saying this now - why didn't we see John for what he really was back then? Why didn't we get the hell away? The truth is I don't know the answer, I'm just telling you how it happened. And it's not like John was a monster, at the time it felt more like he just hated limits, wherever they were. He would search out our limits and push them, test them, force us to go beyond what we were comfortable with. It wasn't just killing crabs. It was jumping off cliffs, he'd make us go higher, it was diving down to explore the rocks when the sea was still, and when there were waves it was making sure we were all looking for the biggest one, or the gnarliest one. Whatever we did he was always pushing us, and that felt... I don't know, intoxicating. He charged the air around him with this charm and energy. We were addicted to just being near him. Because he made us better people. At least that's what he somehow made us believe.

"Come on, you can do it. Here." John often kept a hunting knife strapped to his ankle, and he unsheathed it now, handed it to me. I'd pulled my crab over the pier's deck now and dropped it down, where it continued to eat, oblivious to its fate.

"You've got to do it. If you're gonna fish I mean." He settled back on his heels to watch. I'd seen that John's technique was always much rougher than Darren's. He would just stick the knife kind of casually into the crab's back and then attend to his line and hook, or sometimes just chop the crab straight in two and pick one half up to put on the line. I didn't know which way I was supposed to do it, and felt the weight of the knife in my hand, trying first a stabbing grip, then changing my hand over to more of a cutting action.

"Just stick it in. Come on." There was a curious look on John's face, he was watching me, not the crab.

I changed back to the stabbing grip and held onto the crab at the edge of its shell, where its pincers couldn't reach. I brought the point of the knife down on its back and pushed a little. The shell was too thick to yield and I didn't have the courage to keep pushing. Instead I looked up at John, to check I was doing it right. He nodded with enthusiasm so I raised the knife quite high and then released it, using its own weight to drop down. That way it was like I wasn't quite responsible.

It didn't work, the point of the knife didn't go in, but the shell cracked a little and some greeny yellow slime oozed out.

"Eeewwy, gross," said John.

"Kill it properly Jesse," said Darren.

Kinda horrified that I'd hurt it I turned my head away and brought the knife down again, this time much harder, and then twisted the blade like I'd seen Darren do. I felt the blade crack through the shell and bite into the wood of the decking boards.

"That's it. Now cut it in half and put it on Darren's rod," John instructed me. "Then cast it out, while Darren injures his one."

I normally didn't much like threading the hook through, but I was glad of the distraction this time, and like with the mussels, the thing in my hands already felt like a piece of meat, rather than something with thoughts and feelings, not that I knew if crabs had all that stuff. Even so I was glad when I'd cast it out of sight and it sank invisibly into the flat grey water. But Darren still had his crab fidgeting under his knife and he and John both looked at it, although they were thinking different things.

"Maybe pull one side of his legs off," John suggested. "We could put the hook in one of the leg sockets and out of another one."

The uncertainty was painted all over Darren's face. "I don't know. Ben says you shouldn't..." he began, but he stopped, knowing that mentioning his brother just wound John up.

"We could pull its legs off after its dead?" he suggested. The crab's eyes swivelled from one boy to the other, as if following the conversation, as if it knew this was Darren's last hope.

You could see that John considered this. "In a funny way," he started, "I don't think it would mind being used as an experiment. Its death is for something that way. Something important."

With this the decision was made, and Darren wasn't going to argue any further.

"You keep holding it down, and I'll kind of crunch its legs off." John stepped around and crouched down beside Darren, his knife back in his hand. He poked his tongue out in concentration as he lined up the blade against the side of the crab, and then pushed it slowly down. There was a delicate cracking sound as the steel bit through the outer shell and severed the four legs as one.

"Now let it go, see if it can walk."

The crab had barely reacted, but finally released from the pressure on its back it made a move to scuttle sideways to the pier edge. Its good side still worked and it was able to make some progress, but the stumps of the legs in its broken side just waggled in their sockets while more green juice oozed out.

"If I was a flattie I'd eat that," said John, satisfied. He reached for his own rod and easily caught up with the crab. He picked it up and after a moment's consideration poked the hook into one of the sockets, and forced it through the body until the shiny silver tip reappeared through the creature's belly. John let it go and it swung out from the end of the rod. He walked a few feet to the pier edge and began to swing the line as he manoeuvred the rod out behind his head. When the crab was at the far extent of the swing behind him he cast it forward, pointing the rod out to sea. The crab flew out into the air behind the lead weight, the whole assembly seemed to hover briefly as its momentum carried it away, and then it plopped into the water and John's reel fell silent.

"There. Now we'll see which works better." John settled the rod against the handrail and sat down with his back against the stone wall.

No one talked much for a while. It sometimes took ages to catch anything, and sometimes we didn't catch anything even if we fished for hours. We had a few more mussels, but I didn't want to catch any more crabs for a while and I could see that Darren felt the same. Instead we watched the two rod tips, waiting to see which one would twitch first.

"Fishing is pretty boring," John said after about fifteen minutes had passed.

"Yeah," Darren agreed. You could see the distaste had gone away already. We were back to normal.

"When are we going to get any waves?"

"Dunno."

Surfing was our fall back conversation. I read somewhere that part of what makes it so addictive is that you can't do it every day. It can be flat for ages and there's nothing you can do, just wait and make sure you're ready for when the waves do come. And all you know is that one day they will come again. Maybe that's true, I don't know, but I do know that whatever it was we were doing pretty quickly became boring compared to the thrill of surfing.

"I bet your old beach in Australia has got perfect surf right now," said John.

John did this sometimes, talked about Australia, or about other places he'd read about in the magazines. The way he talked about them was like they were somehow nearly within reach, the sort of place we might go to for a holiday or something. I guess it was because he did disappear every now and then on a holiday, mostly with his mum, he'd come back tanned and full of tales about it, what the pyramids were like inside, or how warm the Caribbean was in February. But it seemed impossible to me by then. I felt like I could barely even remember Australia. I sometimes tried to remember the way from our old house to the beach and I could never do it. I could never quite connect the two. And the beach, that white sand, the azure waters and the lush green of the jungle on the bluff, all that had got mixed up with the images from the surf magazines I binged on.

"We should go there," John went on now. "When we're older and we can go places I mean. Or Indonesia, we should go there and explore and find places that no one has surfed before. We should open a bar in Indo. That'd be cool."

That silenced us all for a while. It would be forever before we were even old enough to drive. Until then we were trapped here. A one-beach town where the waves had to be big enough to push up the Irish Sea before they could get to us. It was a depressing thought. I looked around at the coastline that by then was so familiar. The tide was dropping now and the beach was a thin strip of dirty yellow sand and pebbles, a black line of damp seaweed marking the highest point the water had lapped at an hour or so earlier. There were a few people walking on the beach, and one or two huddled around picnics, mostly families from the campsite. My eyes followed the beach south to where it abruptly met black rocks and above them low orange cliffs. These features curved away out of sight as the coastline took a turn to the south, low green hills visible falling into the sea beyond.

"We could explore a bit more here," I said suddenly. "For all we know there might be better waves somewhere. Better than Town Beach."

Darren's eyes followed my gaze southwards, and when he spoke he sounded alarmed. "No, we can't go there. You're not allowed to go there."

"I know you can't go there," I said, irritated. I'd been looking at the estate which hugged the coast to the south of Town Beach. It was private land, some wealthy landowner had miles of it all fenced off. Even the coastal footpath took a detour inland to go around the estate.

"Everyone knows you can't go there," Darren said again. "It's private."

"Alright Darren," I said. "I didn't mean inside the estate alright? I meant, I dunno, like further away, beyond the estate."

"But how would we get there, it's miles..." Darren started to say until John cut him off.

"Shut it Darren, you've made your point."

Darren closed his mouth and watched John nervously. I knew how he felt.

John had his eyes looking southwards as well now, where the cliffs at the end of Town Beach disappeared around the small headland.

"It can't really be *that* private can it? Not to locals like us." John said.

I almost protested again. I hadn't meant exploring inside the estate, but then the truth was I hadn't *not* meant it either. I'd lived there a couple of years by then, and the three of us had already explored pretty much everywhere else. We knew Town Beach backwards, we'd walked every step of the cliff path to the north, we knew all the coves and the caves, and where it was best to jump from the cliffs into the water at high tide. But up to then we'd always kept away from the estate to the south. But it was probably only ever a matter of time. If I hadn't known that before, it was pretty clear from the look on John's face now.

John's rod tip suddenly jumped down, and without hesitation he scooped it up and gave it a sharp upward jerk, then held it in both his hands, feet widely planted. The tip went still and we watched in suspense as nothing happened for a few seconds, then it bent right over and John grabbed the handle of the reel and began to turn it and wind the line in. We never bothered with playing the fish or nothing like that, we'd just use all our strength to pull it in. Darren and I leaned over the handrail watching the water below as whatever was on John's hook was drawn closer to the pier. He was panting with effort by the time we saw a grey shape underwater pulling the line first one way then the other, then it broke clear of the surface and hung there like wet washing on a line, just giving an occasional flap. It was a big flattie, a really good size to catch from the pier. He hoisted it over the handrail and jumped on it with his knife, severing its spinal cord before removing the hook so that it hardly flapped at all. There was no triumphalism in John's voice when he spoke.

"I guess that proves it boys. Alive crabs are the best."

It was probably just luck that made that fish choose the living crab that day, but maybe things would have worked out different if it had gone for the dead one. I don't know, but I do know that over the next few years, a lot of crabs suffered because of that fish.

twelve

IT WAS ONLY a few hours after Natalie reported Jim missing that the police found the car.

Two officers from the Devon and Cornwall police drove into the car park overlooking Porthtowan beach on the north coast of Cornwall. The interior of the car smelt of the hot kebabs they had just purchased from a nearby takeaway. The officer in the passenger seat was midway through his, a dribble of sauce running down from the corner of his mouth. As he wiped it away he spotted the car. He prodded his colleague in the ribs.

"Hey, over there. Red Nissan."

"Hmmm?"

"There."

"Well, get the list. Have a look."

The first officer re-wrapped his food and reached behind his seat to pick up a clipboard. He flicked through a couple of pages of notes from the morning's briefing until he found what he was looking for. He scanned a finger across the page, then looked over at the car again.

"Yep, that's the one." He glanced sadly at his half-eaten lunch then pushed the door open and climbed out, settling his hat onto his head.

"You're keen," his colleague said, taking another bite of his kebab.

"Well one of us has to fight crime around here."

As he approached the car his feet scrunched in a manner depressingly familiar and he swore out loud. *Bloody thieving toerags.* The passenger window on the Nissan was shattered, fragments of glass lay on the ground like thousands of tiny cubes. He glanced in. There was more diced glass, but here it was scattered across a pile of clothes on the front seat, as if someone had got changed to go for a swim or a surf, which was a common activity on this beach. Or to drown themselves, the officer thought to himself. Suicides weren't unknown either.

There was a parking ticket on the windscreen, a penalty notice. The officer craned his neck to see when it was issued, just a couple of hours previously. He looked around the car but couldn't see any evidence that a pay and display ticket had been purchased.

The passenger side door was unlocked so he opened it, then squatted down. He noticed the ignition hadn't been broken - it was a break in, not a stolen car that had been dumped. The kids around here were getting picky about what they went joyriding in. He stared at the pile of clothes on the seat for a moment, just jeans, a t-shirt and a jumper. Then he stood back up, walked back to his car to finish his lunch and then called it in.

thirteen

A LITTLE WHILE later John turned up at the campsite early one Saturday. There wasn't any swell, and nothing in the forecast. At least it wasn't raining though.

"Is your mum around?" he asked.

"She's gone into town," I replied, still eating toast.

"Good." John walked out of the kitchen and into what was built as the living room but served as the campsite shop. We were open on Saturdays for two hours in the morning. I got the rest of the day off. He browsed for a while, collecting a chocolate bar and a small packet of cereal.

"Got any milk?"

"Use the stuff from the kitchen," I replied knowing John wasn't going to pay. "Mum'll be less likely to notice."

"OK. Where's Darren?"

I shrugged from the doorway. "Guess he'll be around soon. There's no waves again." I meant it like there was no rush.

"Do you sell maps here?"

I thought for a moment. "Uh, yeah, they're in the drawer under the till. Why?"

"Let's have a look at one." He opened the drawer and pulled out a map, checking on the back that it covered the area he wanted. "Come on."

We went back to the kitchen and he stuck the chocolate bar in his mouth while unfolding the map. It wasn't the biggest table and he had to stop and get me to put all the breakfast things onto the side before he could open it properly.

"So we're here right?" He said, stabbing at it. I leaned in. I'd looked at the map before of course, but I'd never really studied it. We'd explored up to then just by wandering, seeing what was there. You didn't need a map for that.

John had his finger pointing at the campsite, behind the yellow crescent of the beach. To the north there was the small fishing harbour, and behind that the blue ribbon of the river cut into the green of the land, the little village spread out along its twin banks. Our world.

"So what's down here then?" John was now poring over the stretch of coastline to the south of the bay. Like I said, all the land down there was privately owned back then, from a few miles inland right the way down to the coast. There was no footpath like there is today either, just signs saying "Private, Keep Out" as you got to the end of the beach. Inland there was a brick wall built along the road that snaked the whole way round the estate, too tall to see over. But on the map the details of the land the other side were shown in just the same detail. You had the contour lines showing where the hills and valleys met the sea, and the actual coastline had different symbols showing how the rocks continued all the way until the next sandy beach, with various jagged inlets and headlands as it went.

I joined John and began to study the section where the fine detail of the land was replaced by the simple colour blue of the sea.

"We need to check out the bits where it faces south west, that's most likely to get the bigger waves," John said.

"Or where there's rock slabs that go out underwater. That'll set the waves up and make them break properly." I agreed.

"If we look now, when there's no waves, we'll need to be able to spot where will work when a swell hits."

"Do you think we'll be able to see?" I asked.

"Yeah, course we will."

"Look here, there's a bit." I pointed at a little kink in the coastline, a small inlet in the rocks where a tiny stream had carved out a notch. "I bet there's a wave that breaks there. I bet it's awesome."

Darren had wandered in by now, and without a word he'd filled the kettle and put it on the hob, and dropped three tea bags into cups. I only noticed him when the kettle began to whistle.

"What are we doing?" he asked.

"We're going to check this place out." John stabbed a finger at the map, his voice filled with energy and enthusiasm.

Darren came over, holding his head on one side to see better. "How?"

"What do you mean how? We're going to hike down there."

"But it's private. We're not allowed to go in there." Sometimes Darren was able to forget things that had come before, it was like he reset himself.

"What did I say to you last week Darren? It's only private to tourists. And we're not going to do any harm."

Darren considered this for a moment and his concerned look formed on his face, like it was John who wasn't getting it. "But it's owned by that old lord guy. He *shoots* people that go onto his land. My dad said so, and his friend used to work in there, so he must know. He saw it happen or something."

Darren rarely said this much, only doing so when he felt there was something urgent to say, and it stopped us for a moment.

"Who is he? This lord guy?" I asked.

"I dunno. He's like this old mad guy whose family died. Apparently he just walks around all day with a shotgun shooting at people who come in. Everyone in the village knows about it."

For all that John knew about the village and the people that lived there, there was no question that Darren was the real local. His family had been there for generations, it was John and me who were the newcomers. And on this one, if Darren said it was a no go, I'd probably have believed him. Maybe we'd have gone fishing again. See who could chuck stones the furthest. The same shit we always did. But John was there that day. No way he was gonna be put off that easy.

"You can't shoot people, even on your own land. I bet he just shoots at rabbits."

"That's not what my dad says." Darren shook his head, trying to make out like it wasn't open to discussion.

"Your dad just doesn't want you to go there. He's just trying to control you."

"No. Everyone knows about it," Darren said again.

John was grinning at Darren now. He found it funny sometimes when people kept on arguing with him, it was always so obvious that John was going to win.

"Well, if he's old, he won't be able to see very well so he won't be able to shoot us. Will he?" Then he went on without giving either of us time to reply. "And he won't be able to run after us. *And* there's three of us, so even if he did we could overpower him."

"He might have dogs or something though. We can't outrun dogs." I said. I didn't mean to, it just blurted out. I didn't like being in the middle of this but I knew the implications of the conversation. If John won - *when John won* - we were going there and I wanted to know what we were facing. I looked at Darren. "Does he have dogs?"

John answered for him. "Course not. We'd hear barking if there were dogs. Like Darren said, it's just one old guy who can't see properly anymore. Everyone knows it." But we both looked to Darren for confirmation. And Darren was too honest to lie.

"I haven't heard about any dogs."

"That settles it then," said John. We all went back to looking at the map. This time I wasn't just scanning it for potential surf spots, but surveying it like it was enemy territory.

"But how will we get there?" Darren asked again, a little while later. There's no path or nothing." Like I said, this was before they opened the coastal footpath and there was no dotted red line to indicate that it was possible to walk.

"Maybe we can just clamber along the rocks? We'd be out of view then as well maybe," I said, hoping this was true. "How far is it?"

John searched the map to find the scale and quickly transposed the distance using his finger. "About five miles to the next bay."

"I don't think we can clamber that far," said Darren.

"Well, let's see how far we can get," John was getting tired of this now. "And if we can't get any further, we'll have to turn back."

And with this both Darren and me were out of excuses.

"Come on. We're going to need supplies and stuff. We'll get some from Jesse's shop and then you can close it up early. Since your mum's away and all."

It was still early when we walked down the beach towards the rocks at the southern end. There was a little path out to the end of the headland, and lots of people used to walk out to it, but beyond that there were brambles and vegetation that had been allowed to grow out of control so that you couldn't get beyond it. There was a big sign planted in the ground just in front with "Private" written in big red letters so there was no way you could miss it or pretend you hadn't noticed. We waited until there was no one in sight on the beach and pushed past the sign, ducking under some brambles that had grown taller than we were. But only a few metres further on they were much thicker and we could go no further.

Darren tried to push his way through it first, kicking at the stems to try and break them, but soon there were little trickles of blood running down his bare legs where thorns had scratched him. He gave up. "There's no way to get through," he said.

But we hadn't seen what John was doing, digging in his backpack. He pulled out a knife with a big curved blade, like the ones explorers used to use to hack through jungles. John had this thing about knives. He had a whole collection of them.

"Stand back," he said and begun to swing at the plants.

Even then it wasn't easy. He made us both help, carefully pulling the creepers back so he could hack at their bases, and then getting us to pull them through, until they untangled from the undergrowth and came free. Then we crawled out backwards and chucked them away, wiping the creamy white sap off our hands. John kept hacking away for ages and slowly he created an opening, more of a tunnel really, into the undergrowth. Once we got through the outer shell of the plants, they got much less dense, here it was just the thick main stems sticking up out of bare earth with most of the plant over our heads. The ground was made up of brown, dead brambles. There was no path, but by keeping to the inside of the bush we could move forward a long way, and John only occasionally had to swing his blade.

In some places the roof of brambles was so thick it was almost dark, but up ahead we could see sections where more light got in because the plant was thinner. John went as far as he could go, and then began to slash away at one of these sections. He was swearing by now, I think he was getting pissed off with the thorns tearing at us. Then his head and torso disappeared in front of us, and then his legs wriggled and pulled him forward, then disappeared into the light. There was silence for a while.

"John." I hissed. I was the one behind him, Darren was behind me.

Nothing.

"John!" I called a bit more loudly, half expecting to hear the crack of a shotgun at any moment.

Then a head appeared through the hole John had created. He held up a finger to his mouth to silence us, then beckoned.

"We're through!" he whispered "Come on."

I turned round to look at Darren and he shrugged then pushed past me and crawled through the gap. I didn't want to be left behind on my own so I followed after them.

You could see at once why we needed to be quiet. We'd crawled maybe thirty metres inside the brambles and come out on the other side of the headland. And the first thing we saw, up a small slope, was this big mansion-like country house. There were no more brambles in front of us to hide behind, between the house and the sea was mostly grass with patches where big grey rocks were poking out. The shoreline itself was mostly rocks, blacker here and less rounded, shot through with fissures and cracks. Where we crouched we were exposed. If anyone had looked from the house's windows they'd have seen us. I felt like retreating back into the brambles.

"Come on," John was already out ahead of us. "Let's get down by the rocks were he won't be able to see us."

I couldn't see anyone at the house but I still half-expected to feel the impact of a bullet in my chest as I ran down to where the grass gave way to the rocks and boulders of the shoreline. There were cracks and crevices in the bedrock where we could hide and sneak looks back at the house. There was still no one about, no faces at any of the windows, so going one-by-one we ran across the open bits until we could next drop down out of sight. You could see we didn't have to go far until we'd be out of sight completely. It looked like we could do it.

John was out in front of course, Darren was in the middle now and I was in last place, waiting until they both beckoned to me before dashing across the open land. There was one particularly big stretch where it took maybe a minute to clamber across this bouldery little beach, right below the house. John and Darren had already made it across and were calling to me, keeping an eye on the house from behind a rock. I was only half way across and caught right out in the open when I heard them calling to me urgently.

"Get down!"

"Stop! Jesse get down!"

There was nothing to get down behind so I just dropped to the ground and tried to fit my body into it. I didn't dare look towards the house but I could imagine the elderly aristocrat fitting the cartridges into the shotgun, his monocle scrunched up in his eye. I closed my eyes and prayed he was as short sighted as John said he was.

"Jesse! Come on. Quick!"

I opened my eyes again and saw them both beckoning urgently to me. I got up, I didn't look, I just covered the ground as fast as I could, stumbling as the smaller rocks moved under my feet. I was out of breath when I joined the others behind the rock.

"I saw someone," said Darren.

I looked at John for confirmation.

"Yeah, there was a guy, he walked from that little building into the main house. I don't think he looked this way though."

"Did he have a gun?" I asked, I wanted to know how close to death I'd come.

"I didn't see one."

From where we were it was quite easy to sneak a look at the house, and I did so now but there was no one about.

"Come on, we can keep going now. We're out of sight for this next bit." John was right, there was a stretch of low cliff here and by keeping to the bottom, there was no way anyone from the house would be able to see us. And although it felt crazy to keep going further into the land, I was in no hurry to go back the way we'd just come.

We made the next headland unseen, and once around it, the going was pretty easy. There were no more buildings in sight and we followed a sheep track along the coast. For some parts we had to drop down onto the rocky foreshore when the gradient was too steep, or the trail petered out, but mostly we could walk more or less normal speed in single file, John taking the lead and me still in the rear. The further away from the house we got, the more we all relaxed until, after about half an hour we came to a part where the coastline cut in. John folded out the map and smoothed it down in a small clearing on the floor.

"This is the place."

We all gazed out at the sea, where small swells, far too small to surf, surged up against and over a shoreline of disorganised and ragged rocks, pushing water up through the gaps and then receding to let it fall back down again.

"It doesn't look much to me," said Darren, sounding a little pleased about this.

"It might be better when there's actually waves though." I said. But I wasn't hopeful.

John didn't reply. He just stood up and hurled a piece of rock out as far as he could. It cracked off a gully in the rocks and bounced out into the sea, dropping in with barely any splash.

"It's no good. It's all just rocks." Darren said. "Let's go back."

John drew back his arm and threw another rock, this time getting more distance and hitting the sea directly. If he heard Darren he made no sign.

"We'll keep going a little bit further. There must be something along here." He set off and the two of us followed.

The rocks got much steeper further along, and we found a section that looked promising for fishing from, since the water was much closer to the path. It was deep too. Although the water was clear so you could still see the bottom, it had that greeny tint that you only got when you looked through a lot of water. There were plenty of sheep here too and our presence unnerved them so that some kept running ahead of us, helping to show a way forward. There was another little headland ahead which was marked on the map as about midway between our beach and the next one to the south, outside the southern limits of the estate, and where another small village lay.

"I think we should turn back," said Darren when we all paused. I might have agreed with him, but John had already pressed on.

"Let's just check out beyond this headland, then we can go back," he called from ahead.

Darren seemed reluctant to move but I slipped past him.

"We've come this far, we might as well have a look," I said to him.

Up ahead John had now made the headland and stopped. He had a huge grin on his face when I got up to him. This look of triumph.

"Check it out," he said.

"What?"

"Down there!"

The coastline was a bit different here. Actually it was a bit weird. We were looking at another small inlet where a valley met the sea, but the sides of this one were much steeper, more like cliffs than sides of a valley, it made a bay that was totally hidden from the land, almost from the sea as well. And there was a strange feature mid way along the cliff on the north end, one part of the cliff had slipped but not quite fallen so it looked like a huge column of rock was suspended in the air.

"How cool is that?" said John, already striding forward to investigate.

On all sides the earth had been eroded down around the rock leaving it resting on a tiny flat section. It almost looked as if you could push it over, but although we tried it was much more stable than it looked.

"It's like it's hanging in the air."

"We should call this place *Hanging Rock Bay,*" John announced. "Let's have lunch here."

So we sat on the grass beside the hanging rock and got out the chocolate bars and crisps that we'd taken from the store. And it was a real beautiful place, totally private. It felt like a closed little world. And we noticed that the north side of the inlet, the side we were sitting on, had this big flat, wide ledge of rock that stretched out into the sea.

It was one of those really weird swells that day, where every half an hour or so you got one or two waves that would come in. You get that around here sometimes, I don't know how it works, it's like they come in at a different angle and find their way up past Ireland. It's no good for surfing because you'd be waiting around for ever in between waves. But as it happened it turned out to be perfect for checking out the potential for new surf spots. Because there we were, munching on chocolate bars, when one of these waves came in, right in front of us. First of all we could see it as a swell out to sea, and John nudged us to watch.

"Here, look at that."

As the swell approached the mouth of the little bay it grew quite distinctly, and where the sea had been totally flat, now a clean wall of water was lining up. It stretched in from the deeper water and bent towards the shore. And as it got closer it got steeper and steeper until it began to break. For twenty, maybe thirty seconds the wave peeled, this perfect little wave that threw out a lip like a silvery curtain being pulled across the reef in front of our eyes.

There were two waves in the set, and we watched in silence as the second wave lined up in exactly the same way, and followed the exact same path in over the reef. It was like looking at a picture from one of John's surfing magazines of some exotic perfect spot. Even just seeing that second wave you could see the lines you'd take, the shoulder sections that you could snap turns off, a bit where it looked hollow enough to get a little tubey cover up. A bowl where the ledge changed its angle a fraction. It looked amazing.

"Fucking hell boys," said John. "Hanging Rock has got a wave."

fourteen

THE DOORBELL AGAIN. This time Natalie saw the black and silver of uniforms through the glass and then her pale hand trembling as it rose to unlatch the door.

"Mrs Harrison?" There were two of them standing there, a man and a woman. The formality of the address was discomforting.

It was the woman who spoke, thirties, curly ginger-blond hair pulled back from her scalp.

"I'm Detective Sergeant DS Venables. This is my colleague PC Ian Turnbull, you spoke to him on the phone earlier today?" They both held up their identification.

Beyond them Natalie saw a police car parked up at the kerb. It looked so out of place, it could have been a spaceship. She tried to read their faces.

"Do you have any news?"

Sue hesitated but didn't answer her. "May we come in?" she said instead.

Natalie looked blank for a moment but then stood back. They came in, crowded together in the little hallway. The man took off his hat and tried in vain to press his hair flat.

"Thank you Mrs Harrison. Is there somewhere we can all sit down? Perhaps in the kitchen?"

"It's Natalie, please call me Natalie."

She led the way. There was something familiar about what was happening, but she didn't have to time to think what it might be.

The table in the kitchen was big enough for four chairs gathered around it. The woman police officer suggested that Natalie sit there.

"I'll make some tea," she said, before Natalie thought to ask. She held up a hand to ward off any protesting. "I've had a bit of practice making tea in unfamiliar kitchens," she said with what Natalie assumed was a sympathetic smile.

"Have you got news?" Natalie said again. Her voice sounded all wrong.

DS Venables waited until she had located mugs and tea bags before replying.

"Yes."

"What is it?" This was Sarah, standing at the doorway. "Hello, I'm Natalie's sister," she said.

The introductions were made a second time around and DC Venables asked Sarah to sit as well. There was some shuffling of chairs to accommodate them all. Another mug was lined up, then filled alongside the others. When Sue had finished she sat down opposite Natalie and spoke softly.

"We've come to tell you your husband's car has been located. The vehicle was found in a car park overlooking the sea in Porthtowan."

Natalie waited, still hoping she was reading this all wrong.

"We put a request in to the Devon and Cornwall Police to check all areas where surfers are known to frequent," PC Turnbull said, as if this had been his idea.

"But have you found him?" Sarah interrupted.

DS Venables shook her head. "No. I'm afraid he wasn't with the vehicle and… And we haven't located him yet."

Natalie's eyes flicked around the room. She recognised now what was happening. The feeling she'd had at the front door, it was a scene they were all acting out. The police, the way they spoke, held themselves, the looks they shared with each other, it was straight out of a TV drama. She fought to suppress the panic of realising what part she had to play.

"Now the vehicle is being examined by the Devon and Cornwall officers but they've already told us there were a man's clothes and shoes left on the rear seat, consistent with someone having gone into the water, presumably to go surfing. I'm sorry to say the vehicle has been broken into, there's no phone or wallet, or anything that could identify the clothes at this stage." The policewoman hesitated.

"But I'm afraid they've also found evidence that the car has been there some time"

"What evidence? Sarah's voice cut into the swirling darkness that was closing in on Natalie's mind. She sounded miles away.

"It had a parking fine ma'am. Issued at," the male PC consulted the notebook he had in front of him. "Zero nine hundred hours, on the third November. That's this morning, nine am," he added.

DS Venables gave them a moment to let that sink in. "We're checking with the council how often their operatives visited the car park, but I have to tell you that a search of the beach and rocks around the car park has failed to turn up anything of significance, other than the car..."

Natalie gripped her mug hard, the heat coming through the ceramic wall almost painful. She wanted to force herself back into the room. She wanted to break the inevitability of this conversation, this drip, drip sequence of simple facts that lead to a single conclusion.

"It's not his car. It's mine."

"I'm sorry?"

"It's not his car, he borrowed mine because his was playing up. I was supposed to take his to the garage. I said I'd do it while he was gone."

The policewoman glanced at her colleague then looked back at Natalie.

"Do you understand what I'm telling you Natalie? We think your husband has been in the sea for at least six hours, perhaps even longer," she added more quietly, "possibly even overnight."

Natalie nodded. She felt chastised, as if she'd been stupid for not realising this.

"The Coastguard has launched a search and rescue operation and they will do everything possible to find him. But at this time of year the water is very cold. I'm so very sorry to be telling you this."

Natalie's mouth felt so dry she could barely speak.

"Is he… Do you think he's…"

The policewoman reached a hand out over the table and placed it on Natalie's wrist.

"We're going to do everything we can to find him."

Natalie stared at the hand lying on her arm.

"At the moment we are treating this as a search and rescue operation. Your husband is likely to be wearing a wetsuit which will greatly extend the period he can be in the water. It will also give a degree of flotation, and he'll have his surfboard for additional buoyancy. We are working against the clock, but there's still reason to be hopeful."

Suddenly the door burst open and a wailing child crashed in, followed by another holding a red toy car. Both ran to Sarah and began to explain the injustice they had suffered at each other's hands. Then, in a moment which might have become a family story had the circumstances been different, both children simultaneously noticed the two police officers sitting at the table and fell silent. The bigger child, four years old, spoke.

"Mum, why are the policemans here?"

"Daniel I told you to wait in the other room." Sarah began to shepherd them out of the kitchen.

"Has Auntie Natalie been bad?"

"Shut up Daniel and come next door. Let your brother have a turn with the car." Sarah gave a look of apology over her shoulder as she led them both out, and the kitchen was quiet, save for the ongoing conversation audible through the living room wall.

"No, Auntie Natalie hasn't been bad. The police are just helping her to find Uncle Jim. But you need to be quiet and wait here."

DS Venables didn't take her eyes off Natalie.

"We are going to do everything we can to find him." She said it again, and this time she squeezed Natalie's arm.

"How many helicopters?"

The policewoman looked at Natalie as if this might help her decode the question.

"Sorry?"

"How many helicopters? How many have they sent up?"

Now the woman's eyes flicked across to her colleague.

"I... I don't know... That'll be up to the Coastguard." She reverted to her comforting tone. "But I'm sure they're doing everything they can."

Suddenly energy flowed into Natalie. She wanted to do something. It felt urgent, like every moment counted.

"His business partner will help look for him. They own a helicopter business. I told you earlier," Natalie stared accusingly at the male officer. Then she jumped up and grabbed her phone from the work surface. She started stabbing at the buttons her hand shaking so much now that she could barely operate it. She thought of the flights she'd taken with Jim, across to Ireland, over the channel to France. She looked the policewoman in the face.

"Do you know how big the sea is out there? Do you know how much water there is? How small things look from the air?"

Her phone connected.

"Dave? Listen to me. They've found my car in somewhere called Porthtowan. Yes, in Cornwall. They think Jim went into the water there this morning," her voice wavered. "He hasn't come out yet." She went quiet for a moment, listening as the man spoke on the other end.

"No, no Dave, just listen. I'm here with the police now. But I need you to get up and search for Jim. Now. I need you to find him Dave. I can't lose him. Not like… I just need you to go up and look for him."

The two police officers couldn't hear the other end of the conversation and they sipped their teas without looking at one another, waiting.

"Search Coordinator," Natalie suddenly turned around, there were tears flowing openly down her face. "He says there must be someone directing the search. He needs to contact them."

DS Venables put down her tea and failed to prevent her face slipping into its look of quiet, understanding sadness, but this time she looked at PC Turnbull. "Well, give her the number Joe."

The man had to radio in to the station to get it, but eventually he relayed a telephone number to Natalie, who wrote it down as she repeated it to Dave. Then she listened for a moment more and rang off. Natalie looked at the two officers in her kitchen, drinking her tea.

"He said he'll be airborne in fifteen minutes."

fifteen

WE HAD TO wait a while before we got to surf at Hanging Rock. Something happened in the meantime that changed things, for a while at least.

School had got a lot easier by then. Darren was there of course, and maybe in a normal school we wouldn't have been in the same classes on account of him being slow, or dyslexic or whatever, but our school was so small that everyone was together all the time. So I got to hang out with him, and the other kids had got used to me by then, but none of them surfed so I wasn't that interested. There was this one girl though. I remember I noticed her right away when I arrived from Oz because she was so pretty, but obviously I'd never talked to her or anything like that.

Her name was Cara Williams, and actually, saying she was pretty doesn't really cover it. She was way beyond pretty. She was amazing. She wasn't the sort of girl you'd expect to find in a small Welsh village. I'm pretty sure she's a supermodel or something now, or married to a billionaire and living on his yacht. She was already tall and slim by whatever age we were then, maybe fourteen? She already had breasts like a real woman. Sometimes she even looked a bit ridiculous going round with her friends at school, like this super hot woman in a school uniform surrounded by sour-faced, ugly girls. Only obviously she didn't hang out with the ugly girls, she was part of a gang of the pretty ones, but she made them look plain because she just *shone.*

It maybe sounds like I'm exaggerating a bit. Well, maybe there are bits of this story where I'm getting a bit carried away - but that's artistic licence isn't it? Anyway, you should believe me on this one. Cara Williams was just amazing.

And there wasn't anyone in the school who didn't see it. All the boys were in love with her. All of us. Lots of them - the honest ones - would talk about how they'd wanked off the night before thinking about her, but you knew that everyone was at it. It wasn't just us kids either, you'd catch the teachers gazing at her when they thought no one was looking, and you can bet they were doing it as well. But anyway. Even though there were quite a few school romances springing up by then, Cara Williams never had a boyfriend at school. And the reason for that was simple, she was so obviously in a different league to any of us, there was no point trying it on.

And maybe this made her lonely. Maybe it was me coming from Australia that made me a little bit exotic too, or maybe she just kinda fancied me a bit, that's not so hard to believe is it? All that surfing was making me fit too. So I don't know exactly what it was but one day, as I was walking between classes I noticed she was in front of me, with her backpack slung on one shoulder, and the zip open. A couple of exercise books were just about to fall out and without thinking I just called out.

"Hey Cara,"

She turned around, as she did so one of the books slid out to the floor. Back in Oz my Mum had been really hot on things like manners and I stooped down to pick them up.

"Thanks Jesse," she said, giving me this smile that made everything else in the world instantly less important. There was no surprise that she knew my name, that's just how small the school was, but I was surprised that she used it.

Her hand brushed mine as she took the books back. I'd never noticed before but even her hands were beautiful.

"No problem," I said. I felt a bit weird and I turned to walk on.

"I'd be in trouble if I lost that," she called out to me. "That's from Mr Johnston's class."

I hadn't been expecting a conversation to start and was already a few steps away, I had to turn back to reply.

"Yeah?"

"He's pretty strict about homework."

She'd slipped her bag off her shoulder to put the books back, and in so doing her white blouse, which was unbuttoned at the top, had also slipped a bit, you could see her bra strap where it pressed into the smooth skin on her shoulder.

"Yeah, I guess." I said.

"Don't you think?"

I couldn't think of anything clever to say so I just said the first thing that came to my mind.

"Back in Oz you wouldn't have called him strict. He'd be average at worst."

"Really?" The backpack was swung back onto her back, pulling her blouse tight against her chest again. The strap forced itself between her two breasts, clearly defining each of them. For the first time I felt awkward as I tried not to look.

"Were the teachers there much stricter there then?"

"Yeah I guess." I said. I made myself look at her eyes, but that was unnerving, looking into those beautiful eyes, I refocused just on her nose, though that was pretty cute too. "I went to school in the city, so you got like, troubled kids there. The teachers had to be really on it."

"That sounds terrible."

I shrugged. "It was OK."

"Where was it you came from? In Australia I mean?" she asked.

"Up on the Gold Coast. Queensland."

"I'd love to go there. I'd love to travel the world," she said and gave this little sigh which made her nose wrinkle. I'd never been this close to her before, and I'd never had a conversation. It had never crossed my mind that as well as being crazy beautiful she was also a real person who had hopes and dreams. And for some reason that washed away my embarrassment.

"Really?"

"Oh yeah. I mean I like it here but," she wrinkled her nose some more so I went back to staring at those eyes. You could lose yourself for ever in those eyes.

"I'd love to see the world as well."

"Yeah, me too," I said. I'd have agreed with anything. She could have said: "I'd love to be buried alive in a coffin with the lid screwed down" and I'd have gone along with it.

"You've got science now haven't you? With me. Do you want to walk together. You could tell me about Australia."

I don't know what you remember about being fourteen, but at that school this sort of thing was considered fucking embarrassing. Whatever it was that was going on I mean, and it wasn't exactly clear what that was. I couldn't tell if she just wanted to be friends, or if we were going to start being boyfriend and girlfriend any minute. But whatever it was she was doing, she was pretty expert at it. For a few weeks after that all we did was say hi to each other sometimes when we passed in the corridors. Occasionally she'd make it so we ended up sat next to each other in class, or sharing the same table for lunch, but never just the two of us. It was like she was gradually allowing me in. If she ever heard anyone joke that she might fancy me she backed right off, but not for too long. And by gradually making it normal to include me within the people she talked to, the other kids got to the point where they accepted we were kind of friends. I guess she was pretty used to being watched and talked about. It made her sensitive to these things.

Her house was up in the village, a little way on from Darren's, and one time after school his mum had promised me dinner and it just ended up the three of us walking together, Cara and me chatting easily. It was weird really, most of the boys couldn't talk to her at all, but because of the way she spoke to me, I could. Even though I was as tongue tied as everyone else with most of the other pretty girls. It helped that Darren was just as embarrassed as I should have been. He just walked along a bit behind us, not saying anything. But even he couldn't keep his eyes off this beautiful creature I was with.

"What you doing tonight?" she asked, as we stopped outside Darren's house.

"Nothing much," I said. And I wish I'd been a bit quicker to see where this was going.

"Me neither," she said. And did that thing with her nose again. "My parents are out until later too." She gave me a smile so powerful it nearly knocked me over and when I recovered the only thing I could think to say was.

"Actually I've got to do some homework for Mr Johnston. You know what he's like." And I laughed like we were sharing some secret joke that Darren wouldn't understand. At the time I thought that was pretty clever, but she just glanced at Darren like she was frustrated he was still there. She waited a while, but in the end she shrugged her shoulders.

"OK, well, I'll maybe see you tomorrow." She gave me her smile again but she'd turned the power right down this time.

"Bye Jesse. Bye Darren." And then she walked off up the hill. We both watched her until she was out of sight before stepping inside Darren's gate and going inside his house. I didn't enjoy Darren's mum's dinner that night. I was already regretting not going with Cara. I think I had a sense then I might regret not going for years to come. I still think about what a dumb fucking move it was today. It's nice sometimes these days to worry about normal shit alongside all the other stuff.

Anyway, for the next week I kept hoping Darren's mum would invite me round to his again after school, so I could have an excuse to walk Cara home again. Only this time I'd walk Cara all the way home first. My teenage mind played out all sorts of fantasises about what would happen next. And that's when Darren put me straight.

We were having lunch, sitting in the school field with our backs to the fence and sandwich boxes open on our knees. I was talking about Cara. What I mean is, I was talking about her again. I think that time I was telling him how she was actually a really nice girl and all, despite being so pretty, and I guess Darren just got sick of me talking about her.

"You know she's seeing some older guy don't you?"

The euphoric little world I'd been constructing in my mind cracked with a jolt.

"Who Cara?" I checked. I felt like my life was on a cliff edge.

"Of course Cara. She just wants to be your friend. She doesn't fancy you. You do know that don't you?"

"Who says I fancy her? I just want to be her friend too." I said, my cheeks flushing even though it was only Darren.

"Yeah right Jesse. Everyone fancies her. Just look at her."

I've already said how everyone was in love with Cara, but I don't think I'd ever connected that with me being friends with her. It hadn't occurred to me that everyone must know that I fancied her too. But Darren had this really simple, plain-speaking way of seeing the world and you couldn't argue with it.

"Who says she's going out with someone?" I asked, my voice sounding strange to me.

"The whole school."

There had been rumours about Cara spreading through the school for as long as I'd been attending there. Sometimes is was minor stuff -

like a buzz of excitement that she wasn't wearing a bra, or was going to be outside a certain classroom doing PE. Sometimes it was more major stuff, like theories about a teacher leaving because he couldn't bear the thought of sleeping with his wife after teaching her maths, or rumours that she'd lost her virginity. So I had no trouble believing Darren that there was a rumour, but that didn't mean it was true.

"Bollocks."

"It's true."

"Alright. Who is he?"

"I dunno. I don't know his name, apparently it's some older guy. Probably got his own car and everything."

I was silent.

"Lucky bastard though. Getting to shag that. Can you imagine?" Darren went on. This was a pretty funny thing to say since hardly any of us knew what it was like to shag anyone at that stage, and certainly not Darren. But that was the way we talked. Like we were at it every night.

"But how do they know?" I asked again. I could feel the panic. I was creating excuses for her in my mind, reasons why this rumour was just the latest false accusation to be thrown at poor Cara Williams. Cara who was actually secretly in love with me.

"I dunno. She tells her friends probably."

As he said this there was a break in the greyness above our heads and a shaft of sunlight lit up the school in front of us. Somehow it brought my panic under control and I even smiled a little. I realised what was happening. It was as beautiful as it was obvious. Cara *herself* had started this rumour. And I knew why. She was doing what she'd done since we first talked. She was doing it because she didn't want the whole school knowing about her true feelings for me.

That weekend there weren't any waves, but John and Darren and me hung out together during the day anyway. Darren had given in to John's pestering and cleaned the caravan, so we were in there again. I don't remember us doing much, but I suggested to Darren that he come back after he'd been home for his dinner and hang out some more. Darren agreed of course, but when I mentioned it to John, expecting a similar response, he got a bit vague.

"Yeah maybe," he said at first, then seemed to make up his mind. "No actually I can't tonight. I'm doing something."

"What?" I asked.

"Just something."

"Just what?" It wasn't like I felt he had to tell me, it was more that we'd never had any reason to keep anything from each other. You either did what you wanted, or what your parents made you do, and there was no reason to keep either of those secret from mates.

"Nothing. I've just got a date." You could tell he was trying really hard to say it nonchalantly, but he didn't really manage it. Even Darren dropped the magazine he was reading in surprise.

"A date?" I asked. "With a girl?"

"Yeah. Course with a girl."

"Who is she?"

"Just some girl."

"From your school?" Darren interrupted and we both looked at him like he was stupid.

"I go to a single sex school Darren." John said. "There's only boys there."

There was an awkward silence for a moment, but I couldn't let it drop, the thought occurred to me that our relationship might move onto a new level, a situation where both John and me were going out with our girlfriends, where we might double date like they did in American movies, whatever that actually entailed. We'd probably drop Darren, you wouldn't want someone like him hanging around, getting in the way, saying stupid things like that all the time.

"Where did you meet her then?" I asked.

John looked embarrassed to be talking about it, but seemed to realise we weren't going to let the subject be dropped in and forgotten as casually as he'd tried.

"She comes to my school some afternoons for music practice," he said. "She plays the flute or something."

"No way?" This was totally incredible news because Cara also played the flute. You'd see her carrying the little case around school sometimes. Half the boys took up an instrument in the hope of sharing music lessons with her. But for me this meant that mine and John's girlfriends had something in common. They could play their flutes together while we went surfing. This was fantastic.

"Actually you might know her," John went on, less embarrassed now that I'd shown my obvious enthusiasm for the subject. "I think she goes to your school. Cara something."

The horrible truth struck Darren before me. I just couldn't make sense of it. Could they even share the *same name*?

"It's not Cara Williams is it?" said Darren.

"Yeah, that's it. Do you know her?" John asked.

"Course I fucking do. Everyone knows her. She's like the hottest girl in school." He was staring at John, who shrugged awkwardly.

"Fucking hell John, you're going on a date with Cara Williams?" Darren was so surprised he'd forgotten how he normally talked to John, he'd left out the respect. "Where are you taking her?"

"I dunno yet," John said. He said a little miserably. Looking back I guess even he was nervous about it. He might have liked to ask our advice, but he knew it was a subject we knew absolutely fuck all about.

"I guess I'll see what she wants to do." John said. Darren shook his head as if he couldn't believe what he was hearing.

"Do you hear that Jesse? He's going out with Cara Williams." He didn't say it in a nasty way, he wasn't trying to remind me how I'd repeated to him every word of the every conversation I'd had with her. He'd forgotten all that. John going out with her eclipsed my achievements in that department.

I couldn't breathe. I'd been plunged off the cliff edge into the abyss, but I *had* to answer. I had to say something appropriate or they'd both know just how deep I'd got myself worked into my own fantasy romance with her.

"Yeah," I croaked. "She's alright I think. She's like, pretty hot." I watched my hand trembling as I reached out to grab Darren's magazine off him, as if the conversation suddenly bored me. I tried to focus on a picture of perfect waves rolling into a blue water point break somewhere thousands of miles away, but my eyes were full of tears and the image blurred. I wanted to be thousands of miles away.

It was horrific sitting with Darren that night, thinking about what John and Cara were getting up to, listening to Darren speculating. John didn't say anything more about his plans, nor did we ask any more questions. So we sat there, Darren moaning about how crap the waves had been, as if this mattered any more. As if somehow life was still supposed to go on as normal. All I could do was see them in my mind, sitting together in some fancy restaurant, her beautiful shoulders bare in a posh dress and John snapping his fingers at the waiter like some sort of fucking big shot. Or maybe her kicking off her high-heeled shoes so she could dance better in some designer nightclub, the crowd parting to give John the room to spin her around and around, her dress rising higher and higher with every twirl. Of course they didn't really do anything like that. They just went to the cinema in the next town and sat in awkward silence before her dad picked her up, but I didn't see it like that. I'm not normally a glass half-empty kind of guy, but that night the glass was dry, it was fucking barren.

Darren loitered around like some bad smell but when he finally went home and I could go to bed I spent the night alternating between miserable insomnia and torturous semi-dreams of John's bare white arse

- that I'd seen a hundred times when he'd changed into his wetsuit - pumping himself into a gasping Cara's beautiful body in the luxury flat that I knew he didn't have.

The dawn brought some relief. Perhaps, I reasoned, the date had gone badly. Maybe she'd even stood him up? I watched out for John the whole morning, but he didn't turn up, and there was no way I was going around to his house. In the end he stayed away the whole day and eventually Darren dragged me off fishing. I think it must have occurred to him by then what I was going through. He wanted to help me out.

In fact we didn't see much of John for a while. Somehow the school rumour mill picked up that Cara was properly loved up with her new bloke, who was definitely much older and drove a sports car. The word was she was definitely having sex with him too, you could see it in the way she walked. I couldn't bring myself to look.

Obviously I didn't talk to Cara at school any more, and she certainly stopped talking to me. I guess she realised that with John and me being friends it was just better that way. A few years later, when I could look back on that time without it feeling like my stomach was being ripped out of my body, I kind of worked it out. She'd probably spotted John some time before and she only really befriended me as a way of meeting him. I'll never know if I did have one chance with her though, that night we walked back together to Darren's house. That was what really got me back then, the thought that I'd blown that chance. Fucking that up dragged me right back down to my lowest point since arriving in Wales.

sixteen

THERE WAS LITTLE Natalie could do but wait. Her sister left, promising to be back when she'd found a babysitter for the boys. The policewoman stayed and tried to re-assert leadership of the situation. She explaining how she was now assigned to the case, and how Natalie's friend Dave had joined two Sea King helicopters and three RNLI lifeboats, from Padstow, Rock and Sennan Cove. She told her about the grid pattern they were working, and how they had to take account of the strong tides found in that area. But Natalie hardly listened to any of it. All she could do was think of those wide open expanses of ocean, far from the beaches and cliffs. She wondered what it must feel like to be out there, alone, with the light fading from the sky, the hope fading from your mind.

Then the policewoman's phone rang. Natalie asked at once what it was, but the officer put up her hand and shook her head.

"It's not news, I'm sorry." She went to the other side of the room and listened for a little longer. A few minutes later she ended the call. She turned to Natalie her face screwed up, puzzled.

"Natalie, I need to ask you a question."

"What's happened? Who was that?"

She answered reluctantly. "That was the officer who found the car. They've undertaken a closer inspection..."

"So?"

DS Venables paused, like she was working out how to continue.

"Natalie I need to ask you about your husband's state of mind. Was there anything troubling him? Perhaps there were money problems?" Again she softened her voice. "Were there any difficulties in the marriage? Had you argued? Anything like that?"

Natalie stared at her blankly. Thoughts flashed through her mind, one burned so brightly she thought the woman must be able to see the image reflected in her eyes.

"No. Why?"

The policewoman paused, then continued carefully.

"They didn't see this at first because they were under the seat, or perhaps whoever broke into the car kicked them underneath by accident. Or perhaps your husband tried to hide them." She watched Natalie's reaction to this.

"Hide what?"

Natalie felt the other woman's eyes on her face.

"Hide what?" She said again.

"There were three packets of painkillers. Paracetamol, on the floor of the car. Empty packets. Natalie was Jim using painkillers for any medical reason?"

The question was so unexpected it took Natalie some time to answer.

"No."

"Are you sure?"

"Yes. I mean he gets headaches sometimes. But no more than anybody. Look I'm sorry but I don't understand. What are you saying?"

The policewoman hadn't put her phone down, she held it in both hands in front of her, as if feeling its weight.

"Do you keep a supply of paracetamol tablets in your car?"

"No."

"Have you in the past? Could those empty packets have been there for some time?"

"I don't think so. I don't remember having any tablets in there."

"Are you sure?"

"No. I'm not sure. I don't understand what you're saying."

"Natalie, the amount of tablets missing from those packets..." The policewoman stopped.

"If Jim took those tablets, there's really only one explanation for what he was trying to do."

"What? No, Jim wouldn't... What are you saying?" A frown was creasing Natalie's forehead.

"I'm sorry Natalie. I have to ask these questions. Has he ever tried anything like this before?"

"Like what?"

"Has he ever spoken of being suicidal? Or made any attempt at suicide?"

"*What*? No!" There was anger in her voice. "Of course not. Why would he... ?" Natalie pushed herself up from the table and strode over to the sink. She took her mug with her, but her hands were shaking so much when she tried to rinse it out it slipped her grip and clattered against the metal walls. She stood there staring at it for a moment and then fired a squirt of washing up liquid after it, but instead of washing it she began to wash her hands under the tap, scrubbing them hard under the cold flowing water.

seventeen

NATALIE KNEW SHE needed time. She felt the presence of the policewoman behind her, she felt her questioning stare on her shoulders. She blew out her cheeks and tried to calm herself down. She didn't know what was going on, but she sensed that how she acted now, how she was perceived as acting by this woman could have an impact on the rest of her life. She turned off the tap and slowly turned around.

"We had an argument, before he left. But it was only a silly thing. There's no way it would make him want to kill himself."

DS Venables said nothing and waited for her to continue.

"He's been working a lot these last few months. Up in Scotland, flying oil rig workers out of Aberdeen. It's just until the business gets enough work in locally. And I guess I've been working too hard as well. I'm teaching undergraduates at the university."

"OK."

"Jim does this thing where he disappears, with absolutely no notice to go surfing. It's kind of an ongoing argument we have. He hadn't done it for a while, I thought he was growing out of it."

She stopped talking and eventually the policewoman had to prompt her to go on. She did so, shrugging as she spoke.

"He had a few days off this week. I was still working and we'd agreed he was going to paint the hallway. Then he announces he's going off surfing instead. I... I kind of blew up at him." Natalie stopped, the memory of it still fresh in her mind. The thought occurring to her as she spoke that this might be the last conversation she ever had face to face with him.

"You're going *surfing*?" She'd said and immediately he was on the defensive.

"It's just for a few days. You're working anyway," he said.

"Yeah but I'm here in the evenings. And it would be nice if you were as well." She glared at him until he looked away.

"Nat, you know what it's like. It's a good forecast. I haven't been in the water for ages."

She knew exactly what it was like. She'd learnt very early on in their relationship that there were virtually no plans that couldn't be dropped at the very last minute if the weather forecast indicated the surfing would be good. At first the idea of this had seemed exciting, free-spirited. But where she'd imagined the two of them dropping everything to explore wild beaches and hidden coves together, the reality was that moments after they'd arrived and 'checked the surf', he'd wriggle into a wetsuit and disappear. She had plenty of time to explore, but it wasn't so much fun on her own. And mostly it was cold so she'd sit in the car waiting for him.

"And what about the money? We've got the house now. What's the point in you working away if you're going to spend everything you earn on surfing trips?"

"I'll camp. Come on. It won't cost much."

"And your car? You said you were going to fix that this week."

He took a deep breath before answering. "I was kind of hoping you might lend me yours."

"Oh fucking hell Jim. You can be so fucking selfish you know that?"

He'd gone anyway. She knew he would, that was what made her so frustrated. He made vague promises to make it up to her, which she pointedly ignored. But even before he'd gone she recognised within herself a little sense of guilt. She knew she was meeting his unreasonableness with an unreasonableness of her own. But instead of backing down, she smothered it with indignation, with a sense of righteous anger.

"And you don't think this was enough to... To explain the painkillers in any way?" The policewoman asked when Natalie had finished.

"No. Absolutely not. It was nothing, just a silly argument."

DS Venables stood quietly, watching.

"Jim's not the type. He really isn't." Natalie felt her eyes imploring the other woman to believe this.

"How about the business. Jim is a partner in a helicopter firm, is that right?"

Natalie nodded.

"Are there any problems you're aware of? With money perhaps? Anything that might have put stress on Jim."

Natalie shook her head.

"Is it possible he could have hidden something from you?"

"I don't think so. He never mentioned anything, and Dave is very sensible, he's very careful."

"Dave is the other partner? The man who's helping with the search and rescue?"

"Yes."

"And how is Jim's relationship with Dave?"

"Fine. Good." The words came out strangled and Natalie glanced across at the policewoman, but she didn't seem to notice.

"Is Jim a private type of man? Would you know if there was something troubling him?"

"No. I mean yes. I'd know."

"Did the two of you have any other arguments? Any problems in your relationship?"

"No. Nothing more than what I've said already. Look you've already asked me all this."

DS Venables raised a hand to calm her down. "I know. I'm sorry. It's just I can't work out these tablets. It's not that unusual for people to use painkillers in a suicide attempt, but like this? It's very strange. I've never seen it before. I'm just trying to make sure we have all the information." With this she turned her head to watch Natalie. "It's very strange."

Natalie felt the policewoman's eyes stay on her, and they weren't entirely sympathetic any more. There was doubt there too, the clear beginnings of suspicion. Maybe that was what made Natalie say what she did.

"You know I might have had some tablets there. Empty packets I mean. I'm afraid I don't keep the car very clean. I think I kept some to help with period pain." Natalie brought her eyes up to meet the policewoman's gaze, and for a moment neither woman blinked nor looked away.

"Three packets?"

"I can't say for sure, but I think so. Like I say, I don't keep the car clean."

"Would you be prepared to make a statement to that effect? This could be important."

"Yes."

"You're very sure about this Natalie? You told me ten minutes ago you were sure you didn't have tablets in your car. It's strange that you're now changing your mind, do you realise that?"

Natalie felt her face beginning to burn, but something made her continue.

"Yes. I'm sure. I was surprised when you told me and I forgot, that's all. I'm sure."

DS Venables looked at her for some time saying nothing, but eventually turned away.

"OK. I understand," she said.

eighteen

IT WASN'T MUCH of a consolation, but the surf got good while John was seeing Cara. Really good. The way it works around here, you sometimes get a run of low pressures that come in from the Atlantic, one right after the other. Big swirls of isobars full of rain and the wind that builds up the waves. When that happens it's like the swell comes in on a conveyor belt. But more often you get the opposite, a big fat high pressure that just sits out there doing fuck all. If you get that it'll be flat for weeks. But when John and Cara were together we had the swell, and for once we got it with good weather too. It was sunny, the wind stayed offshore, sending us the waves and leaving them smooth and clean. The way I remember it, Darren and me went surfing every weekend around that time, most nights after school too.

By then though, the bay was getting crowded. The regular gang had expanded quite a bit already, and we were seeing more and more people driving in from the town inland and from further south. They only bothered to come when the swell was good enough for Town Beach, but it pissed off us locals. They'd leave us alone when the surf was crap, but as soon as we got some decent waves, they'd all be there, parking up right in front of the campsite, ten, fifteen, twenty cars sometimes, each with two or three guys in it. And that was just during the week. Come the weekend it really got silly. The problem was that surf forecasts were getting easier and easier to read. Any idiot these days could see if a good swell was coming, and if it was, everyone round here knew that our beach was the one to head for.

The campsite didn't help of course. It had got a reputation for being popular with surfers, they liked its basic facilities. It meant we had more money coming in, but it all added to the numbers paddling out when the waves were good. And the bay was small remember, it worked OK with just us locals, but add another thirty, maybe forty guys in the water and you started to get real issues with people dropping in, more than one rider on a wave, that sort of thing.

Like I said, I grew up surfing with crowds. I could have lived with it really, but Darren suffered. He was a strange one really. He had this really nice style when he was surfing, and he wasn't scared of any waves, but he really didn't like crowds. He still preferred to sit on the edge of the pack and wait for the waves that came in where no one else could catch them. It worked fine when the beach wasn't busy, but when the pack got too big, if you sat on the edge you were too far away to catch any waves at all.

One Saturday during that time, this really big group of surfers turned up when Darren and me were out there. They arrived in two minibuses with the name of the university up the coast stencilled on the side. They had a small mountain of boards strapped to the roof, and even a fucking kayak perched on top. We watched them from the water and you could see everyone out surfing was watching too, hoping they'd stay in the whitewater, the smaller waves that break right onto the sand, where the kids play. But of course they didn't. We watched as they snapped themselves into wetsuits and paddled out right where we were all sitting, shouting and joking to each other as if we weren't there.

Normally old Gwynn was the friendliest bloke you could imagine and he'd shout out encouragement as people caught good waves even if he didn't know them. And with us guys he knew, he'd always be asking about how you were and stuff in-between waves. Like for example he knew all about John and Cara, in fact he thought it was hilarious that John hadn't been surfing for weeks even though it had been really good, he'd been laughing about it before the students turned up. But even he stopped smiling when these guys started dropping in and ruining wave after wave for everyone. Pretty soon the whole atmosphere had changed. Partly because of the arrogant way the students were surfing, but also just because there were too many people in the water. But then he had a reason to be pissed off.

I saw the whole thing really clearly. I'd just taken a wave right to the inside and was paddling back out. Gwynn was right out the back when the best wave all day came in. It was a beauty, a little bit overhead, and peaking and bending around to give this real steep but gradual wall, you could see it was just going to peel perfectly, and not many waves do that in the bay. And it was Gwynn's wave every day of the week. So he spun around and started paddling, he was in the perfect spot. He jumped to his feet and stepped straight to the nose of his longboard to hang his foot over the front. Big smile on his face, wave walling up beautifully in front of him - he was all set for the ride of the day, lucky bastard.

I guess maybe one of these students thought so too, because he waited until Gwynn was properly up and riding, you know, had a really good look, and then turned around to take the wave as well. There was no way it was an accident, no way he hadn't seen him. He just spun around and paddled for the wave regardless. Gwynn called him off the way you're supposed to, but the student ignored him and kept on going, he made the drop, so now there's the two of them trimming along the wave, Gwynn on the nose of his board and this student flapping around on a shortboard just in front of him.

I heard Gwynn shout out again, "My wave!" He sounded a bit more incredulous now that the guy hadn't dropped off the back, realising his mistake. And I saw the student turn around to look, but he didn't pull out, he just carried on, and then, when Gwynn kept going too, I heard the student reply, I think almost everyone out there heard.

"Fuck off old timer," he shouted at Gwynn, then said it again and gave him the finger. Then he dropped down the face and did a couple of turns. He was an alright surfer too, better than most of the kooky students. It closed the wave out for where Gwynn was riding, and he came off the front and took a bit of a beating as the wave went over the top of him.

Gwynn wasn't having it, not at his break.

"Hey sonny, you don't do that," he said when the guy paddled back out. Everyone else was watching them both, warily like, not wanting to get too involved.

"Share and share alike," the student surfer said.

"What?"

The student said nothing, just tried to ignore Gwynn.

"What? What's that mean eh? Share and share alike?"

The student muttered something that sounded like "fuck off," but real quiet.

"What you talking about boyo? You just dropped in, you don't do that. Everyone knows that."

"Fuck off," the student said a little louder and tried to paddle away a bit.

"Now, where you going?" Gwynn blocked his path with his board. "You don't do that, you don't drop in. I'm sure you know that so let's keep things nice, you apologise and we'll all still be friends. How about that?" As he was speaking the student was still trying to paddle his board around Gwynn, but Gwynn stopped him by putting his arm out and trying to catch hold of his shoulder. I'd seen a few punches in my day, but this was one of the fastest. The guy just lashed out with his fist and connected with Gwynn's face.

"Don't fucking touch me. I said fuck off," he yelled at the water where Gwynn had fallen in backwards. "You're taking every set wave on that fucking log. How about you fucking apologise for that? You fucking cunt."

When Gwynn surfaced there was bright crimson on his face where his lip had split.

A couple of the other locals had paddled closer to Gwynn and helped him back onto his board, and a couple of the other students who were close by went over to the student guy and tried to calm him down. It looked like things might get proper ugly for a moment, but maybe they were studying law or something and realised the first guy could be arrested for assault if they hung around.

"Hey Graham, take it easy yeah? He's not worth it," one of them said. "Let's go in, get out of here."

And they all paddled back in and loaded up their fucking minibuses and pissed off, leaving Gwynn lying on his back on his board trying to stop his lip bleeding.

I might be remembering it wrong, but I think it was that night when we saw John again for the first time in weeks. We were in the caravan, me and Darren I mean, talking about what had happened when the door opened and John just walked in, like he'd never been away.

"Alright boys," he said. "What you up to?" He wasn't cocky or anything, it wasn't a triumphant entrance. In fact I got the feeling he knew it was going to be a bit awkward since he'd brought us something. He put his bag down right in the middle of the plastic table. "You want some of this?"

"What?" Darren reached over to open the bag and John watched without sitting down.

Darren peeled the canvas of the bag down to reveal a six pack of beers.

"Awesome," Darren said. "Nice one, John." He grabbed one at once and opened it, but John glanced at me first and I just shrugged.

We were still too young to get away with buying alcohol in the village, at least Darren and me were. John could sometimes get away with it.

John sat down and pulled out another beer then handed it to me. I didn't want it, not from him anyway, but I took it cos I didn't want him to know how much I'd been hurt. It was stupid really. Looking back it's obvious they knew what I felt for Cara, but none of us wanted to admit it. So officially me and John were still mates, but really at that time I really hated the fucker. John gave me an unconvincing smile and opened another beer for him. Only then did he slide in behind the table next to Darren. And it was him he talked to.

"So what you up to?"

Darren wasted no time telling him what happened to Gwynn and it was perfect for John since it gave him the chance to just slot back in as if nothing had happened. He sat there like a doctor listening to a patient reel off their symptoms.

"You know what? We should be more like the Badlands," John said when Darren had finished. He sounded angry, but to me it was a bit fake. I mean, he wasn't there. What did he care?

"What's the Badlands?"

"Are you for real? Everyone knows what the Badlands are," John said.

"Of course I know what they are," Darren sounded annoyed at himself. "I've just forgotten."

"You're full of shit. You don't know." John laughed. "How long have you been surfing for? And reading all these magazines?" John pointed to the mess on the floor.

"Well, you don't really read surf mags do you? You just look at the pictures," said Darren, which was true really.

"So go on," Darren continued, "what's the Badlands?"

John pulled himself more upright before continuing.

"The Badlands are this secret bit of the coast down in Cornwall. There's loads of reefs and little bays, and it's got some of the most amazing waves in the whole world."

"So?" Darren's face was screwed up like it did when he was confused.

"So, it's really close to like Newquay, which is where there's a million kooks on holiday, and yet none of the kooks dare to go into the Badlands. They all know the Badlands are for locals only."

"So why is it called the Badlands?" asked Darren.

"Because bad things happen to you if you go there." This was me. I felt like Darren was making us both look stupid.

"What kind of bad things?"

"You know," John was beginning to sound pleased with himself. "The locals there won't let you catch any waves for a start. And if you try they'll slash your tyres, or rub wax into your windscreen, and if that doesn't work they'll just beat the shit out of you. Not just one punch like this dude today. Make proper sure you fuck off and don't come back."

John took a swig of beer then belched up the gas. Darren's face was still screwed up.

"But if they slash your tyres, then how do you fuck off? I mean, your car wouldn't go properly. You'd be stuck there."

John sighed. "Well they only do one wheel, so you use the spare to fuck off. The point is you know not to surf there. That's the way the locals get to keep their waves for themselves."

This seemed to satisfy Darren. He finished his beer - he was always a quick drinker - and opened his second, which John had lined up in front of us.

"So we're going to do the Badlands here?" Darren said.

"Yeah, I think so," John said, like he'd sorted the problem, and that annoyed me.

"I think it's a stupid idea."

A little colour flushed into John's face. "Why?"

"It's just gonna be us doing this is it? Waxing people's windscreens and beating them up? Or are we gonna get Gwynn involved? I mean he's just about the friendliest bloke in the whole world. Shall I explain the plan to him or are you gonna do it?"

John looked for a moment like he might punch me. "So you want to let every fucking kook come and take our waves and do nothing about it? Is that it?"

"No. But you didn't even see those uni students. There were like loads of them, and they were all pretty big. And anyway, it's not really a problem for you anymore, you're too busy to go surfing these days." I hadn't meant to say the last bit, it just came tumbling out and even to me it sounded bitter.

John said nothing at first and when he did his voice was quiet. "Well, I guess it is my problem again if you mean Cara. We broke up."

The confused look climbed back on Darren's face, and then replaced itself with one of disappointment. But he was the first to speak.

"You broke up with Cara?"

"Yeah."

"Why d'you do that?"

John shrugged. "I dunno." He stopped then carried on as if he hadn't been going to tell us, but then decided *what the hell*. "I mean she's pretty good looking and everything, and she's got a good body, a really good body actually… But she doesn't have anything that interesting to say."

"Not like us you mean?" Darren said with absolutely no trace of irony.

"Yeah, I guess."

"It's cos she's not into surfing or anything."

"Yeah." John sounded surer this time.

I opened my mouth to say something but the words stuck in my throat. What the fuck did he mean? Nothing interesting to say. She wanted to travel. She'd said so. But what really hurt was the confirmation that John had slept with her. That he knew what her body was like. That felt like having red hot pokers pushed into both of my ears at once. It fucking hurt my head just to sit there listening to it.

"So you're back then?" Darren said, finishing his second beer. He tried a belch of his own but nothing came out so he just sat there opening and closing his mouth like a fish.

"Yeah. Guess so."

"Then I got an idea how we can sort out the crowds in the town bay." Darren was grinning now. He'd gone from fish to cat in one leap.

"What?" said John.

"We could surf Hanging Rock."

nineteen

TIME DRAGGED BY. Later, and still with no news, Natalie pulled open the sliding door to their little garden and placed a cigarette between her lips. She hadn't smoked for over two years, but there was a packet in the kitchen drawer that she'd never managed to throw away. At first the wind was too strong but she remembered how to cup her hands against it and soon she breathed in the stale smoke, the acidic taste was stale and unpleasant, but any sensation was better than how she felt.

She shivered and looked at the sky, streaked with anxious clouds. She blew out small clouds of her own and tried to let her mind empty of all thought, just watching the tip of the cigarette as it glowed red when she sucked, then receded to grey. When it was gone she stubbed it out and came back inside. She drank more coffee and sat. She noticed the weather at last. The policewoman had talked to her about it, but she hadn't listened. Whatever was coming she'd convinced herself that Jim would be back before it happened. Now, as she watched, a black-edged weather front slowly slid over the house, like a lid being closed on the world. And somehow her body could sense the low pressure that was sucking in the weather. Then the rain came, first hitting the windows with drops so heavy she could hear each one, then coating them in streaks like floods of tears. With the rain came the wind.

The storm hit the whole country, but the South West took the brunt. At first the wind came in lumpy gusts which rattled branches against windows and whistled through the wet streets, but soon it was stronger and fiercer. It sent dustbin lids clattering and set off car alarms. People hurried home from work and needed both hands to push their front doors closed. Tendrils of the storm leaked inside and ruffled pictures on walls, sent gates banging in the gaps between houses. By midnight the storm was at full strength, ripping out roof tiles and sending them spinning and twisting through the blackness like crisp new playing cards. An old oak tree in a street near where Natalie lived, a benevolent monster of a tree that had weathered a thousand storms, felt its feet slipping out of the earth and knew its time had come. A mighty gust pushed against its sail of leaves and it eased over. It let go of the earth with a disappointed sigh, then, just when it seemed it might lay down gracefully it felt the full pull of gravity and crashed down onto a car, splintering its limbs and tearing open the car roof like it was made of tin foil. It was during this storm that his body was washed ashore.

There was something in the way that DS Venables waited on the doorstep, the next morning, that told Natalie it was over.

"You've found him haven't you?" Natalie said at once.

The policewoman spoke in her soft voice.

"Can I come in?"

Natalie stood back and the policewoman brushed her as she walked past.

"We think so." She said when they were in the kitchen. There was no tea this time.

"A man's body was found this morning near Bude in Devon. The storm pushed it in. From the description we think it's Jim."

Natalie nodded and wiped at her eye.

"You need me to identify the body," she said, but the other woman shook her head. "If you'd rather not there are other people we can ask…"

"No. I want to. I need to see him."

The policewoman glanced down for a moment before replying.

"I understand Natalie. But I have to warn you, the body has been in the sea for some time… And the weather… You should know he won't look how you knew him. It might be better for you not to remember him like this."

Natalie felt herself floating away and bit her lip to keep her in the present. She wondered why she wasn't crying. She realised the policewoman was still talking to her.

"I'm so sorry for you that this is happening. I'm just so sorry." The policewoman reached out and touched Natalie's hand and for some reason this horrified her. She felt the woman had no right and wanted to snatch her hand away, but with a spike of panic she realised this wasn't a normal response. This was bad enough without having to work out how she was supposed to react.

"I want to see him. I need to see him. To say goodbye." Natalie squeezed her eyes to make them fill with tears and through watery vision she saw the policewoman nodding.

"I understand."

She had perhaps assumed that they would make an appointment, go another day, but they went at once, travelling in DS Venables police car. She'd come out of uniform that day, and the car she was now driving had no police markings, but inside its radio crackled and burped until the policewoman turned it down low. She made a couple of small attempts at starting a conversation, but Natalie couldn't bring herself to respond. She stared dead ahead at the road as the miles ticked by, thinking about Jim. Trying not to think about the week before. Soon they rolled to a halt in the car park at North Devon District Hospital in Barnstaple, the entrance to the morgue was round the back, out of sight from where the living went in.

Natalie stood alongside DS Venables while she signed them in, then they sat together in a waiting area, the only people present. A low table had a small stack of magazines, *Horse and Hounds* and *Hello* mostly. They looked well read. Natalie wondered at that, how could people sit here and do something so ordinary as read a magazine? She didn't touch them herself, but there wasn't time anyway. The receptionist came into the room and asked if she was ready. The policewoman offered her an arm to lean on but she didn't take it.

They walked through double doors into a room she'd seen a thousand times before, in films and TV dramas. But this time she was right there in the room, able to notice the stains on the ceiling, the plug sockets in the wall. For what? Vacuum cleaners? Electric saws to cut heads open? She was trying to fill her mind, to distract it from what she was going to see, but it was impossible, she could already see him.

Instead of a long row of bodies there was just the one, her husband Jim, a year younger than her, lying on a steel gurney, his cold stiff body covered by a green sheet. Natalie found herself led to his head where a small man in spectacles and green surgical scrubs waited for Sue's instruction to uncover it. Natalie noticed the alarming amount of hair on the man's arms, the white strip where a watch had been removed. DS Venables was watching her face and Natalie gave the smallest of nods. Go ahead, she thought. Destroy my life. I agree to an eternity of nightmares.

The man drew the sheet back with almost a theatrical flourish and the head and torso of the cadaver was revealed in a horrible instant. He was naked, the skin was bloated and mottled in purples, yellows and browns. There was a smear of blood leaking from the nose and the cheeks were swollen. The mouth was open and you could see sand, bedded in around the teeth which were cracked and broken. The man had stubble around his chin and neck, and Natalie remembered hearing that hair continued to grow after death, so that sometimes dead people had to be shaved before they were buried. His eyes were the worst. They too were open but unfocused, a hint of cloudiness like a fish going bad.

It wasn't Jim, she could see that at once, but some impulse forced Natalie to continue looking at the horrible face before her. To study it almost. The hair was wrong, dark like Jim's but this man was receding at the temples. Not like Jim. He was fatter too, you could see the extra weight carried on the face. She felt only confusion. And then in a powerful wave the urge to leave at once overcame her. She didn't want to be here.

"It's not Jim." Natalie said, and took a step back, then she turned to the door as if to leave.

DS Venables looked surprised, almost cheated.

"Natalie dear, are you sure? Faces can look different…"

"It's not him. *It's not him. It's not him. It's not him.*" Natalie realised she was crying and felt a stab of frustration that her body was sabotaging her efforts to remain calm, to navigate this process with dignity.

"OK. OK." DS Venables put her arm around Natalie and led her away from the body. She glared at the mortuary assistant and he flicked the sheet back over the man's dead face, shrugging slightly as if it made no difference to him whether this was the right body or not.

"We've got the clothes, if that helps?" he said to the policewoman.

"The clothes?"

"Yeah, he came in fully dressed, we've got the clothes. She might be able to confirm from the clothes."

DS Venables lowered her voice to a whisper, although there was no chance that Natalie wouldn't hear.

"I was told he was wearing a wetsuit?"

"Yeah that's right, a full suit, bow tie and everything. Soaking wet it was."

"Not a *wet suit,* a wetsuit. The man we're looking for was lost surfing. He was wearing a wetsuit."

"Oh right. Not gonna be him then. Not unless he got changed in the water." You could hear in his voice he thought this a funny idea.

The policewoman's face had gone white with anger. She went to reply, but looked instead at Natalie and ushered her out of the room as fast as she could.

"I'm so sorry, that should never have happened," she said at last when they'd rejoined the road east.

"It's OK." Natalie said, she felt calmer now, watching the trees slip by the window.

"It seems that man was washed up exactly where the coastguard was expecting Jim's body to reappear. The ages matched, no one else had been reported missing. I don't think it occurred to anyone that it wasn't your husband. I'm so sorry." She fell into silence, lost at what she might be able to do to improve the situation.

"If you want to file a complaint, I'll make a statement. I think you should consider it."

Natalie pulled her head up at this and looked across at the other woman. She sensed for a moment that this was somehow important to the police officer, but it wasn't something that interested her. She felt relief, not anger.

"It's alright. It can't be easy, your job. For any of you. I appreciate how much you've done. How much you're all doing. The pilots out there searching, the people on the boats, but you as well."

"Thank you," DS Venables said, glancing across at her.

"And I'm sorry for whoever that is, and whoever is missing him, but at least it means there's still a chance. For Jim, I mean."

Now Natalie took her eyes from the road and met the policewoman's gaze, like she was looking for confirmation that all hope was not lost. But all she saw was how she gripped the steering wheel harder.

"There's something else I need to tell you," the policewoman said in the end.

"What?"

"Just before we left the hospital I reported in that you weren't able to confirm the identity… That it wasn't Jim. So the Coastguard could restart the search. But I've been informed that the search won't be restarted."

"What? Why? If he's still out there… Why would they stop?"

"Natalie I know this is going to be very hard to take. But a search like this will only ever be continued while there is a chance of finding someone alive. If Jim went into the water on Monday it's almost impossible…" she hesitated. "And I'm afraid we've had some new information that makes that seem unlikely anyway."

Natalie felt a stab of concern at the phrase 'new information' but forced herself to ignore it.

"What's happened? What have you found out?"

"I told you that your car was found with a penalty notice issued on the fourth November. We assumed that meant the car must have been left there on the fourth, and if that was the case it would mean Jim had been in the water for just a few hours when the search began," she paused. "And forty eight hours now. That's right at the limit of what can be survived with a wetsuit on…"

"So we need to keep searching." Natalie interrupted her, surprising herself as she did so. "Jim's incredibly strong. If anyone can survive it's him. Can you get them on that thing?" Natalie pointed at the radio.

"Natalie, you have to let me finish. The officers in South Wales have now spoken to the council which issued that ticket. They were working on the assumption that operatives would visit the car park several times each day. But it turns out that wasn't correct. Actually the operative who ticketed Jim's car was the first to visit that car park for four days." She glanced away from the road and over to Natalie to see if she was following her.

"I'm sorry Natalie, but it means it's highly likely that Jim entered the water much earlier than we first believed."

Natalie felt blood thundering through her head. She was thinking how they'd last spoken on Friday night, the first of November. They'd made up from their argument and he'd promised to call again on Saturday. But he never did. And it was Wednesday now.

"No. That's not right. That can't be right."

"I'm sorry Natalie. I understand your friend with the helicopter is continuing to search, but I'm afraid it's no longer part of a search and rescue operation."

Natalie stared at her, she couldn't process the words. She could hear them, but it was as if their meaning was separate to the sound, and it had somehow slipped away.

"I don't understand," she said at last, as if this might make a difference.

"I'm so sorry Natalie. But he's gone. Your husband has gone."

twenty

SHE DROVE THERE in Jim's car, the smell of leather from the seats so powerful a reminder of him that it seemed impossible he could really be gone. The garage had done something to one of the filters, or perhaps a valve, she hadn't cared, hadn't been interested in how much it might cost, it was all she could do to thrust her credit card at them and get out of there as fast as she could.

But now she drove slowly, putting off the time when she would arrive. She'd run through her mind how this meeting would go over the last few days. Now it was close, she wasn't sure anymore. She pulled onto the old airport road, past the curved, corrugated iron roofs of the old wartime airman's accommodation now converted into offices and little industrial units. She remembered the last time she'd driven here, just a week ago. And how it had been a different person that drove away.

She parked down the side of the building, where the curved roof flowed windowless into the ground. But she knew Dave was there, she'd seen his black BMW parked out in front, where it always was. Dave had claimed he should get the better space because he was in the office more. He was the one who handled the paperwork, stayed on top of the maintenance schedules, the ever-changing regulations. That was never Jim's strength. But Jim, being Jim, liked to try and park in Dave's space, just to annoy him. Just for the hell of it, even after Dave had put up signs up with their names on in front of each space. It didn't matter now of course, Jim wouldn't be parking anywhere now. She felt the thought nearly crush her, and it took all her effort to pull the handle on the car door and step out.

She walked around to the front of the office, passing the window and glancing in. Dave hadn't heard her arrive. He was sat behind his desk, sleeves rolled up, a frown of concentration on his face. But then something made him look up and their eyes met. She forced herself to smile a sad hello as he got up to open the door.

Inside he said nothing, but held his arms open. She hesitated at first but then let herself lean into him and he pulled her close. They stood together in silence and he stroked her hair, until she pushed herself away and sat down in front of his desk.

"I ran out of flying hours," Dave said. "I already flew more than I should, the coastguard said they'd have to report me if I went up any longer."

"I know," Natalie said.

"I can fly again tomorrow. Do you want me to get back up…?" She was shaking her head and he stopped.

"He's gone Dave. Jim's gone."

He nodded slowly, like he knew this was the case, but hadn't been sure if she had accepted it yet.

"I'm so sorry Natalie. So sorry."

They stood there for a long while neither knowing what to say until Dave went on in a sensitive voice that Natalie was starting to recognise.

"How are you holding up?" He asked.

It took her by surprise, not the question, but her response. It nearly broke her composure and it was all she could do to nod, her chin crumpling up as she tried to hold back tears. He went to hold her again but she pushed him away.

"No."

"No. I need to talk to you. I've come here to talk." Her voice was firm, a little cold.

He rubbed his hand across his face, seemed surprised at the extent of the growth on his cheeks, but he said nothing. Instead he nodded, went back to his own chair behind the desk and sat down facing her. She sat down too, and took a deep breath. But now that the moment had come, Natalie lost her nerve.

"Has it caused problems, you being away from the business I mean?" She said at last.

He answered slowly, he knew this wasn't what she wanted to discuss, but he answered her anyway.

"A bit. I mean, Christ, it's hardly important, but..." He gestured to his desk. "I've called in some favours. It'll be all right."

She nodded, and tried to work out how to go on. But he interrupted her thoughts.

"The guy from the coastguard said that this happens sometimes. It doesn't matter how good a swimmer someone is, or how many years they've been surfing. It's rare, but it happens." He stopped and looked at her, but she didn't respond.

"I know the timing's... awkward."

Her eyes flicked to his up from the desk, then slowly she lowered her eyes again.

"What a difference a week makes," Dave said, changing the tone of his voice, seeing where she was looking. She got the implication but she pulled her eyes up again at once and glared at him.

"I lied to the police Dave. I lied to them."

She watched the colour fade from his face.

"What do you mean?"

"They found empty paracetamol packets in the car. Lots of them.

They thought he took an overdose before he went into the water."

"*What?* Why the hell do they think that?"

"Well I thought perhaps you could tell me?" her nostrils flared and she stared at him, daring him to reply, but he said nothing.

"Perhaps someone told him his wife screwed his business partner last week. What do you think? That might do it."

It was only the two of them there, but Dave's head swivelled wildly from side to side, as if checking they weren't being overheard.

"Jesus Natalie," he said. "There's no need to shout. Just calm down a little will you?"

In reply she just stared at him over the desk.

"Well, have you got anything to tell me? Cos I sure as hell can't think of any other reason why Jim might take an overdose."

"Natalie… Are you suggesting I told him? Because I didn't, I swear to you. Why would I tell him?"

Natalie didn't answer at first. She didn't have an answer for this.

"I don't know."

"It would ruin everything. The business, my marriage…" he glanced at her and added: "Us. Whatever that is now."

Natalie was breathing hard still, but now that her anger had broken free, she felt unsure what to do next. She said nothing and after a moment Dave continued.

"How do you mean you lied to the police?"

She let her breathing slow before replying.

"I told them the pills were mine. I made a statement saying I kept them there in the glovebox, and I hadn't thrown away the empty boxes. That meant they weren't connected to Jim's death. It meant he didn't kill himself. But they weren't mine. I've no idea how they got there."

Dave ran his hands through his hair, as if the thought that was forming inside his head just couldn't make sense.

"But hold on. Jim wouldn't kill himself. Even if he did find out… I mean I don't know what he'd do, but he wouldn't do that. There's just no way."

It was the same thought that Natalie had been having for the last three days. In the six years she'd known Jim she'd hardly ever seen him worried or stressed. And he'd sounded fine on Friday when they spoke on the telephone. He seemed to have almost forgotten their argument when he left, he talked about taking her out to dinner later that week, his way of making it up to her.

"And anyway," Dave went on. "There's just no way he could have found out."

He interrupted her thoughts and she looked at him in surprise, sitting just across the desk from her. The desk that now had such a history, such meaning. The desk on which she had been unfaithful for the first, and now only time, in her marriage.

From the moment Jim introduced her to Dave she knew he liked her. It was obvious in the way his eyes avoided her until he thought she couldn't see them, and then how they followed her around the room. She'd felt flattered at first, it was harmless, a nice boost to her ego. Both these men were catches, Jim better looking, more flashy perhaps, but Dave could hold his own. And here she was, apparently able to captivate one, and still attract the attention of the other. Jim completely missed it of course. He was more excited about how she got on with Elaine, Dave's wife. Jim had grand plans for how the four of them would become best friends, god parents to each other's children. If it wasn't so tragic it would be funny how clearly he saw all their futures, especially now, that he'd got it all so horribly wrong.

And then last week. When Jim had buggered off on his surfing trip he'd left an important folder in his car, which Dave needed. But of course Natalie had the car, she was putting it in the garage for Jim while he was away. Luckily Dave phoned her about it before she dropped the car at the garage. Or perhaps that was bad luck, the way things turned out. She'd driven down to the office then too, in the darkness. Dave was working late again. While Jim had his fun. Bloody Jim.

She didn't usually drink coffee this late, but he talked her into it. He said he had a long night ahead of him and needed the caffeine. Perhaps he implied a little how this wasn't helped by Jim's carelessness in driving off with the papers. Perhaps that gave them both a reason to be a little irritated with Jim, and they were both a little more critical than was normal in discussing him. But Dave didn't talk about Jim for long. Instead he asked about her, something he'd rarely done before. He asked her how her new role was going at the university, and she talked until she'd exhausted the subject, him listening all the while. It seemed like it was the first time that anyone really took an interest. She thought, not for the first time, how Dave was such a nice guy. Jim was lucky to be working with him. She was lucky to know him. Dave wasn't exciting like Jim, but he was handsome, she would still notice him if he walked into a room, and he was reliable, dependable. Everything that Jim wasn't. For some reason they weren't sitting down, but leaning against the front of his desk, their sides nearly touching. The coffee's long finished. And in that moment her mind started playing crazy tricks on her as she wondered how it might feel to slide across a little, so that her thigh pressed up against his. What might he do if her shoulder brushed his?

And at that moment she knew it was going to happen. She could have stopped it, but she didn't. They looked at each other and Dave lifted his hand and brushed the hair out of her face. She tried to stop him in only the most half hearted way, and he caught her hand and held it close to his face. Then he leaned across and she knew he was going to kiss her. She leaned in too and their lips came together. He turned around to press against her and his hands came down from her face to her breasts, cupping them through her bra. And she broke away from him, desperate to let nothing interrupt, to let no moment of fumbling allow her mind to halt this madness she reached behind her back and unclipped her bra and then threw her arms around him and sought out his lips. And then everything that was on the desk, the papers she had brought, it was all suddenly on the floor, Natalie's dress was hitched up around her waist, his hand pushing her knickers down, Dave's urgency to enter her both scaring and thrilling her.

"I just don't see how he could have found out," Dave said, it ripped Natalie back to the present.

"How about Elaine? Did you tell her? Is there any way she could have known?"

"Of course not. Why would I tell her?"

They were both silent for a while, and then, suddenly, she remembered.

"The window."

"What?"

"The window. Remember I made you…"

She didn't finish the sentence, she didn't need to, there was no way he could have forgotten. With her bare back on the wood of the desk her head had fallen sideways and she'd seen the empty blackness of the night outside the office, the blinds up, the way Dave usually had them. And then a flash of red, the rear light of a car, driving away down the road.

"Stop. *Stop.*"

With an effort he did so, his weight pressing down on her, his trousers open at the fly.

"You've got to shut the blinds. Someone might see."

She could sense him hesitate, and wondered if he might tell her not to worry, that no one would be about this late, but instead he pushed himself up and padded to the window, panting all the way. Then he released the cord to let the blinds rattle down across the glass and turned them so the night was shut out. Then he took a long look at Natalie, her legs apart, underwear still caught around one ankle, before turning off the lights. She heard rather than saw him come back to her, still breathing heavily, gently tugging at the cotton of her knickers to free them and kissing the insides of her legs, moving ever upwards.

"You left him a message about the papers didn't you? The ones I dropped off that night. What if he drove back here as well that night, to help with whatever the work was. What if he saw us through the window before you closed the blinds?"

Now it was Dave's turn to stay silent for a long while. She could see on his face his mind working. Eventually he spoke.

"Why would he come back? He didn't have the papers, there was nothing he could do."

But Natalie hardly heard this, with a flash she remembered the red tail lights she'd seen that night.

"I saw a car. Driving away, before you shut the blinds. It must have been him. He must have seen us..." Natalie's hand flew to her mouth, stopping her from going on, but the horror was clear in her eyes. But Dave was shaking his head.

"No. You've got to stay rational. Jim didn't see us. He couldn't have done. There's no way he would have come all the way back from Cornwall to help with a few papers. This is Jim we're talking about."

Natalie didn't move, her hand still clamped over her mouth.

"OK. The light you saw, this car. How close was it?"

Slowly Natalie brought her hand down, and concentrated on her breathing. She looked at the window, the thought that Jim might have stood outside there watching her was almost overwhelming - she remembered with a another layer of misery how she had beckoned to Dave to come back to her just before he turned off the light. But no, Jim couldn't have seen that - the blinds were already down by then.

"Look. *Look.* Out the window. We're the last unit on the estate. But you can see the corner of the main road. That's what you must have seen. A car driving out on the main road, but they wouldn't have been able to see in here."

She tried to calm her breathing and focus on what he was saying. The light hadn't been close she remembered.

"No one saw us Nat. They couldn't have."

Suddenly she got up and went to the window. Outside everything was quiet. Like normal. Most of the other units around them were empty. She saw the main road, some way away, and then a car drove along, slowing for the corner, its brake lights coming on for a moment or two. She began to relax a little.

Natalie went and sat back down. Dave had put a coffee in front of her and she took a sip. The bitterness helped.

"So if you you didn't tell him, I didn't tell him, and he didn't see us through the window, then how the hell did he find out?"

"We don't know that he did. There was no note or anything? Nothing else to suggest…?

"No. Nothing the police have found."

"And you spoke to him after… On Friday night? On the phone?" Dave said. They both knew what he meant. Friday was two nights after their encounter.

"How did he sound? Was he suspicious? Angry?"

She shook her head, remembering the call now.

"No. It was… Good. I think we both felt guilty. Him because we'd had this row about him going off surfing again. Me because of… Well." She shrugged sarcastically, and felt in danger of losing her composure again, but Dave carried on as if he didn't notice.

"So the only suggestion it wasn't an accident is these empty paracetamol boxes."

Natalie considered for a second or two.

"I suppose."

"And they definitely weren't yours? I mean, I've seen your car. It's often quite a mess. They couldn't actually have just been left there?"

Natalie felt herself reddening at this. It was bizarre. She was suddenly feeling more guilt for keeping a dirty car than being an unfaithful wife. "No..." she stopped. "I mean there may have been one packet there, I'm not sure. But not three."

He took a deep breath before replying.

"Then maybe there is a simple explanation. Maybe Jim got a headache. Pulled a muscle or something. That can easily happen when you're surfing. And maybe you had an empty packet or two in the car and forgot to throw them away. And he bought another packet, and used them for something. I mean for something real."

Natalie's face stopped him. Her eyes were wide and pleading. He felt an overwhelming urge to protect her.

"Nat you did the right thing telling the police those tablets were yours. Imagine how much worse this would be for Jim's mum, for everybody if they thought Jim took his own life. And there's no way that happened. This was just a tragic accident. You did the right thing."

Natalie looked away. She tried to look back at him and say something but her nerve failed.

"We'll find out," she said eventually. "When they find his body. They'll do an autopsy. We'll know for sure then. And then the police will know that I lied. What happens then Dave?"

He didn't answer this and it looked for a moment like she was going to cry again.

Dave stood up and came back around the desk. He took her hands and pulled lightly so that she stood up, and for a second time he put his arms around her.

twenty-one

I'D BARELY THOUGHT about our secret spot while John had been with Cara, I was a bit busy wallowing in despair and misery I guess. But Darren had thought about it.

It turned out he'd gone on another reconnaissance trip, alone. He'd taken another look at the map and realised it was easier to get to Hanging Rock if you first went inland following the road up past John's house, and then cut across along a farmer's track by some fields. You then had to jump over the wall that bordered the estate, but it wasn't that hard to do and as soon as you were across, no one from the outside could see you. From there you could scramble straight down the side of the valley and follow it all the way back to the sea and Hanging Rock Bay. It was a bit of a trek, but the big advantage was that no one from the big house would be able to see you, which was much better than the coastal route where you had to pass in front of it in full view.

The problem was the boards. Wetsuits fitted in a backpack, but you couldn't hide three bloody great surfboards, and if anyone saw us on the road, it would be obvious we were headed towards the private estate.

Between them, John and Darren worked it all out. The night before we planned to surf it, we would take our boards as far as John's house. Then we would leave from there early, before there was any traffic on the country lane. If we got unlucky and someone did come along we'd be able to hear then, and we could stash the boards in the hedge. The track would probably be easier, it was unlikely that anyone would be out walking that early. Once we were over the wall it was commando territory - we didn't know what we'd be facing, but we figured that if you were rich enough to have a massive house and an estate, then you wouldn't feel the need to get up early. We hoped so anyway.

It was all Darren and John making the plans. And if it hadn't all taken place at the caravan, I might not have been involved at all. I didn't know how to process the news that John and Cara had split up. On the one hand I was pleased, and of course I didn't buy John's bullshit that he'd split up with her, but on the other it made it difficult for me since John was around more than ever, and I still found it difficult to talk to him like before. I still found my stomach doing these stupid heaves when John mentioned her name. Darren didn't help. He decided he wanted details and would pester him for hours, asking how many times they'd had sex and where and what positions and what it was like. John knew how it made me feel, but that didn't mean he wasn't going to brag about it.

A couple of weeks later, the weather forecast looked good for surf that weekend, and we put our plan into action. I told Mum I was taking my board to John's to fix it, not that she'd have noticed it was gone, and Darren and me peddled up the hill into a freshening breeze, each with a board under our arms. John met us at his gate and we stashed the boards under some bushes just inside his fence. We didn't hang around for long but each went home and set our alarms for five the next morning.

It was autumn by then, and only just light when I woke. My school backpack had been emptied of books to make room for my wetsuit and a few chocolate bars borrowed from the shop. Darren was already at John's when I got there, and we set off right away, talking in whispers even though there was no one else around.

A couple of cars came past while we were hiking single file along the road, and John - in front of course - called for us to quickly lower our boards into the ditch that ran alongside the road. The occupants couldn't have been less bothered, but it was still a relief when we made it to the track, it would be just our luck for one of the local surfers to drive past and stop to ask where we were going. We saw one woman with a dog in the fields, but they were a long way in front and walking away from us so we just stalked along behind, ready to drop to the ground if she turned around, but pretty soon she turned away and out of sight.

It didn't take too long before we arrived at the estate's perimeter wall. It had signs up saying "Private" and "Trespassers Will Be Prosecuted" but that didn't look so likely since the wall was almost falling down in places. It was no trouble to jump up onto it, pass the boards up, and then drop down the other side.

We went from farmer's fields to land that I guess was used for grazing sheep. Just grassland, a few little woods dotted around, and like Darren had said, no buildings or anything in sight.

Even though this was Darren's route, it was still John that took the lead, and we followed him across a half mile of open land and then down into the valley. There was a lot of vegetation down here to push through and the path the sheep used sometimes disappeared, but we could splash through the stream for the few bits that had got too overgrown. Right at the end it got really thick and John had to go through first then we passed him the boards one by one.

And then we turned a corner and we were there.

twenty-two

THE WAVE AT Hanging Rock was special. What happened that day - later on I mean, when things turned bad - that would never have happened if the wave hadn't been something special.

That first day we surfed it the wind was blowing strong and out to sea the horizon was lumpy from all the swell. Even inshore there were white caps everywhere, really it was no day for surfing. But right in close by where the rocky ledge lay unseen beneath the water, in there the surface of the sea had smoothed right off. Maybe it's something to do with the steep sides of the valley, I don't know, but where the wave was breaking it was like a different day. The swells would wallow in towards the reef like bloated whales, their backs ruffled and bothered by the wind, but in close they became spaced out and stretched like a strange creature waking up. And one by one they began to peel off down the point. By the time they were reeling past the Hanging Rock they looked like something out of a surf movie. Only better, for being real and unbound by some little square box in a magazine or on TV.

I don't know about the others but I never really expected to go surfing that day. Not there anyway. I thought we would get there to find the place wasn't like we remembered it, that the wave didn't really work after all. That it was just some crazy dream we'd all had, and we'd hike back without even getting wet and that would be it. We knew Town Beach would be OK later on and that's where I thought we'd end up.

Splashing around in the wind with everyone else.

And because we'd arrived by Darren's inland route it just felt such a shock to see it there laid out in front of us. We'd not seen the sea, just sheep droppings and branches scratching across our faces and then suddenly… this. This vast blueness stretching out in front of us and wave after wave after wave coming through like it had been sculpted by some giant machine. And no one there but us. It looked… I dunno how to describe it. It just looked fucking amazing.

You wouldn't believe how quickly three boys can get into wetsuits, but when we were suited up, we slowed down a bit - the launch was sketchy. The wave broke onto a flat reef that runs up the north side of the inlet, it stuck right out from the cliffs with the Hanging Rock right in the middle. But the reef was studded with boulders and deep cracks so that it was constantly washed by foaming white water surging up and drawing back down again. Getting across wasn't easy. You might make it, or you might stumble on a rock that you've not seen, and there's a lot of seaweed so it's really slippery. Eventually we'd figure out the right way to launch at Hanging Rock - you jump in at the waterfall at the neck of the bay and it's an easy paddle out behind where the waves are breaking. But that first time we didn't think of that. So instead we picked our way all the way along the rocks right out to the point, and tried to make the short paddle out through the breaking waves just before they began their long peel down the reef.

It was hard going walking. You could feel the wind catching at the board, trying to whip it around and slapping the leash against the deck. It was cold too, still early in the day. I didn't have boots and the barnacles cut at my feet. Lower down the seaweed felt greasy and slippery. Eventually I made it down to the water's edge, the point where the last of the wave's energy pushed the water it was carrying onto the rocks. John and Darren were there already, their feet in boots had made the walk a little easier. But something was holding them back.

"Now what?" I asked as I stood close by to Darren. It was pretty much the first time I'd spoken that day.

He said nothing but crouched lower, holding his board in both hands as a bigger swell pushed in, sending water foaming over his feet and up to his knees. He was braced for it and managed to stay upright, but it hit me by surprise and the force of it took my legs away. I found myself carried back up the rocks on my arse, the board clattering off the rocks behind me.

"Shit!" I shouted when I got back to my feet, more to me than anyone else. "It's got a lot of power."

Neither of them answered but Darren was watching me, hesitating. John didn't though. Just as the next swell pushed in he shouted "Motherfucker!" and he leapt forward into the water, holding his board out in front of him. He landed with his chest on the board in his paddling position and began to dig in furiously, strong strokes of front crawl, trying to make ground before the next wave hit. When it did all we saw was a pair of black legs and feet disappearing under a bubbling wall of crisp white foam.

"Fucking hell!" Darren shouted at the sky and he went next, copying John's technique and disappearing the same way. I'd picked myself up by now and retreated a bit to higher ground. From there I could see the two of them paddling as hard as they could. They were paddling straight out, but the rip was so strong they were being dragged sideways faster, back the way we'd just walked. But they didn't even notice. Every few strokes they had to interrupt what they were doing for another duck dive to get under a new wall of water that pushed them back and battered them around. It looked pretty full on.

My heart was pumping like mad and I felt the wetsuit tight against my chest. It didn't feel constrictive anymore, it felt thin, no match for the wind that cut across the headland. I didn't know if I wanted to go in or not, actually that's a lie. I'd have just sat down and watched from the rocks if I'd felt I had a choice. But there was no choice. How could I face John and Darren ever again unless I got in there? So I picked my way back towards the water until the ends of the swells were once again clawing at my knees. I locked my teeth together to stop them chattering, with cold, or fear, I don't know. I got lucky then and there was a break in the waves, just a little lull, so before I could change my mind, before I even knew I was doing it, I threw myself forward and started paddling, ignoring the feel of rocks scraping at the tips of my fingers.

Because I'd seen John and Darren get pulled so fast to the left, I aimed more to the right than they had, much more, and this seemed to help, or maybe I just got lucky. I had to make three fast duck dives, the last a deep one where I could feel the wave sucking hard off my back, like a beast clawing at me as it rolled over my head. When I surfaced you could hear its anger that I'd slipped through, this snarling moan that went on howling as it rolled away from me. Then it went quiet. Eerie quiet. I paddled fast through this long flat section where the sea was bubbling and swirling like a fast-moving river - the air pushed underwater by the waves was finding its way back to the surface. This was the impact zone and I knew you don't want to hang around here. Ahead of me a new set was building and I forced my arms to work faster, ignoring the pain in my muscles as I dragged myself through the boiling water. I had to get over the waves before they broke, that was all that mattered in the world.

Suddenly the first wave was right in front of me, still unbroken, but feathering and about to unload. I put everything I had into pulling my arms through the water. I was paddling uphill and the swell was transforming into a plunging, breaking wave not in front of me but *around* me, to my right it steepened and hollowed and threw itself out and down in a hissing, ugly roar that tore at my legs, way too big to duck dive this one. But for all the fear in my body I knew I was ok, just far enough out to claw my way to the top and over down the other side. Behind it the spray whipped around me and I felt the vacuum in the air try to suck me back, like standing next to a railway track as an express thunders through. There was no way back the way I'd just come. The scream in my arms made me slow my paddling, but I still kept heading out, pulling myself over the remaining waves in the set. Then it all went quiet. I was out the back.

It was massive. There was nothing out there to give a sense of scale, that's why we hadn't seen it from the land, but now I was the scale. The swells were like roaming mountains with great ugly lumps of chop on them the size of cars. There were streaks of foam running like veins across the water surface, and when a wave broke, a way inside of me now thank God, great blizzards of spray lashed downwind for hundreds of metres stinging my face and eyes. My heart was nearly beating out of my chest. I'd have done anything to get out of there.

I know I said I was good, that I ripped, but here's the truth. I might have been OK at Town Beach. But what you've got to know is that Town Beach was the *only place* I'd surfed the last three years. And the wave there was soft as hell. Even before that in Australia I really only went out in small waves. So when I say I was a good surfer what I mean was, I was good at carving little turns and trying to punt airs on soft little waves. Kid's stuff. I had exactly no experience in the type of big, scary pointbreak waves that I suddenly found myself in. And I was out there all alone. The others had vanished.

I was kind of frozen with fear for a bit, just watching the horizon and paddling for my life whenever a set loomed up, but that kept taking me further and further out and eventually I realised I'd actually paddled right outside the inlet and was in danger of being swept down the coast. If that happened I faced a good few miles where big swells were crunching directly onto rocks and cliffs, all the way until I got to the shelter and sand of Town Beach. There was no way I could do that. I'd either drown, or more likely be beaten to death on the rocks if that happened. That thought knocked a bit of sense into me and I started trying to get back into the bay. I hadn't seen the other two since I'd launched myself into the water, but then a swell lifted me up and I got a glimpse of them, sitting there, sort of huddled over their boards. They were right opposite the Hanging Rock, tucked in out of the wind just where we'd said we would sit. It looked miles away.

Like a proper kook I was battling directly against the current and the wind, and I could see from the headland beside me I was putting all my energy just into staying in the same place. And I was tiring fast. I was crying too, it was like half my brain had shut down and was just whimpering inside my head. But fortunately the other half was still just about working. There was this one time back in Oz when the lifeguards came into school to tell us how to beat a rip tide. You never paddled or swam straight against it, but had to go diagonally, or sometimes even let it take you right out and around and choose another place to come in. They handed out these cartoons for us to take home and put on our walls. Panicking Peter did the wrong thing in every drawing, Calm-headed Cindy always got it right, and she looked sexy in her little bikini. I kept mine up until one of my friends laughed at me for having it there. But I still saw it every time I went to sleep for maybe four years. I guess it sunk in. I turned around and started paddling back out into the middle of the bay, even though it felt like the wrong thing to do.

If you stand on the headland you can see what happens to the water. Hanging Rock Bay is shaped like a V, each side being maybe five hundred metres long. It's the only feature in an otherwise straight section of rocky, cliffy coastline so there's little to slow the tides as they rip northwards on the push, and southwards as they ebb. And that tide was always at its worst right there on the corner. That's where I was stuck, still quite close in, but right where all the tide was running and also where all the water flowing out of the bay. You paddle straight against it, you're fucked. You're Panicking Peter. You're this little matchstick figure trying to beat the entire Atlantic ocean pushing high tide up the Irish Sea. But you paddle out and around - it's a long way and still not a nice place to be, but at least you've got a chance.

And sometimes the ocean does funny things to help you out. Another set made the horizon turn black and lumpy, but instead of turning towards it and trying to get over it before it broke, this time I was too tired. I just stopped and lay on my board panting, crying, watching it rumble toward me. Then just before it arrived pure fear made me do something. I didn't want to face any waves, but I definitely didn't want to face a whole set, so I decided to try and catch the first one. It might drown me or it might just tumble me back in through the impact zone. Either way, it didn't feel my life was in my hands at that point.

That first wave still hadn't broken so I spun my board around and just paddled for all I could, trying not to hear the groan the wave made as it stood up around me. I felt it lift the back of my board up and then this flat ocean I'd been paddling in morphed sickeningly into the downward slope of a watery mountain. I felt the board pick up its own speed as it skidded downhill and on an instinct I stopped paddling and tried to stand up. As I did so the board hit some chop and I stumbled, ending up on my arse, hands tightly gripping the rails. But I was lucky too. The board was now facing along the wave, towards the shoulder where it would peel to. Behind me there was this detonation of spray, but it was well behind me. And then it was like being spat forward, the water walled up, the chops were stretched flat and I was right in the pocket of this howling freight train of a wave, the biggest, scariest wave I'd ever seen, and only instead of crouching low like some hero surfer, I was sat on my arse.

All I knew was the longer I could ride it, the more chance I had of getting out of the rip current, so I just straight lined along this beautiful, perfect wall. I dared a glance behind me and glimpsed this blue-black curl as the eye of the wave fought to catch up with me, then I looked forward again at the perfection of a long, sloping shoulder that stretched all the way to the neck of the bay. Dignity came back quick and I tried to get off my bum, but as I did so I steered the board too high up the face of the wave and I couldn't move my weight to send it back down again, so I ended up skipping over the top and onto the flat water behind it.

There was another wave right behind my one, but it didn't look quite as terrifying as the mushroom cloud that I'd caught out at the point, Even so I paddled like fuck to get out past it, as I did so I caught sight of a pair of heads in the water a bit further out, and kept going until I reached them, my arms dying in their sockets when I got there.

"Fucking hell man, these waves are amazing!" John's eyes were wide open and bloodshot from the spray.

"Hey Jesse you were right out beyond the point, almost around the corner," said Darren. "I don't think you should go right out there, it doesn't look safe."

I was panting so hard I could hardly speak and just nodded in agreement. But John didn't care about that. I'd never heard his voice quite like this before, he wasn't talking, he was screaming.

"That was one sick motherfucking wave you caught there Jesse. You rode it on your fucking arse!" He slapped the water with both his hands and yelled at the sky. A roar of celebration. "Can you fucking believe this place?"

On reaching them I'd assumed we'd all concentrate on finding a way to get back ashore, just basically getting the hell out of there and never coming back. however it was clear they weren't moving, but waiting for a wave to ride. Suddenly I was conscious how much I'd been crying and hoped it didn't show on my face. I looked around me. We were about half way along the north edge of the reef, and the water in here was much calmer, we were well out of the current sweeping north by the entrance of the bay. The waves when they came were smaller too, still big compared to anything I'd surfed before and still clean and, well, perfect. I realised I was sitting out there with the sort of waves we'd dreamed of and talked about for years.

John went for one in the next set. He turned around and began to paddle as this shoulder reared up behind him, the wave already breaking further up the point. I hoped he wouldn't catch it as being all together somehow felt safer, but when the wave had swept through he was nowhere to be seen. You could see the curl of the wave working down the reef from behind and as I watched it John's head popped up behind the wave, he must have fallen and let the wave roll over the top of him. He paddled back more amped than ever.

"You've got to catch one of these Jesse, this is way better than fucking sex."

Even out there I felt the lurch. Obedient as Pavlov's fucking dog an image of Cara formed in my mind, she was wet-haired, bedraggled and - get this - wearing Calm-headed Cindy's skimpy swimwear. But this time something was different. This time I was there with John. John who'd fucked the most beautiful girl I'd ever seen. The most beautiful girl I thought was possible. Who'd pressed his face into that mysterious space at the top of her thighs. Who'd slept on those breasts that tortured my dreams. Who'd pressed himself into her so many times that he'd bored himself. And here he was saying that surfing this wave was better.

Suddenly I wanted one of these waves. I'd suffered so much I deserved one. Not on my arse. Not shaking with fear either. I wanted a real one. The next good swell that came along I started to paddle for it, seriously paddle for it and the thing was it was so easy. I had so much time to jump to my feet and then this beauty of a wave just opened herself up to me. I kept low and stuck my hand into the surface as it built up into around me. I was perfectly in control. I stood up high and held my arms aloft and let out this scream that came from somewhere deep inside. The speed was like nothing I'd felt before, I could arc into turns just by thinking about it, it was like I was some seabird riding the winds of a storm. I'd grown up obsessed with surfing but I realised on that wave I'd never really done it. I'd fucked around on little beach breaks but I'd never really *surfed*. And that image of Cara Williams in my head? I just laughed. From that wave forward she looked no better than one of the waves in Town Bay. A good one maybe, but nothing compared to what I now knew. How had I ever fooled myself into thinking she was important? When there was so much living to do?

When I could *surf*?

twenty-three

AT FIRST SHE waited for the call, every time the telephone rang she hesitated before lifting the receiver, allowing herself a moment before hearing that Jim had washed ashore. A moment before the questions would begin about what was found in his blood. Why she'd told the police the tablets were hers. But when the phone rang it was never about that. There were practical calls, handling Jim's affairs - even without a body the nature of his disappearance meant the coroner issued a death certificate after just six weeks. Personal calls, friends, relatives, phoning to see how she was getting on, checking up on her it sometimes felt. The worst were the impersonal calls, strangers asking for Jim as if they had known him, still happy to try and sell to a dead man. But *that* call never came. And as the weeks turned into months and into years, Natalie realised that now it never would. Whatever evidence stayed in a body wouldn't last this long. Whatever happened to Jim would never be known for sure. And then, eight years later, the phone rang, and her life changed forever.

Not too much had changed in those eight years, she was still teaching at university, a lot more confident now with her lectures, settled into her career. The house had been re-decorated, Jim's more valuable belongings long-since sold, the rest given away, or taken to the tip. After eight years the house felt hers. She had lived there alone for twice as long as they had lived there together, the only traces left of him were the photographs on the walls, a bike in the garage, a few folders of papers kept on a shelf, evidence of his life and death.

At first it had felt like her life was in limbo, waiting for Jim's body to come ashore so he could be buried, and so she could finally get an answer to the cause of his death. But equally she didn't want him to be found. She grew to accept that Jim couldn't have known about her affair, but it didn't help. She still felt a hot guilt when she thought about it, and doubts always crept in. And when the months turned into years she knew that the secret of Jim's death would stay a secret. She grieved, and she felt the pain recede into the distance. And the guilt and the shame. But it never quite disappeared entirely.

That morning she had a midday lecture. She got up late. She had time for a coffee before going in. That's when the phone rang. She almost didn't answer it, you get so many nuisance calls these days.

Click. A little bit of wind noise, like the caller was outside.

"Can I speak with Jim Harrison please?"

"I'm afraid not, he passed away some time ago. What's it regarding please?" She sighed inwardly. Another list to have Jim's name removed from.

There was a very long pause on the phone and the man's voice changed when he replied. He sounded confused.

"Oh. I was phoning to say I'd found his wallet."

Her brain was already returning to how she would deliver her lecture that afternoon, but this stopped her dead. Jim's wallet had never been found, the police had assumed it was taken when the car was broken into.

"I'm sorry, what do you mean?"

"Well like I said, I've found his wallet."

"Where? How?"

There was no delay this time. The caller seemed on more expected ground. "Yesterday, out on the new cliff path. We've been putting a bridge in over the stream and there was this bag stashed in a bush. Bit tatty it was, but it didn't look like it was exactly abandoned. Anyways we had a look in, there were a few clothes in there and stuff, and this wallet. It had his name and address in it. You know, if lost please contact this number..." The man left his voice hanging. It wasn't until later that Natalie wondered if he'd been hoping for a reward. But at the time her mind was too busy trying to process the information.

"Are you sure it's the right Jim Harrison?"

"Well I don't rightly know that do I? I'm just ringing the number in the wallet."

"Yes of course. I'm sorry." She stopped.

"And I assume you're working somewhere in Cornwall are you, near Porthtowan?"

Again the confusion sounded in the man's voice.

"*Cornwall?* No love. No we're up by Llanwindus, you know the new coastal path that's going in?"

"Llan...? I'm sorry where is that? Is that in Cornwall somewhere?" Natalie insisted.

"What's all this about Cornwall? Like I told you, we're here in Wales. Near Llanwindus."

"Wales? But that doesn't make any sense. Jim was in Cornwall when he died, not Wales. That's where they found his car."

There was a pause and when the man spoke again she could hear in his voice he was looking for an excuse to end the call.

"Look I don't know nothing about that. Maybe I'll just send the bag onto you, would that be best?"

Natalie answered quickly, beginning to panic. "Yes. No, don't go. Look I'll give you my address."

"I've got it already. Remember? It's in the wallet." The man hung up.

Natalie tried at once to trace where the call had come from, but it was an unlisted number. She replaced the receiver on the wall and stared at it until her coffee went cold.

She didn't mention the call to anyone at work, and by the time she came home later that day she decided she wouldn't tell anyone about it. Not because she wanted to keep it secret, but because, by then, she couldn't be certain she hadn't imagined the whole thing. Better to wait and see if anything actually came through the post, or the man called back. Then no one could accuse her of losing it.

Nearly a week passed. She nearly convinced herself it was some crazy hallucination, but then she saw the postman coming up the drive. He knocked on the door and handed her a parcel wrapped in brown paper. He said something about the weather but she didn't hear what. She'd seen the postmark: Llanwindus Post Office.

She took the package into the kitchen and sat at the table, just looking at it for a while. Then she steeled herself and began to open it. Whoever had wrapped it had used too much tape, the paper tore easily enough but she had to get scissors to break through the taught web of plastic which gripped the contents of the parcel. When she'd pulled it away she recognised the bag inside with a jolt. She'd even noticed it missing, when she cleared out Jim's possessions in those black months after he'd disappeared from her life. It was his flight bag, waterproof and designed to carry enough gear for an overnight stop. It wasn't worn but was faded in places. She undid the twin buckles and looked inside.

She first pulled out a pair of jeans, light blue and battered, underwear bunched up within them. A tee shirt, a black woollen jumper. She raised it up to her face and breathed in, but there was nothing of him there, just dampness. And then out it fell, his brown leather wallet.

It had been a present from her. Special soft leather, hand stitched.

Totally overpriced of course but she hadn't minded that. She'd given it to him to replace a horrible cheap thing he carried around in luminous colours from some surfing brand or another.

She unfastened it and looked inside. His credit cards, personal and business sat in their sleeves. The section for notes held thirty pounds in cash, a handful of coins too. She emptied them out on the table top and watched as they rolled and spun noisily before settling with an unexpected suddenness, the silence returning to the kitchen. His driving licence was there, his face looking off to the left as if in disdain for the bureaucracy of such things, then the slip of card with his name and address on it. Their address, the house that had been hers for longer than it had ever been theirs.

She breathed a few deep breaths and looked again inside the bag, but there was nothing more. And she checked the remains of the packaging for anything, a note, anything that might show who had found it. But nothing again. She sat with her dead husband's clothes spread out on the table in front of her and asked herself, what it meant. Questions she had hoped would slowly fade into the past once again hammered at the front of her mind. And a sadness too, at losing Jim, and the part she might have played in it. She stroked the soft leather of the wallet. She knew there was only one person she could speak to, but she sat there that morning for a very long time before she picked up the phone.

"Can I come and see you?" She said. "I need your help."

twenty-four

WHEN WE WERE too tired to paddle another stroke we let ourselves be pushed ashore on the other side of the bay where the waves bent around so far the water was nearly calm. The small beach there was made up of fist-sized rocks, bleached driftwood and plastic bottles. No one spoke as we emerged from the water. Maybe it was the concentration needed to pick our way up the slippery rocks, but I like to think it was something more. What had just happened, it took time to process it. Our minds had just been opened.

We kept up the silence as we walked back around the bay, across the stream, then back out the other side until we stood beneath the Hanging Rock. Then and only then did any of us speak. And of course it was John.

"This place," he said, quietly, reverently, "We have to keep it secret. We can't tell anyone about it."

Darren was peeling off his wetsuit now and I did the same, pulling a towel from my bag. It was like both of us had lost the power to talk.

"If we tell anyone about this place," John went on. "It'll be ruined. People will come every day, from miles around. This place will be ruined. This is our wave. Our place. We tell no one."

This time Darren nodded and managed to get a word out. "OK," he said solemnly, like he was swearing an oath.

"Jesse?"

John's blue eyes were locked on mine, trying to read me, willing me to accept what he was saying. For a moment I felt trapped as the elation of the last few hours came up against the misery of the previous month and the two cancelled each other out. But I couldn't keep it up, the immovable object was crushed before the irresistible force and the flicker of a smile on my lips burst out into this massive grin.

"*Oh-my-fucking-God!* Do you realise what we've got here?" I was laughing now. "Of course I'm not going to tell anyone, this is the best wave in the whole world. This is winning the lottery. This is the dream, the surfer's fucking dream!"

Then we were all laughing, and I don't know why, but I opened my arms and grabbed John and pulled him towards me and then we were holding each other, laughing and jumping up and down with Darren trying to join in from the side. And the noise we made echoed up above us as it bounced off the Hanging Rock and out over the reef, and the line after line of perfect waves.

When the buzz wore off there was one immediate problem. There was no way we could keep getting our surfboards to Hanging Rock without someone, sooner or later, seeing us and wondering where we were going. It felt pretty safe once we were there. There were no signs that the owner of the estate, or anyone else, ever bothered coming that way, and the valley walls were so steep you couldn't be seen from anywhere else, but we were totally exposed getting the boards to the estate's boundary wall. The obvious answer was to leave the boards there. Right underneath the Hanging Rock there was a little cave, just high enough to walk into if you stooped over, and it got bigger inside so that it was maybe five metres deep. But if we left the boards there, we wouldn't be able to surf the Town Beach. Since we could only get to Hanging Rock at the weekends, that meant no weekday surfing, and if we stopped surfing Town Beach altogether, then people might get suspicious and wonder where we were going.

For a couple of weeks we wrestled with the problem, but then it was John that came up with the solution. His dad was away so we were at his house for once, sprawled out on the white leather sofas with our feet up on the coffee table. Darren had taken a decanter of brandy from the bookshelf and was poking his finger down its neck, tasting it a drip at a time.

"I know what we're gonna do about the board problem," said John, watching Darren but doing nothing to stop him.

"What?" I asked. I expected him to come up with yet another route to get there, the best idea we'd come up with so far.

"We're going to get the boards stolen." He said it, then laughed to himself, probably at how brilliant it was. He stretched himself out on the wide armrests. But we didn't get it.

"How does that help?" asked Darren.

"Because, if the boards get stolen, no one at Town Beach will expect to see them any more."

"But we won't have *any* boards," said Darren. He set the decanter back down on its felt base and came and sat next to me.

"No." John went on. "Then we'll have two boards, because we buy new ones, just like everyone expects us to. And then, because the old ones aren't really stolen, we just make it look like they are, we surf the old boards at Hanging Rock, and use the new ones at Town Beach. Problem solved."

Darren looked doubtful.

"But I can't afford a new board," he began, but I started speaking at the same time.

"My board's insured," I said.

John ignored Darren and answered me.

"That's even better. You get a new board for nothing."

I thought about this for a while then I sort of chuckled as well.

"Actually, that's quite good. Mum would definitely claim if my board got stolen, so it won't even cost anything."

John gave me a golden smile and leaned forwards on the wooden surface of the table, he began to tap his forefinger like he was sending a message in Morse code.

"We need to make it look real. We'll do it from your house. That way it'll look like someone from the campsite has taken them."

"Yeah, there's always dodgy looking guys there, who'd definitely steal boards. Mum's always telling me to be careful."

"But my board isn't insured," said Darren. "And I haven't got any money either." But we ignored him, John just looked at me with a grin that told me he was going to enjoy this. And he did, even more than I'd thought. He loved it.

John insisted it had to happen at night. He said it was when most burglaries took place. So one week later, as the sky grew dark, we left the boards on the lawn in front of the house where Mum couldn't help but see them. Then we retreated to our caravan and kept an eye on them so that no one actually did nick them. We knew Mum had gone to bed when her bedroom light switched off. John gave it five minutes for her to fall asleep and then we moved. But that was when Darren announced he didn't want to do it. He said it was because he hadn't figured out a way to replace his board but I think he was just scared. John just shrugged. Told him it didn't matter, then told me I was carrying Darren's board as well as my own. For a while it looked like Darren might argue but then he just went home so it was just me and John left.

John got changed then, he'd brought clothes in his backpack, black trousers, boots, a black coat and a dark hat that pulled down low over his face. He pulled a pair of gloves on and handed a second pair to me.

"Here you go."

"It's not that cold," I said.

"They're not for the cold."

The moon was three-quarters full but the sky was littered with black clouds that dragged themselves across its face so that our torches alternated from useless to nearly useless. It didn't matter much, John wouldn't let us use them in case someone saw. Anyway, I had my hands full with two surfboards.

I followed John so closely the boards kept knocking together, until he turned around and told me off. We went the inland route and like he'd said, you could see the cars coming miles before they reached us, their headlights like strange yellow cones making their way through the darkness. Even so it was a relief to get off the road and onto the farm track, until the moon went in again the landscape descended into varying degrees of blackness. Every now and then we'd get a scare when a black shadow would baa and bleat at us and hobble to its feet. I didn't have time to be too scared though. John was moving fast and I was hot by the time we pushed our way through the final few bushes at the neck of Hanging Rock Bay. John stopped right in front of me and the only sound I could hear was my breath, coming in gulps.

"Wow," said John, "Look at that."

I did. Hanging Rock Bay looked beautiful that night. The moon was back, hanging big and low over the water, and beneath it a pathway of flickering silver pointed west. The rock itself had one face illuminated, brooded over the view, but its other faces were in shadow, and it was scary going up close to it, it felt like there were too many places for people to hide.

We stashed the boards in the cave. If I'd thought it was dark outside it was fucking dark in there, and every now and then a drip of water would land on my head or go down my neck. Not even John would go in more than a few metres before deciding we'd found the right place to leave them.

"We'll go back the coastal way, it's quicker," John said. He flicked his torch off so we stood in complete blackness, then the light on his watch turned us both eerie and green as he checked the time.

Freed from carrying the baggage we were able to talk more, and with the moon over the sea there was a little more light. Now the Cara thing was over, it seemed impossible it had ever mattered. Our friendship felt closer than it had ever been. I liked being here with John. I liked it that Darren wasn't there, and I could tell John felt the same. We made good progress and too soon we got to the final little beach section where we had to cross in view of the big house. Before we came out in the open John stopped me, showed me with his hands that he was going to take a look, and then rolled around the last rock and looked out over the open ground. A moment later he turned back.

"Torch off. There's a light on. Downstairs window." I could see John's teeth in the moonlight. He was smiling. He slipped his own torch into his pocket. Then he reached up to his hat and began to unfold it down over his face, and I saw it wasn't a normal hat at all but a balaclava. When he was done all you could see were his eyes and mouth.

Then the mouth spoke. "Let's go take a closer look."

"What?"

"It's light inside the house. He won't be able to see us."

"But what if he does?"

"He won't. Come on. Or you can wait here." And he rolled around the rock again, but this time he disappeared.

It wasn't scary where I was waiting, but I didn't want to break the spell with John. So I ducked out from the rock as well and began to make my way up the short rise to the house. It was mostly dark but bright light spilled out from one of the windows. Curtains open. I guess the guy didn't have to bother about neighbours. Up ahead I could see John, keeping low to the ground, he'd found a path up towards the house, but he was still pretty visible. *Fucking hell.* I followed, keeping as low to the ground as I could.

Nearer the house there was a smell of coal burning, and the grassy path gave way to gravel which crunched underfoot, but between footsteps you could hear music playing, loud, classical music. There was nowhere to hide, so I copied John and just ran as fast as I could for the last bit, until we were both tight up against the cold wall of the house, between the grand front door and the window with the light.

"What are we doing here?" I hissed at him, feeling my chest with my hand. I thought the sound of my heart was going to give us away.

"I just want to have a look, see who we're dealing with."

"Why?" I asked, but he'd moved on again, creeping his way along the wall until he was underneath the window with the light on. The scale of the house looked different up close, everything was bigger. It had looked like the bottom of the window was about waist height, but actually you could stand underneath it and still be too low to look in, so I edged along as well until I joined John there, forcing my breath to slow and quieten down. John reached up and gripped the window ledge and pulled himself up, so his head, still hidden in the balaclava, was bathed in the escaping light. He was strong so he could hold himself there for a long time. When he finally came back down he spoke quietly.

"Keep quiet, but have a look."

"I don't want to."

"Have a fucking look." He grinned at me but it looked wrong with his face hidden. "Go on Jesse. Have a look."

I reached up and felt the cold rough stone of the window ledge and slowly pulled myself up until my eyes were just over the lip. Then I felt John grab my legs from below, to support me I guess, but it prevented me from getting down and I panicked so much I nearly shouted out, but then my eyes took in the scene inside the room.

It was the sort of room I'd never seen for real. Only in films and on television. The walls were lined with wood and above that were old paintings, massive, too dark to see clearly but sitting in ornate gold frames like you only saw in museums. There were a few lamps turned on, big brass floor lamps, but the room was so big it was still quite dark. One wall was all fireplace, and there was a fire burning, and pulled up close was a chair. The man sitting there was either asleep or dead. He had his back to us, but you could still see he was old, and dressed that way too, in country tweeds. There was a little table next to him, what looked like whiskey or brandy on it and a book, and something propped up on the floor leaning against it. I suddenly realised what that was and I struggled for John to let me go, he resisted at first but I was too heavy for him. When I dropped to the ground he had his finger to his lips.

"We've got to get out of here," I mouthed, but he shook his head.

"He's asleep, he can't hear us."

"He's got a *gun*." But John just grinned again.

"I know. Cool huh?"

"It's fucking great. Now let's get out of here before he wakes up and shoots us." I went to move away from the window but John's hand stopped me.

"Let's try and break in."

"*What?* Why?"

"Come on, you know you want to."

"What? No I don't. I fucking don't."

"He looks pretty settled in there, we can try the windows around the back. It's a big house. I bet we can get in somewhere."

"Why would you want to? Let's just get the fuck out of here." My voice was getting strained, even I could hear it.

It's funny how you can tell almost everything about someone's expression just from the eyes. Even in the darkness there I could see mostly what John was thinking. Disappointment, but mixed with something else. Something I couldn't make out. I know now of course. Right there and then John was learning that he was different. Not just different to me, but different to nearly everyone else. While we could be persuaded to push our limits, we never really wanted to. But John never really had limits. Not with anything. And he saw other people's limits as a weakness, to be explored at his pleasure.

"If he catches us there's two of us and only one of him." John said and his voice had changed a bit too, like this was his final offer.

"John, the man's got a shotgun leaning up against his fireside table. We're done here. Let's just fucking go home."

John didn't move for a moment, but then his arm across my chest relaxed. But he didn't let me go. Instead he put his other hand on my shoulder and moved his head close to mine so he could look closely into my eyes. I could smell the breath coming from his mouth. We stayed there for a long while, him holding me beneath the window. Then he relaxed again.

"You know I was only joking Jesse," he said. "Let's go."

"Hey Jesse, did you put the boards away last night?" The pitch of John's voice was perfect - curious, but with a note of concern. His face gave nothing away. This was the next morning, just a half hour after I'd woken feeling tired and stiff. I was still nervously spooning cornflakes into my face. Mum was there too of course, that was the point. She was in her blue overalls, getting ready to cut the grass. But John wasn't supposed to be here. It was supposed to be me who discovered the crime. That was the plan.

"What?" I mouthed, spewing bits of cornflake.

"The boards, we left them out the front last night."

I looked at John in confusion, and he gave me the tiniest of nods. I tried not to look at Mum as I replied, my voice sounded all wrong.

"I haven't touched them. Are you sure they're not there?"

John looked worried, like he *really* looked worried and I wondered for a second if it was because my voice had sounded as fake to him as it had to me. He knew Mum wasn't stupid, we couldn't fuck this up.

"Well they're definitely not there now. Judy, I don't suppose you've moved them or anything?"

But it was like Mum had been up all night learning her part of his script. A script he was re-writing on the fly so I didn't have any more lines.

"No, I've not moved them - where exactly did you put them?"

"They were right out in front."

"And you're sure they're not there now? Have you looked under the steps? Perhaps Darren put them away?"

"No I've looked. Oh God." His hand went to his forehead. "I've got a nasty feeling we've been really stupid."

"Oh no John, you don't think..?"

"I do. Anyone could have taken them. You could see them from the car park, and it was busy last night."

"Oh John!"

"Judy," John turned to Mum, "I must tell you this - it was totally my fault, not Jesse's. I told him I'd put them away as I went home, but it got late and I… I forgot all about it." He glanced at me. "I'm so sorry Jesse, I'll replace it, I'll get you another board. Just as soon as I've saved the money."

"Oh *John*."

Then Mum again, this time cast as the hero of John's little performance. "It's insured! Jesse's board is insured, and I think for quite a lot given how battered it looked the last time I saw it. We can claim for a new one. Oh John that's so generous of you to offer but it's really not necessary." She turned to me, me with my spoon hovering in mid air, "Jesse, you are so lucky to have a friend like John."

They were both turned to me now and I could see he was going to do it before he did, he winked at me. Just once.

Mum got me a new board even before the insurance money came through. It was alright, not as good looking as John's which had nice decals all across the deck. Poor old Darren though. It took him nearly two months to beg an old board from his brother so he had to sit watching when we surfed Town Beach.

twenty-five

BUT DARREN DIDN'T care too much, since it wasn't Town Beach where the real action was.

Those first few weeks after we hid the boards at Hanging Rock, the weather stayed in the same pattern where storms would rage out in the Atlantic one after another but never make it over us. That's the perfect set up for surf. You don't see the storms over the horizon, they don't interrupt the light winds, blue skies and sunshine, but they send swell after swell after swell. It's like magic when that happens. I'd never seen the Town Beach working so well, but although we surfed that during the week, it was the weekends we lived for, when we had something so much better.

The excuses were easy to find. As far as Darren's parents and John's dad knew, they were both over at the campsite with me. I'd tell Mum I was either at Darren's or John's. It didn't matter anyway. No one cared where we were by that time. As long as we turned up somewhere for meals once in a while, they were happy.

Maybe the locals at Town Beach missed us, but there were so many surfers in the water by then, so much agro, they would have been happy we were gone. We were always careful getting onto and off the estate, but once we'd dropped down into the valley, there was really no need for caution, it was like our own private world. And we didn't just surf

Hanging Rock, we basically moved in there. We explored the cliffs, the Hanging Rock itself had this magnetism that drew you towards it, like you couldn't believe it was able to balance up there, you couldn't understand how it didn't all come tumbling down to the ground.

We explored right to the back of the cave. It still felt creepy in there, even on the brightest of days. I preferred the waterfall. It was at the neck of the bay where the steam came out and it first funnelled through a perfectly smooth gully in the bedrock, about as wide as our surfboards were long, so you could jump across if it hadn't rained too much, and you couldn't if it had. Where the gully stopped the water flowed out into nothing and dropped a good few metres in a perfect arc. At high tide it dropped directly into the sea, but when the tide was low there was a deep round bowl of a pool left, surrounded by smooth rock. It was deep enough that you could jump in from the top, even at low tide, and so clear and cool we could drink straight from it. I mean you probably shouldn't, but we did.

We built fires. Small ones at first because we were still worried about being discovered, but bigger later on when we realised the smoke dispersed into the air by the time it got higher than the cliffs so no-one could see. We built big fires then, big roaring piles of sticks we collected on the walk in, and driftwood from the shoreline. And that quickly led to ideas about camping out there, since it wasn't easy to make our way all the way home once it was dark.

Sometimes we made reconnaissance missions to the big house. In the beginning the old man scared us, we never knew if he might turn up, so we'd hide in the scrub at the top of the cliff and watch the house through John's binoculars. Sometimes a van would turn up and leave boxes of food on the front step, and it usually sat there for hours before you'd see him open the door and take it in. He was so old he could hardly bend over to pick it up. And John had been right about the shotgun, he only used it for rabbits, and even then he usually missed. We'd watch him limping around on the lawn outside the front of the house, blasting away, and then taking ages to reload, struggling to break the gun down, while the rabbits hopped away. I don't know who was laughing at him more, us or the rabbits. The old man never got near Hanging Rock, the ground was too uneven. He probably hadn't been there for years.

Darren found a lobster pot in pretty good order washed up on the little beach and the three of us built a raft of driftwood to get out into the bay and lay it. We'd bait it with a couple of mackerel, or our old friends those slowly dying shore crabs and more often than not we would pull up a lobster or two. We kept them in an old bucket until the fire had died down so it was just glowing embers, then we'd tip the lobsters on and hold them down with sticks until they stopped crackling. Sometimes we ate them with fresh bread that John stole from the old man's supplies.

But most of all we surfed. The wave at Hanging Rock wasn't magic, it didn't defy physics or create waves, it was just a slab of rock sticking out into the sea. It just happened that it stuck out at just the right angle, and just the right depth to form these hollow, peeling, perfect waves a lot of the time. There were days when it didn't, the swell was coming from the wrong angle, or the tide was a bit too low. There were days when it was frightening, the storm producing the waves too close, the swells too big. There were days when it was disappointing, the waves too weak. But they were the unusual days. The outliers. Most of the time, the wave at Hanging Rock was fucking amazing. And it was all ours.

And so for a few years we'd surf our own private paradise then feast on buttered lobster and grilled fish. And I tell you. If only that had lasted we might all have grown up and been good people. If only that had happened instead of what actually happened. If only. Eh John? If only you hadn't *fucked* it all up.

twenty-six

THEY MET IN a café nearer to the airport than the university. She didn't want the risk of running into any of her colleagues.

"So then. What couldn't wait?" Dave asked when he finally tracked her down. She was sitting upstairs, on a table right at the back, half hidden by a pillar.

She looked blank.

"The party? Elaine's summer party? Next weekend. You're still coming aren't you?"

"Oh. Yeah. I forgot. Of course, I'll be there. Listen, thanks for coming here today. I got you a coffee." She pushed it across to him.

"No problem. It's nice to get away from the office."

A smile from Natalie. She hadn't wanted to meet him there.

"So what's up? How can I help?" He said, sitting down opposite her.

Natalie didn't answer. Instead she reached into her bag and pulled out Jim's wallet. She pressed the soft leather with her hands for a moment, and then tossed it onto the table between them.

"I got a phone call a few days ago. This was found in Llanwindus - that's in Wales. It was stashed in a bush."

Dave didn't say anything but reached forward and picked it up, then turned it over in his hands. Then he opened it and slid out a business credit card. He ran his eyes over Jim's name embossed in the plastic, then looked up at her in surprise.

"This is Jim's?

She nodded.

"Where did you say this was this found?"

"Near a little town called Llanwindus."

"Did you say a few *days* ago?"

Natalie nodded again.

"Stashed in a bush? Just this?" He held the wallet up.

"No. His clothes as well. All wrapped up in his flight bag."

"What clothes exactly - like clothes that he'd packed or..?"

"No. Like he'd undressed from what he was wearing, you know, to put a wetsuit on."

"But I don't understand, the police found his clothes in the car didn't they? The ones he'd been wearing that day."

"Yes."

Dave screwed up his face in confusion.

"And the bag was Jim's? You're sure?"

"Yes. I recognised it."

Dave was silent, staring down at the table. He blinked several times and then spoke again. "And who did you say found it?"

"I didn't. I think it was some workmen. They said they were building a footpath. A coastal path."

"Did they say where exactly?"

"Just this town, Llanwindus. I checked, it's a five hour drive from Porthtowan."

"Did you get their name? Their number?"

Natalie gave a little shake of her head.

"No. I was surprised. And then he hung up. I think he'd been hoping for a reward. Maybe when I told him Jim was dead, he didn't want to get involved."

Dave put the wallet down and began to drum his fingers on the table top. Then suddenly he got up and walked away, over to the wall where the sugar sachets were stored. He took two and returned, when he sat back down Natalie could see his hands were shaking. He didn't open the sugar.

"OK. So maybe he went for a surf in this other place, lost his bag, then drove down to Porthtowan and went for another surf but didn't come back." He shook his head. "No, that doesn't make sense."

"I'm not sure anything makes sense," said Natalie.

"It's a strange sequence of events. I mean if you stashed a bag why wouldn't you recover it?"

"Might you forget it?"

"You said there were clothes in it?"

"Yeah. Jeans and a jumper."

"Did you ever know Jim forget to get dressed?"

Natalie didn't answer.

Dave scratched at his head. "I'm confused Natalie. What are you telling me here? How does this all fit together?"

"I haven't the faintest idea."

"Have you told anybody about this? Have you told the police?"

Natalie shook her head again. "I thought about it, but I don't know what to tell them."

"Have you told anybody else? Have you told your sister?

"You're the only person who knows."

Something in his expression showed this concerned him, but he nodded as if he understood.

They sat for a long time without speaking. Natalie drank from her coffee but he left his alone. Eventually he broke the silence.

"OK. Maybe we should recap. Maybe we can figure this out."

She shrugged but nodded.

"His business bank card is in the wallet. There's never been any money missing from the account. The bank's never contacted me about any attempt to use this card. Is that the same for his private account? Can you check?"

"I don't need to. I closed the account years ago. After I got the death certificate they let me transfer everything."

"So if someone stole the bag from the car, they haven't tried to use the cards."

"No. There's money in there too, cash." Natalie pointed at the back section on the wallet and Dave opened it up.

"Thirty pounds."

"If the wallet was stolen why wouldn't the thieves take that at least?"

Dave didn't answer.

"Do you think maybe someone stole the bag from the car and hid it, meaning to come and get it later."

"But couldn't for some reason?" Dave leaned forward. "It's possible. At least it makes some sense. But why would they hide it so far away?"

"Perhaps that's where they came from? Perhaps they weren't used to stealing and felt guilty, or scared they'd get caught?"

"I suppose that's possible." Dave sat back and thought for a moment. "So. They happened to come across Jim's car in Porthtowan, broke in and stole the bag, then got cold feet and hid it in a bush miles away in Wales and never went back for it." The enthusiasm had gone from his voice. "And that happened by coincidence on the very same day that Jim had his accident and drowned."

"Or on the same day he decided to take an overdose because he found out about us." She kept her voice even and non-judgemental.

"Natalie, I don't believe that's what happened."

"I'm not sure I do either. But you've got to admit you just described a pretty weak theory."

"Yeah. I did."

"Can you think of a better one?"

Dave looked like he might say something, but then turned away.

"What?"

"Nothing."

"What? What have you thought of?"

"I don't know. It's nothing."

"*Dave.*"

He turned back to face her.

"Well, there's one possibility, but I don't know how to say it."

"Just tell me."

He sighed but saw he had to say it.

"Look I don't know if this is crazy, but if Jim's body was never found, and now eight years later his bag turns up. Maybe he didn't die that day in Porthtowan after all. Have you thought of that?"

At first she didn't reply, but then she nodded.

"Yes. I've thought of that."

They looked at each other for a moment.

"But it doesn't make sense either. If he wanted to disappear, how would he do it? What would he live off? Where's he been living?"

Dave blew out his cheeks. "Amnesia?" He tried. Maybe he forgot who he was?"

"With his name and address inside his wallet?"

"OK, not amnesia. Could he..." He paused and softened his voice. "This sounds pretty crazy I know, but could he be one of those guys that has a second wife, a second family. He wanted to disappear?"

"Well," Natalie said after some time. "That's a cheery thought. My husband maybe didn't drown when I thought he did, he just went to live with his other wife." She picked up the wallet and with her elbow on the table, held it aloft.

"So what do I do with this?" She threw it back down on the table between them. "What the hell am I supposed to do now?"

He breathed in and then puffed the air out.

"Well you've got two choices."

She waited for him to go on.

"There's a bin over there. You could take the thirty quid from that wallet, throw everything else in that bin and accept you're never going to know what happened to Jim."

Natalie wasn't sure if he was serious.

"Or..?"

"Or you could try and find out. I don't know how exactly. But you could go to this Llanwindus place. Ask around. I don't know. There might be something that explains this."

Natalie cast her eyes downward.

"That's not much of a choice."

"Then you don't have much of an option."

She was silent until he interrupted her thoughts.

"We could go together. If you don't want to go on your own. We could take Jim's photo, we could ask around. See if anyone remembers seeing him. If nothing else we could find this coastal path, perhaps we could find where the bag was hidden. It might tell us something more. I don't know. There might even be something else hidden there."

She was silent. Was this what she wanted, she asked herself? She glanced up at Dave. Dependable Dave. Still married, still running the business which she held shares in. Still handsome in his own way. Still the last man she'd slept with.

She shrugged. "OK," she said.

twenty-seven

THEY DROVE THERE three days later. It was Dave this time who suggested they shouldn't tell anyone, and she'd agreed at once. It didn't seem likely there would be anything to find, and if that was the case, what good would it do to drag Jim's death out into the open again? If on the other hand they did uncover something, they'd just have to deal with it. Whatever it might be.

The drive felt longer than the four hours the GPS predicted. They got stuck in traffic around Cardiff and then the last part in particular, through the winding roads of west Wales, seemed to take an age. High hedgerows hemmed them in and wooden gates gave glimpses of fields and stone walls. At first the signposts seemed to hint at a place well populated with towns and villages, but then Natalie realised the names were simply repeated in both English and Welsh. Suddenly it felt like an emptier landscape.

It was midday by the time they drove through the thin outskirts of Llanwindus, a few clusters of small grey houses, huddled close together despite the wide open fields which surrounded them. They followed the road down through the main street, a sparse collection of small shops and cafés. It was prettier here. The town looked like it survived on tourism, but it wasn't busy and to Natalie the empty street and the windows watching over it held a vague threat, like their arrival was being observed and noted. Then they arrived at the location Dave had put in the GPS, a small harbour with a great pile of lobster pots heaped on the quay and where dirty squat fishing boats sat alongside. Dave rolled the car into the gravel car park of a pub, the tyres crackled as they came to a stop.

"Funny little place isn't it? Pretty I guess" Dave said, when they were out of the car.

Natalie looked around again. On a sunny day maybe, but under the blanket of grey there was an ugliness to it. It was cold too, she wrapped her arms around herself.

"What do we do now?"

"Well I don't know about you, but I'm starving. How about some lunch?"

The pub was called the *Crown and Anchor*. It sat on the corner of the harbour so that one side flanked the river and a small beer garden ran along the quay. There were tables to take in the view but they were all empty except one with two plates, the remains of a fish and chip lunch that two huge seagulls were now fighting over. Inside it was dark, but at least it was warmer. A fire smouldered in the grate, but the few drinkers inside didn't seem interested. It didn't look like they were there for the company either. They mostly sat alone, sipping pints in silence.

Dave went to use the toilet and Natalie sat down at one of the tables which overlooked the river. Here the weak daylight cut through the gloom and for a moment she watched the river deep and slow below her, boils and eddies gliding past, taking their own path to the sea. Then she reached into her bag and brought the photograph of Jim she'd chosen. It was taken a few months before he had gone missing and showed him smiling, leaning on a wall that cut across the Bristol Downs. In it he looked happy, there was no hint in his face of anything troubling him, certainly nothing that might have caused him to take his own life. Or disappear to start a new one.

But just holding the photograph in this pub in this village unsettled her. She was sure she could feel eyes watching her, even though no one was paying her any attention. She was careful to hold the photograph so that only she could see it and eventually she turned it over and laid it face down on the table. She wrapped her arms around herself, wishing someone would stoke up the fire. Then Dave came back and placed an orange juice in front of her.

"Crab sandwich, fish and chips, or steak and ale pie" he said.

"I'm not really hungry."

"Have the sandwich. You should eat something."

She gave him a little twisted smile, a thank you for the concern.

"You know you look beautiful," he said.

The smile dropped away.

"Let's not bring all that up again shall we?"

He kept his eyes on her for a moment.

"I'm not. But it is true. You really do."

She looked away from him.

"I'm sorry. I'll shut up. Crab sandwich then?"

She thought for a moment, then nodded. When he came back again he squeezed into the chair opposite her.

"Apparently the chef's busy so there's a bit of a wait," he said, rolling his eyes. He noticed the photo in her hands. "You want to get started right away?"

But Natalie shook her head. The words spilled from her mouth before she thought about them.

"Dave. I think this might be a mistake, coming here."

"Why?"

"I don't know. I mean we're not going to find anything are we?"

He answered slowly. "Well we don't know that yet."

"I think we do. I think we both do." Natalie shook her head. "It's all too long ago. No one's going to remember a face of someone who might have stayed here eight years ago."

"Maybe not, but maybe someone will. We won't know unless we try."

"No they won't. We're wasting our time. I'm wasting your time. There's nothing here we can find."

"You're not wasting my time. He was my friend too."

They sat in silence for a long while.

"I'm sorry. I didn't mean to imply otherwise. It's just…" Natalie pushed the photograph away from her, like she wanted nothing more to do with it. "Something doesn't feel right."

"OK, what?"

"I'm not sure I even know. I mean you watch this sort of thing on TV every night, and you think it's going to be easy, but to actually do this… Maybe I'm just scared of what we might find if we start to show that around. We don't know when that bag was put there. We don't know who put it there. What happens if someone does recognise him? Maybe we're better just leaving this all alone."

Dave didn't answer but he watched her until she wished he would look away.

"I mean," she went on. "Why are you here? Really? What do you think is going to happen?"

Dave reached out for the photograph, pushing by its edge to slide it carefully to his side of the table, from where he picked it up.

"I don't know. But I do know this. I don't think you have any choice. We can go home now if you want, but one day we'll have to come back here. You can't just forget this. You'll always wonder if someone here knows something. It'll eat away at you. You need to be sure the answer isn't waiting here."

She didn't look at him for a long time.

"Alright," she said. She looked down at the river again, at how the murky brown water swirled and tiny whirlpools opened up and closed again. Then she turned back to Dave. "Alright. Let's get it over with."

This time they went up to the bar together. She saw that Dave was about to speak but she put her arm on his and pushed gently past him. She slipped the photograph out of his hand.

"Excuse me," she asked of the woman serving, a young woman with tattoos showing on her shoulder. "This is going to sound strange but would you mind looking at this photograph and telling me if you recognise the man?" She spoke quietly so that no one else in the bar would hear, but no one seemed interested in them. "We think maybe he was here some years back. Maybe something happened to make people remember him?"

The woman's eyes widened a little, the only sign which showed she might be surprised, but she stopped what she was doing and held her hand out over the bar for the photograph. Natalie felt her unsettled feeling again as she let the photograph out of her grasp.

The woman studied the image closely, as if it made a welcome change from taking orders and wiping down tables. She took the opportunity to examine Natalie as well, then shook her head.

"No sorry, I don't know him. But then I've only worked here a few months. You might want to ask her. She's the landlady." She pointed to the other end of the bar where an older woman was pulling a pint of dark beer for a man who sat alone on a bar stool. He looked to be a fixture.

Natalie felt a shiver of irritation, but nodded her thanks and she and Dave walked down the bar, and waited just far enough off the shoulder of the local that he wouldn't turn around to them. The landlady noticed them right away and flashed a smile to show she'd be right with them. Natalie felt her heart beating fast in her chest.

"Excuse me," she began again. "Are you the landlady here?"

"That's right." The woman cocked her head to one side then gave them a smile. She had a weathered face, blond hair turned straw-like from cigarette smoke. "What can I get you?"

Already it was easier the second time around. "I wonder if you might have a look at this photograph? It's my husband, he went missing some time ago. We think something might have happened to him here in Llanwindus," Natalie paused. "Or maybe he might even still be here."

An eyebrow shot up on the woman and she took the photograph without a word. Natalie felt the strange feeling again as she let it slip from her hands.

"Handsome looking guy."

"Do you recognise him?" Natalie answered quickly.

"No." She said at once, still looking at the image. Then she looked up. "When did he go missing?" The landlady made no sign that she was going to return the photograph.

"Eight years ago. November third. We know it's a long time ago," Dave stepped in to say this, as if he wanted to justify his presence there. The landlady looked across at him curiously, as if she was appraising the age gap between the two of them, working out where he might fit into the equation.

"We've been here twelve years. Before that in the city. Moved for a quieter life." She looked back at Natalie and gave her an encouraging smile. "Some people have got a memory for faces, it doesn't hurt to ask."

"And you definitely don't recognise him from the photograph? His name's Jim Harrison."

She shook her head. "I couldn't swear I've never seen him before. But nothing comes to mind. Why do you think something happened here?"

Natalie felt a slight flush of relief. If she didn't know him, at least he wasn't a regular, the crazy man with no memory who came in every day. Or the family man who came in here with his wife and kids.

"Well, it's a bit complicated," she said. "He was a surfer, he went missing in the water, originally we thought down in Cornwall. That's where his car was parked, but we found out that maybe he was actually here. We think someone here might know something about what happened." She tailed off and added limply, "but with his car so far away… It's a mystery."

The landlady frowned in a way that suggested sympathy, but mixed with confusion.

"I don't suppose you'd have any records from that long ago? Like if he'd taken a room or something? Could you check for that name?"

"Eight years?" The landlady shook her head. "We don't keep any records that long."

"I didn't… We just thought it might be worth asking."

The landlady offered the photograph back to Natalie.

"I'm sorry I can't be more help, but ask around, we're quite a small village. You might be surprised at how long people's memories are in a place where not much happens."

Natalie smiled her thanks and was turning away when Dave spoke.

"One other thing, I don't suppose you know about the team building the coastal path? It's just that they found something. Something related to Jim, we'd like to ask them exactly where it was."

She thought for a minute but shook her head again. "Sorry. I don't know anything about it."

Natalie was about to thank her again when she went on.

"A surfer you say? The man you're looking for?"

"Yes."

The landlady indicated the local who'd been sitting next to them for the whole conversation. "You should show that photo to young Darren here. He's a surfer. Has been for years."

twenty-eight

ON HEARING HIS name the man froze, his pint of beer halfway between the bar top and his mouth, like he'd been listening but thought no one had noticed. He slowly placed his glass back down, a wobble in his hand sending waves of liquid up the sides of the glass. When he spoke he sounded unsure, defensive.

"I don't know anything 'bout that."

The landlady's eyebrows rose a little in familiar exasperation. There was a motherliness to her tone.

"No one's saying you do Darren, but you could have a look. See if you recognise him. You might have seen him in the water? The lady said he's a surfer. Like you."

The man said nothing but his hand reached out for his drink again, still shaking. His hands were dirty too, black grime around bitten fingernails.

"Go on love, show him the photograph, you never know."

It crossed Natalie's mind that the man might be a bit slow, but she handed him the photograph anyway. His eyes flicked on and off the image before settling. Then he stared for a long time.

"So? Ring any bells?" The landlady said, but the man didn't answer at first. Instead he stole a glance at Natalie, then at Dave, as if trying to place them as well.

"So, do you recognise him?" The landlady said again.

"I don't think so," he said.

"You don't *think* so? So you might?" The landlady said, she sounded encouraged.

"I mean no. I don't know him." he said.

"Are you sure? You haven't seen him maybe surfing somewhere?"

"Surfing? Here at Town Beach?"

"Well maybe." Her patience seemed to be wearing thin.

"No, I definitely haven't seen him surfing here. And I'd remember too, cos I got a good memory for faces," he said, shaking his head. He glanced over at Natalie again as he said this, a little darting look.

"Well, it didn't hurt to look did it?" The landlady tutted a little, then gave a sympathetic glance at Natalie.

"I thought it might be worth asking as the surfers tend to stick together," the landlady started saying. "The locals I mean…" But she was interrupted as the man moved suddenly. He slipped off his chair mumbling something about needing to get to work and was halfway to the door before Dave shouted after him.

"Hey, the photograph."

The man stopped, then slowly turned around, and waited while Dave strode the couple of steps up to him and took the photograph from his hand.

"Sorry mate, I forgot I had it." The man avoided looking at any of them, and when he saw they weren't going to stop him, he started walking again, he was stiff legged at first, like he'd been sitting on that stool long enough to drink too much, or perhaps just to get stiff legs. When he got to the door he glanced back one more time before disappearing. There was a moment of surprised quiet.

"Well that seemed a little bit odd," Dave said, then turned to the landlady. "Is he always like that?"

But she didn't seem to share his suspicions. She reached over and picked up the man's glass, still nearly half full of beer.

"To be honest, he's a bit of a funny one is young Darren. In hindsight, not the best person to be asking about your missing fella. He's..." She stopped and pulled a face, as if that was enough to explain what the man's issue was. Then she smiled at Natalie. "But don't worry, not everyone around here is like him." She reached over and wiped the bar where the man had been sitting. "Plenty of nice people around here."

"You ask around dear. You never know, you might get lucky." The landlady's eyes slid across to Dave for a moment. "Listen honey, I just hope you find whatever it is you're looking for."

As they thanked the landlady a waitress walked out from the kitchen carrying their food. She went to their table and looked around, confused to see it empty, until she saw Dave signalling to her they were coming back. And the distraction of eating was enough for Natalie's slight doubts about the way the young man had responded to settle. Whatever his problems she was glad he had no idea who Jim was. She realised she was hungry, and when she'd finished eating it was what they'd come here to do that she concentrated on. She wanted to get on with it, if only so that she could then leave, and get back to her real life.

They left the pub and worked their way up the small high street, walking together and asking everyone they came across if they would look at the photograph. They went into each business, each time asking the same questions, and as they did so Natalie's unsettled feeling began to fade away. It wasn't just the repetition that helped, it was because no one showed any spark of recognition. She looked into eyes that were filled with interest at being shown the photograph, but registered nothing on seeing Jim's face. He was a stranger here. She began to feel that there was nothing here to find. No terrible secret to uncover.

They worked their way up one side of the high street, then back down the other. It was less than two hours later they were back at the car, still parked outside the *Crown and Anchor*. There had been nothing, no half-remembered sighting, no other leads anyone had suggested they follow.

"So now what?" She said, leaning on the car.

Dave looked pensive, more disappointed than her.

"That little newsagent had a photocopier. We could make copies of the photograph and put it up on noticeboards. Maybe in some shop windows."

Something about this idea didn't appeal to Natalie, but she agreed anyway.

It took another half an hour but they produced four small posters with Jim's image and the words "Have you seen this man?" written in biro underneath. They gave Dave's telephone number to call for information. The village was so small that with just the four posters it felt like they had most of the the village covered.

With that done Natalie was keen to leave.

"I don't think there's anything more we can do," she said when they were back at the car once more. "And no one knows anything anyway. It's like I said, it's too long ago. At least we tried." She smiled, relieved to be leaving. There was still something about the town she didn't like. But Dave seemed reluctant still.

"Have you got any other ideas," he asked, "just while we're here?"

"No." She was firm. "And I've got work tomorrow. Even if we leave now it's going to be late before we get back."

He nodded but didn't say anything. He pressed the button to unlock the car door and Natalie climbed in, but before Dave could open the driver's side his mobile rang, and she watched through the windscreen as he answered it, and then walked over to the river while he talked. The tide had dropped now and the water was much lower, uncovering thick greasy seaweed in greens and browns around the steep high walls of the harbour basin. It didn't improve the view. She thought how hard it would be to get out, if you happened to fall in there, then shook the thought from her mind. When Dave finished the call he had a thoughtful look on his face. He walked over to her side of the car.

"That was Damien," he said, then noting Natalie's questioning expression added, "He's one of our pilots. He's doing a drop off not far away from here. I asked him if he'd mind taking the car back, so we can take the chopper. It's only a forty minute flight."

Natalie didn't understand what he was saying at first.

"You're going to fly us back?"

"Yeah. Saves sitting in the car for three hours."

It made sense, Natalie realised, but the idea brought back her unsettled feeling. She wanted Dave to climb into the car and shut the door and for them to put something physical between themselves and this place. She was on the verge of suggesting they drive away anyway, to get closer to wherever the helicopter was doing its drop off perhaps, when Dave spoke again, and it was like he felt the same thing.

"You know. I think I've seen enough of the village," he said. "How about we take a walk on the beach, until Damien get's here? I told him that's the best place to put down anyway."

She realised he'd arranged it all, so she nodded. Perhaps if they drove away they might not find a site to land, and they'd end up having to drive all the way home. Better to do what Dave said, and they were getting out of the village anyway. She reached for the seatbelt.

"Sure. OK."

It was only about a mile down to the beach, but it felt much more open down there. The car park was empty but for three other cars, parked at the front, near where a wooden boardwalk climbed up and over a pebble embankment. It was so high they couldn't see the sea, just the sky, slate grey and looking like rain wasn't far away. They swung the car doors shut and climbed the steep ridge of boulders. At the top there was a strong breeze blowing in from the sea, making it choppy and rough. Down by the water's edge a figure walked away from them, a dog sprinting through the water ahead of it.

They walked down and onto the beach. The boardwalk stopped a few feet short of the sand, and they had to hop from stone to stone, the largest the size of a pillow, the smallest a bowling ball, like giant grey-black eggs sculpted by the wind and the waves. Then they stepped out onto the firm wet sand. Natalie turned and walked backwards and watched as her footprints disappeared a few moments after she'd left them, water appearing from the sand itself to erase them.

"Look," she said to Dave, pointing at them. "This place doesn't give up its secrets easily."

They walked down to the water's edge, a long way with the tide so low, then turned left, away from the village. Occasionally they had to sidestep quickly to avoid the surges of water where the bigger waves that had broken far out to sea finally reached the land. It was fun, and with each step further away from the village Natalie felt more relief to be nearly done with the place.

"It's a long time since I've been down to the sea," she said to break the silence that had overcome them.

"Because of what happened to Jim?"

"Maybe. I guess so. When I was a girl we used to go on holiday down to Worthing. The beach there is all pebbles that you can't walk on with bare feet. And then the tide goes out and you have to walk out over a mile of mud. Then if you get there the sea is freezing. I never did see the point of it."

"No one knows the point of Worthing."

She laughed. "You know what I mean. It was different with Jim. He had this strange connection with the ocean. Sometimes he just needed to see it. At times I felt it was more important to him than I was. I guess I came to resent that a little."

Dave said nothing but she felt him watching her. She swung her hair to keep it under control in the breeze. It felt nice to be there, walking on the beach, with Dave. A crazy image formed in her mind, the two of them walking barefoot on different sand. Turquoise water, palm trees, a different beach, a different world. She shook her head again, to clear the thought.

"For a while after Jim died I hated the sea." Natalie continued. "I hated it for what it had done to me. I wanted to try and live my life without ever seeing it again. Without ever hearing about it ever again. But do you know how hard that is?"

He shook his head.

"It's impossible. There's always something on the news, or it appears in films when you least expect it. Someone takes a journey, or becomes a fisherman or something silly like that." She laughed.

"What do you feel now? Do you still hate it?"

Natalie stopped walking and turned to face the waves. She took a deep breath of the wet, salty air.

"Maybe I don't hate it anymore, but I resent it. I want to know what happened to Jim. I want to know why my life had to change like this, and the answer is out there, hidden by the sea. And it won't ever tell us now. It won't give us back his body now. The sea just took him, somewhere, somehow. I guess I resent that. But I don't hate it anymore. I don't hate being here."

As she spoke the first few spots of rain splattered onto their jackets.

"See, why would you come to the beach? It's always cold or raining or horrible! Let's go back."

They both turned and looked up the beach looking for the nearest shelter. They'd walked a fair way and they were past the end of the pebble embankment by now. Up above them inland was a low grass ridge, studded with bushes, and at one point a large sign, its orientation blocking the worst of the rain. It was the only shelter in sight.

"It looks like it's just a shower," Dave said, scanning the sky. "We're best off waiting behind there and heading back when it's passed." They broke into a run.

Natalie reached it first and stood with her back towards it. The wind had picked up with the rain, blowing it more sideways than downwards so that the sign made a pocket of protection. When Dave got there too she moved over to give him room. He was puffing from the effort of the run and began to wipe the rain from his head. The water had plastered his hair down, it highlighted how he was thinning, and for some reason it made her think of his wife. So she turned away, examined the sign instead. It showed a large map of the area with a red dotted line indicating the line of the new footpath being opened up along the entire coastline of Wales. Grainy pictures of men in suits shaking hands accompanied a short text explaining how the funding had been won for an unbroken route around the coastline. There was information on the wildlife that visitors could see, puffins, guillemots, dolphins and porpoises, and wild flowers. She read it absently before making the connection.

"This is it. This is the footpath."

Dave looked lost then understood her meaning and read the sign with her.

"It's two hundred and fifty miles long," Dave read. "That's going to make it pretty difficult to find the guys building it."

"Maybe. But we could always just phone them?"

"What?"

"Look there. Where it says 'for information ring this number'."

Dave looked at her with a small smile of satisfaction then reached into his pocket and pulled out his phone. "Ok then," he said as he keyed the number in. Natalie leaned in when she heard the ringing tone.

"Ceredigion County Council?" The woman who answered had a thick accent. Behind it they could hear the telltale sounds of a call centre. Dave explained how they were trying to trace the team building or repairing the coastal footpath around Llanwindus. At first she had no idea what they were talking about, but after more explaining she understood.

"So why do you need to speak to them?" She asked. It was clear that not many people had taken up the opportunity on the sign to call.

"One of the workers making the path found a bag that was lost, and returned it to us. We just wanted to thank them personally," Dave explained.

This seemed to satisfy the woman, in fact more than satisfy - she was suddenly enthusiastic to put Dave in touch with the 'footpath team' and she asked them to hold on. They waited with the rain blowing around them while the tinny sound of Tom Jones played from the speaker of Dave's phone. Tom got through almost a whole song before she came back on the line.

"So. I've spoken to the team in footpaths. They said it's a commercial contractor but they do believe they're still in the area. I can't actually reach them myself, but I do have a mobile number if you'd like?"

Natalie nodded her head. She pulled a pen from her bag and held it ready to write on her palm.

When they had it Dave hung up and immediately dialled the number now written on Natalie's hand. After a moment though he held his hand over the phone to mouth *"answerphone."* She shrugged and mouthed back *"leave a message."*

Dave quickly explained why he was calling and left his number, asked for someone from the team to contact him at their earliest convenience, then hung up again.

"Well that was a good find. Now what?"

It had nearly stopped raining by then, but it looked more like a short break in the bad weather before things got worse.

She shrugged. "Isn't that helicopter of yours due pretty soon? We could wait in the car before that lot unloads on us?"

They walked, more quickly now, back along a footpath which gently climbed the pebble bank, giving them a view over the beach on one side and the countryside inland on the other. But as they neared the car park Damien called again, and this time Natalie got the gist of the conversation from what Dave said. It seemed the pilot had been delayed, only by an hour, an hour and a half at the most. She worked out while they were still speaking that it still wasn't worth their while driving home, but this time she felt much less concerned. It was only irritation she felt at the delay. Then she noticed it. When Dave hung up and started explaining the call she waved him away.

"I'm sorry Natalie..." Dave began, then stopped. "What is it?"

"There. Look at that."

"What?"

"That there. That's a campsite," she said.

She was looking behind the car park where a low wall marked off a few fields. Some were dotted with caravans, dirty and abandoned, grass and weeds grown thick around them. There was a building too, a house, a scruffy road leading up to it through the grass.

"He was camping. Jim was camping. I'd almost forgotten. And we've tried everywhere else. Come on." Natalie cut away from the path, working her way down the pebble bank and into the car park, but instead of walking towards their car, she walked towards the back of the car park, where a gate was drawn closed across a gap in the wall. It led to the house. Dave followed behind her, struggling to keep up.

The gate was half off its hinges. At first Natalie thought it couldn't have been opened in a long time, but then she noticed a small bronze padlock that chained it to a post. It looked too shiny to have been there that long. She shook it, confirmed it was locked shut, then looked for another way in. It didn't take long, the wall next to the gate was low and easy to climb. Even so she didn't climb walls much these days and she felt awkward swinging her leg up, her hands slipping on the wet rock.

She jumped down on the other side and her feet sank into the boggy earth. She was surprised at the length of the grass, it reached her knees.

"Where are you going? It's obviously abandoned." Dave called to her, but she ignored him and pressed forward. Behind her she heard him muttering something about a café in the village, but when she glanced back he was climbing over as well.

Closer to the house now she could see green paint peeling off the walls. The windows downstairs were boarded up, upstairs the curtains drawn shut. For a horrible moment she thought she saw a face at one of the upstairs windows.

What are you doing? She thought to herself.

She stopped, certain that it was just a trick of the light, but it broke her enthusiasm. Dave was right. The house was clearly derelict. So what if Jim had been camping? Even if it was open a campsite would never keep records. And this one didn't look like it had been open in years.

She gave up. Instead of the main house she walked over to what must have been the shower block. She moved closer to investigate. In front of her stood four shower stalls, three of them had no door, the final one was creaking as the breeze moved it on rusty hinges. It sounded like a child crying, or an animal in pain. Inside each cubicle she could see a layer of mud and slime on broken tiles with a scattering of litter. There was the sharp tang of urine. Dull silver pipes hung in the air where they had been ripped from the walls. She sensed Dave arrive beside her and was glad of it.

"Looks like it's been closed for a while," he said. "I'll never understand why some people want to take a shower in a field anyway."

She turned to him and smiled.

"Not everyone can afford five star hotels and private helicopters you know."

"Surely there's a reasonable middle ground though?"

She laughed.

"Anyway, there's no one here." Dave said. "How about we find a coffee in the village?"

Dave must have thought she didn't hear him, and said it again.

"Let's go and get a coffee… Natalie?"

She stood dead still.

"There's someone there. In the house watching us."

Her hand was at her mouth and there was fear in her eyes. She grabbed Dave by the arm.

"I think it's him."

twenty-nine

"WHO?" DAVE ASKED, and she could hear the sudden tension in his voice.

Natalie looked down at her arm, gripping Dave by the wrist. She let go quickly, as if the limb had acted on its own accord.

"Nothing. No one," she said, reddening despite the coolness of the air. She wondered if he knew who she meant.

"Who?" he said again.

"No-one. I just thought I saw someone in the house. It's nothing. I just find this whole place a bit creepy. It's been a strange day." She was about to turn away and lead them back to the car when she stopped again.

"There! Up in the top window." The colour drained from her face.

"I saw him again. Someone I mean. Up there watching us. He's hiding behind the curtain, look you can still see their outline against the curtain."

"Are you sure?"

"Yeah. Look, there again!"

Dave was squinting over at the house.

"Man or woman?"

"I don't know. Man I think."

"Well we're probably trespassing on his land."

"Then why not tell us to leave? Why hide behind the curtain? Why be in a derelict house with all the curtains shut in the first place?"

Dave didn't answer at first and they both stood looking at the house, feeling suddenly exposed.

"Well, let's go and find out." He stepped towards the house.

"Find out what?"

"We've asked pretty much everyone in the village already. Let's see if this guy knows anything. Have you got the photograph?"

But Natalie didn't move. "I'm not sure Dave. I don't think I want to."

"Why not? It's probably just someone wondering what we're doing in their field. Come on." Natalie wondered if Dave really felt as breezy as he sounded.

"I don't know. Maybe this is why no one in the village recognised him. What if he's been hiding out here all alone?"

Dave took her hand. "Come on. We've been through this. If we don't ask you'll only wonder if there was more you could do." Gently he took her arm and led her forwards towards the house. And then they both saw the curtain twitch again.

As they neared the building the state of disrepair become more obvious. There was a small sign above a doorway which read 'Reception' but that was obviously out date. The nearby window, the only one not boarded up, had several cracked panes. All the glass was covered in grime so that without putting their faces right up against it they couldn't see anything inside. A second sign hung on the inside of the window, its thick red letters just visible: 'CLOSED'.

Further round the house was another door, this one accessed via a flight of wooden steps. It looked like it was, or had once been, the main entrance. There was a doorbell at the top of the steps.

"You know, if this was a horror movie, this is where you'd suggest we split up," Natalie said.

Dave gave a dry laugh. "That's a good idea. You ring the bell, I'll wait in the car." But he put a foot on the first step, was about to put the other on the second step. But then there was a sharp *crack*. The rot in the wood gave way and the step collapsed under him. He stumbled backwards, only just managing to stay on his feet.

"Jesus fucking Christ."

Thc humour they'd just managed was swept away.

"Are you OK?"

"Yeah, just." He bent over and swept wood splinters off his trousers. "Guess no one's been up those steps in a while."

Natalie took a few steps back, giving her a better view of the back of the house. "There's another door around here."

She led the way this time. Around the other side of the house they saw a lean-to shed and the nose of a vehicle inside, a red pick up truck, battered and muddy, but looking like it could still run. The side door, when they reached it, also looked in better condition, like someone still used it. Dave glanced at Natalie as they both stood before it.

"Are you ready?"

He nodded.

She knocked twice, loudly, and more confidently than she felt.

She saw his feet first. Dirty brown boots, heavy boots that looked like they could do damage. Trousers with a grey and white camouflage pattern. A green knitted jumper, tight enough to see he was slim, skinny even. Tall too, about Jim's height. But he looked younger than Jim would be now. And the face was wrong. Dark brown, nearly black eyes stared out from narrow slits in a face where the skin was pulled back hard on the bones. The hair was long and greasy, the chin bore patches of stubble, but unkempt dirty growth. It wasn't Jim.

"What do you want?"

"Hello sir. We're sorry to bother you," Dave started. "I wanted to explain, I think you just saw us wandering around your grounds..."

But Natalie interrupted him. It felt appropriate as the man was staring directly at her, he appeared to not even have registered that Dave was speaking.

"My friend and I are looking for someone who went missing some time ago. We wonder if he might have stayed on the campsite?"

"Campsite's closed."

"I can see that. This was some time ago. A long time ago actually."

"Closed a long time ago too."

"We're not here to go camping."

The man smirked a little. Then he shook his head.

"I've not seen anyone."

Natalie realised she'd been holding her breath. "Perhaps if I could show you a photograph?" She quickly fished out her image of Jim and held it up for the man to see.

He glanced at it quickly, but instantly took his eyes of it. He fixed his eyes back on Natalie.

"Don't know him."

"You didn't look very hard."

The man sniffed. He snatched a quick glance at Dave, the first time he'd shown any interest in him.

"It's better you don't show that around here."

"What? What do you mean by that?"

"Shown that around a bit have you?"

"I'm sorry?"

"I said, who you shown that to?" The man spoke with a flat voice, something nasal in his accent different to the lyrical norm of the village.

He scanned the empty field around them. Then he turned away from them and seemed to swear under his breath. He seemed to consider what to say next for a long time before speaking.

"Look, if you're here. Maybe it's better you come in."

Natalie glanced over at Dave but his face gave little away. She could see his hands screwed up into fists.

"OK." She said. There seemed nothing else she could say.

thirty

I KNEW EXACTLY who they were when I saw them from upstairs. I didn't know what they were doing, poking around in the shower block but I knew who they were. A man and a woman, it had to be them.

I'd only just got rid of Darren half an hour before that, stinking of booze, panic in his eyes, telling me this wild story about the guy's wife being here, asking questions in the *Anchor* after so long. And Darren said they knew things. He said they'd found something on the coast path, or someone had, and they were looking for us. *A body*, he said, *it had to be a body.* I told him not to be so stupid. If they'd found a body the police would already be involved and then we'd be proper fucked.

At first I thought it might be just another of Darren's drunken nightmares. He got them sometimes, especially when he'd been spending too long in that fucking pub. But it was a bit early even for Darren to be proper pissed, so I kept a watch out. And here they were. A man and woman just like he described them. Actually standing at my door and asking me about that man. And somehow they did look like they knew. Or maybe me and Darren just both had the same fucking nightmares.

I sometimes wonder what made me ask them in. They showed me this photograph and I could have just said I'd never seen him before. I nearly did too. But then where would I have been? They could have talked to anyone, and I wouldn't have known anything about it. So I don't think I ever really had a choice. I asked them in because I had to.

And if I'm being honest, I guess I was curious to meet her, *the guy's wife.* I wondered what she looked like, what she was like to talk to. From how the man had been I thought she'd be a bit coarse. I'd pictured her as a blond. Obvious looking, red lipstick and big tits. But she wasn't like that. She was pretty though, with these green eyes and long dark hair. But not pretty in a common way. She looked refined.

I guessed the man with her must be her new husband. She looked over at him like she was saying *this is strange* and then she led the way in when I opened the door. I thought he must be rich, cos he was bald and a bit fat. A woman like her could do much better than that.

I was trying to think as I led them towards the kitchen, but it was hard because she was asking questions the whole way. "Do you recognise the man in the photograph? Can you tell us anything about him? His name was Jim Harrison."

I didn't answer her.

"I could get you a drink?" I said when we got there. "I've got some cups somewhere."

They looked at each other then the man spoke. "Would you mind just telling us about the man in the photograph. Do you recognise him?" He had a much deeper voice than I'd expected. I was trying to work out who he was, where he fitted into all this.

"Do you recognise the man in the photograph?" he was saying again.

"Alright alright."

"Alright you do recognise him?" she said. She was staring right at me, so close I could have reached out and touched her.

I stalled. "Let me see it again."

She handed me the photograph but they were both still standing up and the kitchen isn't very big so I told them to sit down and made a point of not looking at the photograph until they did so. Eventually they gave in and sat.

"Jim Harrison you said?"

"That's right. Do you know anything about him?"

This was it, my last opportunity to say no. But I knew now I wasn't going to.

"Jim," I said, watching her reaction to the name. "Well I know something about him."

She jumped as I said it. Actually bounced on the chair it was such a shock to her. Then she stared at me for ages, right into my eyes, and in the end I had to look away.

"What do you know?" She was calm but her voice was icy.

The man stood up again. He was a bit shorter than me, and he stood up real straight like he didn't want me to notice. "I think you'd better start talking right now," he said. And that pissed me off, you know, taking that tone in my kitchen.

"Look do you want that tea?" I replied, I was speaking to her. I wondered if he might try and hit me. I figured she'd try and stop him if he did. She wanted to know so badly. "It's a long story. You might want some tea."

After a while she nodded and then he sat down again while I got the mugs out of the cupboard and set the kettle to boil. I could tell they were both staring at me but I didn't care about that. I needed time to think.

I needed the time you see to get it all straight in my mind. How I was going to tell them, so I made sure they were the best cups of tea they'd had in a long time. I washed up the mugs and then warmed them with some hot water and while that was happening I asked them about how strong they liked it, whether they wanted milk and sugar, even if they preferred white or brown sugar. I didn't really hear what they said though because I was thinking so hard, so I had to keep asking them the same questions over and over. It took a long time, but eventually I put a steaming mug in front of them both and waited until they'd both taken a sip and told me it was ok. And then I began.

And in the end I told them everything, and I mean everything. It felt like I was unburdening myself. It all just flowed out.

By the time I actually got to the part about the man, those teas were long cold, but by then they'd stopped interrupting me and just sat there listening. It was almost like I was someone important making a speech or something, like what I was saying really mattered. So even though John had made me promise never to tell about what happened, *never tell anybody about that day,* I found the words were flowing out of my mouth and I just couldn't stop them.

"It was a Saturday, I told them. A Saturday in November. We were sixteen years old..."

thirty-one

I NOTICED HIM right away. I mean I noticed he was a surfer. I was serving in the little campsite shop. I still had to on Saturdays, but I'd negotiated with Mum that I'd open from seven in the morning till ten only. If people wanted something after that they could go over to the village.

Me serving in the shop meant I'd sit behind the till with my head buried in a magazine. I'd only put it down if the customer was a pretty girl, or if it was someone who looked like they might be into shoplifting. This guy maybe looked a little like that. He was much older than me, but still a young guy. He had sharp eyes, they didn't look like they missed much.

"You're a surfer right?" He'd picked up a tin of beans and some bread and presented them to me. We didn't have a scanner or anything fancy, I had to add things up on my pad.

"Yeah," I saw he was looking at the magazine article I'd been reading, all turquoise waves and palm trees. "Maybe."

"I saw you in the water yesterday. You're good."

"Thanks." I replied as sarcastically as I could. I knew I was good, didn't need this guy telling me.

He shrugged as if it hadn't been a compliment, just an observation of fact.

"You got a forecast?"

I always had a forecast. All of us made sure we caught the end of the news on TV, hoping to glimpse tightly-packed rings of isobars mid-

Atlantic, which was usually behind the presenter's arses while they went on about weather for ducks or some other irrelevant shite. The rings were how the charts showed Atlantic depressions, the weather systems that sent us waves.

"I don't have a TV see, I'm camping," he explained. He gave me a smile that matched my sarcasm.

"It's doesn't look good," I told him. There was something about the way the guy was staring at me that I didn't like. It was like he knew my secret and was testing me. "There might be a little wave later. Maybe waist high."

His eyebrows went up in surprise. "That all?" he asked. "I thought it'd be bigger."

This time I shrugged. "The headland blocks the swell." I meant it as a way to end the conversation. It wasn't that I was always a miserable sod with the campers, but we had a rule to be as rude as we could to visiting surfers. John called it the 'Badlands Rule'. But it wasn't the brightest thing to say in this case.

"Yeah I noticed that. Say, you're not from round here are you?"

"That's one pound forty nine."

He ignored my outstretched hand at first, but then stuck his hand into his jeans to get his wallet.

"Here you go," he handed me a ten pound note. He was one of the day's first customers and I didn't have much change.

"Got anything smaller?"

He shook his head. "Australia right?" He smiled thoughtfully. "The accent. I was trying to place it. Guess you're used to better waves than here eh?" He dipped his head in the direction of Town Beach. "Sorry kid, that's all I got."

I let out a long sigh even though I didn't have to go far to get change, since Mum was counting cash for the bank in the kitchen.

"I'll be back in a minute," I said getting up.

"Hey don't worry, I'll get something else." He turned around and grabbed a couple of packet rice meals and a bottle of Coke, then plucked a postcard at random from the rack.

"Say, you don't have maps do you?"

I'd been adding up the new items but stopped as I heard the words.

"Maybe," I replied slowly. "Where do you want to go?"

"It sounds a bit small for a surf. I thought maybe I'd take a walk, see what's around the headland," he indicated the one to the south of the bay with a twist of his head. I don't know how he knew, but I really got the sense he was testing me now.

"You can't go that way," I said. "It's all private property. The best walks are over the river, north of the bay."

"Yeah I heard that." I didn't know if he meant he'd heard where the better walks were, or if he knew the headland to the south was all private.

"There's big signs and everything," I said, and immediately regretted it.

"Big signs huh?" he said. "I wouldn't want to mess with big signs." The sarcasm bubbled a bit closer to the surface. "You got that map then?"

We sold maps every day, but something made me not want to give this guy a map. I considered telling him we'd sold out, but realised he'd only have to stroll over to the village shop to get one, and we sold them for a quid more, so it would be a victory of sorts. I pulled open the drawer and handed one over.

"Thanks kid."

With the other items I had enough change, and I handed it over. He gave me a sarcastic smile while balancing his food on the map and clutching it to his chest. I hadn't offered him a bag.

"I'll see you in the water, kid," he said, pushing open the door with his free hand.

I watched from the window what tent the guy went back to, he was pitched up by the shower block, a red Nissan parked along side it with the white curve of a surfboard just visible inside. I knew cars by then, I'd been driving Mum's around the campsite for years and was counting the days till I was old enough to take my test. To put a surfboard in a car that small you had to wind down the passenger seat and push it in through the boot. There was only room for one driver. It meant the guy was here on his own. I don't know why I noticed this at the time, maybe just the fewer surfers around the better.

I don't know what it was, a premonition maybe, but I felt uncomfortable for the rest of the morning. I was planning to head straight down to Hanging Rock once I'd closed for the day. My comment about the headland blocking the swell probably came out because I'd been thinking about that. That day there was the sort of smallish swell that didn't get into Town Beach, but would be working nicely at The Rock. Darren and John would be there already, but it would be better that afternoon on the pushing tide, so I wasn't really going to miss much.

I tried to remember how long the tent had been there, but I hadn't noticed it before. I guess that meant not long. His car was parked parallel to me so I couldn't see the number plate and check in the book. But I didn't want to go out and look, because I still felt as though the guy was somehow watching me. A while later once I'd become distracted by some other customers, I saw the car had gone.

We were going to spend that night at the Rock. I'd told Mum I'd be staying at John's, while he and Darren told their parents they might stay over in one of the caravans with me. We always did this really vaguely so there was less chance of getting caught out. We thought we'd probably surf Saturday afternoon's high tide, get in again early on the Sunday and then a late afternoon session before coming back to real life Sunday night. That meant I had to fill a backpack with quite a bit of gear, wetsuit, food and water. So it was near midday by the time I was hiking out on the road past John's house. It didn't matter if anyone saw me since I just looked like a normal hiker making the detour around the private estate. You saw people doing it all the time. So I wasn't paying much attention, even when I heard the noise of a car behind me. But it slowed down instead of overtaking, and I decided to stand back on the verge and wave it past me. I thought it was probably some old dear from the village who was too old to drive properly. But when I turned around I saw the flash of red from the bonnet and was too slow to drop my head or look away. The guy from the shop was in the driver's seat, a pair of dark glasses over his eyes. It felt like he hesitated for a moment before driving past, and I could feel his eyes on me in the rear view mirror as he continued down the road.

thirty-two

IT FREAKED ME out a bit, but even so I'd almost forgotten by the time I got down to Hanging Rock. I could see right away I was wrong about the morning not being that good. There were long lines of swell stretching far out to sea and inshore it was peeling so well there were sometimes two or three waves breaking down the reef at the same time, each following the same line as the first. They shimmered in the sunlight and it looked almost like Oz, the sea was so blue and the sky so clear. Darren was out there, he'd just paddled back into position as I walked clear of the undergrowth. I couldn't see John anywhere but I stopped to watch Darren get a wave. I guessed he'd been in a while because his paddling was slow and tired, but he made the take off and I had to smile, even though we knew the place so well by then, sometimes you still just had to stop and smile at how good it was.

I wasn't sure now if the afternoon would really be better. But I quite liked that Darren and John would be surfed out from the morning, while I'd be fresh. We maybe didn't talk about it that much, but we were pretty competitive about who was best.

By the time I got to the Hanging Rock itself there was a bit of a lull in the swell so I set down my bag and got my wetsuit out to dry it. I laid it out on a rock and as I did so I saw John picking his way up from the beach by the stream, his board under his arm. He must have ridden a wave in just before I got there. We had these really comfy chairs there by then made from driftwood - old pallets mostly - and I stretched out on one, waiting with my arms behind my head, trying to decide whether I should get in now for a quick surf or wait with the others.

"You should get in there," John said when he arrived. He'd stripped off the top half of his wetsuit and his blond hair was dripping water down his chest. You could see he was breathing hard from the exercise. "It's pretty decent."

"You going in again?"

"Yeah, in a bit. You got any food?"

I pointed at my backpack. "Help yourself." Then I pointed out at the waves, a new set was coming in now. Together we watched Darren paddle out through them, not turning around to catch any. "What's up with Darren? Why's he wasting waves?"

"Cos he's a pussy." John grinned at me. "Actually we've been in all morning, and he's surfing pretty good. He got this barrel earlier for maybe four seconds. Bet you he tells you about it first thing he sees you." As he was speaking John had torn a chunk from a loaf of bread and was busy fitting the key to a tin of ham, the type where you have to wind it around to remove the top. Normally he was pretty good with those, but maybe his arms were still tired because the key snapped off halfway around.

"Fucking hell," he said and I watched him digging around in his pile of clothes for his hunting knife. He slipped it out of the sheath and prised the tin open with the thick blade. Then he cut a big slice of the pink meat and held it against the side of the knife, eating it carefully right off the blade.

Out on the reef the last wave in the set was lining up to roll down the point, and Darren turned around to take it. You could see his little arms digging deep and his feet thrashing around. He nearly missed it, it looked like it was going to roll right underneath him, but just at the last moment it steepened enough that his board began to accelerate and he sprang up, one hand keeping hold of the board's rail. It always looked so beautiful from up by the Rock, you could see the whole wave stretched out, you could see exactly where it was going to go hollow enough to ride the tube and where it slowed a little to leave a steep wall for throwing in some turns. It was much easier to imagine yourself riding the wave well from up there, than it was when you were actually on it, all the noise and buffeting from the whitewater chasing you down the reef.

"Come on Darren, pull in, pull the fuck in," John had turned to look too. It was obvious that Darren was too far from the breaking part of the wave which was setting up to throw a big, easy tube, he needed to stall the board and kill a bit of speed to let the best part of the wave catch him up. Darren did, a little, but we both saw he could have been deeper. Instead of disappearing from view behind the curtain of falling water, we could see him the whole time on the flatter part of the wave, doing some nice Darren turns, as we called them on account of how he held his arms out like he was pretending to be an aeroplane. But just before the wave finished, we both saw something that meant we stopped looking at Darren. No, not something, someone.

"What the fuck's that?" John said. I don't think I ever heard his voice like that. It had shock and anger and fear and panic all rolled up together in it, and I knew right away there was going to be trouble.

The man was right by the water's edge, about fifty metres away from us. He was wearing a wetsuit and holding a white surfboard, a little shortboard thruster just like ours. He was turned towards the sea, watching the wave that Darren was surfing, and once Darren dropped back into the water the man moved again, walking below us, out towards the point. He must have thought he was going to have the surf of his life.

"There's some fucking guy there," John said. Not to me, it was like he was telling another part of himself.

I hadn't said anything so John turned to look at me. "You see that? There's some fucking guy thinks he's gonna surf our break. Hey!" He shouted the last word, not so loud at first but then he stood right up and shouted it loud. He wasn't thinking, he was just acting.

"Hey! Who the fuck are you?" I'd never heard him sounding so angry.

The man stopped and turned, I don't think he'd seen us before then. He seemed to hesitate for a moment but then he carried on walking the way he'd been going, stepping carefully from one rock to the next.

"Come on Jesse," John said to me already setting off. "Come with me."

I was thinking about the way this guy was in the shop. I'd already seen he had this attitude. I was thinking how this was going to be messy. I just didn't want to even be there.

"What are you gonna do?" I said.

"Fucking come with me and you'll see," and he turned and went. When John spoke like that, you didn't argue. You just didn't.

I could hardly have kept up with John if I tried, and I wasn't trying too hard. He practically ran down the rocks, his wetsuit arms still flapping around his waist. The guy had stopped again, he must have seen John coming by now and knew he was going to have to talk to him at least. John shouted at him again when he was maybe five metres away, way too loud.

"You better fuck off right now, this place is private."

It was him alright, I saw that now. I saw the same sarcastic look too. He thought this was funny. "Calm down son. There's plenty of waves here for everyone." And he looked at me and gave me a nod, like he'd seen an old friend.

"I said this place is private," John said again. "Now turn around, *fuck off,* and don't ever come back. Do you understand?"

It was only then I noticed that John still had the knife. I don't know if he just forgot to put it down when he started running or what. We were all into knives then, you know for making things out of wood or cleaning fish. But John's was the nicest. The biggest too.

"And I said there's plenty of waves to go around," The guy had seen the knife as well. I was close enough to see how his eyes changed, the pupils got smaller.

"Listen, I'm gonna have one quick surf, then I'm away. No harm done." The man began to turn like he was going to keep walking out to the point, but he kept his head half turned, not looking away from John.

"I don't think so. It's locals only," said John.

The guy laughed at this, he actually laughed. "Look kid, I don't know what you think this is. I know this place is private but I'm pretty sure you're not the lord of the fucking manor." He looked at me again, he was smiling.

"I get it, I do. This is your spot. But there's only one of me, no one knows I'm here and I live fucking miles away. I swear I won't tell a soul about this place. Now I'm gonna have one surf and you'll never see me again. So how about you relax?"

I knew this day was going to come, there was just no way we could keep Hanging Rock secret for ever. Really it was amazing that no one had come earlier, amazing that none of the crab fisherman had seen it, when they were working their pots. Hanging Rock was only secret because it was in the estate, but, a wave that good? People were still going to find it, in the end. We all knew that. But John just shook his head.

"I said it's locals only." And he shifted the grip on his knife so that the blade was concealed up the inside of his wrist, like you saw people doing on films when they knew how to handle themselves. "Now get the fuck outta here."

For a little while we were all just standing there, then the guy spoke again. He wasn't laughing anymore.

"You pull a knife on someone son, you want to be sure you know how to use it."

Without taking his eyes off the blade he slowly bent down and placed his board on the ground, it didn't rest down easily because we were all standing on all these uneven rocks. He stood up again and faced John.

"Cos you might accidentally pull a knife on someone who knows something about fighting with knives and who will break your fucking arm right off." He'd started to move very slowly towards where John was standing, getting himself on a flatter base.

"You know that even threatening someone with a knife is a very serious thing to do? There's a witness here. That kid behind you. I know him, he works in the campsite shop over in the village." All this time he didn't take his eyes off John.

"Now I don't know what bullshit you kids have been reading in your little magazines but I promise you this, you're gonna be in a shitload of trouble if that knife doesn't go away pretty soon."

John said nothing, but he held his arm out bent in front of him so the blade was pointed right at the guy.

"I'm serious kiddo. You put that away and we'll have a little chat about all this, straighten it out." A lot of the cockiness had gone out of the guy's voice by now, he sounded nervous.

"How'd you know that?" John asked. His voice sounded weird too, like for the first time since this began he was back in control of himself.

"Know what?" The guy asked.

"How'd you know he works at the campsite shop?"

"I talked to him this morning. He told me about this place."

"That's bullshit," I blurted out. "He's lying John. I didn't tell him shit."

"He said the headland blocks all the swell, he said I should go for a walk." The man took his eyes off the knife for the first time and looked into John's face. "He even sold me a map." The guy smiled again.

And that's when John made his mistake. He turned around to look at me, tried to focus on my face like he wanted to work out if it was true.

I was looking at him too, trying to say the guy was making it up, so I didn't really see what happened, not properly. But the guy made a move. There was this blur and suddenly it was like they were hugging, and it looked like they were going to fall. You don't want to fall on rocks like that. Never mind John's fuck-off hunting knife, you could really get hurt just falling down on rocks like that.

Then they went down together. There was this sound, like a thud and then a real nasty crack and then these grunting, whistling noises. Then John started yelling and sort of rolled off him all the while holding onto his arm. You could see right away it was all at the wrong angle, his arm I mean. It was snapped at the wrist. His face had gone totally white, and I saw it and felt instantly sick and like I needed to crouch down and just not look in that direction.

"Oh shit, your arm. Man, your fucking arm."

He didn't say anything, he was just panting, trying to find a way to hold his arm so that his hand didn't dangle horribly down. That's when I realised he wasn't holding the knife any more. And for some reason I needed to find it. It was like I feared the worst. Probably from watching so many movies or something, I kind of knew where I would see it and there it was. When the guy had rushed John he'd put out his hands to keep him away, it meant the knife's blade went out too. So maybe it was an accident where it ended up, buried right up to the hilt in the guy's stomach. Maybe it was an accident.

thirty-three

"MOTHERFUCKING BASTARD BROKE my fucking arm." John was sitting down now, his back against a rock and he'd managed to find a way to hold himself that let him speak.

"Did you see that? Did you fucking see that?"

I didn't answer. I was just staring at the knife.

"I said did you see that?"

I must have shook my head because John started talking real loud. "He jumped at me. He fucking jumped at me! Why did he do that?" There was spit coming out of John's mouth, he was talking so fast.

"Jesse, you saw that didn't you? I know you saw. He just fucking jumped right at me."

I stepped a couple of rocks forward to get a better look at the guy. His mouth was opening and closing like a fish did when we pulled them up onto the pier. As he breathed he blew bubbles. At first they were white but then they started coming out red.

"Oh Christ," I said. Then John started to make this retching noise and when I looked at him he was puking up, his good arm cradling the broken one.

Everything started spinning and I think I was moaning out loud. I knew I was going to fall if I didn't get on the deck so I lowered myself onto the rocks and held my head in my hands. I stayed like that for a while listening to John throwing up. And then I heard something else.

"Kid. Kid, you hear me? Get some help." I lifted my head from my hands and looked at him. He was staring right at me, croaking the words, a little bubbly puddle of blood formed on the rock by his face as he spoke.

"John, it's alright, he's alive. It's gonna be alright he's alive." I looked over at John, I felt so relieved I was nearly laughing, but John wasn't smiling. It was like he wasn't there at all.

"John?"

Then Darren turned up. That bit was just surreal.

"What's going on?" he shouted before he got to us. "Is that a dolphin?" Darren came closer and said it again. "Have you guys found a dead dolphin?"

John didn't answer so I had to. "No mate, we haven't found a dead dolphin."

"What's that then?"

"It's a guy that John's stabbed." I said and Darren laughed.

"Shut up, what is it?"

"I just fucking told you, alright?"

Darren came closer again and stared for a moment. Then he looked at me, at John with his fucked up arm and puke down his chest.

"Who's that?"

"I don't know."

"Where did he come from?"

"I don't know."

"But John stabbed him?"

"Yeah."

"Why'd he do that?"

"I told you Darren I don't know, alright?"

It was a beautiful day all around us, the sky hardly had a cloud in it, the air was crisp since it'd been raining the night before, and the autumn colours on the bushes were beautiful, dark greens and yellows and browns. All around I guess there was the sound of waves peeling down the point, seagulls hawking overhead. But it was like we'd torn a huge hole in the middle of it. The only thing I could hear was this rasping noise coming from the stabbed guy as he tried to breathe. And for a long while that's all that happened.

I sometimes wonder what would have happened if I'd had the courage to take over then. Before John pulled himself back together. If I'd said then that it wasn't too late to save the man, if I'd ordered Darren to go and get help, told John we were gonna stop the bleeding or something. But that's not what happened. I guess it was always John in charge, never me. And I was paralysed by the thought of where we were, it was a half hour hike to get back to John's house, and we certainly couldn't carry him all that way. And what would people think? The guy had John's hunting knife stuck into him.

"He was cutting out the ham, up by the Rock," I said. "I think he just forgot to put it down."

Darren didn't say anything for a moment but then nodded his head hard.

"Mate, it's alright," Darren said to John. "If he dies, it's alright. Your dad's got lawyers and stuff who work for him. He'll get you off, you won't have to go to prison or anything."

John didn't even seem to hear Darren so he turned to me and said. "Jesse? His dad will get him off won't he? It's going to be alright?"

It had all just happened so quick I couldn't keep up. I certainly couldn't work out the consequences yet. I didn't know if it was all going to be alright. It didn't feel like it would.

"What do we do?" Darren asked, it was like he had to fill every silence.

"What do we do Jesse? We should do something."

I tried to pull myself together, but every time I thought of something that people did in times like this it didn't seem to make sense.

"We could go to the road. Try to flag down a car." I said after a while.

"Yeah. Yeah. Good idea. It might be a doctor. They could come and fix up that guy and sort John's arm."

"It's a long way to the road though," I went on. "And the tide's coming in now." The guy was laying among the rocks at the very edge of the low water mark, that was why it was so slippery down there, all the seaweed and stuff.

"Yeah, but maybe we can drag him up a bit," said Darren. "Enough so the water doesn't get him. Before we go to the road. We can both go to the road can't we Jesse? You and me I mean?"

"But he's got a knife sticking out of his stomach," I said, it was like I just couldn't figure this out. "What are we gonna say?"

"We tell them it was an accident. You said it was an accident didn't you? You saw it all Jesse."

"Will you two shut up?" John suddenly cut in with this weary voice. "Will you two just shut the fuck up?"

And of course, we shut the fuck up.

Then John began to shake his head, wincing as he did so. "I just need you two to shut up. I gotta think about what we're gonna do."

We waited while John shuffled his back against the rock he was leaning against to bring himself more upright.

"No one goes to the road," he said when he'd finished.

"What?" Darren looked about to cry.

"You go to the road. We're all going to prison for murder."

"What are you talking about?" I said. "What did we do?"

"I'm telling you. We gotta think properly about this. We gotta do the right thing here."

"The guy's not even dead," I said. "Look at him."

John did. He turned back to the man and watched him for a while. There was a lot of blood now, leaking from where the knife cut into him, it was bright red and so thick it clung to the smooth black rubber of his wetsuit.

"Yeah but he's gonna die. You can tell, wounds like that, in the stomach, it always takes a while to die. They can't do anything about those wounds, even in hospitals. I've seen it in films," said John.

We all watched the man some more. He was staring right back at us, and his mouth was moving like he was trying to speak but he couldn't, he didn't have the breath to get any words out and every time he opened his mouth, it was just blood that came out.

"If we try and get help, he's still gonna die, the only difference is we'd go to prison," said John.

"What's with the 'we'?" I asked. I don't know how I dared say it to John but the thought of going to prison scared the shit out of me.

"Well I am aren't I?" For a moment his eyes were pleading with me. "You ain't gonna help him if you go to the road, but you're gonna send me to prison. My knife's stuck in his stomach. Who's gonna believe it's an accident?"

"I saw it, sort of. I can tell them."

"They won't believe you. They'll have you for assisting, or lying to them. They'll get you too Jesse."

I felt panic rising up in me. I could see he was right.

"What about me?" Darren said. "I could go, I didn't see anything."

"Then you'd put us both away," John said. He sounded suddenly tired. "And the guy still dies."

"Face it. We're in this together."

We were all quiet for a long while. I was dizzy with it all.

It seemed like a long time until John spoke again, but when he did it was like he was back. Our friend, the problem-solving, calm and dependable John, the guy who always knew what to do. Always told us the right thing.

"I've got to make a sling. Jesse, give me your jumper." I must have hesitated since he said it again. "Jesse, give me your fucking jumper." I struggled out of it and was about to throw it at him but I saw he wouldn't be able to catch it. His good hand was holding the broken arm.

"Tie the arms together. Right at the ends of the sleeves. That's it, now put it over my neck. Carefully."

I did what I was told and he gently slid one of the jumper's arms underneath his own. He winced then swore out loud as he let its weight fall into the sling, then he puffed out a few deep breaths and held out his good arm.

"OK. Now help me get up."

When he was standing he checked out the rest of his body and seemed relieved there were no other problems. Then he slowly made his way over to where the man was laying. He crouched down and inspected where the knife went in. I couldn't even look at it.

"Jesse," he called out to me without turning away. "He said he talked to you at the campsite, is he staying there?"

I nodded. "Yeah but I didn't tell him any..."

"That doesn't matter," he cut me off. "Was he with anyone?"

"I don't know, how would I know..." I suddenly remembered the car. "No. He had his board in his car. The passenger seat was wound down and the back seats aren't split on those cars, so there were no other seats." I felt pleased to have worked this out.

"Good. He said he was on his own here too, before the accident, he said no one knows he's here." John nodded to himself.

"Good," he said again. "So no one knows he's here. No one knows we're here either. We know that. So how did he get here?

I thought back to what happened as I walked down. "I saw him drive past me, just before I turned off from the road."

"Do you remember what car it was?"

"Yeah, red Nissan."

"OK, very good. So we know he parked somewhere south of here in a red Nissan. We can find it so we can sort that. So we've just got to do something with the body."

I must have been looking cos I saw the man's eyes when he heard that. He could definitely still hear what we were saying and his face moved at those words. He tried again to mouth something, I think it was to me but I looked away again.

"He's not really a body though is he?" I said. Part of me didn't want to interrupt John in his flow, but this seemed kinda important. "Look at him. He's still moving."

This time John spoke really quietly. "Jesse I've told you, people don't survive things like this." As he spoke he reached out with his good hand and touched the handle of the knife, then pushed it slightly so the blade moved in the wound. The man gave out a low moan, then you could see him gritting his teeth. John held the knife delicately between the fingers of his good hand.

"Not so cocky now are you? You fucker." He shook his head. "You should have listened to me. I told you to fuck off. Now we've all got a problem. We've got to work out what to do with you." He gave the knife a little push, playfully, then stood up awkwardly.

Then the man made a big effort to speak to me. I could barely hear him but it was something like "kid, your friend's crazy. You gotta get…"

"Shut up or I'll put a fucking rock down through your head," John interrupted him, and we were all quiet, waiting for what John was going to do next. Finally he bent down again and settled his fingers around the handle of the knife. When he was happy he looked the man in the eyes and spoke again.

"This might hurt a little."

Then he pulled the knife out. It must have been wedged in harder than he anticipated because it got stuck half way out, a smear of bright red on the shiny silver blade. Then John had another go and this time freed it. Then he calmly washed the blade in one of the rock pools, and then the arm of his wetsuit, which still had a bit of sick on it. He totally ignored the man who was groaning now and had moved his arms over his stomach.

"Shit John. What'd you do that for?" Darren sounded dismayed. Where the knife had been the wound was steadily dripping blood, but now blood was gushing out of a three inch gash in the wetsuit and the flesh beneath it, coming out in little pumped spurts.

"It's better this way," said John. "It'll be quicker."

You could see the life slipping away from the man now. It looked like he didn't care about whether we got help now. All his body was concerned with was damage limitation, emergency shutdown procedures. His eyes fluttered but he wasn't seeing anything. He'd been holding his head up off the rock, but now it dropped down, a sharp angle of rock pressing into his cheek and forcing his mouth open, teeth grating on the barnacles. We just stood there watching while the rock pool filled up with crimson, treacle blood that turned dark like the thick ribbons of seaweed.

"It's a body now." John said a few minutes later, but neither Darren nor me replied.

"Come on. We can't leave it here, the tide's coming in, it'll get washed away. Someone will find it if that happens." John said.

I had one more go. "John this is fucking mad. We got to go and get some help."

"No we don't."

"Yes we do. This is crazy. You're crazy."

"You and Darren, you're gonna move the body up to the Rock."

"You're fucking mad. I'm not doing anything you say."

John turned on me, real angry now.

"Jesse I'm not saying this is fucking pleasant for any of us. But we've gotta do this. Unless you wanna be put in prison for a very long time we've gotta stick together. Now you get his fucking legs, Darren get his arms. Let's move the fucker and get on with this."

John was still holding onto the knife. I opened my mouth to argue again but he interrupted me, he held the knife up to my face and he was yelling like he'd never yelled at me before.

"He's fucking dead Jesse. Do as I fucking tell you."

I felt my lips quivering and tears at my eyes but I nodded and did everything just like he told me.

thirty-four

AT FIRST I took the guy's arms and Darren took his legs, but that was never going to work. You wouldn't believe how hard it is to carry a body over rocks like that. Every time we tried to move him, we either couldn't lift him over a boulder, or we slipped on the seaweed. We were going to hurt ourselves, and his teeth were getting cracked, falling out even and lumps of hair and skin were getting ripped off on the barnacles. But John made us keep going and in the end we just took a foot each and dragged him. We tried not to watch as his body slipped and skidded across the rocks. It was pretty gross. I nearly lost it, but John somehow kept us going. He'd stopped shouting at us by then and was encouraging us instead, telling us what a great job we were doing and how it was all going to be OK. I think he was enjoying himself by then. But anyway, eventually we had the guy up there in our little camp at the foot of the Hanging Rock.

"You're doing great boys. Fucking great." John said. We had the guy's body spreadeagled on his back right in the middle of the little grassy patch where we used to hang out. He looked a sight. His face was ruined, there were rips in his ears and cheek and his nose was half gone, what was left was just a bloody mess. I think maybe even his neck had broken because his head was at a weird angle staring up at the sky. I wondered what the hell we were supposed to do now. It didn't take long to find out.

"Now you got to dig a hole to stick him in."

I didn't say anything, just dropped to my knees and started scratching at the grass with my hands. But Darren didn't move. Tiredness and shock had left him pale. He'd just got off the water from a long session remember.

"We just gonna bury him here? Is that it?"

"Come on Darren. Just dig." John started kicking at our driftwood chair and broke out a plank which he gave to Darren, I guess to use at a spade.

"How's that going to help? It's basically just rock."

Darren had a point, as I was finding out. The little flat hollow underneath the Hanging Rock was the only patch of grass on the whole section under the cliff, but dig down and you hit rock right away.

"And we can't just leave him buried here anyway. It'll be weird, knowing he's there all the while."

John looked frustrated and he took the plank of wood back from Darren and started hacking at the earth one handed. He only got a few inches deep before he hit something solid.

"Fuck it. In the cave."

"What?"

"We'll put him in the cave. We'll have to leave him there for now."

Darren opened his mouth to protest but I nudged him and shook my head, and he sighed and took his place on a leg. We hauled the guy in backwards as far as we could, his lifeless head bouncing from rock to rock with dull thuds. When we came back outside you couldn't really tell that anything had happened there, except for the trail of blood leading right up to the entrance. It didn't feel like we'd exactly solved the problem.

"I told you we can't just leave him here." Darren said again.

"We're not going to. But right now we've got to find the car. Get your stuff and follow me."

John led us at a pretty fast pace so we didn't get to talk much. But it didn't take that long anyway. There was only really one place he could have parked, and sure enough, the car was there. Red Nissan, sitting on the verge where the farm track left the road. We were lucky with the keys. I went down on hands and knees to look around and there they were, a little silver key ring dangling from the suspension coil. I pulled them out and went to give them to John, but he shook his head.

"You're driving." He held up his arm in my jumper sling.

"But I don't have my licence."

"You've been taking lessons though haven't you? You've been saying how fucking good you are for ages."

"Yeah but," I stopped. "What about Darren?" I said.

"I'm not trusting Darren."

I opened my mouth to protest but he had a point. "Oh fucking hell."

I opened the driver's door and climbed inside, then reached across and opened the passenger side as well. John told Darren to roll the seat up - the guy had it flat to take his surfboard like I remembered - then he made Darren get in the back and sat down beside me. He shut the door. The little car smelt of pine and warm plastic.

"Where we going then?" I asked.

John didn't answer at first, and when I looked at his face I could see he wasn't sure himself. None of this was planned remember, he was making it up as he went along, and even John had his limitations.

"I dunno. We've got to find somewhere to hide the car so that no one finds it. A scrap yard or something. Or like a lake we can push it in." He stopped and I could see him thinking hard.

"We could push it into the harbour?" Darren suggested. "You can drive right to the edge."

"What? In the middle of the fucking village? No, it can't be anywhere around here." He flipped open the glovebox and started searching around while I looked at the car's controls, wondering how far he was going to get me to drive. I'd probably overstated my driving skills to them at that stage. I watched John pull out a road map which didn't make me feel any better.

"That'll help," he said. "How much petrol is there Jesse?"

I looked on the dashboard and felt a flood of secret relief when I saw it. "*Oh fuck*. It's empty. Totally empty. We probably can't even get to a petrol station." I turned to John to see how he'd take this, but then I heard Darren from the back.

"Turn the ignition on," he said. "You need it on or the dial doesn't register."

Darren was right. When I turned the key the needle climbed at once to just over half full.

"See? I told you," Darren began but I told him to shut the fuck up.

"Half a tank." I said to John, hoping the plan was going to be finding somewhere to ditch the car long before we used all that up. But he didn't answer, he was flicking through the map, his lips were moving as ideas ran through his head.

"I've got it." He turned to me with a grim look on his face. "It's a bit of a trip though."

"A bit of a trip?" I said, feeling sick now. "Where we going?"

"Buckle up. We're going to the Badlands."

You know I've read a bit about murders and murderers since then. You could say I developed an interest in it, that's understandable isn't it? Anyway, it turns out the murderers who get caught, most often they do so because they make silly mistakes. They panic basically. They don't think things through. They get rid of the evidence as quickly as they can, instead of as carefully as they can. It's understandable, believe me I know, you get scared, you don't want to be there, dealing with what's happened. You take shortcuts. That was what me and Darren were like, but John wasn't. And that's what made him so good that day. His arm must have been killing him, but he hardly mentioned it. He wasn't panicking, he was thinking. So he wasn't making mistakes. And to come up with the plan he did, that young, that inexperienced, that was nothing short of genius. The only problem was it meant I had to drive most of the night.

"What are you talking about? What are we going there for?"

"OK Listen. He's a surfer right? This guy. He's here on his own. He *told* us no one knows he's here. So he could be surfing anywhere. So where's the most dangerous place to surf?"

Both Darren and me stayed quiet, blank looks on our faces.

"The Badlands. You're asking for trouble if you surf there, everyone knows that. We just have to leave the car somewhere in the Badlands. When they find this guy missing they'll think that the locals there did him. That's where they'll look for the body."

I wasn't thinking that far ahead though. "Cornwall? You want me to drive to Cornwall?"

John looked at the map before answering. "It's three hours. Three and a half tops. You'll be alright."

"But I've never driven further than the village."

"We'll be fine. We'll do it together. But we've got to go to the campsite first to get his stuff."

I didn't say anything. All I was thinking was I had to drive this car for four hours. For a moment I wondered if I could come up with a plan of my own to stop this madness, but I knew I could never outthink John. I stared out the windscreen for a little while then started the engine.

There was no one else on the road but I still indicated to pull out, might as well start out properly. I pulled away, revving a little high and Darren started telling me what to do from the back.

"You're still in first gear. You've got to change gear."

"Fuck off. I know. I'm changing now."

"That's fourth. You've put it in fourth. It's going to stall."

"Fuck off Darren."

John was just sitting there giving me this encouraging look, willing me to do this.

I drove the mile or so back down the road to the campsite and slowed just outside the gate. I could see Mum's car was there parked outside the house. John flipped down the sun visors and told me to keep going, over to where the guy's tent was pitched. I swallowed hard and did what he said. There was a little turn you had to make right by the house where you had to slow right down. We always used to glance out the kitchen window to see who was coming, whether they'd paid, whatever. I tried to get a bit of a run up to get through here fast, but I messed it up. I tried to change gear just before and missed it, and the engine juddered and stalled. We all just sat there staring at the kitchen window to see if Mum's face would appear. Even John looked worried, but he stayed calm and told me to push the clutch down and try the engine again. It wouldn't catch, just kept turning over with us sitting there right outside mum's kitchen window. There was washing on our little line. Mum was definitely there.

"You're gonna flood it Jesse," Darren said. My hands were shaking. I knew she was going to come out at any moment to see what the noise was.

"Calm down," John said. "Slowly." He reached across and put his good hand on my arm. "Try it once more."

It was like the car did what he told it, just like we did. The engine caught and I pulled away like old people do, the clutch still half in, the engine revving way too hard, but we moved forward.

I pulled up at the tent so the car was between it and the house.

"Fucking hell that was close," Darren said, and I just collapsed forward on the steering wheel, but John was onto the next challenge.

"Careful when you open the tent," he said. "We don't know for sure there's no one in it.

So I got out again and looked around a bit. It didn't look like anyone was there but I called out a tentative 'hello' and gave the tent a bit of a shake. No one replied, so I slowly unzipped the tent door. I don't know what I would have done if there'd been someone in there. I expect John would have thought of something.

It was empty apart from a camp mat and a sleeping bag and a few clothes scattered around, they guy wasn't exactly camping in luxury, but that was good as it meant we could pack his stuff up more quickly. I ran around the tent pulling out pegs so it flopped down onto the grass. John opened the Nissan's boot and got me and Darren throwing things in, putting the tent away neatly because John told us we had to make it look normal. When it was done I shut the boot and we all climbed back in. I put my shaking hands back on the wheel. That's when I had an idea.

We had to drive right through the village to get to the main road. And there's a police station at the end of the main street. Wherever John wanted us to go, we had to drive right past it. I suddenly realised there was nothing John could do if I stopped. If I stopped and got out and ran inside and told them what had happened, then it wasn't too late. For John maybe but not for me. If I drove John right to them, surely I wasn't an accessory to murder or whatever John was saying I was. I'd be a hero. The boy who caught a murderer. That was all I was thinking as we left the campsite and drove up to the village. I had to do it. I wasn't even thinking about the driving by then, just whether or not I could get out the car in time. But as we approached the police station and I slowed a bit, I could feel it was written all over my face what I wanted to do. I felt like he must be reading my mind.

"What are you doing Jesse?" He gave me this look. I'd seen it plenty of times before, like when he wanted me to get more wood for the fire, or finish off a rabbit that had got caught in our traps. But it was darker this time.

"Why are you slowing down?"

The truth is I just didn't have the nerve to do it. With his broken arm I could have stopped and run in there to the police - how was he gonna stop me - but my courage let me down.

"I'm not. I'm just keeping to the speed limit. We don't want to get busted for speeding do we?"

He kept that look fixed on me for a long while, until we were all the way out of town. I couldn't stop then, it was way too late.

That trip, Jesus Christ. I'll never forget that trip. At first there weren't any junctions and we just had to follow the road. Even so I got a little traffic jam on my tail, and on every straight bit people overtook me and honked their horns. Then we got to the motorway, and we either went so fast I thought we were going to crash, or so slow cars nearly piled into the back of us. I nearly freaked out so much John had me stop at the first services. He made me drink coffee and talked to me until I calmed down. He also bought aspirin or something, for his arm. He took four pills dry as soon as he got in the car and then he wound down the window and popped all the rest out of the packet onto the road. Then he did the same with a second packet, but he threw the boxes on the floor of the car.

"What you doing?" Darren asked him.

"A little misdirection," he said. "Come on. We gotta get going."

That trip took easily double what John had said it would. We pretty nearly all died around Cardiff when a lorry joined the motorway, I didn't know I was supposed to get out of the way and it fired it's air horn at us, which made me swerve right across into the fast lane. I went right over the path of this old volvo and I could see the driver, white faced with shock fighting the steering wheel to keep control. But slowly I kind of got the hang of it.

Even so it was way past midnight when we even got into Cornwall, and the Badlands were way down the bottom. John took us to a beach called Porthtowan. I wasn't really part of the conversation by then, just following the white lines and going whichever way John told me to go. We found a car park overlooking the beach. There was no one around of course, it was three in the morning by then but even so we parked it in the corner, right out of the way.

The idea was to dump the car there, but it was pretty cold so John told us to get some sleep first, and I was so tired I was out straight away. The next thing I knew it was getting light and John was shaking me awake. He made me pull some clothes from the guy's bag in the boot, and leave them on the passenger seat, like you'd do if you were surfing. Then John made us wipe everything to get rid of fingerprints. Then he told me to lock the car and hide the keys. As I was kneeling down to do so there was this massive bang and glass started falling about my ears. As if I wasn't shaken up enough by that point.

"What the fuck was that?" I said rolling back on the floor. John was standing above me, looking into the passenger window that he'd just stoved in with a brick.

"What the fuck did you do that for?" I asked.

"I told you, a little misdirection. " Then he said:

"Come on. Let's see if we can find some breakfast and get outta here."

It was still so early we had to wait a bit, but eventually we found somewhere that did a full English, and me and Darren ate while John figured out how to get us back home. We got a bus first, I don't remember where to, but then we got on a train up to Bristol, and then Carmarthen. Again I slept most of the way. But when we got there John made us leave the station and go to the high street. We went into every shop that looked like it might sell fireworks and we bought as many as they'd sell us. It was coming up to bonfire night so there were loads available. John did all the talking, he passed for eighteen pretty easily by then, and it cost a load, but like everything else he just put it on his credit card. If I'd known he had access to so much money I'd have stopped him stealing so much from the campsite shop. Anyway. He bought so much I had to make more room in my bag by snapping the sticks off from the rockets and throwing them away. We didn't get back on the bus until we each had a backpack filled to bursting with fireworks.

It was late by the time we finally got back to the village so we sneaked into the campsite and spent the night in our caravan, not putting the lights on in case Mum saw we were there and came out to offer us food or something. I don't think any of us slept much.

John woke us up at first light again. He looked tired that day. His arm was all sorts of blue and purple and swollen so it was twice the size it should have been. For a moment I didn't think he was going to be able to go through with it, and that scared me, the thought that Darren and me might have to do it on our own. But he fitted his sling again and got on with it. He made me sneak over and get all the petrol from the campsite's sit-on mower, then we had to hike back out to The Rock. The jerry-can of fuel weighed a ton. Our last expedition to the wave at Hanging Rock.

It seemed unreal walking down there that day. It was a stunning dawn, the sun rose up behind us and the oranges and reds and browns of the leaves were crisp against the lightening sky. It made it all the more ridiculous what we were setting out to do. I remember thinking I didn't want that walk to end. I didn't want to see what I knew we'd find at the end of it. I don't exactly believe in God but I was praying that somehow the guy hadn't been dead after all, that he's woken up from his trance, scrabbled around to put his teeth back in and walked off somewhere. That maybe all we'd really done wrong was steal the guy's car.

But when we arrived back at the foot of the Hanging Rock it was all like we'd left it. The only difference was it looked like some animals had been in the cave and had a go at the body. It's not like he was hard to find I guess.

We all sat down around the bags of fireworks and one by one, we opened each one up and poured the black power into Darren's backpack. We filled it up and then packed it down hard, we got maybe twenty kilos of the stuff in there. Then John carried it to the bottom of the crack behind the Hanging Rock and wedged it in as far as he could reach. He poured half the petrol into the bag as well, so that it sagged and it sat there in a stinking oily puddle. Then he laid out one of the ropes we used to anchor the lobster pot as a fuse, splashing that with petrol as well. He was concentrating so hard the whole time he didn't speak. Darren and me just stood there watching and waiting.

"Ready?" John stood half way between us and the towering Hanging Rock, at the end of his trail of rope and petrol. He held his lighter in his hand.

For a moment I was taken back to the last time I saw my Dad, and I thought that it would be kind of ironic if this was the last time I saw John alive as well. But I just shrugged like I didn't care anymore and then nodded.

John struck the lighter and cupped the flame with his other hand. Then he crouched down with the flame. For a while I thought nothing was going to happen, but then I saw a little flicker of yellow and blue dance away from him in the sunlight.

He jogged backwards until he was standing next to us. Then the flame reached the petrol-soaked bag of whatever the hell they put in fireworks to make them go bang. I'd been half sure that nothing would happen but I was way wrong. It went up instantly with a big 'whumppp' that made the entire cliff face shudder. The whole thing moved, shuddered, then the toe that the Hanging Rock rested on had nothing to push against and it bulged out, held for a moment and then spluttered forward. A few pathetic sized rocks blew out but no more than we could have heaped upon the body in five minutes of effort. I looked at John and started to say "What now?" But he didn't answer, he had his head back and was watching the top of the Hanging Rock.

It was swaying. Actually swaying. Then, at the base, there was a crack, a tiny thing at first, but growing and spreading and splitting so fast it was like your eyes couldn't keep up with it. It raced up the rock and then across and then the whole thing was moving. The whole enormity of the Hanging Rock, and a good deal of the cliff face behind it were suddenly in freefall.

"Get the fuck back!" John yelled and didn't wait for us, he turned and ran out on the smooth rocks towards the point. Darren grabbed my wrist and began to drag me away. All I could hear behind me was the thunder of a massive avalanche of rocks. I only went a few steps before tripping and I put my hands over my ears and eyes and wondered if I was going to die.

But we'd already been standing out past the end of the cliff, so the avalanche went right past us. The noise was immense though. It roared and boomed and it shook the ground, and then it did it again when the noise echoed back from the other side of the bay. I opened my eyes to see tidal waves heading out to sea, smacking into swells as they arrived into the bay. They slapped into each other and fanned upwards, stopping each other dead in their tracks. But then slowly, everything settled back down and then I was watching a new set of waves come in, and when the did they were different. The rocks had slumped out much further than we thought they would and gone right out onto the reef underwater. The next wave to come in, and the wave after that, and all the waves after that for ever and ever, instead of peeling the way we knew so well, they got half way down the reef and then they just stopped, crashed into the rocks like this wasn't anywhere special at all.

And where the Hanging Rock had been there was only a cloud of quickly clearing dust and hazy blueness. A slump of gently settling rock stretched from the bright new cliff face right down and out into the water. The black, rounded, seaweed-covered rocks by the water's edge that were so familiar were suddenly replaced by crisply outlined new ones. There was no fire left, that too was buried under rock. The body of the man, his surfboard, our camp, it was all buried underneath. And you could see right away, it was gone forever.

thirty-five

NATALIE SAT AT the table in silence. Half thoughts chased themselves around her mind like leaves caught in an eddy of wind. Then she closed her eyes and like the wind was shut off, her thoughts began to settle.

At last she knew. Jim was dead. There was no longer a residue of hope that something else might have happened. He wasn't living somewhere, his memory erased. He hadn't left her in punishment at what she had done. He was just dead. Dead for nothing. Dead because of one of his stupid fights, picked at the wrong place and the wrong time. She felt empty. Not sad, not angry, not even particularly curious. Just empty, letting the story wash over her as if it were one of the waves the man had described at this Hanging Rock place.

Dave was different though, he did look angry. And when he spoke he sounded incredulous. "You could have saved him." he was saying. "If you'd have got help, you could have saved him. Why the hell didn't you?"

The man didn't answer. He didn't even look up from the table at first. As he'd told them the story he'd been animated, his eyes darting around the room. Now he was slumped in his chair. Then he shrugged.

"I told you. And it probably wouldn't have made any difference."

"I'm going to phone the police." Dave said and he pulled his phone out.

The man glanced at him, then at Natalie but again he said nothing, just watched while Dave began tapping the screen on his mobile until it purred at them in the quiet, the same tone three times. A voice answered loud enough so they could all hear it.

"Emergency operator, which service do you require? Fire, police, or ambulance?"

Dave asked for the police and the woman said she was connecting him.

A new look had come onto the man's face now, uncertainty, and then a new voice came through the speaker of the phone saying "Police, where are you calling from please?"

Suddenly Jesse looked directly at Natalie and shook his head urgently. "Not the police. Not yet. You don't know everything yet. Make him hang up."

His eyes seemed to be pleading with her.

"Make him hang up," Jesse spoke a little louder this time, and there was panic in his voice.

"Make him hang up," he said again. "Someone could get hurt. You've got a sister haven't you? With little kids? Two boys?"

Natalie snatched at Dave's arm, knocking the phone from his hand and onto the tabletop.

"How do you know that?" she hissed.

The voice on the phone asked Dave again where he was calling from and they all stared at the phone.

"Hello caller?" it said. "Is there anyone there? What is the nature of the emergency?"

"Hang it up Dave," Natalie spoke very quietly.

He watched her for a moment then very slowly picked up the phone. He breathed a couple of times, then he spoke into the phone. He told the woman he was sorry. He said kids had got hold of his phone. The voice sounded doubtful, reluctant to end the call, but he pressed the button to silence her.

"How do you know about my sister?" Natalie said to Jesse.

He looked resigned.

"I need to tell you the rest of the story."

"How do you know about my sister's boys?" Natalie's voice was angry now, but her face was white.

"Is that a threat? Are you threatening her? Is that what this is?" There was plenty of colour in Dave's face.

"No. Not from me anyway." Jesse put out his hands in front of him. "You don't understand."

"Then I think you'd better tell us right now," Dave said.

Jesse took a deep breath. He looked around the room as if there might be something there to help him explain, but finally settled his eyes on Natalie's. "It's John. You've got to understand this is all about John. You talk to the police, you're making a move against John. And you do that if you want, but you better understand what you're up against. You better know you're gonna take him down properly, because if you don't, he's gonna come after you. And you really don't want that to happen."

Dave still had his phone on the table. He looked like he was itching to use it.

"Just what exactly are you saying?"

"Let me tell you the rest of the story. You'll understand."

Dave looked at Natalie and their eyes locked for a moment, then she nodded.

"Go on," said Dave.

thirty-six

JOHN SPENT A few nights in the hospital, but even after that, when I called his house, it was always his dad who answered. And he never let me speak to John. He said he was resting or something. That was weird. Normally he'd just sound pissed off that he was acting like John's answering service and call up the stairs. But whatever his dad thought, with all that had happened I needed to see John. So I decided to go round anyway.

When I got to the house his dad's car wasn't even in the driveway. I thought for a minute there was no one there, but the kitchen door was open so I let myself in, but then I thought that maybe John's dad was there anyway, just his car wasn't. That thought made me nervous so I was really quiet. I went upstairs but quietly, and right away I felt better because I could see John in his room, or his back at least. The door was open and he was facing away from me, doing something at his desk. I couldn't see what it was at first, so I moved closer. He was struggling to tear something out of a newspaper, the fact that one of his arms was wrapped in plaster almost from the armpit wasn't helping.

"What you doing?" I said.

He jumped.

"Fucking hell Jesse. What are you doing here?"

I didn't really understand the question. Just over a week before we'd covered up a killing together. It felt to me like we had something to talk about.

"What do you mean, what am I doing here?"

"How did you get in?" He asked. He was holding himself funny. I thought at first it was the plaster cast, but then I saw he was trying to hide the paper.

"Through the door. Like normal people."

He ignored this. "My dad's here," he said instead. What he meant was, what was I doing just walking in when his dad was home.

"His car's not here."

"He's back any minute I mean. He just went out to the shop."

"Yeah maybe." Since that subject was done I asked him again.

"So what you doing?"

"I'm not doing anything." He said again, but I was standing over his shoulder now, and he couldn't hide the paper without it being obvious. Besides, I'd already seen what he was doing.

"That's about the guy isn't it? What you're reading. What does it say?"

For about a second it looked like he was going to deny it. Then he slid the paper over to me.

"Here."

I read the story. It was a local paper, but not local to here so I don't know where he got it. And it didn't say much either, just a few lines that a search had been called off, and the guy was presumed to have drowned. It did have his name though. It gave me a funny feeling reading that.

"Jim Harrison," I said. "I didn't really think of him as someone with a name."

John gave me a funny look at this and I felt a bit stupid.

"I mean, not like a person with feelings and stuff. You know, a family. I wonder if he had any kids?" I looked at John like he might know the answer.

John continued to look at me for a little while. Then he ignored me, and went on tearing out the article. When he'd finished he pulled open his desk drawer and took out a folder. He opened it and I could see a couple of other clippings from newspapers. He put the new one with the others and closed it again.

"No. No kids. Not his anyway."

I didn't understand that, but I knew it meant John was in one of his weird moods. He got like that when he wanted to freak you out a bit, to play with you.

"What do you mean by that?" I said. But I didn't really want to know.

"I mean there's kids at the house, but they're not his. From what I could tell they're his wife's sisters."

There hadn't been anything about that in the article I just read, and it didn't sound like the sort of detail you'd read in a paper.

"How d'you know that?"

A smirk appeared on his face. It twisted his features so that for once he didn't look handsome. He looked nasty.

"I went to have a look."

"You did what?"

"Calm down. I wanted to check they didn't suspect anything. I just waited outside, had a look in the windows. I didn't knock on the door or anything."

"Why?" I said again. For some reason I remembered that time we sneaked up to look in the old house. The old man asleep with his shotgun.

"Look it's no big deal. I just wanted to have a look. I went down on the train to check it out. I just wanted to be sure. It's just a bit of insurance."

"Insurance for what?"

"I don't know. That's the point of insurance isn't it?"

The smirk was gone, replaced by a look of calm assurance. Like he was helping me to understand something that was hard to grasp. But I don't know, even then I didn't get it. To me it just seemed, I don't know, it just seemed kind of wrong.

Then there was a noise downstairs. "My dad's back," he said, and he slipped the folder back into his drawer and locked it. "Come on, we've got to go." Before I could ask why he was leading the way downstairs, and out of the side door, so we didn't run into his dad.

"What's the problem?"

"Shut-up Jesse. Just come with me,"

He stepped outside and closed the door behind him, then led the way out into the garden where we hardly ever went.

"What are we doing?" I said. Then I had a horrible idea.

"*Shit!* Have you been found out? Does your dad know? Is that why you didn't want me to come around?" I felt my gut contract at the thought and I jerked my head around to see if there were any police cars on the drive. I hadn't seen them when I turned up, but they could be sneaky, like in the films.

"No one knows." John said.

"Are you sure?"

"Yeah."

"Then what are we doing in the garden?"

He didn't say anything to that. But he looked at me like he was deciding something and kept walking away from the house.

"We're in the garden cos you've gotta understand something. Two things actually. First, no one knows. No one knows and no one's gonna know. OK? Two: Everything *has* to change now. It's just the way it has to be."

I didn't say anything but there must have been a look of confusion on my face, because he went on.

"Look I know this is hard. But we've just got to deal with this. This was just an unlucky accident, but we've got to accept it."

"I do accept it," I said, looking at my feet.

"Good. That's good. And we've gotta accept the consequences."

He kept walking me away from the house. I turned around then and I saw his dad at the window, watching us.

"John, what's going on?"

We'd reached the trees by then, what John's dad called the apple orchard.

"Jesse, things have to change now. You know that don't you?"

"Change how?"

"We can't see so much of each other for a while. In fact we can't see each other at all."

"Why?"

"That's the way it has to be now." He didn't look at me.

"I don't understand. Why?"

For a while he just stood there, looking off into the distance. Then he shook his head.

"There's lots of reasons. Someone could have reported seeing three young guys driving that car. We can't be those three young guys any more."

"But no one saw us."

"The way you were fucking driving, lots of people saw us."

If he meant that as a joke I didn't take it as one. I jumped in, my voice high pitched and angry.

"But no one saw us, and anyway, everyone in the village knows we all hang out together. It's gonna look more weird if we stop."

"No Jesse. You're wrong."

"Why?"

He ignored me. He reached up and pulled an apple off one of the trees, and held it in his bad hand while he twisted the stalk out with the other. "You want one?"

I ignored him back, but he just shrugged then took a bite. Then he looked at me and smiled.

"Don't be angry Jesse. This sets us free. We did something special back there. We smashed the ultimate limit. And we did it perfectly. We can do anything now." His eyes sparkled, and for a second it felt like the way things had always been.

"Just we can't do it together?"

He smiled.

"We were never going to do it together. Not for ever."

My brow furrowed again, but before I could say anything he threw his good arm back and hurled the apple as far as he could down the garden. It burst through the leaves of the trees and out of sight.

"In a way it's good you came to visit. I've got something to tell you. I'm moving to London. I'm going to live with my mum for a while."

"*What?* Why? You hate London."

"No I don't."

"You always said you did."

"Well... It's not so bad." He glanced down at his arm. "I can't surf for a while anyway."

"But that'll get better. You don't have to move. You don't have to *go away*." I could hear how high pitched I had got, how whiney I sounded. In contrast his voice still had its usual deep calmness.

"And when it does? What then? We all go back to surfing Town Beach like little kids? Hanging Rock's gone Jesse. That was the only thing that made this place worthwhile."

"I don't understand," I said after a while.

"Come on Jesse. You understand. Maybe Darren wouldn't, but you do. You get this."

"I don't." I felt the panic welling up again. "What else is there?"

"What else is there but some shitty little village in Wales?"

I stayed quiet while he went on.

"I'm gonna start working for my dad. In his property business. I always was, you knew that."

"No I didn't"

"Jesse...," he started, but he wasn't about to start arguing with me.

"But what about surfing?" I asked. "You can't surf in London."

A look passed over his face. Something like irritation. Boredom. Then his focus shifted off me and was on the horizon, you could see how his pupils contracted.

"Did you really not feel it at all?"

Now I was just confused. "Feel what?" I said.

He looked at me again, and this time he smiled, a deep, broad smile - we called it his superhero smile cos when he did it he looked like the guy who played Superman in those old films. "The thrill. Bigger and better than anything before."

"Thrill?"

"You know. When it happened. Driving that guy's car when he was lying there cold and still. Burying the fucker under tons of rocks. Didn't you feel it? Didn't you get anything from that?"

We'd stopped by now and he was facing me. I tried to look away from his eyes but I couldn't.

"Didn't you like it just a little bit?"

I didn't say anything. I couldn't say anything.

"Come on Jesse, you can admit it. It's only me and you here." Those blue dancing eyes bore into me until I had to look away.

"I got sick and scared is what I got," I said.

His face changed into an expression of mock sadness, then he laughed. "Liar," he said.

"Come on." Then I found him turning me around with his plaster cast on my back, and we walked in silence for a while until we arrived at his front gate. I realised he didn't plan on going any further.

"So that's it? I mean you're just going? Just like that? You're just going to leave me?"

He looked at me again and the light was gone from his eyes this time. They were cold and dark.

"Don't be like this Jesse."

"Like what?" The anger I'd bottled up over the week suddenly burst out again.

"*Are you for real?* You fucked everything up and now you're just gonna leave us here?"

"It's not forever Jesse. We just can't be those three guys for a while. Trust me."

"So how long's a while? How long's a while John?"

But he didn't answer, instead he swung the gate shut.

"How long's a while?" I said again. I thought he wasn't going to answer me, but maybe he saw that I wouldn't have left. I'd just have stayed there, screaming the same question over and over.

"When the time's right I'll call for you. Just keep your head down and your mouth shut." He backed away from the gate, then raised his good hand and held his whole arm straight, pointing right at me.

"I know I can trust you Jesse," he said. "Don't let me down."

thirty-seven

I DIDN'T SEE or hear from John again in six years. I picked up rumours of course, especially early on, that he'd joined another school in London, that he took his exams early and started working for his dad. But after a while even the rumours dried up. So it was a surprise when John's name came up again. Even more so because I read it in the papers.

Things had moved on a bit here of course. I didn't do too well at school after what happened at Hanging Rock, so I was working full time at the campsite by then. I still hung out with Darren and he was working too, fixing engines or something at the garage in the village. We'd stopped missing John by then, at least, we'd stopped wondering about him, and talking about him. But we still felt his absence. Every night that we just sat about reading surf magazines in the caravan. Every weekend when we waited in vain for something exciting to happen.

It was Mum who saw it, a small photograph in one of those magazines you get free with the Sunday papers. There was an article about the actress, Sienna Rowlands - this was before the tits-out photo-spreads in the lad's mags, she was known then for doing those films about the teenage detective - anyway the magazine talked about how she was dating a mysterious, handsome young man. It printed a photo, and Mum showed it to me since it looked a lot like John.

The photo was taken in the street, outside 'her London home'. The couple were holding hands and she was looking towards a shop window, so you couldn't even see who she was. But he was looking straight towards the camera. His clothes were different. He looked like one of those fashion victims we used to laugh about, with expensive jeans and a surfer t-shirt. His hair had grown long and was styled into a blond wave. We always had this thing about hair. If there was ever anything on TV or a movie about surfers they'd always have long blond hair, but real surfers never did. The thing was long hair would get in your eyes, and it would take ages to dry once you got out the water, and the salt would make it go all crusty. So we'd always kept our hair short. But there John was looking every inch the fake surfer.

But apart from that it was clearly John, the same square jawline, those same clear blue eyes. And whether he'd worked on the look or not, he did look like a film star's boyfriend, whoever wrote the article thought so anyway. They tried to get Sienna to talk about him but she refused. She wouldn't even say what his name was. The article wrote it up like this: *"Sienna giggles coyly when asked about her new, and completely gorgeous, beau - but all she will say is they've been together a few months and they're very happy. Lucky Girl..!"*

It felt weird as hell, seeing him in that photograph and I thought about it the whole afternoon. I was serving in the shop but it wasn't camping weather, so we weren't busy. I don't think a single person came in, so I just sat there, wondering what his life was like. How he might have met that girl from the *Teenage Detective* films. And what they might be doing, right at that moment, when I was surrounded by boxes of cornflakes and buckets and spades. I was still thinking about it later too, when Darren came round after work. We sat in the caravan drinking beers and not talking, just like we'd done the night before. And the night before that.

Maybe that's why I got a bit obsessed with searching for more information on what John was up to those days. I didn't have much else to do.

We still sold magazines and newspapers in the campsite shop, so it was easy enough for me to scan through them every day. I'd make a pile and work my way through them, ignoring the news pages and going straight to the gossip parts, I was looking for anything I could find on Sienna Rowlands. Mostly there wasn't anything, but every now and then she'd get a mention, or a photo. She'd be outside a nightclub, getting out of a taxi in a little dress and high heels, or with her arm around someone else who was famous. I soon learnt Sienna wasn't the sort of girl to miss out if there was a party happening anywhere in London. And she seemed to be linked in some way to nearly every film that was coming out. Everything I found I cut out and kept in a box under my bed. I hid it because I didn't want Mum to get the wrong idea and think I was using those pictures for jerking off.

This way I managed to piece together a few details about John. It was *The Sun* which first found out a name for '*Sienna's Fella*' - that's what they had been calling him. What they wrote about him didn't make much sense though. It said he was the son of a property developer but it also made him out to be some sort of business genius or something. It talked about how much his company had grown since he'd taken over, as if that was all down to John, when really he'd just been given it all from his dad. And whoever wrote it was more interested with his looks and that long blond hair than checking their facts. A few weeks after his name was out there Sienna did a full interview where she 'revealed all' about how they met, at a party somewhere, and how much in love they were. She moaned that he was always working but she said he made it up to her by taking her away to all these tropical places and teaching her to surf.

My box of cuttings grew quite a bit when her next film came out. It was some arty thing where she had her kit off more than she had it on. I watched it a couple of times but I couldn't understand it. But some people must have liked it since she got some award. I saw John in the background when they gave it out in some big ceremony somewhere. He was sitting at a table in this flash dinner jacket and people were clapping and patting him on the back like he'd done something clever.

For some reason I never told Darren, but he found out soon enough anyway. I remember it was raining hard. Darren came into the caravan soaking wet. He'd come straight from work, but he didn't have his normal bags from the takeaway and the off license. Instead he just had this magazine. And he was upset, you could always tell with him. He didn't even sit down, he just thrust this magazine under my nose.

"You seen this?"

I didn't say anything but took the magazine from him. It was one of those hundred-most-beautiful women features you get in mens' magazines. I looked at Darren and shrugged, and he just said:

"Go on, read it."

So I scanned through the women in their underwear and swimsuits. It didn't take me long to find her, a new entry in at number thirty six. The way she looked in the picture I'd have put her a little higher than that.

"This?"

"Read it," Darren said.

"I just have."

"No *read* it." Darren wasn't great with reading and writing. So I read it out loud.

"Sienna Rowlands: The hotter-than-hot actress from the *Teenage Detective* series and now star of arthouse sensation *The Black Hole.* Sienna is also developing a career as a model and it's easy to see why with such fine attributes. But before you get too excited, Sienna is in a serious relationship with millionaire businessman John Buckingham."

"That's John."

"I know."

"They said so at work. Dan was talking about the girl who was in *Teenage Detective,* that she was going out with someone from round here, and Lloyd said he didn't believe him, so Dan brought this in to prove it and he showed it to Lloyd... And that John they're talking about, that's John. That's *our* John."

"I know."

"And it says he's a millionaire."

"Yeah, I know. "

"And it says he's going out with the *Teenage Detective* girl."

"Yeah."

"I always really liked the *Teenage Detective* girl."

I looked at Darren. "I know Darren, I know."

But I didn't resent John's success, not at that stage. OK, maybe I didn't exactly like how I was the one stuck in the campsite with Darren, looking at the pictures of John's girlfriend in her underwear, and reading about the parties they both went to. And maybe you might think me pretty naive, but at that point I still believed what he told me that day when we walked in his garden. About how us splitting up was only temporary. I mean it had to be right. With what we'd shared together, with what we knew about him. So I didn't resent his success, the higher he climbed the better it was going to be when he called for me. I saw from the papers that Sienna had some pretty gorgeous friends. Soon John would be introducing me to them. Soon I'd be going to those parties. I'd be in those photographs of laughing, smiling beautiful people in the VIP sections of nightclubs.

So I didn't resent John, instead I started waiting for the call. Every time the phone rang I felt a rush of nervous anticipation, wondering if it was him. Every time a car pulled up in the campsite I'd wonder if it might be some flash sports car with him in, come to pick me up. But it never was.

Then, about seven years after what happened at Hanging Rock, I finally did see him. I was walking down the high street in Llanwindus, and he stepped out of a shop, nearly stepped right into me, a bottle of wine in his hand, wearing this smart suit with ironed creases. His hair was pulled back from his face and held in a pony tail behind him. He had no chance to avoid me, and just stood there staring for a moment, then finally said 'Hi'. He gave me this smile with teeth that were too white.

"Jesse? Is that you? Man how you been?"

There was enthusiasm in his voice but I'd caught how his eyes had searched for a way to move past me before the charm had clicked in.

"OK, I guess."

"What you doing with yourself? Here, help me with this." He thrust the wine into my hands and patted his jacket pockets until he found a set of keys. A white Range Rover with blacked-out windows half blocking the pavement winked its orange lights at us.

"Climb in, let's have a chat."

He went round to the driver's side and I opened the door to reveal a cream leather interior. I was wearing a set of overalls from the site, they had the name of the site embroidered on them, and they weren't exactly clean so I tried to brush myself down before getting in.

"Shut the door," he said, and I swung it closed, trapping me in luxury.

"You still working at the campsite then? Thought you'd have moved on or something,"

"Nah, not really," I said, and it kind of died in the air between us, so I added "I'm thinking about college though," even though this wasn't true.

"Oh yeah?" He didn't try to hide his lack of interest.

Despite everything, the way we'd met, how obvious it was that he hadn't meant to see me, it still occurred to me that this was the moment I'd been waiting for. I didn't know how it was going to work, just that I had to somehow keep the conversation going.

"So I saw you on TV a while back. The Oscars or something."

His forehead furrowed in slight confusion. "I think you mean the BAFTAs. With Sienna right?" Then his face broke into a smile. "That was a fucking night that was." I thought for a moment he was going to tell me about it, but he lapsed back into silence.

"She's nice. Sienna I mean," I said. "I mean she looks nice." I got flustered since he knew I hadn't met her, and I thought he might be thinking I meant she was good for jerking off over or something like that. My face began to burn red.

"Yeah. She's OK." he said and then seemed to think about it for a while. Eventually he went on.

"You got yourself a bird Jesse?"

"Nah. Not really."

"No?" He looked over at me, one eyebrow raised.

"I mean yeah, loads of birds, just nothing serious. You know?" I took a risk and tried a hint. "I mean there's nothing tying me down here, is what I mean." After I said this he looked forwards again and didn't speak for a while, and I wondered what life would be like working with John in London. I thought of myself with a girl like Sienna. There was one of her friends I saw her with in lots of pictures, a dark-haired girl. I liked the thought of her.

"I was just back to see Dad." he said at last, still staring forwards out of the windscreen. He put his hands on the padded steering wheel like he wanted to get moving. The arm of his suit jacket slipped back to reveal this expensive-looking watch. I was reading the situation so wrong I was still thinking how in just a few months maybe I'd have a watch like that.

"Yeah, I'm sort of hanging out, waiting to see what comes up." I tried again.

Then his phone rang and he looked at the screen. He made this clicking sound as an apology, then he answered it and had some pointless conversation with someone called Brad.

"Sorry mate, that was just Brad," he said when they'd arranged to do lunch when he was next in town.

"No worries."

"So, you're doing well then? That's good. That's good to hear."

"Yeah. Real good." Suddenly it occurred to me I had to reassure him - remind him - just how trustworthy I was, how I could be relied upon in a crisis.

"I'm just, you know, keeping an eye on things. Making sure no one does anything stupid. You know, Darren or whatever."

His eyes narrowed. "Keeping an eye on what?"

"Making sure Darren doesn't, you know, doesn't mention anything to anyone."

He didn't say anything but then he raised one of his fingers to his lips and shushed me and really gently shook his head.

I gave him a grin. "Hell yeah sorry. There's nothing to mention is there?"

We both fell quiet and he put both hands back on the wheel. Then he sniffed loudly like there was something stuck in his throat.

"And Darren? You still see much of him?"

Before I could answer his phone rang again.

"Shit," he said this time, then: "Jesse mate this one's a business call. I gotta take... Would you mind?"

"No, I got it. I understand." I opened the door and stepped outside, and John didn't start speaking until I'd shut the door again. There was a little wall by the car so I sat down on it, thinking he'd invite me back in when the call was done. As I sat there I even wondered if he maybe wanted me out cos he was going to ask whoever it was on the business call where I could be given a job. I mean clearly we hadn't finished speaking, and that's how fucking deluded I was at that point. But then about five minutes later the engine started and he revved it up hard and then he just drove away. He just left me there, sitting on the wall and fucked off again. I couldn't see him because the glass was all blacked out. But I'd been inside. I knew he could see me sitting there.

thirty-eight

I KNEW THEN that John was never going to call for me. I had to give up the little fantasy that had grown in my head, that someone was going to save me and take me away from my life. And the ironic thing was, once I'd stopping thinking that was going to happen, it did.

It was seven years since we brought the Hanging Rock down, and I couldn't believe all that time had gone. All I'd really done was hang around the campsite. Even Darren was getting ahead of me, he'd done some exams through the garage, he was qualified now. And Mum had been nagging me for years to get out and do one of those adult education courses, or do anything really. Just to get on with my life. So after that time I met John, something made me sign up.

The main town around here is about ten miles away, and the courses were there, in the draughty basement of the council offices. Most of the students were old, you know, in their thirties or forties, a right bunch of fuck-ups really. The teacher told us to call him Paul. I think this was to make it seem different to a school, but whether that was for our benefit or his I'm not sure, since Paul wouldn't have lasted five minutes in a real school. He was really skinny and he spoke with a girl's voice. He had a beard, maybe to make him look more manly, it hadn't worked. Paul was such an obvious wuss I'd have walked out if I hadn't sat myself so far from the door. But then I'd have missed her walking in.

She had long red hair. Bright red, not ginger, the sort that's dyed rather than natural. She was wearing this horrible long skirt with embroidered flowers and leaves on it, and big lace-up Dr Martin boots. She sat down near the front of the classroom and at first she ignored me, but after Paul made everyone introduce themselves to the class she kept turning around and glancing back at me. She was pretty too. I mean not really pretty, John wouldn't have looked twice at her, but she had nice eyes, and she could smile a nice sarcastic smile. I would have walked out that class if she hadn't walked in, but with her sitting there, I stayed.

It wasn't till after the lesson that she spoke to me. I was waiting for the bus back to Llanwindus, and I was thinking adult education probably wasn't for me when she came walking past pushing this old bicycle.

"Hey you," she said. It was only me there, so I guessed she meant me. I nodded back.

"You're that moody guy who was sitting at the back and didn't talk to no one." She pushed her hair out of her face. She had brown eyes. Up close they still looked pretty.

"Yeah maybe."

"Hi moody guy." She raised a hand from the bike and waggled her fingers.

"Hi," I said back.

She watched me for a bit.

"Angel."

"What?"

"That's my name. I'm Angel."

"Oh. Hi Angel."

She stood again just watching me, until I realised.

"I'm Jesse," I said.

"I know. You said so in class, remember? When our *class leader* got us to introduce ourselves." That was what he'd called himself, instead of a teacher. She smiled the same sarcastic smile I'd seen earlier.

"Doesn't sound like you were paying much attention."

"Well it was a bit boring."

"Paul's a twat isn't he?"

"He looks like a twat."

"Everyone there's a twat."

I couldn't think of anything to say to that, and I thought she was going to walk on, but she didn't.

"Do they make you come here too?"

"Who?"

"Dole Office. I have to attend the whole course or they stop my benefits."

"Really? That's shit," I said.

"Very shit. So do they send you too?"

"No," I said. I thought about saying my mum sent me, but that didn't sound very cool, and then I was saved by the bus coming.

It wheezed to a stop a few steps in front of us but I didn't move.

"That your bus then?"

"Yeah."

"You gonna get on it?"

"Yeah probably." I was struggling for something to say, something memorable. But nothing was coming. Fortunately Angel was a bit more straightforward than me.

"Or you could come to mine and get wasted? It's just down the road."

I had to struggle to keep the shock off my face. "Yeah OK," I said with a locked jaw.

The bus stayed empty and the driver gave me a dirty look as we walked away, her rusty bicycle clanking away between us.

We went back to her place. As we were walking along I was pretty sure 'come and get wasted' meant the same as what people in films meant when they say 'come in for coffee', so when we got into her crowded little hallway, I wondered if I should just jump on her there. But she'd brought her bike in with her, and that would have made it pretty awkward. Then she showed me into the little lounge and I saw she really did mean 'come and get wasted'.

We sat on her little sofa and she pulled out this plastic bag with cloudy yellow crystals in it and she chose a couple to put into her pipe. Then she put the lighter to the bowl and lit it, while pulling the smoke hard into her mouth. It was almost all gone when she passed it to me and the smoke was sitting at the top of the room like a cloud. I wasn't even sure what it was, but I figured I had to do some too if I still wanted to be staying there that night, so I took the lighter and copied what she'd done. Within seconds the room, the whole fucking *world,* melted away as if my eyes were gas-torches and everything I looked at burnt in front of me. I don't know if it was seconds or minutes later I managed to speak.

"What the fuck?" I coughed.

"Isn't it *amazing*?" She leaned in towards me. "It makes you go for ages."

I just sat there panting with the room coming and going whenever it wanted. Then she leaned over and put her hand on my cock. I tried to put my hands onto her, to feel for her breasts but my arms were moving real slowly, like I was swimming though honey. Then there was a noise in the hallway and this head appeared round the door while I still held my arms out, like I was pretending to be some sort of zombie.

"Hi Angel - Oh hi."

"Hi Meg. Jesse, this is Megan, my housemate," Angel said. She'd slipped back across to her side of the sofa and her voice still sounded normal. I wasn't even sure if Megan was real or a hallucination. But I nodded hello to it and managed to get my arms back down.

"I'm going to cook some pasta, do you want some?" Her eyes took in the meth pipe which had found its way onto the coffee table, and I thought I saw a slight frown pass her face.

"No thanks. We're alright here aren't we Jesse?"

Megan walked through to the kitchen and started banging around before I could answer, and when I looked back at Angel she gave me a naughty smile then fished out another good-sized rock from her little bag.

I can't remember how many we ended up smoking but I was way too fucked up to have sex with Angel after that. Megan came in for a bit and ate her pasta from a bowl on her knees, she didn't seem to notice I was basically comatose. When I woke up it was the morning and I was still on the sofa. Alone.

My head hurt and my mouth felt like someone had laid carpet on my tongue and nailed it down. But worst of all I assumed I'd blown it with Angel. I forced myself up and went to the kitchen for a drink of water. I thought I'd sneak out quietly. I'd ditch the course and go back to working at the campsite. I couldn't come to town again. But then Angel came in. She was barefoot, wearing a big t-shirt with Mickey Mouse on the front and nothing else but a pair of orange pants. I saw them when she bent over to get something from the fridge. I don't know if she meant it to be sexy but it sure as hell was. When she straightened back up and I'd dragged my eyes back to her face she was holding half a joint, and her eyes twinkled with success. She lit it up and then holding it in her mouth she took my hand and led me out of the kitchen. We edged past her bike in the hallway and went up the narrow stairs and into her room.

It was like a weird purple cavern, filled with stuff, feathers dangling from the ceiling, candles, trippy psychedelic posters and purple cushions and teddy bears everywhere. Everything smelt of joss sticks. I stood for a moment feeling lost then she kissed me and blew smoke deep inside me.

When the joint was finished she undid my belt and pushed my trousers to the floor. Then she pulled her t-shirt up over her head and she had nothing on underneath but those orange pants and she grabbed my hands and put them on her tits.

The meth hadn't totally worn off and she was right. I did last for ages. We fucked on her single bed against the wall. At first we were surrounded by all these teddies, but one by one they fell onto the floor, till it was just me and her, with her legs spread so wide they nearly touched both walls of the room at once.

Angel confused Darren. She and me were together a lot after that, and he didn't understand why I suddenly wasn't in the caravan when he turned up most evenings, plastic bag of beers in hand. Darren confused Angel too. He was too slow to follow her caustic comments when she came down to visit. She liked to get stoned in the sea air, she just didn't see why we had to wait until Darren had finished his six pack before we could pull the little bed down and get the old van creaking. I thought at first there might be some future in Darren and Megan, it turned out she wasn't a hallucination, and she was ugly enough to be just Darren's type, if he really had a type. But when I mentioned it to Angel she just lifted her eyebrows and said *"Megan? Darren?"* and I knew I'd got that wrong. And slowly Darren got the message and didn't turn up every night, and I could sense the balance of my life had shifted. I'd started on a new path.

And who knows? If things had just stayed as they were for a little while longer my whole life might have got established on this new path. A path that had nothing to do with Darren and John and all the shit that had happened at Hanging Rock. Maybe if I'd stayed on it long enough I'd have got to a point where there was no way back. But fate wasn't having that. It played its ace card. It made something happen that forced me right back onto the path that led ultimately to John. Maybe I'm kidding myself now if I thought there was ever any other way.

It seemed to me to come out of the blue, but when I thought about it Mum had told me lots about the pains she was having in her armpit. When she finally went to the doctor he had her drive right to the hospital in the city that same day. They told her the lump in her breast was the biggest they'd ever seen. I think they were quite impressed in a way. The scan showed the cancer had already spread to her lungs, her heart and her kidneys. They asked if she wanted a prognosis and when she said 'yes' they told her she had a thirty percent chance of being alive in six weeks.

She'd always said the women in her family were tough but didn't last long. Her mother was dead by sixty, her mother before her too, so I suppose Mum had lived her life expecting it. It still came as a shock though. Two months later she would be dead.

And the funny thing was, while Mum was dying, it was Darren who understood, not Angel. She thought me and her smoking a big bowl of crystal meth would sort things out. But Darren came and talked to Mum. He sat with her and talked about times when we were kids. The times she'd shouted at us for ripping up the grass skidding our bikes. The times we'd brought flatties back from the pier and she'd cooked them. And when he talked like that she smiled through the pain. And even I, fucked up on the dope like I was then, I could see that was a good thing.

It was Darren's idea to tell John. He convinced himself that John would want to know, because of the way they'd always got on through the years. At first I said no. I was still pissed off with him for what happened in the Range Rover, but in the end I agreed. Mum had always liked John, it might be nice for her to see him one more time. But then I didn't have any contact details for him, so I had to go to his dad's house to get them. Then for a few weeks I just sat there with John's address written on a scrap of paper in my room. By the time I got to sending him a letter, it was a bit late to ask him to come and see Mum before she died. Because she was already dead.

thirty-nine

ANGEL STAYED OVER with me at the campsite the night before the funeral. It was the first time she slept in the house instead of the caravan and we made the most of it. But Darren turned up before breakfast, and right from the off they were getting on each other's nerves. We spent the day killing time, the two of them bickering and dipping into Angel's big bag of grass.

The church was depressing. It wasn't quite just the three of us, but we didn't even fill half of one side and the vicar didn't know who we were. There were a few ladies from the village that Mum had got to know. Gywnn, the old surfer with the longboard came as well, but that was it. John didn't come of course. I kept looking towards the back of the crematorium in case he was going to come in late, but he never did.

It didn't matter. Even in his absence, it was John we ended up talking about back at the house. I had the fire lit and Angel was curled up on the sofa, her long skirt stretched tight over her legs, and just her orange socks visible. Darren was in the armchair, his face both angry and sad, watching the logs as they burnt. It was Darren that brought the subject up.

"I really thought he'd come," he said, not taking his eyes off the fire. "Or send flowers or a note or something? You're meant to do that at least. Why didn't he do that?"

I shrugged and joined Angel on the sofa, letting her rest her legs on my lap. Normally I'd have liked this, but her legs felt heavy, I thought about dumping them on the floor. "We've not seen him in years. What did you expect?"

"After what you did for him Jesse? I expect a bit more than this."

"He was probably busy." I was tired and stoned and I glanced at Angel, but she didn't seem to be interested.

"Yeah. Probably busy with his film star girlfriend."

Darren grabbed the poker from the fire tools set and started stabbing at the logs.

I ignored him and looked again at Angel, but she was watching now with more interest. She swung her legs off me and pulled herself more upright on the sofa.

"So is it really true then?" She asked. "You two properly knew John Buckingham when he lived here?"

We'd never properly talked about John by then, but most people in the village knew about him by now. People who didn't really know him I mean. They saw him in newspapers with his film star girlfriend. People were proud that he came from around here.

"We still do know him," Darren said.

"Obviously," she said. She rolled her eyes.

"What's that mean?"

"Obviously you know him really well. That's why he's here with his whole entourage."

I just watched the fire eating through its meal of logs.

"We do know him," Darren said. "We know him better than anyone."

"What does *that* mean?"

"We know things about him that no one else knows." Darren said.

Angel laughed. "What? Like the time you all wanked onto a digestive playing soggy biscuit?"

"No, like…" Darren started to say, but I cut into him.

"Hey, Darren, put another log on the fire will you?" I stared at him, a warning to shut up.

"Go on then," Angel said, after he'd thrown the log on and a million sparks had spiralled their way up the chimney. "What do you know about John Buckingham? If there really is something, you could sell it to the papers. It's pretty clear he's not really your mate after all. You might as well make some money out of him."

Darren glanced at me but kept quiet.

"Come on Darren. Either you know something or you're full of shit. Which is it? What's the big secret?"

Darren didn't look at her when he replied. He dropped his head and mumbled, something. He spoke so quietly I barely caught what he said.

"We went surfing together."

Angel heard it though. She raised her hands to her face like she'd seen a ghost.

"Oooo. Big fucking story Darren. Hold the front pages." She looked at me for encouragement and I could see Darren opening his mouth to say something else so I had to jump in.

"Fuck's sake Angel, will you just leave it? It's not really the night for this." This pissed her right off, and she snatched her legs away from my lap, then grabbed her dope from the table and announced she was going to bed. From the way she said it, I wasn't welcome to come with her, so I let her go.

"I don't get you sometimes Jesse," Darren said when Angel's banging upstairs had stopped. "Don't you ever feel betrayed?"

"What?"

"Betrayed. We help him out like that, and then he just disappears. The next thing we hear he's some big shot with no time left for us. Doesn't that piss you off a little bit?"

I sighed. "A little bit."

"Sometimes that pisses me off." Darren said.

"Yeah well there's nothing we can do about it." I wanted to change the subject. Or just sit there staring at the fire.

"Especially since it wasn't even an accident."

"What?"

"At Hanging Rock. He made us help him out like that and it wasn't even an accident."

"Course it was."

"No it wasn't." He shook his head.

"You didn't even see it happen," I said.

"I didn't need to. I thought about it. You don't stab someone like that by accident. It's obvious."

"John said the guy lunged at him. It was slippery. John said it was an accident."

"Yeah, that's what he said. But I don't think what he said adds up. At least it doesn't to me."

"He was in shock about what he'd done. He'd broken his fucking arm Darren. He was in pain, in shock."

"Well what about when you went to see him? Before he went to London. That we all just had to be apart for a little bit. That was bullshit too. He didn't even bother coming to see me." He shut up for a bit and I thought he might drop it, but he didn't.

"It's not fair Jesse. It's not fair what he's doing with his life and what we're doing with ours. Not with what we know about him."

I could get a sense with Darren sometimes. This wasn't something he'd just thought of. He'd been working up to this for some time. A long time. I was glad that Angel had gone to bed.

"Yeah well like I said. I didn't really see it either. I was looking at you when it happened, so I don't know."

"But you do now, because I've told you."

I said nothing and for a time I thought he'd dropped it. We had a few drinks and watched the fire. But all the time I could feel Darren watching me. Then he started again.

"It wasn't no accident Jesse."

"What does it matter anyway now? It's not like we can do anything," I snapped.

He leaned forward, swirling his drink around in his glass.

"He stitched us up. Making us help him like that. Making us drag the guy's body over the rocks, driving his fucking car down to Cornwall and blowing up the Hanging Rock. We couldn't go to the cops after that. We didn't do anything and he made us as guilty as he was."

"Well… There's nothing we can do now."

"And then he couldn't even be bothered to come for your mum's funeral. We help him out and he couldn't even come for that. Didn't even send a letter to say he was sorry. No flowers, no…"

"Maybe he was busy." I cut in.

Darren considered this for a good while, nodding his head gently the whole time.

"Yeah, busy. Probably."

"I don't get why you don't see it Jesse. He owes us. He owes us big time."

He looked at me, his little eyes all hard.

"He owes us Jesse. And I reckon we should do something about it."

He told me his plan that same night. It wasn't sophisticated. It didn't even make much sense. We were supposed to write him a letter, telling him we're going to the cops unless he paid us. Darren didn't know how much. Just enough money so we could go and do whatever we wanted.

At first I didn't think he was serious. It was so stupid, but I knew him too well. It made sense to him.

"How can we go to the police? When we were involved? They'll put us in prison too."

He shook his head. "Not if we both tell them the same story, that we saw John do it, then they'd put him in prison. We'd be on the witness protection scheme or something."

I looked at him, sitting there leaning forward over the table. "So you want to blackmail John?"

He looked surprised by this, as if it hadn't occurred to him that what he was suggesting might have a name. Then he nodded.

"Blackmail. Yeah. That's right."

I stayed quiet.

"And he'll do it, he'll pay us Jesse. He'll have to, cos of all the things he would lose."

Still I didn't answer him.

"And just think what we could do with money Jesse. We could go away. We could move out to Indonesia or something, just you and me. We could open a bar by the beach. Just you and me Jesse."

But I just got up and went to bed.

forty

I SHOULD TELL you something about Darren's bar. According to him, that's what we were saving for. He'd read a story in a magazine once about two guys who moved to Indonesia and opened a beach bar. They went surfing in the days, and they worked at the bar every night. He'd been going on about it for years. How we'd surf these tropical waves, and serve cold beers to beautiful girls all night. Sometimes he'd even adjust the daydream to allow Angel to fit in with it. In his fantasy she wasn't allowed behind the bar, but he could just about cope with the idea of her wiping the tables down.

Sometimes I went along with the daydream, but other times I told him to get real. You had to have loads of money to do something like that. I never had any money, and even though he was working, he never actually saved anything. Whatever he got paid from the garage he spent right away in the pub or at the off-licence. Darren's Indonesian bar fantasy was just that, a fantasy, and at first I figured his blackmail idea fell into the same category.

But I also figured that with Mum gone, quite a lot was going to change. It's not like I wanted Mum to die or anything, but now she was gone the campsite was mine. Which meant I could sell it and do something else. I never seriously considered Indonesia, but I did think I could do something with my life. Maybe I could follow John's path and go to London. Anything to get me out of Llanwindus. But I got a nasty shock a few days later. I looked through the accounts of the campsite. And even though I wasn't great at maths I could see it wasn't that good. I finally understood why Mum had climbed into her overalls to sort out the drains instead of phoning a plumber for all those years. Ten years after she'd bought the place, we still owed more on the campsite than it was worth.

If that was depressing, it soon got worse. With Mum gone the work began to pile up pretty quick. For a while I did what I could, but it was impossible. I was running the shop and checking the campers in and out, while Angel was padding round in her bare feet, puffing on a joint and helping herself from the shelves. There was the grass to cut, all the stock taking, the fucking showers that never ran hot. And you've got to remember I was the owner of the site by then. I wasn't going to be the one cleaning the toilets too. Anyway, we seemed to get a run of people who just complained all the time, so one day I just closed the gates and didn't let anyone else in.

Except Darren. He kept coming. And whenever Angel was out of earshot he never let up on his new idea.

He tried to draft the blackmail letter. He showed it to me and I could see it was hopeless. He wasn't completely illiterate, but writing wasn't his strength, and this wasn't the sort of letter where you could get help at the local library. But even allowing for all the mistakes he'd made, there was something convincing about the letter. When I managed to understand Darren's points at justifying *why* John owed us so much, I had to admit, it made sense. We *had* helped John a lot that day, and it *was* all John's fault. And, unlike him, for some reason we hadn't been able to shake it off so easily. It *had* affected us. We'd both fucked up our exams soon after it happened, it's hard to give a fuck about maths and shit when you're worried the police are going to arrest you for murder. John did owe us something for that. And now John had so much. And we weren't asking for a fortune. Just enough to get us set up somewhere. Make a fresh start. Then John could forget about us. He wouldn't have to worry about how we were getting on. It made sense when you thought about it.

And on top of all that I also figured out that if *I* didn't help Darren write his letter, then he'd eventually get someone else to help him. He'd promise someone from the garage or the pub a share of the money, cos he was easily stupid enough to do that. And if I let that happen we could lose control of the whole situation real quick. And I suppose I thought that if Darren was going to get some money, then I should get some. That was only right. That was only fair. After all I drove the car for John. I helped him more than Darren did. So in the end, I didn't really have a choice. I guess that's how I ended up helping Darren to write his blackmail letter.

Darren agreed to have it all done in his name. He even wanted it that way. Since Mum had died it was like he wanted John to know how much he hated him. He really wanted John to believe it was just Darren screwing him over. Like he was smart enough to do that. That was fine with me, but when I looked John up on the internet and found out how much he was worth, I told Darren we had to ask for more money. And he was OK with that too.

We were excited the night we finished the letter and put it in the envelope. I wrote his name on the front and then added *strictly private and confidential, to be opened only by Mr John Buckingham* underneath. I underlined the *only* three times to make sure it went right to him. We took it to the postbox in the village and bought eight cans of beer to celebrate. Darren spent the night talking about how we were finally going to Indonesia. For a little while I started to believe it too.

The letter was pretty simple. It told John to pay the money directly into Darren's account, a one-off payment to buy his silence for helping to cover up his crime. If John didn't pay, Darren would go to the police and tell them everything. But we were convinced he would pay. And when he did, Darren would give half to me. I'd tell Angel the money came from the campsite. She didn't know it was in debt at that point.

Every night that week we checked Darren's account on the internet, each time expecting to see the money showing up, but each night it was the same. He had a few hundred quid in the account but the transactions were all the same, twenty quid at the off-licence or at the Spar. No big deposits. Darren thought the letter might have got lost in the post. I started to worry something else might have gone wrong.

Then John made his move. One night Darren didn't come around. He practically lived at the campsite by then, so I had to phone around to find where he was. Eventually I found out. Darren's brother had been killed. He'd got into a knife fight near a club in Cardiff. A knife fight for fuck's sake. Darren's brother the pacifist. The vegetarian. The biggest pussy you could ever meet. There was no way he'd got into a knife fight. It was John. This was John giving his answer to Darren. He must have slipped out into the city night and stalked Darren's brother until he left some night club, then pulled him into an alleyway and stabbed him over and over again.

But that wasn't enough for John. I got a message too. Since I'd been a bit closer to Darren for a couple of weeks Angel had been a bit pissed off with me and she'd gone back to her flat. The same day I heard about Darren's brother I got a call from Megan, Angel's housemate. She'd never called me before so I knew it had to be bad news. And it was. There was a scummy little park near their flat, and sometimes people used the toilets there to inject. Not Angel, she was never into heroin. She wasn't a junkie or anything like that. But that's where they found her anyway. She was on the floor in a cubicle, the needle was still stuck in her arm, the plunger pressed in. For once her blue lips were nothing to do with make up.

There was nothing to connect the two deaths. At least nothing we could tell the police. But we knew it was him. The knife he stabbed Ben with had an eight inch blade. It was a hunting knife, just like the one John had used at Hanging Rock all those years ago. I don't know, maybe it was even the same knife. There were no fingerprints, no other evidence, no witnesses. He must have gone from there straight to see Angel. We never told her what John was really like so it would have been easy for him to get her to follow him. I don't know how he got her to take the drugs, probably he just forced her. The toilet cubicle was open at the top, so once he'd done it he could have just climbed out. But the police didn't accept that, they said that because the door was locked it must have been an accidental overdose. They didn't care really. Good riddance. To them she was just a junkie who came from a care home and who no one was gonna miss. To me she was my only chance of ever getting away from John.

forty-one

"THAT WAS SIX months ago. It was when I finally realised what John was. The kind of person he really was. He's not like other people. He doesn't have the limits other people have." Jesse shook his head, as if he still couldn't quite believe it. "It's like something out of the movies."

The others said nothing, and after a moment Jesse went on. "I still think the guy at Hanging Rock - your husband," he glanced at Natalie, "I still think he was the first, but I know he's killed others since then, not just Angel and Ben but others as well. He likes it. It's how he gets his kicks. If you go after him you'll make yourself a target. He'll hurt you too."

Jesse sat back against his chair and it took them a moment to realise he'd finished.

"Well?" Dave spoke finally. He still sounded angry. "Is that it?"

"Yeah. That's about where we are."

"Well I'm sorry. I'm sorry to hear about all that's happened to you, but this doesn't change anything. We still have to call the police. Right now." But as sure as he sounded, he didn't touch the phone, instead he glanced over at Natalie. She didn't look back, her eyes seemed to be focussing on a small point on the far wall.

Jesse sighed, even rolled his eyes a little bit. But he sounded defeated.

"OK. Whatever. I guess it's your choice. I'm only trying to help." He gave Dave a weak smile.

"Whatever he'll do, maybe you can deal with it. You know?"

Dave glared at him and picked up his phone but he hesitated again.

"I just thought she'd want to know. What with her sister's kids and all." Jesse went on.

Dave's head snapped back around to Jesse. "You say that again I'm going to wring your filthy neck."

"Christ man, calm down. Shoot the messenger and all. I'm just trying to explain it to you." Jesse had his hands out in front of him, palms up.

"Sometimes I want to tell the police too. I want to find a way to end this nightmare. But then I think a bit more and I know I can't. The police won't believe me, they won't do anything to him, and he'll just punish me more. Maybe I'll get lucky and he'll just kill me. Maybe it won't even hurt too much. But there's other people. Darren, his mum and dad. John knows all about them. And if he wants to hurt me more, there's plenty of ways. And he won't hesitate. He doesn't *fuck around*. Don't you understand what I've been telling you?" Jesse's eyes were staring at Dave. Pleading with him.

"Look, Mr… Jesse. I understand the situation perfectly. But we cannot let a threat stop us doing the right thing - this is a police matter. I mean how do you think this is supposed to end?"

For a moment Jesse said nothing, then his shoulders slumped, and it looked like he might cry. "You're still not getting it. It's not just me now, is it? Her sister and the…"

Dave cut in quickly. "Don't you dare say that again."

"What am I gonna say?"

"You're going to spout some nonsense about Natalie's family being in danger, but it's ludicrous."

Jesse opened his mouth but didn't speak. Instead his tongue explored his teeth.

"He came to my house," Natalie said. Neither of them could tell who she was speaking to.

"After they killed Jim he came to my house and watched me. What did you say he called it? Insurance."

Jesse nodded, not taking his eyes off Dave.

There was a long silence. Eventually Jesse broke it.

"Let's try it your way. You tell the police. What are they going to do? If you manage to convince them you're not mad they *might* go and interview John Buckingham, successful businessman with a famous girlfriend. They might politely ask his side of the story. Maybe they'll show him photographs like you've shown me. Does he know Jim Harrison? He'll say he's never heard of him, and he'll be convincing because believe me he can be *fucking convincing* when he lies to you. Maybe he'll call his lawyers, expensive lawyers. Maybe it'll all be so friendly he won't even need to. And when the police walk away, he'll get to work. I don't know that he'll start with the kids. Maybe he won't. Maybe he won't fuck around this time and he'll just kill us all. Move on. But I doubt it. I know John and that's not the way he works. I think he'd enjoy himself. I think he'd find where they go to school. I think he'd lure them into his car, or an old van. I think he'd gag them, tie them up. I think he'd make sure they knew they were going to die, he'd show them the knife, he'd stick it in slowly and..."

"Stop. Stop it will you? Just stop it." Natalie brought her hands from her lap and pressed them against her ears.

"Do you get it now? Do you get the problem?" Jesse was staring at Dave.

For a moment the only sound in the room was breathing. The sucking in and pushing out of air like waves on a beach. It was Dave who recovered first.

"Well if we can't go to the police, what exactly do you suggest we do about all this? We can't just walk away."

Jesse pushed his chair back and stood up. "I'm gonna make more tea," he said and he turned to the cupboards.

"I don't want more tea," Dave said, but Jesse ignored him, and began to fill the kettle. He collected the empty cups from the table without looking at them, and only when he'd dropped a fresh tea bag into each did he speak again.

"I don't know." His head was bowed, his eyes on the floor. "If I knew what to do, don't you think I'd have done it by now?" Jesse glanced over at them both and then continued. "I've thought about the police so much, I've even picked up the phone, written them letters, but I've always held back because I know how it ends that way. I *know* John. I grew up with him."

The kettle boiled and in silence Jesse filled the cups, then fished out the tea bags with his finger, and splashed in some milk. He put a cup each in front of Natalie and Dave.

"You really want to know what to do? You gotta kill him. That's the only way to stop him. You wanna go back to your lives and not worry that John Buckingham's gonna break into your house one night and cut your throat? You go to the police you *make* that happen. You wanna stop him, the only way is to put him in the ground."

He stopped and stared directly at Natalie. "I'm sorry for what I've done and sorry that you're involved, but that's the truth of it."

She saw now that he had a single tear upon his cheek. It looked strange and unreal, and as it fell to the ground he sniffed and looked away.

There was a noise outside, a low hum that Dave recognised first. He got up and went to the window as the sound clarified into rotor blades chopping heavily through the salty air. For the first time Jesse looked confused.

"What's that? What's going on. You haven't called the police already?" He said.

"Stay here," Dave practically growled at Jesse. "Natalie, come with me. I'm going to go and help him down."

Silently she followed and they went outside. The chopper was hovering over the car park, but the pilot saw Dave, who was making signals with his arms. Natalie didn't understand the exchange, in truth she paid little attention but it resulted in the helicopter landing gently on the driveway leading to the house, where there was plenty of room. Only when it was down did she notice Jesse hadn't stayed inside but had joined them, staring wide eyed as the red and blue painted machine wound down its engines, its skids at right angles to the road. Eventually the rotors slowed so that you could make out each blade as it spun around. Then finally they stopped altogether and the only sound was the quiet whines and ticks of the machine as it settled on its perch.

"What's that?" asked Jesse.

"It's a helicopter," said Natalie.

"I know, I mean what's it doing here?"

"It's Dave's. We're going to use it to fly home. Dave's business is a helicopter firm. Jim's was too," she added the last part as an afterthought.

Jesse looked incredulous. "That guy can fly a helicopter?"

Dave walked back to them and led Natalie away so they were out of Jesse's earshot.

"I'll give Damien the car. Then we've got the chopper for as long as we want. It's not needed for a couple of days now." He looked at Jesse to make sure he hadn't followed again. "What do you want to do about this?"

"I don't know," she replied. "It's all a bit much to take in isn't it?"

Dave nodded.

"I suppose, you know, since we've waited this long so we might as well not call the police right away. Let's think about it first."

Dave said nothing and his gaze stayed on Jesse. He stood half way between the house and the helicopter, he seemed unable to take his eyes of the machine. Then he gave Natalie a curt nod.

They gave no explanation to Damien, and he didn't even look curious. As the firm's most junior pilot there was nothing unusual in swapping one aircraft for another, or indeed for a car to enable his employer to run the business effectively. The three of them watched as he started the car and swung out of the car park.

And then Jesse walked up to the helicopter and put a hand out to touch its glossy paint.

"So can we go up in this now? Cos if so I can show you where he is. Where your husband's buried I mean. I was going to ask if you wanted me to take you there, but it's an hour's walk and we wouldn't get there before dark. But in that it would take no time."

Dave glanced at Natalie and read something there that made him nod. "I don't know if we'll be able to land, we may only be able to look from the air."

"There's a big open space at the top of the cliff," Jesse said. "You could land a plane there. Easy."

"What do you think?" Again Dave spoke only to Natalie.

"I'd like to see it."

Dave gave Jesse a look of open contempt and walked over to the chopper.

They put Jesse in the back seat, cooing over the leather seats and excitedly adjusting the volume levels on the ear defenders that hung in racks from the ceiling. Dave told Natalie to keep an eye on him, then turned his attention to preparing the aircraft for flight. With the engines already warm it wasn't a long process. He glanced across at Natalie and nodded to let her know they were taking off and he pulled up on the cyclic. The helicopter rose up in a steady hover and Dave pushed it gently out towards the beach.

"I'll follow the coast south," he told Jesse through the headphones. "You tell me when we're there."

Jesse made no effort to hide his sense of amazement and delight at taking to the air above the land he was so familiar with, but Dave didn't waste time with giving him a pleasure flight. He dipped the helicopter's nose forward and settled into a flight a hundred metres above the sea keeping the rugged coast on his left hand side. A moment later Jesse's voice came through the headphones again.

"There. It's down there."

Now Dave pulled the nose up to kill their forward speed and made a left turn so the aircraft was facing the land. Ahead of them was a vee shaped inlet, a bluff of cliff on one side and leading inland from it, a heavily wooded ravine.

"There, on top of the cliffs, you can park there," Jesse's voice came again through the headphones.

They edged closer until they were in a steady hover just in front of the cliffs, Dave leaning forwards inspecting the ground.

"I thought you said it was flat?"

"Flattish."

"You could land a plane here could you?"

"It looks a bit smaller from up here. Looks a bit more overgrown as well," Jesse conceded. "How about there?" He pointed a little further inland where there was a clearing.

Dave didn't reply but he allowed the chopper to drift towards it, and then held them in a steady hover over the clearing as he looked around. He didn't look happy but he muttered that it would do. They dropped the final few feet and regained the ground with a slight bump, and when the helicopter's engines had quietened again they climbed out. Jesse walked off at once, towards the cliff edge.

"That there, that's the rockfall, you can still see it pretty clear," Jesse said when they joined him. "There's a path where we can get down."

He led and they followed down a footpath that switched back upon itself several times as it tracked down the steep ground. And although the slump of rocks to their left clearly wasn't fresh, you could see from the vegetation and the paler colour of the rocks that it was recent in geological terms. It was also huge. Hundreds of thousands of tons of rock. And if what Jesse had told them was the truth, that somewhere underneath it all was Jim, it was overwhelmingly clear he wouldn't be found. Natalie looked at it and tried to imagine a police team excavating the cliff. It was too big. It was impossible.

"You blew this all up with gunpowder?" Dave asked when they reached the bottom.

"Yeah. The Hanging Rock was up there," Jesse pointed into the air above their heads. "When it came down it took a whole section of the cliff with it. The rocks went right out into the sea. It changed the wave right away, and then over the years, it's just gotten worse. I reckon it changed the currents or something. Stopped the whole wave working." Jesse looked saddened as he spoke.

"I don't really give a fucking shit about your wave," Dave said, and then there was silence. The three of them gazed out across the slew of rocks and earth. The helicopter was still visible at the top of the slope, fifty metres above them.

"And Jim's under there." Dave went on. "Somewhere."

"Oh yeah. He's in there alright." Jesse said.

forty-two

FOR THREE DAYS neither Natalie nor Dave spoke to anyone about what they'd learnt. They didn't even speak to each other. They needed time to assimilate what they had learnt. And it was easier not to think.

But Natalie found it impossible not to think. During the day the thoughts interrupted her work. She'd find herself losing the thread of conversations with colleagues and clients. At night the first thing she did was open a bottle of wine, and when that was gone there was nothing to distract her. Nothing to deflect the thoughts. And once she began to think, her mind quickly filled itself with a strange new world of fears. Once the gears and cogs of cognition began to move, they accelerated quickly, until they were racing out of control.

She felt once again the loss of Jim. But it was not the same hurt as when he had first disappeared. The aching hollowness of not knowing what had happened to him was settled. She felt some relief that he hadn't taken his own life. She felt a hot shame that he hadn't felt forced to do so because of her actions. But she did not weep again for how her husband had died. Too much time had passed for that.

What she felt now was different. At first she could not recognise what it was, this ever growing sense, but as she sat alone and thought, whatever it was threatened to overwhelm her. Occasionally it exploded, a flash of emotion so bright it was like a bolt of lightning cracking through her brain. Eventually she realised, it wasn't pain any more, it was fear.

On the third night Dave called her and said he needed to talk. She found herself almost unable to answer, and at first nodded dumbly at the phone. Eventually she managed to reply, and half an hour later she heard his car pull to a halt in her driveway.

"He checks out," Dave said grimly, by way of a greeting. "I don't know if you've searched on him, but pretty much everything that Jesse said checks out. There is a character called John Buckingham, famous girlfriend. He comes from Llanwindus, runs a string of companies. Restaurants, hotels, that kind of thing." Dave stopped. "I know I shouldn't say this, but you look terrible."

"Thanks Dave." She half laughed, half cried.

"You don't look so great yourself."

It was true. He'd not shaved since she last saw him, his chin and jowls hung low as if pulled down by the weight of the dirty grey stubble.

"You better come in," Natalie said. She led him back into the kitchen and without offering poured him a glass of white wine.

"Thank you. I'm sorry, I should have asked. How are you?" Dave asked.

She gave a weak smile and raised her own glass to her lips, and then seemed to change her mind. "I don't know."

"I'm not sure I do either. This is a bit unreal isn't it?"

She nodded.

"I'm afraid I'm not here just to talk it through. I've found out something else. I think it's important."

She felt her heart rate increase and almost told him she didn't want to know. But she inclined her head onto one side in the lightest of shrugs, and Dave sighed before continuing, his voice quieter now.

"I tried to find out about him online. There isn't much, mostly it's about his girlfriend. It seems he's… secretive, doesn't seek out the press at all. But his company still makes the news every now and then. When it does it's usually for acquisitions. He's got a reputation for being ruthless, in business I mean."

Natalie didn't say anything, but from the look on her face this didn't surprise her.

"There's more."

"What?"

"You're not going to believe this." He sighed. "He's a client."

"What?"

"He's a client of the business. John Buckingham is a fairly regular client of ours. He's even got a flight booked for the end of next week. We're flying him to Ireland."

Natalie narrowed her eyes as if the light was hurting her.

"How? Why?"

"I don't know. It could be a coincidence. Most of his business interests are in London, but he also has some here, and in Cardiff." He shrugged. "If you're involved here and you need a helicopter, we're top of the list. But I think we also have to consider whether this could be his way of… I don't know. Keeping an eye out or something. I don't understand it though. Why take the risk of using our firm? Why would someone do that? Natalie?"

Dave wondered if she had heard him, her eyes looked to have lost focus and she stared at nothing. But then she replied.

"I've been doing some thinking too," Natalie said. She rolled her head around as if her neck hurt her. "And some research."

"Go on."

"I looked into psychopaths. Psychopathic people. They're not just something you see in horror films, they're real people. Some you get to hear about. People like Ted Bundy in the States, he killed nearly forty women before they caught him. Jeffrey Dahmer, he killed fifteen. There was a man called Gary Heidnik. He kept young women in a cellar. He took them out at night and raped and tortured them. He tortured them to death, and when they died he cooked their limbs and ate them. He fed the bones to his dogs. They're real people Dave."

When he didn't reply she went on.

"People think they're incredibly rare. And the ones like those are. They're the outliers. With most psychopaths, you just never get to hear about them. They're known as 'high-functioning psychopaths'. The high functioning part just means they're able to hide their psychopathic traits from other people. No one knows how they enjoy other people's pain. Sixty five percent of murders are never solved. Some people think that undiagnosed psychopaths account for a lot of them."

Dave said nothing.

"It's not exactly my area of expertise, but I know a little about it. Everything that Jesse described. It's extremely plausible. Christ he might have been reading it from some of the case files I see from time to time. These people, they kill, they steal, they rape… And sometimes they get caught but most often they don't because they're not panicking when they're acting, like normal people would. They don't make lots of mistakes. When they kill people they're enjoying themselves. So they get good at it. Normal people don't expect them to behave as they do. Because normal people wouldn't do what they do. What I'm saying is…"

She stopped and rubbed her face with both hands.

"What I'm saying is. If this man is a psychopath as Jesse described - and I think he is - then flying with Jim's firm, it's exactly the type of behaviour we should expect. Not to keep an eye on us as you say. Not despite the risk. He'd do it *for* the risk."

"I don't understand," Dave said after the room had fallen silent.

"Good. I'm glad. You shouldn't. A normal person shouldn't understand the motivations of a dangerous psychopath. They might have a drive to hurt or kill that makes no sense at all, to us. But to them it's all that matters."

"So what do you do, you psychologists, when a psychopath walks in looking for treatment? I mean what happens to these guys? What do we do here?"

Natalie drew a deep breath. "They don't. It doesn't happen. We see plenty of people *affected* by psychopaths, but they almost never present themselves for treatment. They don't know that they have a problem. And why would they? You know there are studies that say one in eight of chief executives of major companies and top politicians are psychopaths? I'm not saying they're necessarily killers, but they're psychopaths nonetheless. Their traits help them in life. They don't feel the same limitations normal people do. They don't come looking for help because their ability to inflict pain and suffering upon other people without feeling anything themselves is an enabling thing for them."

Dave said nothing, so she went on.

"And do you know what we say to people who have been affected by a psychopath? How we treat them?"

"How?"

"We tell them to get as far away as possible. We try to patch up what's left of their lives and tell them to run away. That's it. And now we're stuck with one. You and Elaine and me and my sister, and God knows who else, we're all stuck with one of these real life monsters, watching over us. Waiting for us to find out about him."

"So we go to the police." Dave said.

Natalie's body stiffened at the words. She shook her head.

"What do you mean? We *have* to go to the police."

"You're not understanding Dave. Jesse was right."

"Oh damn Jesse. You shouldn't be listening to that … that scumbag. He needs to be locked up too."

"No. I know you didn't like him but he's just as much a victim in this as Jim was. As we are. In a way he's more of a victim. He's lived most of his life being manipulated by this man. And he's right because he's had years to think it through…"

"No. No. You're wrong. He's wrong. He's smoked too much I don't know what, and you, you're…" Dave left the sentence unfinished and it hung there between them.

"If John Buckingham uses the firm's helicopters, then he knows all about us. He watched me when Jim went missing, so he knows about my sister and the boys. He'll know he can control me by threatening them. He'll know about you too. He'll know about your wife. He'll know about Elaine."

Dave was breathing hard, as if he'd been running.

"Then we tell the police. Dammit this is why we *have* to tell them."

"*Oh tell them what Dave*? What do we tell them? A multi-millionaire, the partner of a film star is a psychopathic murderer? And what proof do we have? Are we going to show them that rock fall? You saw it. They'll laugh at us. They'll lock *us* up."

"We can show them the bag. Jim's file shows the car was left in Cornwall."

"What does that prove? Nothing."

"Then we give them Jesse. We make him speak to them, tell them what he told us."

Natalie sighed. "Even if he would go, which I doubt given how scared he was, why would they believe him? They'll see him as just another bitter, drug addict fantasist."

"*So why do you believe him*?" Dave's voice was higher and louder than normal.

They stared at each other until Natalie looked away.

"Because I know something about these people." Natalie closed her eyes hard for a moment, and when she reopened them she looked at Dave, her voice calmed now. "OK. Say he does convince the police, it doesn't help us because there isn't enough evidence to act. So all it would do is alert Buckingham that we know about him. It's probably why he's been watching us all this time. God knows what he might do."

The way Dave was looking at her, Natalie wondered for a minute if what she was saying was crazy.

"So what then?" He said at last. "Please don't tell me you're considering Jesse's… His *solution?"*

Natalie paused before answering, and the longer the silence went on, the more ominous it sounded to her. "I'm… I'm trying to think of another way. But I'm not getting anywhere. What if there isn't another way?"

forty-three

IN THE BUILD up to the weekend the forecasts had talked of rain, but when Saturday morning arrived the sky was settled, the few clouds that hung about were wispy, high altitude affairs that the late summer sun would probably burn off. In her preparations for the party, Elaine had fretted about the weather with her husband, or at least had tried to do so - to her frustration he seemed disinterested, preoccupied by something, what it was he wouldn't say. She wondered at first if she was just imagining it. After all, he had always been less interested in the social side of life than she had.

Elaine liked to throw one good party each year. It was a habit she inherited from her parents, who had entertained throughout her childhood in a similar, if somewhat grander manner. And like her parents she would tell people - anyone who would listen really - that the purpose of the party was to share some of their good fortune with friends and family. To give something back.

Elaine grew to understand that for her mother there was another, less wholesome motive for her summer parties. They happened to allow her to show friends and family, and local councillors, prominent business people - the movers and shakers of the town - just how fortunate she had been in marrying into money. But the same could not be said for Elaine. Despite her accident Elaine did still consider herself lucky in life, and perhaps the whole experience changed her. Whatever the cause, Elaine's parties were less pretentious than her mother's, no less exclusive but aimed at a different circle. They weren't a place to be seen at, more an event to enjoy. They were just more fun. And over the years Elaine and Dave's summer party had grown into an important annual event, not just for her, but for all their friends and family.

That said, Elaine had never fooled herself that Dave entirely shared her enthusiasm. He would normally huddle up with his pilot friends, drinking beer and talking flying while she circulated, but that was OK. That was what he enjoyed. And he at least took the preparations seriously. He'd help to choose wines that were appropriate for the food. He'd see to it that the pool was cleaned. Generally he'd take an interest.

But this year, something was different. For several days Dave had been distracted and distant. And she'd hoped he would snap out of it but he'd got worse. He was totally disinterested. And it wasn't just the party, he seemed to have lost all interest in everything. He wasn't shaving, in fact he was hardly speaking to her. He was out a lot, which helped to hide it, but when he was there, it was as if he alone knew that the world was about to end. And when she asked him about it he simply denied there was anything wrong. When she pushed him - and Elaine knew how to push - he mumbled something about a problem at work. This in no way satisfied her. She had little interest in how the latest model of Eurocopter differed from its predecessor, and she'd sat through enough discussions of flight levels and rudder yaw to last her a lifetime. Nonetheless, when Dave told her not to worry because it was about the business it pissed her off. Not least because it was her father's money and connections which had helped to make the business what it was.

And this morning - the morning of the party - she finally lost patience and snapped at him. She reeled off a list of jobs he should have done and hadn't, and then wheeled herself around with an angry flourish. He muttered something in reply, she didn't catch it with the noise of the rubber wheels on the tiled floor, but five minutes later she saw that he had finally stopped what he'd been doing all morning, hiding in his study hunched over his desk. Moments later she saw he was scrubbing the barbecue griddle, the bag of charcoal at his feet. She calmed down a little. She rolled around their huge, adapted kitchen putting the finishing touches to beautifully dressed tables, loaded with canapés, flowers and rented champagne flutes. She felt both vindicated yet still dissatisfied.

Perhaps she shouldn't have shouted, but really, it had been Dave who insisted on not employing caterers for the event, and now she had to nag him to help getting things ready. And after almost ignoring her all week. But then she began to feel a little more guilt than anger. Dave wasn't given to bad moods. And she knew he worried about the business. He'd taken the whole thing on since Jim died, and it had grown so fast since then. Plus of course he found social events more stressful than she did. They weren't really his thing. Not like Jim. She stopped what she was doing and smiled. Jim. She remembered the things he'd got up to over the years. Jim liked to party. She bit her lip. Strange to think of Jim suddenly after all this time. Of course, it was probably because Natalie was coming this afternoon. With her sister too, along with the boys. They'd be, what? Nine and ten now.

Dave interrupted her thoughts by walking into the kitchen. He began folding back the doors that separated the kitchen from the patio area. In warm weather they could be pulled almost completely out of the way. It was one of the few jobs she was unable to do in the heavily adapted kitchen, but they'd drawn the line at the extra thousands to install electric ones. She decided to forgive her husband for the ill-natured exchanges of earlier. She would be understanding of how he felt, even if she didn't understand it. She smiled at him warmly.

"We should keep the main tables indoors just in case it does rain," she said.

He looked at her blankly, like he hadn't understood a word.

"What?"

Two hours later and the party was underway. The tables were now half emptied, a score of Champagne bottles stacked up empty underneath. The barbecue was alight, flickers of yellow-blue flame dancing up through the heap of coals. The band were taking a break, drinking bottled beer and talking with Damien, one of the younger pilots who seemed to know them from somewhere. Most of the guests had arrived, Elaine's neck was aching a little from having to stretch upwards to receive welcome kiss after welcome kiss, and the doorbell went again. She excused herself and spun around, propelled herself to the hall. She opened the door and held out her arms.

"Natalie, Sarah. It's great to see you."

"Hi Elaine, we're sorry we're late," Sarah said and shot a glance down to her children. The elder boy looked furiously embarrassed to be holding a bouquet of flowers. He gripped them close to his chest until his mother pushed him from behind, then he held them out to Elaine. "These are for you," he mumbled.

"Oh Daniel. They're beautiful. Come here and give me a hug." The boys took turns to do so, their awkwardness compounded by the difficulty in leaning into the chair.

"Thank you Sarah," Elaine said when it was over. "They're getting big. They're taller than me now."

Sarah looked unsure how to answer this so smiled instead, then said: "Thank you so much for inviting us. The boys are very excited about the swimming pool."

Daniel took this as a cue. "Can we go mum?"

"It's not me you need to ask. It's Auntie Elaine's house."

But Elaine didn't wait to be asked. "Have you got your swimmers?"

There was a chorus of "Yeah".

"You remember where it is?"

"I think they do," Sarah said laughing, already being pulled backwards by her children. Then she stopped laughing and added: "Will you be alright Nat?"

Until that moment there had been nothing out of place in the greeting, but Sarah asked the question with a tone of such concern that Elaine turned to Natalie in surprise. She seemed to be staring at nothing. Elaine's smile changed to a frown.

"Such lovely boys," she said, to break Natalie's trance.

It was a quite innocent remark, and quite true as well, they were good kids - unusually polite and kind for boys their ages. So why the comment made Natalie wince Elaine couldn't tell. She smiled again at Natalie, who still hadn't stepped inside. But the smile she got back was brief, and weak.

"Are you OK? You look a little tired."

Natalie blinked her eyes, and for a second it looked to Elaine like she was blinking back tears. "I'm fine." When she saw that Elaine was still staring at her she added. "I'm sorry. Work's a little stressful at the moment. That's all." Again the smile came, but this time it was even weaker than before.

Elaine tried to look sympathetic and understanding, then reversed a little to allow Natalie to come in the door. "Well do come in, let me get you a drink," she said.

A little later and Elaine sat with her hands resting on the top of her wheels and watched them. Natalie and Dave, standing together and apart from everyone else. They both carried themselves the same way, shoulders tensed, heads a little bowed. Shooting glances around, as if to check no one could hear them. She kept on watching as one of the pilots wandered over to them, browsing for whatever might be cooked. He chatted for a while, flashing a white-teethed smile at the pretty Natalie, whose demeanour had changed suddenly. She was smilier now. Polite, but somehow still managing to make her body language dismissive. The man hung about for a minute but then walked away, glancing over his shoulder as he did so. Natalie had always drawn attention from the men. *Her* tragedy, the loss of a husband, somehow seemed to enhance that. The same certainly couldn't be said for being left sitting in a wheelchair for life.

The thought gave her a bitter feeling. A vaguely familiar bitter feeling, and she wondered if there could be any other explanation than the thought hammering in her mind.

Could it be happening again?

Elaine started seeing in sixth form college and they stayed a couple the whole time, until they split up and went to separate universities. Dave said it was because he couldn't handle a long distance relationship, but Elaine suspected that the true reason was his dissatisfaction with the physical side of their relationship. Or rather the lack of. It wasn't that they hadn't slept together, but rather how long it had taken to build up to the event, how frequently she had stopped him, and when it had finally happened, how infrequently she seemed willing to repeat the performance. But throughout university they stayed as friends, and several years later, at a party they happened to attend together, they both drank too much and ended up back in bed together. Elaine vowed not to make the same mistake twice.

Now back together they did it frequently enough, she made sure of that, and she slowly learnt to relax. She could never quite make herself behave like the women in those magazines that she and her friends used to swap. But they grew together as a couple. They made it work for them, even if it was generally carried out in near-silence, with the lights off.

And then she had the accident. The long stay in hospital, the hopes that after her physical injuries healed she might regain some movement of her legs, the disappointment when that didn't happen. Months afterwards a doctor sat down with her and talked about sex. It was a very matter-of-fact conversation, she was amazed at the time that the man could just sit there and talk with apparently no sense of awkwardness. It was all to do, he said, with how we have a set of nerves that links the genitals to the brain, totally separate to the spinal chord. He seemed fascinated by this, as if it were some brilliant extra on a new car. In some cases, the doctor told her, a person could feel an orgasm only in the parts of the body that had feeling left. A lucky few could experience orgasm in the whole body, just as they had before. But there were also an unlucky few, those who felt nothing.

Given how things had been before Elaine was pretty sure she knew which group she fell into, and perhaps such an attitude stacked the odds against her. But sex became both very different and much less frequent, she just hoped that this time Dave would understand.

And then there had been that night. Dave was late back from the office, and she had just passed the test to drive the new car, adapted for her disability. So she decided to go for a drive. She'd surprise him at the office. She got there with no problems, but as she approached she saw there was nowhere to park - Jim's car was there as well. So she stopped across the road. She was just about to start the long process of moving the chair to exit the car when she'd glanced across at the office, through the window, to see if Dave had noticed her.

Clearly he hadn't. He was half-standing half-perched on his desk, Jim's wife Natalie beside him. They looked - close - too close. As she watched he reached up and touched her face, and then they were kissing, his hands were all over her. Elaine's hand went up to her mouth. She felt sick. Short of breath. She wanted to scream, she wanted to burst in there. But that would take ten minutes, and what would it achieve? She forced herself not to look again. She restarted the engine, left the lights off so they wouldn't see her and drove away, slowing only a little at the junction with the main road. She never told him. She never challenged him about it. But she did understand. She looked now at how pretty Natalie looked standing there. *Standing.* Shapely legs shown off by her short summer dress.

Elaine thought of her own body and felt a sense of mourning for what she had been. But she forced herself to smile. We're all animals, she repeated to herself. We all have our needs. And she accepted that it was probably happening again.

forty-four

DAVE AND ELAINE'S party was just about the last place Natalie wanted to go, four days after learning how her husband had died, and that the man who killed him continued to pose a threat to her and her family. But since she could tell no one, she had no reason not to go. She considered faking sickness, but a text message from Dave changed her mind.

Are you coming tomorrow? I have to speak with you.

Natalie walked through the house in a daze. Most of the guests were gathered on the patio, outside the kitchen. A band were playing and the garden was strewn with chairs and loungers, many occupied and pulled into smaller circles. Natalie knew most of the people there, at least by sight. It was the same crowd each year. She nodded to a couple, but didn't go over to speak to them. She saw her sister further away, where the lawn gave way to the kidney shaped pool, shouting at the boys not to splash people. Normally she'd have joined them, but she'd spotted Dave, by the barbecue, a little out of the way by the fence, Dave with his back to the party.

He turned and saw her, then watched as she walked over. He looked like a man incapable of smiling.

She saw what he was grilling - strips of marinated steak, skewers of vegetables and prawns, thick sausages.

"Hi. You want something?" He said.

"Not really."

"Me neither. Kind of hard to get in the party mood isn't it?"

She smiled, the same weak smile she had earlier, but with Dave it had more understanding in it.

Dave turned back to the grill. He gripped one sausage with his tongs and gave it a quarter turn, then worked his way down the rest doing the same. When he'd finished Natalie was still there. Watching him.

"Have you thought any more about what you want to do?"

"I've thought about nothing else," Natalie said. "I still don't know."

There was a table next to the grill, a heavy concrete plinth supported by a wall of bricks at each end and inlaid with terracotta tiles. Dave's drink rested on one of them, a tumbler of something, the syrupy swirl of its alcohol evident. He lifted it now and swirled the ice around before taking a sip.

"Get you a drink?"

"I'm driving."

"I'll get you one anyway. We need to talk."

By the time he'd handed her a tumbler of strong gin and tonic the food on the barbecue was ready, and a raggedy, jovial queue formed. Natalie picked at a plate of salad for the sake of it and joined her sister by the pool. The boys were diving. They'd come prepared with goggles and could swim the length of the pool underwater. She sat astride a sun lounger and nursed her drink, glancing over at Dave. When all the food was cooked he looked for her, nodded, and then disappeared inside.

"I'm not sure I can keep this up. Nothing seems real anymore." They were upstairs where Dave had a small office, its window overlooked the back garden. The decoration was all Dave, presumably since it was hard for Elaine to get up there. Natalie was sitting in his chair, a leather high-backed executive model festooned with adjustment levers. He was leaning against the plain white wall, a drink in his hand. Natalie spoke again.

"I can't talk to people. They don't even seem real. It's like I'm living in a bad dream."

Dave breathed heavily. "I know."

A silence drew out between them.

"And if that wasn't bad enough, I think Elaine suspects we're having an affair or something. She keeps staring at me."

"I know."

"So what was it you wanted to say?" Natalie asked.

He gave another sigh. Then he rolled his head back and looked at the ceiling. He stared at it for a very long time before he began to speak.

"I don't know a way to say this," he said at last. "Once these words come out I can't take them back. And I've thought of a dozen ways to begin, but every one seems wrong." Dave didn't go on but he turned to look at her. The expression on his face was ominous. It scared her.

"You want to do what Jesse says don't you?" She shook her head away from his gaze. "You want to bloody kill him."

"No. Of course I don't," he said quickly. "I don't want to. There's nothing I want less. But..." Dave stroked his chin. He'd shaved for the party. It made him look even more tired.

"Look, the way I wanted to put it is like this. The law allows a person to... to *kill*," he lowered his voice on the word, "to kill another person if it's in self defence. And that's the situation we find ourselves in. Through no fault of our own. That's just the truth of it. Our lives and the lives of entirely innocent people are at risk if we don't act. Now normally the correct course of action would be to go to the police, but in this case, we can't."

"I agree with you," she said quietly.

"I simply cannot believe I find myself saying this, but..." he stopped, only just registering what he'd heard. "What?"

"I agree with you. If we could do it, it would be a way out of this."

Now Dave turned around to look at her.

"It *would* be?"

"If we could, yes."

Dave checked her eyes, confusion had edged into his expression.

"I think, Natalie." He stopped. Breathed hard for a moment. "If we're seriously going to consider this... option. We need to talk in certainties. It *can* be done."

She didn't answer but she kept her eyes on him.

There was a small leather sofa on the back wall and he walked over and flopped down on it, his head back. He talked to the ceiling above her head.

"I need to tell you something. I need to tell you a story. Will you hear me out?"

She shrugged. "Yeah. OK."

"You know when I really worked out that life is unfair? Really fundamentally unfair? It was after Elaine's accident. Not the accident itself, that was just bad luck. But afterwards. The police hardly even looked for the driver. Did you know that? It was before the days when everything was covered by CCTV I suppose. Maybe it would have been different if Elaine had remembered more of the car. Maybe if there'd been a witness. But there wasn't. It was dark, it hit her from behind. The bastard never stopped. There were no clues. When no one turned themselves in, that was it. But *he'd* have known of course. You don't drive straight through someone on a pedestrian crossing and not notice."

Dave glanced down to check Natalie was still listening.

"They gave up on the case before she even came home from hospital. They moved onto things they could solve. It didn't even matter who her father was. She would never walk again, she couldn't have children. That didn't matter to them. The driver got away with no punishment at all. Maybe a dented bumper. A few sleepless nights maybe." He glanced at her again.

"For years I thought about the man driving that car." At this he dropped his eyes from the ceiling and stared at her. "Or the woman, it might have been a woman but I always pictured him as a man. And I fantasied about what I would do if I ever found him. Not about reporting him to the police. That wasn't the kind of justice I wanted. My fantasies were always about what *I* would do to him. At first it was more about doing to him what he had done to Elaine. Something to do with all those Catholic masses my parents made me sit through I suppose, an eye for an eye. A baseball bat for a hit and run. But that never seemed practical. Actually it never seemed *fair*. All that would do was land me in prison. I'd lose again. Elaine would lose again. So I began to think instead about *removing* him. Killing him I suppose." Again his voice quietened on the word. He stopped again and this time he stared down at his hand. It was resting on the arm of the sofa but still holding his drink, but his hand was shaking so violently the ice was rattling against the glass. He leaned forward and set it down.

"It seemed harmless, helpful even, these fantasies. An outlet for my frustrations. I never thought it was real. I never thought I'd actually find him, how could I? But even so I'd work out how to do it, so I wouldn't get caught." Dave began to smile now. An ironic smile.

"And it's entertaining, it's like a puzzle. Working out how you might do it. A puzzle with an infinite number of right answers. I could spend hours thinking about it. I whiled away many a long flight thinking how it might be done. And once it's done in cold blood, once your victim doesn't even know you're coming for him - it's not so hard. Not once you commit yourself. So it's not a question of *could* we do it. The question is should we?"

Now that Dave had sat down, their heads were at the same level.

Natalie blinked several times before answering. The only response which came to her was a professional one.

"It's not an uncommon response," she said, her voice was flat, as if she'd switched off from anything emotional. "Fantasies like that. Everyone has an inner world that's kept private, where we explore options that we'd never actually consider doing for real."

Dave nodded, then when she didn't continue, he answered.

"There is no chance with Elaine. The man who wrecked her life is long gone. But the man who killed your husband isn't. He's all alone on one of our helicopters next week." Suddenly Dave stopped and bit hard on his knuckle. He screwed his eyes tight shut for a second.

"I've been skirting around the subject so I'll just come out and say it. I think we have no choice. I think we have… The *moral right* to take this matter into our own hands. The moral obligation. I think we should take him out Natalie."

They stared at each other for a long while until Dave went on, now his voice was much quieter. "And I know how we're going to do it."

Natalie, already shrunken into herself, felt her body shrivel even further. She felt the blood drop from her head and her vision began to close in, she wondered if she was going to faint, and she didn't care, she wanted to. Anything but this. Anything but being here in this room listening to this. But then her body began to recover. She could feel her heart hammering in her chest but her eyes slowly regained everything around her, Dave's pokey little office, the distant sounds of the party below. She was cornered. There was no way out of this, apart from the one, horrible, final solution. She recovered enough to open her mouth.

"How?" she asked.

forty-five

THE FLIGHT JOHN Buckingham had booked with the firm was from his home in the west of London direct to Ireland. It was the second such flight he was taking, and like the first it was to visit his girlfriend Sienna, who was in the final weeks of shooting a movie over there. She was playing the romantic interest lead in an IRA thriller.

It hadn't been easy for the director to find a location which allowed for the beautiful wide open shots of the 1980s landscape minus the many wind turbines which had popped up since then, and which they were allowed to blow up as comprehensively as the script demanded. The spot they chose also had to house the nearly one hundred people who were working on the film in decent accommodation. Sienna's Hollywood-based co-star demanded a house of his own. In the end they found somewhere perfect, and the only caveat was that it was a three-hour drive, down twisty roads, from Dublin International airport. It was for this reason that John had the helicopter booked. Or more accurately, that his PA - a woman called Carol - had booked it for him. Dave knew all this from her rather chatty email, and he also gambled that over the years John's reason for using the firm's helicopters had shifted from primarily a means of keeping an eye on Natalie, to a habit born of convenience. If you can afford to travel by helicopter, the speed, comfort and point-to-point nature of it really is very handy.

He checked the logs. During John's first trip, nearly three weeks previously, the chopper had flown from London to the film set, picked up the actress and then the pair had spent two days flying around Ireland, first visiting the Ring of Kerry for one night, and then heading north for a second night on an island in Strangford Lough. Damien had been the pilot. Carol's instructions this time around, which assumed Damien would once again be flying them, were that he should pick up Sienna from the same location but this time head to Dublin, where she - Carol - had reserved a suite at the Hilton Hotel.

Thus Dave's first task was to tell Damien he wasn't needed for this trip. He got lucky with the excuse. A late job had come in, a corporate hospitality golf gig that Dave would have had to fly since there were no other pilots available. It was plausible enough that Dave preferred to fly the Ireland trip himself, and Damien wasn't surprised when he was told of the change in plans. The only thing that did surprise him was when Dave also mentioned that he would take the Eurocopter, but it wasn't a big surprise. The Eurocopter was the largest helicopter they operated, capable of taking seven guests, and too big really for the two clients who were booked to use it. But it was also the newest, and Dave mentioned to Damien, as casually as he could, that he just wanted to spend a bit of time getting to know her. Dave didn't mention that Natalie would be coming with him. It would have sounded odd to do so.

Actually Dave knew the chopper very well, he'd spent enough time researching it before signing the payment schedule to add it to his fleet. And he knew it was the only chopper they operated which would allow them to carry out his plan. What made the Eurocopter unusual was its interior layout. The two seats up front faced forwards, for the pilot and co-pilot. The paying passengers travelled in a separate rear cabin where six white leather seats - armchairs really - were arranged facing each other around a low table. Below its beautiful cherrywood top were two glass-fronted cabinets, one was a small keep-warm oven, the other an ice box. When clients booked the Eurocopter they could choose from a range of light meals to eat onboard, each prepared by a ground-based team of Michelin-starred chefs and designed to stay at their best for a flight of up to three hours. There were no cabin crew, the passengers had to serve themselves, but if this was a hardship, there was complimentary champagne to sooth ruffled VIP feathers.

Dave advised Carol of the upgrade to the aircraft by email, noting that it was complimentary, and attaching the menu and drinks list, along with a request that she let him know ASAP so they could ensure his order was ready for the flight. Then Dave had waited nervously for four hours until she replied, during which time he had begun to fret that the man might suffer from airsickness, or eat at unusual hours, or even that there had been something in his email which somehow raised her suspicions. Dave's heart beat faster when her reply had pinged into his inbox. He needn't have worried. She was brief but enthusiastic:

"That's no problem! John loves an upgrade! Please no food, but Champagne would be perfect!"

She even added a smiley face after her name.

That done, Dave moved onto the next stage of the plan. It was harder than he imagined to force the needle of the hypodermic through the bottle's cork. He had to take it out to his workshop, place the bottle in a vice - swaddled in a towel so as not to mark the label - then load the syringe into his table-mounted drill. He broke two bottles and three needles before he tried heating the needle with a blowtorch. Once it was red hot it burnt its way through the foil and cork. It barely left a mark.

It wasn't easy either choosing what to inject. He knew a little about pain killers from living with Elaine for so long, and he had a medical cabinet full of options. Natalie had some expertise too, but neither of them knew how to adapt their knowledge to be certain of knocking a man unconscious. They were also unsure how well their concoction would be disguised in a glass of Moet and Chandon. This was complicated since they didn't know how much their victim would drink, nor how quickly. In the end they put a little more in than they thought necessary.

These preparations were carried out with a light-headed sense of unreality. The relief that there was a route out of the nightmare overwhelmed any opportunity to consider that the plan was insane. A sense of paranoia took over. They put nothing down in writing, no texts, no emails. They used the telephone only to arrange where to meet. They didn't talk again with Jesse. Dave insisted it was better he knew nothing about it. The short timescale, the subterfuge and the preparations conspired to make them feel better already, at least in the daytime. Only during the nights did real doubts creep in, and each morning they both felt the need to make contact, to reassure each other they were doing the right thing.

But now they were nervous. Obviously nervous. Sitting in silence, feeling sick nervous. They were in the air, en-route from Bristol to West London. The journey only took forty minutes and Natalie counted the minutes down. In front of her a GPS screen showed their location, the time to destination ticking down far too quickly. Then the one dot on the screen was joined by a second, the small hotel, near John Buckingham's house, where it was possible to land the Eurocopter. They were five minutes away and she could stand Dave's silence no more.

"I can't believe we're going to do this." She said, only to have something to say.

He looked across at her then reached over and put a hand on her arm.

"We've been though it Natalie. We've covered every angle."

"But what if he recognises us? He knows our faces. Isn't he going to be suspicious that we turn up in his helicopter?"

"He probably won't even see who we are. From what Damien said he spends every flight with his head down going through papers."

"But what if he doesn't this time?"

"We just have to act totally natural. There's no reason why I wouldn't fly the helicopter, it's my business, I'm a pilot. And you're a shareholder, come to check out the firm's new toy. And this flight has been booked for weeks, long before you were sent Jim's wallet."

"But what if he knows we've been sniffing around Llanwindus? Showing people Jim's picture?"

"He doesn't."

"He might though."

"But he probably doesn't. That's why we're hitting him now. Before he gets to know. We have to do this Natalie. We've been through it."

"I know," She sounded sad.

"Breathe. Take ten deep breaths," Dave said. "We've just got to get through this. Get him in the back and drinking and it'll soon be over. And remember. Remember what this man has done to you. What he's taken from you. And what he could still do if we don't do this."

She closed her eyes and gave a couple of quick breaths. Then she took some deeper ones. She felt herself calming down, then she looked across at him and nodded.

"This is the only way we get our lives back intact. This is the right thing to do."

The screen in front of Natalie showed them as one minute away, and Dave began to slow the big machine down. They were over a golf course and ahead of them the hotel slipped into view, its garden held a large ornamental pond and the painted H of a tarmac helipad.

"We're here."

They landed at two forty five, fifteen minutes earlier than arranged but as Dave was dialling Carol's number to let her know they were there Natalie pointed out of the cockpit towards the Range Rover, its windows tinted on the sides, but clear through the windscreen. It came to a halt a few car lengths away, and a lady in the passenger seat waved at them through the windscreen. Dave put his phone down.

"This is it Natalie. Just stay calm. Stay with me."

He unbuckled his straps and pushed open the door, suddenly the low hum of the engine, muffled by soundproofing, was replaced by a roar of noise. Dave climbed the two steps down to the ground and walked over to the car, one arm held high above his head to protect from the downdraft. Natalie stayed where she was. She watched the car as the driver's door opened and John Buckingham stepped out.

She recognised him from photographs on the internet, but was surprised at his size in real life. He wore a blue suit that looked expensive, but it did little to hide the powerful frame underneath. He was tanned and his blond hair was pulled back from his head in a neat ponytail. Even so he was strikingly handsome. The PA got out of the other side and they were walking past each other, she presumably to drive the car away, he to join Dave who had closed most of the gap from the chopper to the car. She watched the two men shake hands, and then lean in close to each other, presumably to try and be heard above the noise. She could see Dave moving to pick up John Buckingham's small valise but the younger man waved him away. Instead Dave moved his arms to show him the way towards the helicopter.

If she had really felt calm during any part of this madness, she didn't now. And had there been any way of abandoning the plan at that moment she would have taken it, but now he was just a few steps away. She realised for the very first time that they really were doing this. It wasn't panic she felt now, but sickness. An intense sickness that rooted her in the seat. Took away her final chance to end this madness.

Dave opened the door, and the flood of noise returned. She realised why the gestures had been so obvious - the noise was so loud they wouldn't have been able to hear each other. John Buckingham climbed in and Dave slammed the door shut. For a moment it was just the two of them inside the helicopter, she could smell his presence. Aftershave. She noticed he wore cuff links on his shirt, heavy lumps of gold. John Buckingham chose a seat - facing forwards, and looked around the cabin. He settled himself, ran a hand over his hair to check it was still in place. And then he noticed her.

forty-six

HIS FACE FROZE. At first he seemed too surprised to hide an expression of shock, but then he did. An easy smile appeared on his lips, which pulled back to show his teeth, even and white. He leaned forward, crouching in the cabin, held out his hand.

"Hello."

Before Natalie could think she was extending her own arm behind her seat, as if some power outside her were propelling it. As if he were able to draw her over to him. Before they touched she felt the shake in her hand.

"I'm John Buckingham." He looked calm now, totally in control. He gazed into her eyes and his smile widened. He took her hand and she wondered if it were a trap and he would pull her in to the back and demand to know what she was doing there. But he didn't. He just shook her hand, perhaps he held onto it for a moment too long, but then he let it go and sat back down.

She still hadn't spoken.

"I didn't see you there. I wasn't expecting a second pilot."

Natalie was spared from answering when the noise flooded back in as Dave opened his door and climbed in beside her. He was talking, presumably continuing their conversation from outside.

"I'm sorry about that sir. It's always a little loud outside."

"That's all right," John said, still looking at Natalie so that she couldn't turn around without looking rude.

"I hope we haven't kept you waiting at all?"

"Not at all, I was a little early. Carol keeps me to a tight schedule." He smiled again, his eyes still on her although he was speaking to Dave now. Natalie knew she had to start acting normally right now, or he would certainly notice something was wrong. She forced her face to flash him a smile and pulled her hand away. He watched her as she did so, but she turned to the front anyway.

"Say, Dave, what happened to the other guy? Damien? He flew me last time. Said he was booked for today as well."

"Yes I'm sorry about that," Dave said a little too quickly. "I'm afraid he injured himself at the weekend, playing five-a-side football. Nothing serious, just a rash tackle. You know what it's like." They'd gone through countless possible ways to answer this question if it came up. Natalie didn't dare turn around again to see how he took it.

"Ouch," John said.

"Indeed. I hope the upgrade goes some way to compensating?" Dave continued, his voice steadier now. "The Eurocopter is new to our fleet. We're trying to upgrade our more important clients when we can. It really is the last word in VIP travel at the moment."

John Buckingham looked around the cabin, its acres of cream leather and polished walnut.

"It's nice."

"Please do make yourself comfortable."

"Thank you. I will." John Buckingham sat back and rested his arms on the chair's rests. He was a big man, even in the spacious cabin it was obvious, his handsome head not far from the ceiling. That smile still in place.

"We can take off right away," Dave went on. "We have a bit of a headwind but she'll cruise at 143 knots, so we'll make good time." It sounded to Natalie like he was trying to forget what they were doing by focussing on the aircraft. Then he surprised her by adding:

"Please do help yourself to a glass of champagne. There's a bottle on ice in the cabinet in front of you."

"Thank you." John Buckingham said, but gave no sign whether he planned to do so. Instead he looked back at Natalie.

"So you're what? The co-pilot?"

Dave answered for her. "That's right, we're familiarising all our pilots. I hope you don't mind?"

"Not at all. I didn't catch your name though?"

They hadn't discussed this question coming up, and as Natalie opened her mouth to answer she realised she had no idea what she was going to say. Half-formed invented names gathered in her throat but she realised she was already speaking.

"Natalie," she said, her voice little more than a croak. It felt wrong to stay facing forward so she turned around again and tried to smile. He grinned back.

"Natalie." He repeated the name again as if testing how it felt to say out loud. "Natalie." He smiled to himself this time. "Well it's nice to meet you Natalie," he said and then settled himself back deeper in his seat. She turned back to face the front, but felt his stare on the back of her head.

"We're ready to go sir if you are," Dave's voice sounded too far away when he spoke, John Buckingham's was somehow much closer.

"Absolutely *Dave*. I think we're all introduced now. Let's get on with it."

Natalie watched Dave on the controls. The knuckles on his hand gripping the cyclic were white where the blood had drained away. She hardly felt the big helicopter lift off and pull them smoothly into the air. Then the nose dipped. Before they'd gathered speed she watched the Range Rover below pull out from the hotel car park and onto the main road. Then they were gone, flying over the trees of a small forest. She looked across at Dave and mouthed the words:

"He knows."

Dave didn't reply, nor give any sign that he'd seen, but concentrated instead on flying the aircraft back towards the west. It was late in the afternoon by then, and sunlight streamed into the cabin, giving them both an excuse to wear sunglasses. For a long while none of them spoke. Behind them their passenger had now pulled out a set of papers and was working his way through them, scrawling notes with an expensive pen. Natalie waited until she thought she had Dave's attention and mouthed again.

"He knows."

This time Dave shook his head in reply. Then he cleared his throat and called out more loudly.

"Sir? Sorry to interrupt sir. I just wanted to tell you we're up to cruising speed now. It should be a very smooth flight all the way out to Ireland." Dave shot a glance at Natalie.

"Do please help yourself to refreshments. Champagne. There's a flask of fresh coffee as well, and some danish pastries in the oven in front of you."

Buckingham looked up from his papers. Then he pushed his shirt cuff up his arm and glanced at his watch.

"Four pm. You know that's not a bad idea." He put everything he was holding down on the seat next to him and linked his fingers together inside out, then stretched them in front of him.

"This is supposed to be a break after all." He reached forward now and opened the ice box. His broad tanned hands pulled the champagne bottle and he expertly stripped the cork of its foil, the bottles were fitted with a cage to catch the cork when it popped.

"You'll find glasses in the tray in front of you sir."

"Thank you." He pulled it open, lifted a crystal champagne flute out and placed in on the table. Its base was wider than normal for stability. Then he hesitated.

"I'm guessing neither of you two are able to join me?" He asked.

"No sir," Dave smiled.

"Not even you Natalie? You don't seem to be doing much flying?"

"No, sir," she said glancing back at him.

"A shame. But I admire your sense of duty." He gave the cork a half twist and then there was a loud *bang* when it came free from the neck of the bottle. Buckingham filled the flute with ivory bubbles which quickly settled back to a half glass of golden liquid. Then he topped it up so that the glass was nearly three quarters full. He pushed the bottle back into the ice bucket and sat back again. The glass rested on the table. Untouched.

Up front Natalie could barely sit still. It felt as if a game were being played where Buckingham knew exactly what was going on. She felt the panic rising again. He was going to taste the chemicals they had dissolved in it. Of course he'd taste them now. He was already suspicious. God only knew what he was thinking. She could see something of what he was doing from the reflection on the inside of the windscreen, but she felt rather than saw him lift the glass now. He'd picked up the papers again and he held the glass by his side. Then he lifted it and put it to his lips. He sniffed. Not a sniff of suspicion, not even a sniff of appreciation, just a sniff, like he had a bit of a cold. And then he put it to his lips and took a sip.

He took a sip, and he was still lost in his papers. He didn't look at the glass. There was nothing in his face to suggest the champagne tasted unusual. And then he took a second sip, bigger this time. Natalie thought she was going to scream out at Dave to do something to stop this, or even to John Buckingham himself, to make him throw it on the floor. That he mustn't drink it. Instead she made herself grip her own armrests as hard as she could. She told herself to breath and tried to remember. The man behind her had killed. A young girl forced to take an overdose in a public toilet. A man stabbed to death outside a nightclub. Jim. Her own husband. Stabbed to death for no other reason than he wanted to go for a surf. The man behind her was responsible for all those empty nights of crying she had suffered. There were probably others as well. Others he had killed, other people who had suffered because of who he'd killed. And this was a man who would kill again, she knew that from her work, from her training. So she didn't scream, she didn't say anything. Instead she prayed, not that a god would stop this, only that he would hurry up and get it over and done with.

It was a journey of less than an hour to clear the Welsh coastline and strike out over the Irish sea. Halfway there and Buckingham had emptied his first glass. And soon after that, as Natalie sneaked little glances behind her, the drugs looked to be taking effect. At first he'd put down the papers, it looked as if he'd become tired of them. He even poured a second glass, but he hadn't drunk any of it before he seemed to sag forward, he looked confused. And then his eyes closed and his body slumped sideways, held up only by the side of the helicopter. After five minutes of this Dave spoke to him.

"Sir? Sir, are you feeling alright sir?"

There was no reply.

"*Sir?*" Dave spoke louder now. Still no answer. No movement at all.

Dave looked across at Natalie.

"OK. Let's finish this."

She was dimly aware of how her whole body was shaking but it felt easiest to go along with what they'd planned. She reached beneath her seat and pulled a bag onto her lap, then from it she took out a small zipped pouch. Even though she knew he was unconscious, she still held her body to prevent Buckingham from seeing what she was doing. She unzipped the pouch and there, held in place by two elastic loops was a syringe, a plastic guard over the needle. Its barrel was filled with a colourless liquid.

This was the second stage of the plan. They had been so concerned over whether he would taste the drugs in the drink, that they had used only enough to sedate him. Now they needed to finish the job. It was the most unpleasant part of the plan, but they had not been able to think of any way around it. Natalie would have to inject the contents of this syringe - powerful drugs skimmed from the top of Elaine's medical cabinet - into John Buckingham. They were much surer about this dosage. Once this was injected he would never wake again.

In the rear of the helicopter Buckingham sat now with his head rolled back, eyes shut, a line of drool hanging from the corner of his mouth. His legs were slightly splayed apart, the material of his trousers pulled tight over his upper thighs. Thick powerful thighs. They were the perfect target, but out of reach of Natalie from where she sat. She held the syringe with her thumb resting against the plunger, and looked at the man behind her. Then hesitated.

"I can't reach him."

Dave glanced back at the situation, then forward again at the controls. "You'll have to squeeze through back there."

"No. I can't"

"It's alright. He's out cold. Come on."

Natalie heard the urgency and fear in his voice and asked herself why it fell to her to do this part. She told herself. Because you can't fly a helicopter.

"Fuck, fuck fuck," she said. "Hold this." She gave Dave the needle and unbuckled her seat belt. She pushed her arms through the gap between the two front seats and stepped through, squatting on one of the rear-facing seats facing Buckingham. Now in the back of the aircraft she could hear his breathing, a rasping sound. She reached forward and took the syringe from Dave and without hesitation slipped the plastic guard from the needle. Her heart was hammering in her chest, but outwardly she felt calm. Like she was acting out a dream, it didn't matter what she did because it wasn't real, couldn't be real.

Buckingham's eyes were still shut, his handsome face looked relaxed now, his skin tanned, the thick cotton of his shirt was slightly open, revealing his chest. A few yellow hairs had escaped and shone where the sunlight hit them. She reached out with the syringe and slowly held it over his leg, the needle pointing downwards. A drip formed on the tip and then fell onto the fabric of the trousers where it instantly spread out and began to be absorbed. She watched his eyes. They didn't flicker. She held her breath.

She knew about injections. How un-tensed muscles would allow the slender metal to pass unnoticed between their fibres. How she could then gently depress the plunger and the deed would be done. She knew he wouldn't wake up. It would be painless for John Buckingham.

But that had been how it would work when discussing the plan in her kitchen. Here, in the back of a helicopter a few hundred metres above the Irish Sea with the softened growl of the engine and the wind noise, with this man so close to her, the smell of him in her nostrils, it suddenly felt impossible.

She forced her hand to move but it wouldn't. She wondered in a wild moment if she might need to use her other hand to make this hand obey, use two hands as if pushing against an invisible force. But then her arm dropped, as if on its own, or like there had simply been a delay in receiving its instructions. The result was not the smooth, firm action she had planned, but a half-hearted jab with a needle, it penetrated the leg, bounced out again and then jabbed in again under the weight of her arm. This time it stayed in place, but only just under the skin. She panicked and pushed the plunger in some way and the material of his trousers turned wet and dark.

She realised she was screaming. An inhuman sound of frustration and fear. She tried to push the needle deeper but she did so at an angle and the needle stuck, but she pressed the plunger harder anyway. Anything to be done with this. And then Buckingham's eyes flicked open and met hers. She snatched her hand away from the syringe as if it had electrocuted her. It nearly came with her hand, instead staying there, lying flat now on the top of his thigh, still one third full. He looked down and saw it.

Buckingham stared at it for a moment, then turned his eyes towards Natalie, sitting opposite him, her hand over her mouth, her frightened eyes staring at him.

"What the fuck?" he cried. "What the fuck is going on?" His voice was slurring wildly. "You just stabbed me?" He went to brush the syringe off his leg but the needle was embedded and he only succeeded in sending it deeper, pushing a little more on the plunger. He cried out in pain.

"Jesus!"

Dave spun around so fast he nearly lost control, and the helicopter juddered underneath them, slewing sideways through the air. Somehow John Buckingham was the first to recover.

"What is this?"

Dave looked forward to correct the aircraft but then turned around again. "Don't play innocent. You know what's going on."

"The fuck are you talking about man?" Buckingham's eyes were wide awake now. His nostrils flaring. He glanced down again at his leg.

"What have you stuck in me?"

The noise in the helicopter seemed to have grown louder. "We know all about you," Dave shouted through clenched teeth. "We know you killed Jim Harrison. We know all about you Buckingham. The champagne was drugged. She's just injected you with enough tranquilliser to drop a horse. You're fucked. This is where you pay for your crimes."

John stared at Dave in amazement then opened his mouth to shout something back, but then closed it again.

"Shit," he said at last. "You're… You're killing me?"

"Too fucking right. What did you think? We'd just let you take us out one by one?"

"What the fuck are you talking about. Are you insane?"

"It's no good lying," said Dave.

Buckingham looked down at his leg again, his breathing coming fast and hard. "Lying? What am I lying about? What have you stabbed me with? What the fuck is all this?"

He was looking at Natalie now. But she said nothing, she stayed pressed into the opposite corner from him, she wasn't screaming now, but panting hard, bringing herself back under control.

"I said what is this? What have you stabbed me with, bitch?"

"What does it matter?" Dave shouted back.

From somewhere John managed a laugh. "This is insane. This isn't fucking happening. You're lunatics. You're what? A pair of crazies? Is that it?" He looked around as if there might be some way out, and then there was a silence in the cabin. Natalie didn't know why she spoke, only that he had to know what this was about. She had to justify her actions.

"You killed my husband. You know what we're talking about," she said.

When he answered his breath was coming in heavy lumps. "The fuck you mean lady? You just fucking stabbed me for no reason."

"You killed my husband."

"Fuck you." He screamed it this time. "I don't even know who you

are."

"Llanwindus. Eight years ago. The *Hanging Rock*. The man you killed was her husband. My friend. We know all about it," said Dave.

This stopped John. His mouth hung open. "The Hanging Rock? Oh shit." He held his hand to his brow, then pushed against the seat in front of him, as if trying to make more room to breathe. "This is about Jesse. Jesse's sent you to kill me."

Suddenly a huge spasm rocked his body. He tensed up, the muscles on his neck bulging, his head jerking back and forth. Natalie, watching from the back, thought he was dying, but then he banged his hand to his chest and he roared out in pain. Then he sat back taking shallow breaths, sweat dripping from his face.

"Jesse. You've been sent by Jesse. *What the fuck has he told you?"*

It was a strange form of guilt that was driving Natalie now. Guilt becoming infused with uncertainty.

"He told us you killed Jim," she said. "My husband. That you stabbed him at your secret place. Hanging Rock."

Buckingham didn't answer and Natalie wondered if he could still speak. After a moment she continued.

"He said you made him and his friend cover it up so they were involved too. They tried to blackmail you about it and you killed again. His friend Darren, you stabbed his brother, and you made Jesse's girlfriend take an overdose. Jesse said there were probably others…" She stopped as Buckingham closed his eyes.

"I fucking bet he did."

"What do you mean?"

There was a long silence, but eventually Buckingham opened his eyes again and looked straight at her. "And you believed him? You believed that sociopathic fucking…" He shook his head. "I bet he did say that. And a whole lot more. Whatever it took."

There was another silence. But this time the truth began to dawn.

"Look lady, you better believe me. I never killed anyone. That man, your husband, it was Jesse who stabbed him."

For a moment there was nothing but the thrum of the engines and the sound of breathing. Then Natalie replied.

"What?"

John Buckingham's shoulders sagged forward a little as he spoke.

"I was there at Hanging Rock when it happened. But I didn't kill anyone. It was Jesse. He had this obsession with how we were the locals there and we had to protect it. Then one day this guy turned up and Jesse went apeshit. He grabbed his knife and tried to scare him off. The guy even tried to walk away but Jesse ran after him and stuck the knife in his back. Then it went crazy, the guy was tough, somehow he broke Jesse's arm, but Jesse got his hand on the knife again and then he just kept sticking it in, again and again."

Buckingham stopped talking and the only sound was the growl of the engines and the wind buffeting the front of the aircraft.

"I helped him cover it up though. Darren and I both did. I shouldn't have. I was young, scared. I was supposed to be his mate. And Jesse can be pretty persuasive." John gave a short laugh. "He got you to try and kill me, didn't he?" He glanced down at the needle still lying flat on his thigh.

Natalie looked at it too, wondering how much could have leaked onto his trousers. How much had slipped into his bloodstream. "What about the others?" She said suddenly.

Another spasm seemed to hit Buckingham and he screwed up his face to resist it. When it passed he answered, but his voice sounded weaker, more distant.

"Darren's brother was a nasty, violent little shit. I heard he got into a fight outside a nightclub. Maybe that's all it was, maybe it was Jesse. Jesse always hated him, so I wouldn't be surprised. And Jesse's girlfriend? She was a junkie. Maybe she took an overdose? Or maybe Jesse helped her take one. I don't know. After Hanging Rock I just tried to get as far away from him as possible."

"But that can't be right," Natalie was speaking quickly now. "Why would Jesse try to blackmail you if it was him who had killed Jim? That doesn't make sense."

"I don't know about any blackmail. I do know he asked me for a job."

"What? I don't understand."

"About six months ago. After his mum died. And he doesn't need money, believe me. That campsite's worth a fortune. No. He wanted to come and work with me. He wanted it to be like the old days, the two of us running around London together. Going to parties. Probably with Darren hanging on as well." He shook his head.

"Did you give him a job?"

"Did I give him a job? Did I give a job to the man I watched kill someone when he was sixteen for no fucking reason? No. Funnily enough I didn't. I bought the biggest fuck off alarm system on the market, I warned security at the office that he was a stalker and I told him if he ever came near me again I was going to the police even if it ended up with me in prison as well. I thought it did the trick. Until now."

Natalie shook her head. There was too much new information. None of it fitted. Nothing made sense.

"But you recognised me when you got in the helicopter. I saw you. If you're innocent how would you know me?"

"I'm not innocent lady. I'm not innocent. I found out about the guy Jesse killed. I read he had a wife. All that. So yeah. I knew who you were. Didn't expect to fucking see you sitting up front today. But I figured it was just a weird coincidence."

"But it's not a coincidence that you used this company. You chose to use this company. That proves you're lying, it proves something anyway." Natalie's voice fell away, uncertain.

"Yeah maybe. I just thought giving you business… It was like a little way of… I don't know. Making amends."

Buckingham closed his eyes again and no one spoke for a minute while Dave piloted the chopper further out to sea. Then he sniffed and opened his eyes again. "What is this? In my leg. Am I going to die?" He turned to Dave. "There any point turning around and flying to a hospital?"

Dave hesitated. Finally he said: "We're about sixty nautical miles off the Pembrokeshire coast. We could get back over land in maybe a half hour." He didn't make any move to turn them around though.

"I understand," Buckingham said. "I get it. I mean why you've done this. Jesse makes you do things you wouldn't normally do. He did the same to me. You get me to hospital, I swear I'll say this was all an accident. Some fucked up weird accident. I won't press charges."

Dave looked around at Natalie. They stared at each other for a moment and then she nodded. "Turn around Dave," she said.

Buckingham looked at her. "Thanks," he said.

For a few moments no one spoke and Dave threw the chopper into a hard looping turn. As he did so Buckingham's face split into a grin. "So what were you gonna do anyway? How were you going to explain the dead guy in the helicopter?"

Natalie didn't answer and Buckingham turned to Dave. "Huh?"

"We were going to say you opened the door and jumped out. They'd assume it was suicide. When the police looked into you they'd realise what you were. Maybe they'd figure your conscience caught up with you. Who cares? There's no reason for us to have anything to do with it."

"Wow. Simple. But fucked up."

Buckingham allowed his head to fall sideways against the window. He looked like he was ready to sleep, but then he spoke again.

"You know the first time I ever met him he told me he killed his own dad. Some science experiment thing that went wrong. He told me how his dad beat him up when he was little. I don't think that was true either. But I wasn't getting on too well with my own dad then and he thought it gave us something in common. It was weird. I guess I was impressed in some way. He said he only meant to hurt him, but it went wrong. He put too much gas in, ended up making a bomb. But that's why he came here. Cos he fucking blew his dad up. If that hadn't happened he could have lived out his psychotic little life thousands of miles away. None of this would have to happen. Not to us anyway."

He spasmed again, only harder, and this time it never looked like he was coming back from it. His neck locked again and his limbs jerked. His face turned from red to purple, then a white froth formed at his mouth. His eyes stared at Natalie the whole time, and then they burst red as the blood vessels split open. And then his arms and his chest stopped jerking, he just stopped. His head fell back, his mouth left open. His fingers continued to twitch, but nothing else moved.

For a while the only sound was the *thump thump* of the blades overhead and the muffled roar of the engines. Dave stared straight ahead, his fingers light on the control as though the smoother they flew, the less real the moment was.

Eventually Natalie leaned forward. She held a hand close to his neck, and after a moment's delay she touched three fingers against it. She watched his mouth and chest. When she spoke she sounded matter of fact, distant. "He's not breathing."

The blades thumped on. Dave didn't turn his head.

"Say something Dave? Did you hear me? He's not breathing. I've killed him and he didn't do it."

Dave still wouldn't speak.

"Dave, talk to me. Please talk to me."

forty-seven

"We've got to go through with the plan." It was the first thing Dave had said for fifteen minutes and it finally interrupted Natalie's hollow sobbing. She had her hands over her eyes, her body curled up as far away from the dead man as she could get in the small cabin.

"We don't have enough fuel to fly around thinking about it. And we can't explain. We can't land with… We can't land with that. We have to go through with the plan."

"What do we do about Jesse?" Natalie's could hardly get the words out.

Dave didn't answer.

"Are you going to convince me to kill him too?"

They flew onwards for another ten minutes, the only sound over the wind and engine was Natalie's cries. Eventually Dave interrupted her again.

"Look I don't know what to say Natalie. I don't know what to think. But we've got to deal with the situation we're in now. We've got to stick with the plan. There's no choice."

She turned to look at him, streaks of tears visible on her face. She couldn't speak but she managed to nod.

Dave took one hand from the controls and wiped his brow, leaving his hand there as if he just wanted to shield his eyes from what they were witnessing. "There." He pointed to the seat next to where John Buckingham's body was.

At first she didn't understand, but then she realised that he was telling her to get on with it. Without speaking she knelt down on the floor of the cabin and, with two hands, began to drag Dave's bag out from under the seat. When it was free she unzipped the top and looked inside. It contained lead weight belts, the kind used by divers.

"You're going to need to slip them around his waist, one by one. They're heavy, be careful."

Without a word Natalie pulled out the first belt, thick black webbing threaded with four dull silvery weights, each two kilograms. The way Buckingham's body was leaning against the window there was a gap between the small of his back and the seat and it was easier than she feared to pass one end of the belt through the gap and around his stomach. Then she pulled the belt tight around him and buckled it up.

"Put them all on," said Dave from the front. "I've read there's something about gas that makes them float after a while. We don't want that happening."

She pulled two of the other belts out and did the same but there wasn't room for the final one.

"Do his legs. Put it around both of his legs. That'll be fine."

"I am Dave. I bloody am OK?" She did so, and when she was finished she sat back and stared at what she'd done.

"OK," Dave said. "Now hook your arm through the seatbelt. When he goes the weight will shift. The autopilot might not keep it stable."

Without replying Natalie threaded one of her arms through the straps in the seat next to Buckingham.

"OK," she said again.

Dave looked around until he was satisfied the horizon was empty. Then he flicked a switch down and sat for a moment with his hands above the controls, not touching them. Then he carefully climbed out of his seat and squeezed through the gap into the rear cabin.

"Let's do it," he said.

She looked into John Buckingham's face as he reached across to pull open the door. The skin had gone very pale and the eyes were still open, the mouth as well, in a way that looked as if he were about to speak, but his chest was still, there was no breath moving in and out of the body.

Dave slid the door open. The noise of the engines flooded in, and thick wet air was forced into the cabin. Natalie recoiled from the opening and the drop below, she was glad Dave had made her hook her arm through the seatbelt. Together they pushed, only needing to roll the body over towards the door before gravity took over and pulled it out and away. The helicopter rocked first one way then the other, so they saw the last part of the fall. The arms and legs tumbling, spinning so that the head was going to hit the water first. It hit in a trough between swells, a strange white splash on the blue-back surface of the ocean. It sank at once but left a residue for a few moments. And then that too was gone, erased by the action of the wind and the waves.

Dave chucked all the food out afterwards. He emptied the champagne bottle out of the open door, then tossed the bottle down, and then did the same with the coffee flask. It might have looked odd had they landed with no supplies, so they had others, not laced with poison. Then he slid the door back closed, and the noise and buffeting disappeared. Dave flew the chopper north, back towards the path they would have flown had they ever intended to travel to Ireland. Then twenty minutes later he took a deep breath, and flicked open the radio channel.
"Mayday, Mayday, Mayday." He gave the tail number and position. He said that their passenger had just jumped out. He told the Coastguard they were holding position over where the man had hit the water but there was no sign of him. They stayed for there for half an hour, talking intermittently on the radio until a Coastguard Sea King helicopter took over. Then, low on fuel, they headed back to Bristol.

They were met by two police officers. They both gave a statement, separately. They'd rehearsed, so their stories matched. John Buckingham had said nothing other than a polite greeting. Neither of them had noticed him unbuckling his seat belt. They'd both looked around when they heard the door opening. No. There was no chance to stop him. No. He hadn't say a word. Could it have been an accident? It didn't look like one. It looked like he jumped. Any idea why? No. None at all. It didn't take much to look shook up. That came naturally.

epilogue

I'M SITTING ON my board in the clearest water in the world watching Darren pick off a small wave. We're over a coral reef, a few hundred metres out from a beach where palm trees are swaying in the morning offshore. There's a bar there. Just a few tables really, and a fridge packed with beer, but it faces the ocean and it's right on the break. I can just make it out when the waves go flat.

It's warm. Warm enough that I'm just wearing shorts, and I can feel the salt drying on my back, pulling my bare skin tight. It does rain here, but not like Wales. And I don't think it's going to rain today.

We'll surf for a couple of hours and then go in. We've both got things to do before we open up. I've got a few investments to check. After that, well, we've both got girlfriends here and I was planning on spending the afternoon with mine. They're local girls, dark skin, dark hair. Young. Mine's the prettier one but the funny thing is, they both cost the same.

We won't open up until it gets dark. We could do. But I'm not in it for the money. No point killing ourselves.

What happened next I'm guessing from what got reported in the papers. It was quite a story for a few days. Not really because of John. Businessmen kill themselves all the time. Deals go wrong. Shit happens. It's hardly news.

No, it was the Sienna angle that made it newsworthy. Heartbreak for Hollywood's golden girl. Lots of opportunities to print more pictures of her looking sad. Sad with her cleavage hanging out. Sad in skimpy shorts. She looked pretty good sad. There was suspicion too at first. Not that she was involved, no one suspected John's death was anything but suicide. But some people wondered if she'd been a little bit of a naughty girl and that had pushed John over the edge, so to speak. No one seemed to suspect the pilot of the helicopter had the slightest thing to do with it. Why would they? Suited me just fine though. If I ever run out of cash I've got a number to call.

And her heartbreak didn't last too long. No reason why it would of course, it's not like there was anything special about John. Not really. And a few months later she was photographed being consoled by her Hollywood co-star in the Caribbean. Sad in a bikini. Actually scrub that. She didn't look sad. It was just her in a bikini and a 'steamy embrace'. And the publicity was great for the film. It was a big hit. I watch it most days.

But I can't talk any more. Darren's paddling out again. I shout out to him and he smiles at me. He always smiles at me when I call him Darren. And I only do call him that since I can't pronounce his real name. He turns around as soon as he reaches me and takes another wave in. It's funny really because that's just what the real Darren would have done. It's a shame in a way. He'd have loved it out here.

A message from the author

Hello! I'd like to say a big thank you for taking a chance on a totally unknown author and reading this book. *The Wave at Hanging Rock* is my first novel and I'm genuinely delighted it's fallen into your hands and you've apparently read it all the way through. I hope that means you enjoyed it. Either that or you're stuck on a really long flight and there was nothing else to do. Either way, thank you (and have a nice trip).

If you did like the book I'd like to ask you a favour. By some estimates over one million books are uploaded to Amazon each year. The few thousand that stand out are those which Amazon's algorithm 'thinks' people are interested in, and one of the factors it uses to determine this is how many reviews a book has. Therefore it will be a huge help to this book's chances of succeeding, and hence my chances of writing another one, if you can leave a review. Obviously if you would like to do more and tell all your friends, recommend the book on facebook or have the title tattooed on your forehead - that's all fine by me.

It's very easy to leave an Amazon review. You can just give a star rating, write a few lines or write a full-length book review. You can leave your name, or be anonymous. You'd be surprised (or at least I was) by how much every single review can help a book's chances of being discovered.

To post an Amazon review type "The Wave at Hanging Rock" into any Amazon webpage and click on the book's listing. On that page you need to click the button that says "Create a review". It's pretty straightforward after that, even my mum can do it. In fact, many of the reviews are from her.

If you'd like to stay up to date with my other books (which don't exist yet, but I'm working on them) please follow me using the links below:

On facebook & Twitter you can find me @greggdunnett

Or sign up for my mailing list at:
www.greggdunnett.co.uk

Thank you again for reading.

Gregg Dunnett
September 2016

acknowledgments

I never thought I'd write an acknowledgements page for this book, not unless it got published properly. It just seemed a bit pretentious. But as time went on I realised there was quite a long list of people who helped to get it into a publishable state, whether that was the self publishing or traditional route. And so it would be wrong for me not to acknowledge them, even if it made me end up looking a bit self-congratulatory. Plus, I realised, an acknowledgments page gave me the advantage of spreading out the blame for those people who didn't think the book was any good. With that seed firmly planted, here goes:

First those kind people who agreed to read an early version. Jane Lavery, Jenefer Roberts, Colin Bainbridge, Helen Gleed, Maria Lopez & Lucy Clarke. Particularly Lucy, who tore the early manuscript to pieces, but told me how to put it back together again so that it made sense. Lucy knew how to do this because she's a real, properly published novelist with four brilliant books selling around the world. That's invaluable, inspirational help to an amateur like me. If you've not come across her books yet, check her out at www.lucy-clarke.com

Also deserving of a special mention is Jane, whose enthusiasm was infectious, and encouragement relentless. Thank you Jane. Later readers were Ian Leonard, Colin Bainbridge (again), Jono Dunnett, Alun Williams, Sue Williams, Tez Plavenieks, and Maria Lopez (again). Thank you all for wading through and pointing out the many bad bits that still remained.

Thanks to Rob Earp for all the work in putting the cover together and designing my website. Thank you to Jono for building the website and all the other bits that independent authors need these days, like decking. It all looks so professional I'm counting that no one will notice the book's only average, at best.

Thank you to Maria & Allegra for your proofreading eyes. I re-inserted a few typos once you were done just to make you doubt yourselves…

And finally to you if you've read this far. Thank you for being one of my early readers and I hope you liked it.

CPSIA information can be obtained
at www.ICGtesting.com
Printed in the USA
LVHW04s1143040918
588652LV00001B/36/P